More praise for
BLACK MOUNTAIN...

"*Black Mountain* is a fabulous tale. . . . What begins as a simple hike in the woods for a group of city dwellers quickly turns into a perilous trek where every step is more harrowing than the last. Just when you think it's safe to take a breath, Standiford tops himself with another pulse-rattling surprise. Complex and stylish, *Black Mountain* makes James Dickey's *Deliverance* seem like a frolic in the park with the local Cub Scout troop . . . this is Standiford's richest and most compelling work yet. And that's saying something."
—James W. Hall

"*Black Mountain* is a fine, intelligent thriller with sharp detail work and nicely complex characters, innocents abroad in a western landscape as treacherous as a minefield."
—James Crumley

"Les Standiford is at his best in *Black Mountain.* It will discourage you from ever going backpacking—but never mind, it will hold you in your chair so that you won't want to go anyway!"
—Ridley Pearson

"[*Black Mountain*] boasts vigorous writing with lots of action. . . . Standiford makes terrific use of his spectacular setting."
—*Publishers Weekly*

"Standiford's work has from the beginning been distinguished by believable heroes who are defined as much by their limitations as their strengths, a sure, somewhat understated sense of place and action scenes that are among the most heart-stopping and compelling ever written. All of these qualities are evident in *Black Mountain.* . . . Beautifully crafted, combining poetic descriptions of the threatening beauty of Wyoming with action sequences that will have readers leaving fingernail impressions in the cover, *Black Mountain* is a stunning achievement by a hugely gifted writer."
—*St. Petersburg Times* (FL)

continued . . .

continued ...

BLACK MOUNTAIN

Les Standiford

BERKLEY PRIME CRIME, NEW YORK

This is a work of fiction. Names, characters, places, and incidents either are the product of the author's imagination or are used fictitiously, and any resemblance to actual persons, living or dead, business establishments, events, or locales is entirely coincidental.

BLACK MOUNTAIN

A Berkley Prime Crime Book / published by arrangement with the author

PRINTING HISTORY
G. P. Putnam's Sons hardcover edition / 2000
Berkley Prime Crime mass-market edition / February 2001

The Penguin Putnam Inc. World Wide Web site address is
http://www.penguinputnam.com

ISBN: 0-425-17853-6

Berkley Prime Crime Books are published
by The Berkley Publishing Group,
a division of Penguin Putnam Inc.,
375 Hudson Street, New York, New York 10014.
The name BERKLEY PRIME CRIME and the
BERKLEY PRIME CRIME design are trademarks
belonging to Penguin Putnam Inc.

PRINTED IN THE UNITED STATES OF AMERICA

10   9   8   7   6   5   4   3   2   1

Thanks to Scott Waxman, for believing;
and to Neil Nyren, Jim Hall, and
Rhoda Kurzweil, for all the help.
I couldn't have done it without you.

This book is dedicated to
Kimberly, Jeremy, Hannah, and Xander.
And to Phil Sullivan,
who taught me about books . . .
and about the mountain.

In the mountains, the shortest route is from peak to peak,
but for that you must have long legs.
—NIETZSCHE

1

August 29
Absaroka National Forest, Wyoming

Bright had been trailing the black Suburban for nearly thirty miles, ever since it had left the gun shop in Sheridan, something called Mighty Malcolm's Arsenal and Ordnance. August was nearly gone, now, but there'd been a boldly lettered sign still hanging in one of the shop's barred windows, red, white, and blue: HAVE A BLAST ON THE 4TH OF JULY—ALL HANDGUNS DISCOUNTED.

Patriotism, Bright thought. Always a useful concept.

Take those proclamations pasted to the bumper of the big vehicle up ahead. TAKE MY GUN, KISS MY BUTT. THE NRA'S FOR CANDYASSES. And another sticker featuring a rendering of a fist with the middle finger extended, which Bright wasn't close enough to read.

An actual hand appeared briefly at one of the passenger windows of the Suburban, and a can sailed back in the slipstream, jouncing onto the pavement. Bright felt it pop under his own wheels. He'd seen perhaps a dozen other cans sail by in the last hour.

They'd turned off I-90 onto the state highway several miles back, had passed through two wide spots in the road known as Ranchester and Dayton, then turned northward again just shy of a flyspeck called Burgess Junction. They were deep in the heart of the Bighorn wilderness, now, on a winding, everclimbing, two-lane blacktop that would give out to gravel before long, somewhere above 9,000 feet, somewhere in a vast spread of peaks and pine near the Montana line, population per square mile steady at zero. Bright, having spent far too much of his adult life in human ant piles, the past several months in Hong Kong, the most recent in New York, found the prospect pleasing.

There had been an exotic game ranch up there once, a fact he had learned in the course of his considerable research. The Roosevelt Preserve, named with unabashed irony, it had sprawled across the shoulders of Black Mountain, the most formidable of those angry-looking peaks and one that had been sacred to the Lakota tribe, the original settlers of the area.

The Lakota once had hunted the area, too, but they had taken only what they needed for survival and had offered up apologies to their gods each time an animal had fallen. Things had changed, of course. The Lakota long since slaughtered, the few survivors displaced. For a time, their sacred mountain had become a place where world-class high rollers had come to stalk ibex, gazelle, bison, bighorn sheep.

Were one to pay enough, Bright mused, one might have shot oneself a rhino up there, chased after a snow leopard with an automatic weapon, tracked down some bewildered elephant too old for the circus or stolen from some zoo, finished it off with a bazooka or a Sidewinder missile, whatever turned the hunter in oneself on.

The ranch had finally gone under, but there was talk of what storybook creatures had escaped or been left behind and were still roaming that far-flung wilderness. All of them fair game, free game, now, for the intrepid hunter, and for what seemed to be the freelance expedition such as that traveling the lonely road just ahead.

Time to bring that party back to its senses, Bright thought. Time to remind them how careless men can be. He nudged the accelerator of the big Ford Expedition, brought his window down, and reached to place the magnetic lamp onto the roof. It wasn't actually a policeman's light, of course, just as the uniform and the siren belonged to no jurisdiction, but they would help him get the job done.

At first, the Suburban ignored the flashing blue light, but Bright had expected that. He nicked the siren a couple of times, then held it, its unearthly squawks and whoops doubling and redoubling off the deep canyon walls.

Another mile, and the Suburban finally slowed, then bumped down grudgingly onto a turnout a hundred feet or so above the stream that sawed with timeless patience at the canyon floor below. Bright had turned off the siren but allowed the flasher to continue its whirl as he got out.

The moment he emerged into the still air, the heat struck at him. The better part of two miles up, but it was ovenish hot, as close and as hot here, it seemed, as it had been on the plains below. What kind of hunting weather was it, anyway?

"Some kind of problem?" It was a burly man who addressed him, the driver of the Suburban stepping down onto the gravel, so quiet Bright could hear the crunch beneath the man's spit-polished boots. Five-eleven, maybe six feet, a close-shaved head the shape of a concrete block, no discernible neck. With a massive chest above a formidable gut, he went perhaps 240, and Bright, himself six-two, his 200 pounds easily concealed in the loose uniform he wore, knew what it would feel like to hit him.

"Please take your hands out of your pockets," Bright told him evenly.

The man glanced down, then back inside the open compartment of the Suburban, rolling his eyes.

Bright heard something spoken inside, an answering guffaw of laughter. There were four of them altogether: one standing by the road in front of him, three hidden behind the smoked windows of the Suburban. Convinced he'd taken enough time to make his point, the driver took his hands out of his fatigue-fashioned pants and opened his palms to Bright.

"You worried I was gonna shoot you?" the man said. He offered a smile that came across as a leer.

Bright's own expression was neutral. "I'd like to have the others out of the truck," he told the man.

"What the hell's this about?" the driver said, taking a step toward him.

Bright didn't back away, simply held up his hand. Something in the gesture must have communicated itself to the man. He gave Bright an exasperated glance, then turned to the open doorway. "He wants you to get out," the man called.

A chorus of groans and muffled curses. The door nearest Bright swung open, and a tall man with a camouflage cap mashed atop his unkempt dark hair got out, kicking a beer can onto the gravel.

Hamm's, Bright noted. From the land of sky-blue waters.

They were driving a $40,000 vehicle, drinking special-of-the-week beer. Possibly it appealed to their proletarian instincts.

The tall man looked at Bright. "He ain't been drinkin'," he said, jerking his thumb at the driver.

Bright nodded, as if it mattered. Then two others, the first a younger-looking, pseudomilitary version of the driver, and the second—something of a surprise to Bright—a stocky, light-skinned black man in jeans and a T-shirt, emerged around the back of the Suburban.

"What kind of cop are you?" the younger man said, and Bright assumed from his voice that he was the driver's son.

And a fair question, Bright thought. His vehicle was unmarked, his uniform, such as it was, unadorned. Pale green canvas trousers, a matching shirt, a badge that seemed vaguely official in its shape but offered no explanation as to his affiliation.

"Forest Service," Bright said. "I noticed your erratic driving."

"And I'm a Chinese aviator," the young one said. He glanced at his father. "This isn't any traffic cop."

"Take it easy, Simms," his father said.

"You mind if I just have a look in the back?" Bright said. Unnecessary, really. He'd had a look while the group had shopped at Mighty Malcolm's. They'd brought along everything he was interested in already. Whatever they had added there would be a bonus.

"You got a warrant?" This from the tall man, an unlikely-looking litigant.

"That why you stopped us, to have a look in the back?" the driver said. He affected calm, but there was new color flushing that close-cut scalp.

The black man had been staring closely at him. Bright noticed that the man's nose was unnaturally flattened, that a fine crosshatching of scars thickened the tissue above each eye. Maybe that explained what he was doing with this crew of self-appointed militia. Take enough punches, your natural enemies might seem to be allies.

"This fellow is a long way from home," the black man said abruptly.

There was something forlorn, something resigned, in the way he said it. Or perhaps it was just the shadow of the great mountain that sobered him. Either way, Bright thought, he'd sensed the truth of what was about to happen.

"Yeah, well, let me just get my license, Officer," the driver said, turning toward the cab of the Suburban.

The black man also had turned, and was heading around the corner of the Suburban when Bright withdrew the pistol from the holster at his belt. The first shot took the black man in the back, just beneath his left shoulder blade. He staggered forward, spine bowed as if he'd been kicked, then pitched over the side of the canyon.

The driver was turning with a pistol upraised when Bright shot him twice in the chest. He went backward into the cab of the Suburban, squeezing off a round that blew through the roof with a whang. The roar of the unsilenced shot echoed again and again off the narrow canyon walls.

Meantime, the driver's younger double was bent over, scrabbling for a pistol sheathed in an ankle holster. Bright shot him squarely in the top of his shaven scalp, and the young man fell back into a sitting position, his head lolling against the side of the Suburban as if he had had just too much beer and hot sun to bear.

The tall man had bolted around the back of the truck with an agility that seemed surprising for his awkward stature. Bright knew he'd be going for something inside the vehicle. Instead of pursuing the man, he stepped over the inert form of the young man before him and slid into the backseat, just as the opposite door was swinging open.

Bright kicked hard, heard the surprised grunt from the other side of the door. The man would have been yanking that door open with desperate force. Bright's kick was all it took. The tall man flew backward, lost his grip on the door handle, and sailed out into space, his arms windmilling. Bright caught a glimpse of his surprised face, was on through the passenger compartment in time to see the man land on the rocks below, his hands upflung in permanent surrender.

All done, well done, Bright found himself thinking. Then felt something grip his ankle, felt his foot fly from under him.

Stunned, he caught a glimpse of the face of the black man as he went down hard on his back. Bright felt his breath fly from him, felt his hand bang against the side of the Suburban, heard his pistol clatter away in the gravel.

The black man, his face twisted up in pain, was pulling himself up over the lip of the cliff, now, his gaze on the pistol, which had come to rest a few feet away. There was no question who would reach it first.

He saw the man's hand close on the weapon, saw the look of satisfaction on his face as he swung it toward him. Still gasping, Bright swept his hand through a skiff of gravel, stinging the man's face and raising a cloud of dust between them.

The black man cursed, and squeezed the trigger. Bright heard the familiar chuff of his own pistol, then a great, odd sigh from behind him, the sound of one of the Suburban's huge tires deflating in an instant. The black man was wiping the grit from his eyes with one hand, steadying himself for a second shot, when Bright braced himself against the flattened wheel and drove his heel against the man's forehead.

The man tottered, but clearly he had taken harder shots. He was bringing the pistol down once more when Bright kicked him again, this time high on the chest, where a bright stain had blossomed on his shirt. The man groaned and fell backward, one hand clutching at his wound, the other locking on to the leg of Bright's billowing trousers.

Bright kicked him again in the chest, then a third time, but though the man's eyes dimmed in pain, his grip on Bright's leg held firm. Bright slung one arm backward, clawing for a hold on the deflated tire with one hand, reaching for his belt with the other. His feet were sliding in the loose gravel, struggling for purchase like dream appendages. He yanked hard at the clasp of his belt, tore at the fastener of his waistband, his zipper.

He rolled onto his back, forced his shoulders hard against the wheel of the Suburban, kicked once more, this time giving it everything. He arched his hips off the ground with his follow-through, felt the cloth of his pants peel down his legs in an instant, felt weightlessness for a moment, then heard the man's cry as he sailed off into space. Bright's trousers were still clutched in his hand, flapping above him like some faulty parachute.

A tree limb jutting from the cliff tore the fabric from the man's hands and flipped him, end over end, toward the stream below. Had it been a true river, the man might have had a chance. Instead, he went head-down into water that might have been a foot deep, the apotheosis of a Do Not Dive Here warning. The crack rose to Bright as if two great stones had been clapped together.

Bright got to his feet, breathing heavily, and stared down at the crumpled figures below. After a moment, he retrieved his pistol, then went around to the other side of the Suburban to be certain there were no more surprises waiting.

The canyon had regained its former quiet. Heat waves shimmered above the mute asphalt road. No hum of sixteen-inch tires, no clack of cans tumbling toward the steep shoulders, no raucous, steel-edged laughter. Bright smelled the tang of pine in the still air. A pair of jays swooped overhead, their cries a harsh counterpoint to an otherwise peaceful scene.

The man who had been driving the Suburban lay half in, half out of the cab, his pistol clutched rigidly in his hand. The one Bright had taken for the driver's son still sat upright against the side of the truck, his porcine eyes bloodshot and protruding, a bottle fly making its way down the bridge of his nose, where a trickle of scarlet had dried.

Bright glanced at his watch, checked the angle of the sun, let his breath out in a sigh. He would have to find a way down that cliff and scale it again, would have to change a sizable tire, and so much else.

It was his own fault, of course. The matter could have been handled simply, with far less risk. But he had allowed himself an inexcusable breach of caution, given his line of endeavor and his considerable experience. Was boredom to account for it? Some lapse attributable to such thin air? He might be getting too old for this line of work, he thought. Perhaps he would have to start picking his jobs with more care.

He glanced out over the tops of the pines clinging to the roadside canyon, toward the distant line of peaks. Maybe it *was* the mountain, he thought, maybe some lodestone deep inside its mass, some essence that tugged at the workings of any man's inner compass. The Lakota had died, but not because they were stupid about such things.

He opened his hands to the mountain, bowed his head briefly. He had no idea if the Lakota had behaved that way, but he offered up his apology anyway. *This is what I must do.*

And then he turned to regard the men on the ground beside him and shook his head, driving superstition from his mind.

They had died, he had not. He would not be so careless again. He had accomplished what he'd set out to do, and he could go on to the next step of the plan, now.

He bent down to pry the pistol from the hand of the man who'd been driving the Suburban, removed its clip, jacked the remaining round from the chamber. He was about to turn his attention to the arsenal in the back of the vehicle, when he thought of something.

It took him a moment—it was always difficult undressing a corpse—but it turned out that the pants fit perfectly. He tucked in his shirt, then glanced down at the man who had been so fond of his weapons.

Bright bent down, applied his lips to the tips of his fingers, and tapped the rigid buttocks of the driver. Acknowledge the spirit of your victim, was that not the Lakota way?

"Take my gun, kiss my butt." Bright nodded. He had his equipment, now; he had the bodies of the men upon whom everything would one day be blamed. All that remained, then, was the work itself. So he rose and began to do it.

2

Now, I have not heard from the president lately. . . ." The sonorous voice boomed from the massive loudspeakers and was almost immediately swallowed by a wave of appreciative laughter from the holiday crowd that filled Sheep Meadow.

Fifty thousand of them, give or take, Corrigan thought. Almost as many as Simon and Garfunkel might get, though those would be paying customers, of course. He doubted many of the folks sprawled out there in the bright late-summer sunlight would have spent very much just to listen to Fielding Dawson.

The only reason Corrigan was there, for instance, was that he was getting paid. Then again, he supposed you could say Governor Dawson was getting paid, too. All those potential votes, all those cameras working, it'd have to pay off, if the governor ended up making his move, that is.

"This man, he is good," Rollie Montcrief said at Corrigan's shoulder. Montcrief was only six months out of the police academy and was still enthusiastic about a lot of things. Even the fact that he'd been lottoed into the Transit Authority hadn't fazed him. "Hey, I could have ended up with Housing, man. Every night working the projects."

True enough, Corrigan thought, watching a father chase down a toddler racing across a grassy swale. The duty could have been worse.

Technically, he and Montcrief were members of an equivalent public agency, with a comparable pay scale, benefits, and the like, but everyone knew that despite all the talk of upgraded images, better equipment, and boosted morale, of the three police forces—Housing, Transit, and NYPD—only the latter were truly considered cops.

Corrigan stepped forward, caught the toddler before he could reach the fascinating trash can he had his eyes on, and lifted him up to the grateful father. "Thanks," the father said, hustling back toward his spread blanket with his child tucked under his arm.

Corrigan felt a vague stickiness on his hands, and wiped his palms on the back of his trousers without looking. Some things were better left unknown, he thought. Meantime, Fielding Dawson must have delivered another zinger up there, for the crowd was laughing again.

Corrigan had missed it. He'd suddenly found himself thinking of his own father, had been wondering with a pang how many errant children his old man had delivered back into the arms of a parent. One of the many little things they'd never had a chance to talk about.

His old man had been a real cop, one of the city's finest, and though Tom Corrigan had never voiced his disappointment while he'd been alive, Corrigan knew it had hurt him to see his son a mere cave cop. "We should be happy, Richie-boy, happy you're any kind of cop at all, what with the eye and all."

That line, with a downcast gaze and a stretch for another splash of Bushmills, that was as close as his father had ever come to voicing his real concerns, Corrigan thought as he gazed out over the crowd, about as close to an apology for his part in the accident as the man had ever come. And nothing to be done about that, now; even though Corrigan, four years on the force, had applied for a transfer, was working toward his bachelor's, was hoping that this time the doctors might be willing to overlook the issue of an old eye injury for a veteran officer and all. His old man was dead and gone, and even the wearing of the blue could never bring him back.

Nothing really wrong with his eye these days, anyway, Corrigan thought, nodding idly, barely glancing at his chattering partner. Nothing that affected his work. He could see just fine, the only real lingering effect of the injury a certain flattening of his depth perception, a slight washing out of distance. It was something he'd tried to forget, something he'd just as soon not think about.

Right now, for instance, he could see what he needed to see

just fine. Governor Dawson up there on stage, doing his thing, all the happy people spread out on the fields beyond, listening with one ear and enjoying life. Just like Corrigan and Montcrief, happy to be goofing, for as long as it lasted, the two of them standing just beyond the west wing of the temporary stage, soaking up sun, backs to the stone wall that separated them from Central Park West and the subway station entrance that they'd been assigned.

Once the governor finished up, Corrigan and Montcrief would be among the gauntlet shielding Dawson, escorting him down the steps of the station to a rendezvous with a special downtown train: a big-shot express straight to the World Trade Center, where he'd address yet another gathering meant to help propel the as-yet-unannounced candidate into the thick of the race for the presidency.

After they had Dawson and the rest of the prominences safely tucked away, things would go more or less back to normal: He and Montcrief would spend the rest of the shift back in the ozone-laden caves, doing what they could to lend order to the chaos sure to come when the families started home. But right now they could take advantage of some rare paid time up top, out in the fresh air, sun on their faces. It had to be good for them both, even though they had to listen to Fielding Dawson's bullshit, even though Corrigan couldn't shake the feeling that in their distinctive commando-styled sweaters they stood out like a couple of cave fish tossed unaccountably to the surface of the earth.

Nobody was paying any attention to him and Rollie, however. All eyes were on Dawson, up there on the big platform, his silver mane so prominent, so shiny, you could probably spot him on the moon, flattened depth perception or no. The governor had his arms raised like some television preacher, turning this way and that to the still-roaring crowd.

Larger-than-life Fielding Dawson, an ambitious attorney who had parlayed a record as an outspoken member of the state legislature and a marriage to wealthy socialite Elizabeth Richardson into the governorship, was a curious mixture of pull-yourself-up-by-your-bootstrap-isms and Kennedy-esque concerns for the common welfare. He had not exactly broken ranks with the lame-duck president, but he had taken enough shots at Washington to endear himself to the cynical New

York voter and, apparently, to sufficient numbers of the voting populace elsewhere. The world was aching for a hero, that's what Corrigan thought. And it seemed that's what Dawson intended to be.

"He talks the talk," Corrigan said grudgingly.

"And *she* walks the walk," Montcrief said. He'd already lost interest in matters political and was nodding at a young woman in a yellow halter top and skin-tight pants switching past them toward a line of Porta Potties. She cast a sidelong glance at Montcrief, seeming to add an extra jounce to an already energetic motion.

"Not bad," Corrigan said.

"'Not bad'?" Montcrief said, his hand to his heart. "I am dying, here."

"Don't die while you're with me," Corrigan said. "I don't need the paperwork."

"That one could kill us both," Montcrief said, probably loud enough for her to hear if it hadn't been for Dawson's voice, finally carrying on.

"Now, *if* the president *had* called me," Dawson continued, the plosives blasting out of the speakers with a force that made Corrigan happy they were in the wings, "I would have told him that all his recent troubles could be traced to a simple source. . . ."

"We know what *that* is!" a heckler bellowed over several other catcalls.

Dawson smiled, again holding up his hands for quiet. "I'm serious, now," he called. "I would have reminded him why he had been elected in the first place. I would have reminded him that there is vast, unfinished business before us."

He paused and swept his gaze over the crowd. "We need, once and for all, to enact strong gun-control legislation, and we need to rededicate ourselves to the preservation of the natural environment," he added, in brief reference to the two issues that he had hammered on since he'd taken up residence in Albany. He jutted his formidable chin toward the crowd to finish. "I would have reminded him that he was sent to Washington to lead, not to try to please everyone. . . ."

Dawson broke off as another cheer erupted. "*You* do it, Governor," the same heckler bellowed, and Corrigan wondered for a moment if the guy might be a plant.

"You the man!" the guy added. Sounded like the same ass-hole in the background at all the golf tournaments.

"I'm weighing all the options," Dawson called out over a general roar of approval. "I'm going to take a much-needed vacation, out West, where I can get out of the eye of the storm for a few days. But I assure you that I will make a decision sometime in the next few weeks."

More cheering, then, and Montcrief was shaking his head. "Why don't he just say the word?" he wondered. "Why not just come out and run?"

Corrigan shrugged. "It's always better when they come to you, Rollie. Like that *chiquita* you were looking at."

Montcrief cut his glance toward the Porta Potties. No sign of the girl in the yellow outfit, but Montcrief nodded anyway, a smile crossing his handsome features. With his Latin-lover looks, he'd never had any problem getting the girls to come to him, Corrigan thought, and wasn't that a nice quality to have? It was not so easy for himself: He might have been born and bred in Brooklyn, a half dozen miles from where Rollie had grown up, but with his reddish-brown hair and fair complex-ion, he'd long ago pegged himself as a poster child for Mid-western life. Girls looked at Rollie, they probably had immediate notions of romance and intrigue; with Corrigan it was probably more like "ear of corn."

He turned back to the stage, then, his attention drawn by something he'd sensed more than focused on at first. He saw what it was, now, though. A tall guy there, approaching the back of the stage, apparently having emerged from the tangle of trees and underbrush along the boundary of the park, a place where the terrain rose up sharply to the north.

"My *chérie amour,*" Montcrief was saying at Corrigan's shoulder. Probably the girl had finally popped out of one of the toilets.

"Look here," Corrigan said, his gaze fixed on the tall guy, nudging Montcrief with his elbow.

The guy was at least six-six, maybe more, and was moving awkwardly but intently toward the back of the stage, like a big water bird wading toward something enticing in the shallows. The temperature outside was probably nearing eighty, but the guy had a knit watch cap mashed down over his ears, a long overcoat flapping from his skinny frame, and what looked like knitted gloves on his hands, with the fingers cut out. Hard to get a fix on the guy, really, because everything about him—his clothing, his features, his entire aura—was indistinct, smudged.

"Looks like one of ours," Montcrief said as he turned.

"That's my guess," Corrigan agreed.

The very image, Corrigan thought, of one of the many who lived in the underground, moving from platform to platform, from maintenance tunnel to maintenance tunnel, kept on the move by Corrigan and the rest of the troops, one of their principal occupations in the course of a day, really, and a hopeless task it was. Keep the legion of the homeless moving, that's all they could do. Like setting off a bug bomb in your own apartment, which only sends the things you don't want to see scurrying into the hidey-holes next door.

"What's he got in his hand?" Montcrief was asking, but Corrigan was already on the move.

Fielding Dawson must have just delivered a humdinger, Corrigan was thinking as he ran, for the crowd was roaring, now, overwhelming anything that had come before, and the brass band up on the stage had erupted into a rousing fanfare.

"Hey, you!" Corrigan cried at the tall man bearing down on the stage. "Hold it! Police officer!" But his words were swallowed in the din.

There *was* something in the guy's hand, he saw, and Corrigan hesitated, wondering if he should go for his own weapon, which, in deference to the sensibilities of the governor, was snapped this day inside a holster at his ankle. To reach it would have meant having to stop, though, to spend a precious second or two, and Corrigan saw now that the governor had indeed finished up with whatever he'd come to lay on his adoring public and was making his way through a pack of back-slapping, high-fiving admirers up there on stage, his personal security occupied with fending off the crush.

The tall guy—smudge man, Corrigan found himself thinking—must finally have noticed Corrigan's approach. His awkward gait shifted, and he turned, squaring himself, bringing his raised arm down . . . just as Corrigan left his feet, driving his shoulder into the guy's midsection, sending them both to the ground, the perfect open-field tackle. Not much weight there, not much resistance at all, Corrigan thought, almost like taking down a shadow . . . .

But as they tumbled, Corrigan felt his chin crack painfully off the man's knee, felt those bony legs twisting from his grasp.

They must have finally noticed something up on stage, Corrigan thought. He heard shouts of alarm from that quarter, felt someone collide with him from behind, saw Montcrief, his feet taken out from under him, crashing heavily into the risers beneath the corner of the platform.

Corrigan rolled to his feet in time to see the tall man already running away, vaulting over the rock wall that bounded the park, his long coattails flapping in his wake.

Corrigan glanced at Montcrief, who stirred groggily amid the steel supports, then at the pandemonium that had erupted on the stage itself: handlers diving for cover; the governor going down beneath a crush of bodies, some intending to protect the man, others just trying to save their own asses, Corrigan supposed.

But by this time he was up on his feet and off after smudge man. A dozen strides to the wall, up and over himself, in time to see those flapping coattails disappearing down the subway entrance. Several passersby gaped as Corrigan raced across the broad sidewalk, shouting: "Police officer! Stop!" his lungs already burning with effort.

He caught the top rail of the entrance, turned himself around, soared, hit the stairwell a dozen steps down, on the first landing. He slid across the gritty surface and banged off the wall, hearing the sound of rasping footsteps rising from the dim tunnel below.

He steadied himself, then was down the rest of the steps two and three at a time, his legs starting to go rubbery, as much from the adrenaline as fatigue. He hit the bottom at full speed, had to jump over a panhandler sitting there—a guy on a blanket spread out so you couldn't avoid him coming or going, one trouser leg pinned up, and a violin—a frigging *violin*—tucked up under his chin, the other holding a bow suspended in amazement as Corrigan flew past.

He caught sight of a couple of Transit cops and a supervisor chatting idly at the far end of the platform, down where Dawson's gleaming train idled at the ready. No sign of smudge man in that direction.

He spun about, surveyed the other end of the platform, saw a heavy-set woman with a pair of shopping bags hustling his way, glancing nervously over her shoulder. There was nothing visible behind her but a series of support pillars marching away toward the dark mouth of the tunnel, but Corrigan figured that's where the man had to be.

He felt a vague stirring in the ozone-laden air, felt the rumble, presonic, growing beneath his feet, knew an uptown train was on its way. The woman, who'd probably been waiting for it, passed by him quickly, shaking her head before he had a chance to say a thing.

"*No se,*" she mumbled bitterly as she hurried away. "*¡No se! ¡No se!*"

Corrigan started forward, moving cautiously, now, aware that his mouth had gone dry. He remembered his pistol, then—earth to Corrigan—and might have been about to go for it, when the man stepped out from behind one of the massive supports.

It could have been only an instant that they stood frozen, their stares locked, but to Corrigan it seemed to last forever. There probably had been color and detail in the clothes the guy was wearing, but those had long ago disappeared. Even his eyes were hard to make out: the pupils wide, the irises indistinct, the sclera the dusky red of old, old blood. Hard to tell where the dark fabric of his coat left off and his skin began. But one thing was clear: There was no weapon in his hands.

"Take it easy," Corrigan said, feeling himself being gauged.

That was one of the things about tunnel rats, he thought, certain of whom he was dealing with, now. They developed a supersensitivity to the nuances of the life forms around them: hostility, docility, insanity, who might hurt you, who you could scam. How else could you survive down here?

The guy's gaze sharpened, his tongue flickered, moistened his cracked lips. "We don't need more trouble," Corrigan said, trying to sound reassuring.

The guy began to back away, his eyes widening.

Corrigan felt the press of ozone-laden air from the opposite direction, knew the train was about to burst free of the tunnel.

The man had begun to make wheezing sounds, as if he were having a hard time breathing.

"Just hold it, now. Hold it right there," Corrigan said, struggling for the right tone. If it wasn't commanding enough, he would lose this one, for sure. Then again, come on too strong and he'd send him flying off again.

The man was gasping, now. Instead of answering, he turned away, suddenly broke into a run.

"Goddamnit," Corrigan called. "Stop. . . ."

The man glanced back, panic in his face, but he wasn't about to stop. He'd jammed his hand back into his pocket, seemed to be struggling for something.

The arriving train burst from the uptown tunnel. Corrigan hesitated, then charged. He had almost reached the man when it happened.

The man's foot caught something—a rift in the pavement, possibly, or maybe even the corrugations on the plastic safety line. He stumbled sideways, wavered for an instant, then toppled.

Corrigan lunged for him, felt his hand brush down the sleeve of the man's flapping coat, felt the leathery skin of the man's palm against his. He clutched frantically, but it was like trying to catch hold of a dream figure, like trying to gather smoke in his hands. In the next moment, Corrigan lost his grip altogether, and the man fell over with a cry.

Corrigan's mouth had opened with a shout of his own when he saw the man's body slam against the train, midair. He felt as much as heard the impact. He threw his arm up against the hail that enveloped him.

In the instant his eyes were shut, he saw his father once again, his old man glancing up as Corrigan came through the doorway into the kitchen of his parents' place in Brooklyn, drawn by who knows what premonition.

Barely two months before, it had been the same evening of the same day they'd buried his mother, the last well-wisher gone home, time to have a heart-to-heart. His father, six months retired, sat at the Formica table, a bottle of Bushmills close by, a jelly jar for a glass, nothing left in either.

His father had his service revolver out and cocked, had his mouth open and the barrel upraised, like maybe he wanted to pick something out of his teeth with a blue cylinder of steel, and who was Corrigan to interrupt?

"Dad," Corrigan said—all he could think of, all he had time to say—before his father—that sad-eyed, mournful gaze—finished the gesture, the hammer slammed down, and wetness was everywhere, a wave that blew over him like the force field of a subway express roaring through a station.

When Corrigan opened his eyes, when he could see again, the platform about him had been transformed into a scene from a charnel house.

The doors of the train hissed open. Corrigan stood transfixed, gaping dumbly inside the car. If his own father had been there, sprawled dead across a puke-green table, he would not have been surprised.

But it was not his father, of course. Just one elderly black woman alone on a bench, a thin woman in a dark blue suit, and a pillbox hat with a veil. The car's sole passenger. She sat with a twine-wrapped box between her legs, staring out at him as if she were viewing the most normal sight in the world.

His face was wet, his chest soaked. Something warm dripped from his chin.

The woman's expression did not flicker. She stared at him quietly, without surprise, without judgment. And then, as the alarm began to sound, she gathered her things and strode out across the awful platform, a person on her way toward some piece of business, passing him without a word.

3

"The boys from the precinct are on their way, Richie. You need to talk to me."

Corrigan, who discovered he was now seated on one of the platform benches, stared up into the eyes of Jacko Kiernan. They were kindly blue eyes, he thought, set under a fine network of worry lines that fanned out across his temples, beneath his snowy white hair. The look of a confessor, of a Santa, his father's long-time friend on the force, Saint Jacko.

"I told you already," Corrigan said, wiping himself with the towel Jacko had placed in his hands. He checked himself as best he could: There was still a bit of blood on his pants, but he'd pulled off his sweater, which had taken the worst of it. He wiped his face and hands again. The awful part was over, he told himself. But his head was leaden, his thoughts bleary, disconnected.

"I know what you told me," Jacko said, looking around. "But it'd be better if you'd seen a weapon."

Corrigan shook his head. "He was running, that's all. I identified myself, told him to stop. He fell." Corrigan rubbed at his face until his skin was fiery.

Jacko nodded, glancing about the platform. The stairwells had already been blocked, and a technician was stringing yellow crime-scene tape from support girder to girder. The two trains had shut down, their silent, lightless presence as incongruous as a pair of buses left stalled in a thoroughfare.

"There's no problem with this, Richie. We just want to be sure. Get this over with quick and clean, right?"

Corrigan realized he was staring at a dark streak of blood that had dried on the back of his hand. He picked up the towel again, glanced up at Jacko as he worked, nodded.

"Look here," Jacko said.

Corrigan saw that Jacko was holding a pistol. A battered .32 caliber pistol, its butt crusted with gore, dangling from his finger by the trigger guard. Whatever had been in the black man's hand up top, it had not been this weapon, Corrigan felt sure of it.

"Where'd that come from?" Corrigan asked.

"Looks to me like it went up his windpipe and out his ass," Jacko said, glancing at the pistol.

"Don't do this," Corrigan said. "It's not necessary. I told you what happened. The driver will back me up. It was an accident."

Jacko cocked an eyebrow. "The driver didn't see shit," he said.

There was a commotion on one of the stairwells, where a pair of steel-jawed types in suits descended, a half dozen more cops in blue scuffling noisily along with them. They might have been on their way to the Yankees game, Corrigan thought.

"You want to get yourself home, get cleaned up, now, don't you?" Jacko was saying.

Corrigan nodded.

"Then just leave the fine points to me, Richie-boy," Jacko said. He clapped Corrigan on the shoulder. He moved off with a spring in his step toward the cops from the world up top.

Corrigan noticed something on the floor of the platform nearby. He bent and picked it up, holding the item between his thumb and his forefinger. A curved piece of plastic casing, cracked, the whole of it smeared with blood.

An inhaler, he realized. About the size and shape of a derringer. Something you might shoot yourself with, *if* you had bronchitis or asthma. Corrigan glanced up.

"Jacko," he called, but the man dismissed him with a backward wave.

Jacko conferred briefly with the group at the foot of the stairs, then turned to glance at Corrigan with an odd look on his face. Jacko turned back, said something to what must have been the lead detective, then came toward Corrigan again.

"They need you up top, Richie," Jacko said. His face was a mask.

"What?" Corrigan said, feeling a fresh wave of dread. "What's happened now?"

"Just get a move on." Jacko shook his head. "It's the governor wants to see you, right away."

4

That's him!" Corrigan heard someone cry as he came up the last set of steps, surrounded by the knot of cops who'd come to fetch him. A sea of reporters and cameramen were gathered about the station entrance, many of whom seemed to be shouting at him, whatever they were saying lost in the sudden din.

He stared about, fighting the urge to shield his face as the cameras began to whir. Like he was a ~~perpetrator, Corrigan thought, some hoodlum~~ dragged up out of the underworld to face the music.

"This way," one of the plainclothesmen said, taking his arm. They shoved their way through the clamor, Corrigan's head swiveling this way and that. He caught sight of Jacko struggling after him near the back of the pack.

"Were there shots fired?" one reporter bellowed, thrusting his microphone at Corrigan like a blunted sword.

"Fuck off," the man propelling Corrigan along said, clubbing the microphone away with a swipe of his forearm.

Corrigan saw that they were heading back toward the stage where the governor had been speaking. The stage itself was empty, but there was a cluster of cops and suits gathered near the foot of the steps where Dawson had been scheduled to make his departure.

A couple of the uniformed cops stopped to lift a nylon barrier rope that had been stretched across the entrance to the park. One of them, a florid-faced guy with graying temples, gave Corrigan the look. He didn't have to say it: *Nice knowing you, asshole.*

Then Corrigan was ducking under the rope along with the plainclothesman, leaving the reporters behind. "Worst part of the job," the burly man at his elbow said.

"You're a cop?" Corrigan asked as the din faded behind them.

"You could say that," the guy answered. Corrigan glanced ahead, saw that the gathering of cops and suits near the foot of the stage steps had parted. He saw Fielding Dawson standing there, his silver mane pressed back in place. He had his chin tilted back and seemed to be sighting down his aquiline nose at Corrigan's approach. "I'm the governor's chief of security," the guy was saying.

"Officer Corrigan." Fielding Dawson's voice boomed all about them.

Corrigan turned from the guy who'd been escorting him, back toward Dawson, dumbfounded by the sound. He stared, realizing now that Dawson was holding a microphone as he strode forward from the pack gathered by the stage. He came at Corrigan like a talk show host on location, microphone in one hand, thrusting out the other in hearty welcome.

"I want to be the first to thank the man who has saved my life." The words echoed all about them.

Still dazed, Corrigan started his own hand forward in reflex. He realized then that he still held the plastic inhaler casing he'd picked up from the grimy floor of the subway platform below.

He had a sudden flash of smudge man, then: just one more poor, addled bastard backpedaling from the law, his mouth popping like a fish's as he went in front of the train. He saw his father slumped across the kitchen table of his boyhood home, the back of his head gaping open like a passage to hell.

"Officer Richard Corrigan," Dawson's voice boomed over the still-thronged meadow. "One of New York City's finest."

"Not exactly," Corrigan heard himself saying.

But his words were lost in the cheers that arose. And he felt—as he extended his own hand toward the governor's well-tanned paw—the plastic casing that might have been a pistol go tumbling to the ground.

5

Rather slow for a holiday, isn't it?" Bright asked the man behind the counter.

The man, clearly Native American, was resting his backside against an ancient Coca-Cola cooler. "We're off the beaten track," he said.

Bright nodded, looked again at the thing in his hand. "What is this, anyway?"

The man glanced at Bright, then at the dusky object he held. "Chip," the man said.

It was a dusty, cavernous place that seemed to swallow sound as well as light, and at first Bright thought the man had misunderstood the question, that he might have been offering his name.

Could it be? A creature out of a Frederic Remington painting with a name like Chip?

There was a black-and-white television on the counter, offering a wavy picture of a baseball game. The Indian had turned the sound down when Bright entered the store. WILD WEST SOUVENIRS, the sign outside promised. FLOTSAM AND JETSAM would have been more appropriate, Bright thought, surveying the junk arrayed on flimsy card tables, discarded cable spools, a pair of battered picnic tables.

"Chip of what?" Bright said, though it was beginning to dawn on him.

"Buffalo chip," the man said.

Bright stared at the thing in his hands. Dull brown, hard, almost weightless, with an odd, burnished quality that gave it the appearance of having been machined. So, he was holding a piece of buffalo shit. He tossed it back into the cardboard box, along with what looked to be a hundred others that had come from the same elemental stamping press.

"People pay you five dollars for a piece of shit?"

The Indian's expression did not waver. "Some people do."

Bright nodded. "I like the profit margin."

The Indian's attention had drifted back to the television set. There might have been a batter crouched at the plate, waiting for a pitch, but then again it could have been a samurai lurking in a snowstorm, waiting to strike.

"Follow the herd around, pick up five-dollar bills right off the ground," Bright said.

The Indian turned to him. "Haven't you heard? The buffalo's all gone. White eyes killed 'em. Every last one."

Bright found himself smiling. "So, we're talking *antique* shit, then."

"What we're talking about is buffalo chips," the Indian said. "Five dollars apiece."

Bright nodded, picked up the chunk he'd been holding. Something in the notion appealed to him. He peeled a ten off the folded wad in his pocket and put it on the counter by the television. There was a commercial on now, or so he thought, perhaps a ghostly image of a woman in a tight sheath dress with her hand on the flank of an automobile. Or perhaps it was nothing, just imaginary patterns in a constantly whirling mass of snow. They were hundreds of miles from any city, and there didn't seem to be a cable attached to the set. Perhaps the Indian only *believed* he was watching television.

"You have any drinks in that cooler?"

The Indian glanced down over his shoulder as if he had just realized where he was sitting. "Coke, Sprite, Diet Coke, Yoo-Hoo," the Indian said. "Dollar each."

"Yoo-Hoo?" Bright asked, letting the question linger.

The Indian regarded him. "You *look* like a white man," he said. "But I'm guessing you could be something else."

Bright nodded. A few hours before, he'd killed four men who'd considered themselves experts in matters of violence. He suspected the one standing before him could have handled the job just as easily and probably wouldn't have lost his pants in the process. You met your equals in the most unlikely places, he thought. Next time he got to pick a partner, maybe he'd come back and talk to this man.

"Coke, then," Bright said.

The Indian shoved himself off the cooler, reached inside without seeming to look, and pulled out a dripping bottle. He handed it to Bright, flicking the cap off with his thumb as easily as if he'd used an opener.

"Ted Turner," the Indian said, nodding at the snowy television. Bright glanced over, saw nothing but an electronic blizzard. "You ever notice how much he looks like Custer?"

"No," Bright said. "Who does he play for?"

"He sits in the stands," the Indian said. "But someday he's going to make a mistake, take a trip out West."

"You think he'll come in here?" Bright said, taking a swallow of his drink.

The Indian nodded. "It's destiny," he said, and the two shared a smile.

Bright nodded, waiting as the Indian counted out his change. Bright picked up a quarter. "The sign out front says you have a pay phone."

The Indian nodded, and used his chin to point over Bright's shoulder. Bright started off.

"It's thirty-five cents, now," the Indian called.

Bright stopped, came back to the bar, found a dime among the coins. "Ted Turner's fault," the Indian said, then turned back to his game.

"It sounds as if you're on a cellular," Bright said as the connection was made.

"Don't worry," the voice on the other end assured him. "It's encrypted."

"Why should I worry?" Bright said.

"There's a reason you called, I'm certain of it."

"What's your take on buffalo chips?" Bright said. There was silence on the other end.

"You must be using code left over from some other assignment," the voice said finally.

"There's a killing to be made out here," Bright said.

"I certainly hope so," the voice replied.

Bright glanced over his shoulder at the counter. The Indian was gone, the television dark. Outside, the light seemed to be fading.

"This is to inform the client," he said. "Everything's in place."

"It is understood," the voice replied.

"You won't be hearing from me again," Bright said. "If there's anything to say, say it now."

"Have you made that other contact yet?"

"Very soon, now," Bright replied.

"You'll proceed as planned, then," the voice said. "And good luck."

"Luck doesn't enter into it," Bright said, and the connection broke.

Outside, he found that the sun had indeed sunk behind a distant, ragged ridgeline. A fiery band of red split the horizon: darkness below, pale blue sky above, as much sky as he'd ever seen. One star up there, or maybe a planet, given the brightness; from time to time, he regretted his lack of knowledge of the heavens, but practicalities dictated where his expertise must lie.

He scanned the parking lot, the nearby sentinel pines, but found no sign of the Indian. No car, no apparent trail, no shadow of a departing shapeshifter. There was a battered aluminum mobile home at the far edge of the lot, but something in its aspect suggested that no one had lived there for years.

If he wanted, he could walk back inside, fill his pockets full of antique buffalo shit, help himself to all the Coke and Yoo-Hoo a man might drink, carry off the quiet TV and anything else he might fancy, as well. There'd be no one to call after him, no angry shopkeeper on his tail.

He laughed at the prospect, then started toward his car. Those idiots he'd dealt with earlier in the day, they might be stupid enough to try such a thing.

Bright was in his vehicle, turning the key, about to drive off the map. He glanced off toward the great mountain that loomed in the distance. Yes, such men as those might try almost anything. And look what had happened to them.

6

But don't you feel just a little bit ashamed of what you've done?"

This from Montel Williams to one of his guests, just as Corrigan wandered back into his cramped living room. In another life, the space had served as the common area of a two-person dorm for students at nearby Columbia Law School. His cousin Victor, then a scholarship student, now in practice in Albany, had still been in residence during the re-privatization and these days rented to Corrigan at 10 percent over his net.

Corrigan didn't resent Victor for charging him the 10 percent. He'd sold his parents' house within a month after he'd buried his father, hadn't been back in the kitchen since the day it happened. Another consolation of death: His former hour's commute to work, with a change of trains, had shrunk to a quarter of that, one straight shot downtown.

So, everything has a bright side, Corrigan thought, glancing down at the copy of the *News* that lay on his coffee table. GUV LUVS CAVE COP—the blaring headline, a big picture of him with the governor's arm around his shoulders, the governor all teeth and gleaming hair, Corrigan looking a little bewildered, like a guy who'd been mistaken for someone else.

The story, so far as Corrigan had read into it, recounted some pretty heroic deeds. According to the writer, Corrigan not only had saved the governor from possible harm but had shielded his partner, Rollie Montcrief, from gunfire with his own body, then single-handedly pursued the would-be assassin into the bowels of the subway station, where he had overtaken the assailant and managed to wrest the man's weapon away. In the hand-to-hand struggle that had ensued, the assailant had lost his footing and fallen to his death on the tracks. While the normal departmental investigation of the incident was ongoing, blah, blah, blah . . . .

Yours truly would be furloughed for a few days, now, Corrigan thought, flopping down on the musty couch Victor had left behind. And he would be free to watch as much daytime television as a man might stomach. Just now, for example, he'd been to the bathroom, then wandered to the kitchen for a fresh beer, and had come back to discover he'd missed the end of *Springer,* which had somehow morphed into the opening of *Montel.*

The kid Montel was talking to wouldn't raise his chin off his chest. He looked to be in his early twenties, a few years younger than Corrigan. On the chair next to him sat a petite blonde about the same age, in a tight skirt that extended about an inch below her panties, her hair chopped short, her eyes sporting too much mascara.

Corrigan wondered what the kid could have done to his partner to earn such censure from Montel. After airing the confessions of barnyard-animal humpers, where was there to go with these programs, anyway? Maybe he could get a shot on one of the shows: "Made My Day: I threw a homeless man into the path of a subway train."

He snapped off the set, leaned back into the ratty couch, had a slug of his beer. *Today is the first day of a lot of days off. Whoop-de-do.*

He reached back toward the battered coffee table where he'd had his feet propped, brushed a few scattered Chee-tos aside, and picked up the bankbook he'd tossed there. Fifteen thousand one hundred and twelve dollars, and sixteen cents. Plus whatever interest had accrued since the last entry, which was a couple of weeks before his old man had pulled the trigger, surely a tidy addition by now, he thought.

Richard and his mother were named in joint tenancy of the account, and she had never mentioned it. She might have failed in a number of bodily functions during those final months, Corrigan thought, but she hadn't lost her sense of what moral actions smelled to high heaven, that much was clear.

He hadn't been able to bring himself to visit the bank where the funds were kept, either, even though there were plenty of things he could use that his salary wouldn't quite cover, a new couch and coffee table among them.

He tossed the book back on the table, finished the beer, stood, and stretched. He walked into his stuffy bedroom, found a fresh shirt in the laundry bag he hadn't unpacked. He donned it, went to the equally stuffy bathroom, splashed water on his face, smoothed his hair. He was wondering if someone had come to replace Montel yet, when the telephone began to ring.

"Lotta people over here," the voice on the other end was saying.

"Over where?" Corrigan asked.

"Looking for *you*," the voice continued, the tone beyond aggrieved. "Reporters!"

By now, Corrigan had realized who it was. "Yeah, Mr. Blanco," he said to the man who'd bought his parents' house. Five grand down, just about enough to cover the costs, Corrigan carrying the paper on the balance. He hadn't gotten around to changing the home address on his Department records; somebody had probably leaked the information to the press.

"I work in the nights, okay? They waking me up for you. . . ."

"Listen, I'm sorry, Mr. Blanco. You didn't give them my number, did you?"

"No number," Blanco said. "I couldn't find."

"Great," Corrigan said. "Now, I want you to do me a favor. . . ."

"My wife tell them where you live," Blanco was saying. "Say, 'Get the hell out of here,' you know? She don't like."

"She gave them my address?" Corrigan said, a sinking feeling in his stomach.

"And chase them away with a broom," Blanco said. "I tell her, 'Come inside, Luisita,' but she don't like. . . ."

Corrigan heard a banging at his door, then. Some enterprising reporter already there, already past the lock that rarely worked in the foyer?

"I gotta go, Mr. Blanco. But don't give out my number, okay?"

"I'm not gonna," Blanco said. "But Luisita, she don't like. . . ."

"Good-bye, Mr. Blanco," Corrigan said.

The knock was sounding again, louder this time. He dropped the phone back into the cradle, turned to consider the alternatives. He could use the fire escape, he supposed, but somebody was probably climbing up the ladder already. On the other hand, he could just ignore the knocking, get himself another beer, go back to the couch. He was trying to calculate how long before he'd have to send out for more Chee-tos when a familiar voice sounded through the door.

"It's me, Richie-boy. Open up."

Corrigan felt himself relax. He hurried to the door and flipped off the lock, then swung it open.

"Man, am I glad . . . ." he began, then broke off when he saw who was there with Jacko.

"Mind if we come in?" The blocky guy who'd yesterday called himself the governor's security chief was already moving toward the open doorway. It didn't seem exactly like a question.

Corrigan glanced at Jacko, who shrugged helplessly. "Why not?" Corrigan said, and ushered the two inside.

"The governor wants me to go *where*?" Corrigan said. He'd just come back into the living room with a fresh beer for himself, a glass of water for Jacko. The governor's man, who'd introduced himself simply as Soldinger, had declined Corrigan's limited choices.

Soldinger opened his palms neutrally. "The Absaroka is a wilderness area in north-central Wyoming," he said patiently. "I haven't been there myself."

Corrigan shook his head. "Why would he want me to go there?"

Soldinger closed his eyes briefly. "I suspect that's a question better suited for the governor," he said.

"It's one of these outward-bound trips for the well-heeled," Jacko Kiernan broke in. "The governor's had his own private expedition planned for some time."

Corrigan stared at him. "Is that supposed to explain something?"

"Officially, you've been added to the security detail," Soldinger said. "In reality—"

"It's a publicity stunt," Corrigan broke in.

"The governor would simply like to acknowledge your accomplishment and the fine work of the Department," Soldinger said, unfazed.

"You're on furlough, anyway," Jacko chimed in.

"This is bullshit," Corrigan said.

"Captain Zinn's already authorized your leave," Jacko added. He was staring down at the picture of Corrigan and the governor on the cover of the *News*, had spoken without glancing up.

Corrigan started to say something, then paused.

"Kid takes a good picture, don't he?" Jacko said to Soldinger in the awkward silence.

Soldinger shrugged.

"You mean Zinn *wants* me to do this," Corrigan said to Jacko, finally.

"It redounds to the image of his operations," Soldinger said.

"You've been bucking for a transfer, Richie," Jacko said, finally meeting his gaze. "This can't hurt a thing."

Corrigan stared back at him for a moment, holding himself in. Then he turned to Soldinger. "I don't know squat about the wilderness. I wouldn't know a bear if it bit me in the ass."

Soldinger waved his hand. "The outfitters are in charge of the trip itself. They pitch the tents, cook the food, paddle the rafts."

"Rafts?"

"I've got a list of some personal items you'll need to pick up," Soldinger said, glancing at Jacko as he reached into his coat and withdrew a folded sheet of paper.

"I'll help you out with that," Jacko added. "The Department's picking up expenses."

"You have got to be kidding me," Corrigan said.

"I'd be sure I got myself a comfortable pair of hiking boots," Soldinger said, standing up. "You may not have to do too much, but you will have to handle your own walking, as I understand."

Jacko nodded. "First rule of the cop business," he said, taking a quick swig of water as he stood along with Soldinger. "Gotta love your shoes."

Corrigan stared back, was still trying to figure if there was some translation of "No!" the two of them might understand, when the buzzer from the foyer began to ring.

"You expecting someone?" Jacko asked.

Corrigan sighed. "No one I care to see," he said wearily. He turned to Soldinger. "So, when's this trip supposed to happen?"

"There'll be a car here to pick you up first thing in the morning. The governor's plane leaves La Guardia at ten A.M."

Corrigan nodded, the buzzer an uninterrupted whine. "You might have to get me out of here, get me someplace else," he said, glancing at Jacko, who nodded his assurances.

"Whatever," Soldinger said.

"Me and Jacko," Corrigan said, "we'll just go out the back, if you don't mind. Maybe you can talk to the people down there in the foyer."

"I'll take care of it," Soldinger said.

"Yeah," Corrigan said. "I know you will."

And he followed Jacko Kiernan out.

7

Elk River Pass, Wyoming

You're no cowboy, are you?"

The voice was authoritative, though not accusatory. Bright turned to regard the woman who had taken a stool at the bar beside him. She wore her dark hair in braids wrapped tightly at her ears, something that a nineteenth-century schoolmarm might have affected.

But this was otherwise no schoolmarm. The crimson blouse opened an extra button, form-fitting jeans, a pair of ostrich-skin boots, by Lucchese, perhaps. She ran her tongue over her lips, adding a bit of gloss to flesh that had been glossy enough already.

Bright thought of a succession of vampire films he had seen, and decided this woman might have played in any one of them. He also decided that there would be no shortage of candidates for her attentions.

"No," he told her. "I'm not a cowboy."

She smiled and had a sip of her drink, something with a slight bluish tint swirling in a martini glass. It seemed an unlikely choice for this bar, an oversized roadside cabin filled with locals in jeans and checked shirts, most of them with bottled beer in hand.

Her eyes met his in the mirror behind the bar, and she lifted her glass in salute. "It's a Blue Glacier," she told him. "Half gin, half vodka, with a touch of blue Curaçao. The bartender at the Four Seasons in Seattle invented it."

Bright glanced about the room, then back at her. "Are you with the local Welcome Wagon?"

She arched an eyebrow at him. "I'm all alone. Something tells me you're alone. I thought we might share some laughs."

"Why not say something funny?"

She smiled. "I can do that. Would you like one of these first?" She raised her glass to him.

Bright shook his head, indicated his tomato juice. She shrugged, had a swallow of her drink, put the nearly empty glass down before her, and clasped her hands. "Here goes," she said, offering him a brief smile.

"This cowboy's sitting in a bar, you see: hat, chaps, spurs, the whole bit. A good-looking woman spots him, comes to sit beside him." A group of genuine-looking cowboys had a spirited game of pool going in a nearby corner of the bar, and she'd leaned in close over the hubbub. Bright could feel her breath warm against his neck. Right about where she might sink her teeth, he thought.

"She asks if he's a real cowboy, and the cowboy turns in surprise. He admits he probably is. He tells her he's spent his entire life on a ranch, roping cows, riding horses, mending fences." The woman tossed her hair, baring her own neck momentarily. "She seems to accept this."

The bartender came by, and the woman made a circular motion with her finger, suggesting she'd like another drink. Bright was thinking about the sound of her voice, the unusual accent, the odd formality of her speech. When the bartender had gone, the woman leaned even closer, her breasts brushing Bright's arm. He watched her through the mirror. From that angle, she seemed poised, about to strike.

"So after a bit," she continued, "the cowboy asks the woman what *she* is." The woman ran her tongue over her lips again, held her gaze steady on Bright's. "The woman tells the cowboy that she's a lesbian. She spends her entire day thinking about women. She awakens thinking of women, thinks of them when she eats, when she showers, when she watches television. In short, everything seems to make her think cf women."

Her face was so close now that Bright really could not focus. It was easier to watch her through the mirror. He sensed movement, then felt her hand come to rest on his knee.

"The woman leaves the cowboy a little while after this, and a couple comes to the bar to sit where she'd been sitting. The couple study him for a moment and finally ask if he is a real cowboy. 'I always thought I was,' the cowboy tells them, 'but I just found out that I'm a lesbian.'"

Her hand, which had risen to the inside of his thigh, squeezed slightly, then left him as the bartender delivered her drink. Bright swiveled on his stool, watched her lift the nearly full glass neatly, watched her sip.

"So, what's the punch line?" he asked.

She put her drink down and regarded him quietly for a few moments. One of the pool players sent the cue ball flying wildly off the table, and she watched, unmoving, as the young man bent near her stool to retrieve it.

The young man came up with his face inches from her knees. She smiled, and the young man tipped his hat as he rose.

When the pool game had resumed, she turned back to Bright. "In my experience," she said, "a man who lacks a sense of humor turns out to be a disappointing lay."

"I just wondered what happened to the woman in your story," Bright said. "Did she come back for the cowboy? Was she waiting outside as he left? Or perhaps he went home with the charming couple who liked him for his spurs and boots."

She regarded him for a moment. "What's in that drink of yours?" she asked finally.

"V8," he said.

"Interesting," she said.

"It was invented by an Italian steamroller operator one afternoon in Siena, when a crate of vegetables fell off a truck in front of him."

"I meant your take on my joke was interesting," she said, staring off in the direction of the pool table. The cowboy who'd had his face inches from her knees a few moments before grinned back at her.

"Unusual country, don't you think?" she said thoughtfully.

"It's the wilderness," he said. "You're not supposed to feel at home here. That's the point of it."

She turned to Bright. "I feel very much at home."

He thought of the forest outside, the unbroken sweep of rugged country that ran for hundreds of miles in every direction. She had the sharp features of a cat, the gleaming teeth, the shining, hungry lips.

Perhaps she *was* at home here. Perhaps she had been spawned here, had come down from the great distant mountain to claim some necessary thing.

"Did you have a purpose in mind when you sat down here?" he asked.

"I think you know what my purpose is," she said. Her gaze held his for a moment.

"I am Nelia," she said, extending her hand. "Nelia Esteban."

"Bright," he said, extending his own. Hers was a cool grip, and a firm one. Anything caught in it alive would have pause, he thought.

"I know who you are," she said.

"I hadn't expected a woman," he replied.

"I'd been hoping for someone with a sense of humor," she said. She motioned to the bartender, stopped Bright's hand when he went for his wallet. "Let me get this."

"Why not?" he said. "At the end of the day, it's coming out of the same pocket." He finished his drink, then turned to follow her out.

At the exit, Bright found the young cowboy holding the door open for her. The young man's grin turned to something of a sneer as Bright followed after her.

"You're lucky to be alive," Bright said as he passed the young man.

The young man gave a humorless laugh. "You some kind of badass, mister?"

Bright glanced at him mildly, then at the disappearing backside of Nelia Esteban. "Not me," he told the puzzled young man. "It's *her* you ought to be worrying about."

"Towel," she gasped, twisting her hand around behind her back. She was facedown in the big bed, her other hand clutching a wad of sheeting she'd torn loose from the mattress. "What have you done with the towel?"

Outside the windows of the hotel room, it was storming. A bolt of lightning haloed the drapes in the darkness, and a peal of thunder splintered the skies, rattling the walls of the room. He groped about with one hand, found the towel, managed to place it in her hand. The motion seemed to take the last of his energy.

He let his head roll over, glanced at her, at the vague shadow of her long black hair, unloosed from the braids, now, fanned out across the dim white glow of her flesh.

"A nice touch, those braids," he said as the sounds of the thunder faded. "Very Hester Prynne."

"Gwyneth Paltrow, actually," she said. The air-conditioning had kicked on, and a band of light from a vapor light outside leaked past a gap in the curtains. She raised herself up on one elbow, tucked the towel deftly beneath her. "Just like her hairdo at Cannes. I'm not familiar with the other actress."

Bright nodded. Perhaps she was putting him on. There was no way to know with Nelia.

"That cowboy getup you were wearing," she said. "Was it *High Noon* inspired you?"

"When in Rome . . . ." he said.

"I very nearly missed spotting you," she said. "Imagine."

"I can't," he said. "I can't imagine you missing anything."

"Then I saw you at the bar, and I thought, Of course, he thinks he's in *The Wild Bunch* this go-round."

"Those films are from before your time," he said, ignoring her jab.

"Not in my country, *señor*," she mimicked. "There they are *steel* first run."

A fresh gust of wind swept over the hotel, splattering rain against the wooden siding. Another, more distant peal of thunder sounded, but the storm seemed headed away.

"Pehaps next time we should pretend we're in *Casablanca*," he said, thinking of his own favorites. "Or perhaps *The Maltese Falcon*."

"Not bloody likely," she said, mocking his own accent. "Morocco, San Francisco"—her tone was dismissive—"*this* is the only place in the world where life still looks like a movie set."

True enough, he supposed, but he didn't feel like saying so. "Or possibly we could just meet like ordinary people," he said. "Hello. How are you. Good to see you again. A peck on either cheek before bedding down."

"Who have you dispatched lately?" she chimed in. "Care to have a look at my new garrote? We're hardly ordinary people, Bright."

He nodded, grudgingly amused, but his mind had drifted to the dilemma presented to the great Bogart late in the film, where he'd played a detective who had realized he'd been sleeping with a killer. The writing had been particularly true in that regard, Bright thought. The issue was not that she had killed. If anything, that had only inflamed Bogart's passions further. It was just that she had killed his partner. There was where the moral issue lay.

"I *can* count on you," he said at last, his words floating up toward the invisible ceiling.

This made three times that they had worked together. The first time they'd met in Brunei, where he'd mistaken her for one of the Sultan's coterie, and she had played along, just to see his surprise when they were sent off to do the necessary work together. The second assignment in London, he'd been idling in Harrods, no idea who he'd be working with. He'd decided to have himself fitted for a suit, saw the salesperson going out, found her there suddenly in the dressing room playing tailor, brandishing a tape measure, her smile around a mouthful of pins.

"So long as we're employed by the same side," she said, breaking into his thoughts. Her hand had snaked its way to him, gave an affectionate squeeze.

"Tomorrow's a busy day," he said.

"How long since we've been together?" she said, dismissing him. "Tonight's a busy night."

"I'm already thinking how much there is to be done."

"Be quiet," she said, sliding closer. "You could be fucking some ordinary person. Where's the fun in that?"

"I wouldn't be fooling around at all," he said. "Not at a time like this."

"You sound like a football coach: 'Save it for the big game, men.'" Her leg swung over his.

"Normal people next time," he said. His mind was drifting, despite himself. "That's how we should be."

"Like *Last Tango in Paris,* then?"

"I'm afraid I missed that one." He was biting his lip. "I'm not much for dance."

"Oh, don't worry," she said as she turned atop him. "This is a step you're going to love."

8

"You got everything you need, Richie-boy?" Jacko Kiernan didn't seem too concerned about the answer. He had his mug of coffee in his hands and was staring out the café window at a woman in leopard-skin pants standing near the curb as if she were waiting to hail a cab. He turned back to Corrigan as a sedan pulled up, and the woman slid smoothly inside.

"I'm fine," Corrigan said. As it had turned out, the list Soldinger had provided him stipulated more of what would be provided for him than what he would need to bring. No tent, no sleeping bag, no backpack, no serious equipment necessary.

He'd been told to show up in uniform for the big sendoff, but after that, he was free to wear whatever he chose. Practical enough, Corrigan supposed, but just one more sign this was all for the sake of public relations. He'd picked up some jeans, some extra socks, a couple of sweatshirts, a light parka made of something called Gore-Tex, all of it stashed with his toiletries in a nylon bag there on the seat beside him.

They were sitting in a place not far off the Grand Central Parkway. Go one way, you'd be on your way out to Rikers. Just to the east was La Guardia. He'd been in the café with his old man a couple of times. Tom Corrigan, he thought. Never missed a spot where a cop could get a cup on the cuff.

"You get that pair of hiking boots?"

Corrigan stretched his leg out from beneath the table between them. Jacko glanced down.

"Those are tennis shoes."

Corrigan shrugged. When the clerk at Outdoor World had opened the box, revealing the mesh uppers, the stitched Nike swoosh, Corrigan had said the same thing. "The kid told me these were the latest thing in boots. *Très* hip."

"Tray, my ass," Jacko said. "You want a pair of shoes you can kick something when you have to."

Corrigan nodded, glancing at his watch. "Sounds like something my old man would have said." He noted that the sedan outside hadn't pulled away, but the woman's head had disappeared. Jacko had his chin raised toward the café window as if he were trying to get a look inside the car.

"It was, in fact," Jacko said, still staring out the window. "I always liked the line. Now it's mine." He gave Corrigan a smile.

Corrigan reached into his shirt pocket and tossed the bankbook down on the table between them.

"What's that?" Jacko asked.

"Take a look," Corrigan said.

Jacko opened it, flipped the pages. He folded it closed, slid it back across the table to Corrigan. "Your father was a thrifty man," he said.

"My mother never mentioned this money," Corrigan said.

Jacko shrugged. "She was in a lot of pain there at the end. She was taking a lot of pills."

Corrigan shook his head. "The doctor bills had been mounting up a long time before that, Jacko. She could have used that money. But she wouldn't."

The waitress came by to refill their coffee, and Jacko waited until she was gone to reply. "What do you want from me, Richie?"

"I spent all of a half hour with Internal Affairs yesterday," Corrigan said. "They couldn't have cared less about that poor bastard who died. They don't even know his name," he said with a significant pause. "But they sure as hell had to know where that gun came from. . . ."

"On my soul, it was right there on the platform . . . ," Jacko said, lifting his right hand.

"Can it, Jacko. You wanted to take care of me, the Department's just happy to avoid a black eye. I'm the one keeps getting to see the guy's face going over the side."

Corrigan paused, and glanced down at the table. "The other thing I thought about was this." He tapped the bankbook with his finger.

Jacko glanced briefly at the bankbook. "I'm not with you, son."

"Just tell me, Jacko. How'd he get the money? Who'd he squeeze? Who was he shaking down?"

"You're making a lot of assumptions over fifteen thousand dollars, boy-o. If your father had been crooked, he'd have come away with a lot more than that."

"My old man never thought big," Corrigan said. "I'd just like to know how he came by it. Just what scams he could stomach. We didn't get much of a chance to talk there at the end, you know."

The woman in the leopard pants was out of the car already, blotting her lipstick with a handkerchief as the sedan pulled away. "I remember when I could go as quick as that," Jacko said, turning to Corrigan with a wistful smile.

He saw the expression on Corrigan's face and broke off. He put his palms on the table, leaned forward. "That was a terrible thing you had to go through, Richie. A terrible thing. But it had nothing to do with you. And your old man was no crook. He was a stand-up guy who didn't know what to do with himself once he was out of harness. When your mother died, that must have finished him."

"He still had a son," Corrigan said.

Jacko stopped, drew a deep breath. "He thought the world of you, Richie."

"It must have killed him, me stuck in the caves."

Jacko shook his head. "He was proud of you. He felt as bad as anybody about . . ." Jacko paused, searching for words. "About you getting hurt."

Corrigan nodded, and felt his hand go unconsciously to his eye. "He never said anything about that, either."

Jacko studied him for a moment, then finally clasped his hands together. "Your old man had his problems, Richie, but what's past is past. You got to take advantage of what's laid in front of you. You go off on this trip, go someplace where you can breathe fresh air, get your head cleared out, know what I mean? By the time you come back, you'll feel a lot better. I wouldn't be surprised to see that transfer waiting for you."

Corrigan stared at him. "Everything swept under the rug, I put on the blue, wait my turn to blow my own brains out? Maybe I'm barking up the wrong tree, Jacko. Maybe I ought to explore another line of work."

Jacko stared at him. "Aye, but you're a tough case," Jacko

said, his descent into brogue only underscoring how deeply he felt. As a child, Corrigan had been able to gauge just how drunk Jacko and his father had become, just how close to some dream of Ireland they had drifted, by the same measuring stick.

"Just take this opportunity, son."

"Go wander in the wilderness with Dawson, we can sort out our lives together?"

"You deserve some pleasure in life."

Corrigan sat back in the booth, too weary to continue. He pocketed the bankbook and stood, tossing some bills on the table. "Thanks for the heart-to-heart, Jacko. It was life-altering. And thanks for everything, okay? Trying to keep me out of trouble, putting me up last night, keeping the reporters away. . . ."

"Richie-boy . . ."

The woman in the leopard pants had turned full-face toward the window of the café and was running her tongue about her glistening lips. Just checking her reflection, Corrigan told himself, but it seemed her gaze was burning into his. You take the hand that's dealt you, that look seemed to say. You take the hand that's dealt you.

"Let's just go to the airport," Corrigan said. "Like you say, I need a change of scene."

9

"I want to reassure the people of New York that the commitment of my administration to the welfare of this great state continues undiminished," Fielding Dawson said as flashes popped and cameramen jockeyed for position in the claustrophobic section of the departure lounge set aside for the press conference.

Corrigan, who'd been delivered to the proper concourse only moments before by Jacko, stood off to one side of the podium, part of a coterie that included Soldinger and a burly-looking type in plainclothes who looked like he'd spent far too much time at the steroid bar.

Dawson, who was clad in a sport coat and a checked shirt without a tie, looked uncomfortable in the getup, like some judge who wasn't quite sure how to act when he wasn't behind the bench. But the guy had undeniably rugged good looks and kept himself in careful shape, Corrigan had to admit. It was probably an image that would play well in the heartland.

"My wife, Elizabeth, and I have been planning this trip for more than a year. Despite all the talk that's going around, nothing has changed in the Dawson camp. We'll spend a few days in the wilderness doing some considerable soul-searching. . . ." Here he broke off, while the cameras turned for a wave from his wife. "And then we will make our decision known.

"Until then . . ." he added, raising his hands in apparent benediction, "I am the governor of the greatest state on earth, and I am very proud of it." A cheer arose from a group of supporters near the front of the room, with one heavyset man leading a chorus of wuffing that quickly died out.

"Now, one more thing before we go . . . ," Dawson was saying. Corrigan wasn't paying much attention. He'd been scanning the crowd, noting Jacko's encouraging visage toward the back, idly assessing the pert figure of a young female reporter near the front of the crowd. Unlike most of her more formally attired peers, she was dressed in jeans and flannel shirt; instead of jostling with the rest of the mob, shouting out questions that tended to blur into one unintelligible roar, she kept her head bent, scribbling continually on a pad she carried. He particularly liked the way she paused to lick the tip of her pencil from time to time. It was a trait of his mother's, he realized abruptly. Dawson's voice reduced to a background drone in his mind. A somehow endearing piece of business he'd forgotten until now.

She glanced up suddenly, her gaze locking on his, and Corrigan quickly looked away, feeling his cheeks begin to burn.

". . . so you can understand why I am not about to venture into such uncharted territory without him, one of this city's finest, Officer Richard Corrigan."

Corrigan blinked as a wave of applause came from the crowd, accompanied by a fresh round of wuffing from the man who was assuredly a member of the Dawson camp. It had dawned on Corrigan by now what he'd just tuned out of in Dawson's speech, why the girl's glance had been drawn to his.

Dawson had turned to him, with his hand extended. "These people have been dying to hear from you, Officer. Come on up and say a few words."

Corrigan stood transfixed, staring at Dawson. The man held his megawatt smile intact as Corrigan hesitated, but there was a sinister edge in his eyes, it seemed. Corrigan felt a nudge at his back, Soldinger's big paw shoving him forward. He glanced out at the crowd again, saw Jacko's beaming face, his spirited thumbs-up. The young reporter he'd had his eye on a moment before had left off with her note-taking and was regarding him with interest.

Already there were shouts from the others, a cacophony of questions that clearly would only grow. Corrigan took a deep breath and felt his feet carrying him toward the podium as the flashes popped anew.

He leaned toward the microphones clipped there, cleared his throat, stepped back as a squeal of feedback sounded. "I just wanted to clarify that I'm a member of the Transit Authority Police," he said. He glanced around nervously, seeing nothing, now. "So I don't get out much. . . ." There was a wave of appreciative laughter.

"Did you think you were going to die?" someone bellowed from the pack.

Corrigan hesitated, turned to the governor, whose posture seemed to be urging him on: *Hell, yes, man. Braved a hail of bullets, dodged a fusillade of fire.*

He turned back to the podium, then, leaned close to the bank of microphones. "I was just doing my job," he found himself saying. "There's really nothing more to it than that."

He stepped back, and though Dawson had to have been disappointed, he was quick to jump in. "A typical selfless statement from a true hero, ladies and gentlemen. Let's hear it again for Officer Richard Corrigan."

There was a fresh burst of applause, but Corrigan wasn't really aware of it. Somehow, he managed to make it back to his place by Soldinger, where he stood with his face flaming, his eyes fixed firmly on the floor.

After a few moments, Corrigan realized that Dawson had uttered some wrap-it-up farewell, and he allowed himself a glance toward the podium. The attention had shifted back to where it had been, of course: The governor had turned to embrace his wife, ignoring the reporters crying out for any scrap of confirmation that he had in fact decided to seek his party's nomination for the presidency.

"Leander Polk says he's stepping aside for you, Governor," a network correspondent with a particularly commanding voice called.

Dawson turned for that one. "Last month, Leander Polk wanted Colin Powell to be his running mate," he said. "I wouldn't put much stock in these rumors."

The correspondent tried to get in a follow-up, but he was drowned out by his colleagues, who were advancing on the Dawsons like lepers toward the gates of Lourdes.

"Let's get him out of here before they eat him," Soldinger grumbled to the steroid abuser at Corrigan's shoulder, and then they all were being hustled toward the doors.

10

Corrigan, who had a row to himself, had been leaning against the blurry window, nearly lulled to sleep by the unending roar of the big plane's engines. He'd been halfheartedly trying to calculate how much of the continent they'd covered, but with the ground obliterated now by a screen of clouds, he'd been reduced to the grossest level of guesswork.

He'd flown to Chicago once to visit his cousin Victor and his family, the summer after his eye had been injured, and he'd spent the whole trip out and back trying to trace the features of the landscape below, somehow imagining that he'd be able to distinguish one state and region from the other in the same way he'd been able to in his school atlas—he'd probably expected dotted lines and squiggly topographical features. It had been quite a disappointment when he'd discovered the truth, he recalled, staring down at the vague landscape below him, now.

"Mind if I talk to you?"

He glanced up, bleary-eyed, doing a double-take when he found the reporter he'd had his gaze on at the press conference staring down at him.

"My name's Dara Wylie," she said, smiling, extending her hand. "I work for *USA Magazine.* I did a piece a few months ago about the mayor's efforts to upgrade the image of the subways . . . ?"

Corrigan had no idea what story she was talking about. But he did find her even more attractive at this close distance, and was trying not to gawk. She had straight sandy hair cut just above the shoulders, no makeup that he could perceive, and a pair of guileless hazel eyes that regarded him carefully, seeming to take his measure. He saw a spray of freckles across the

V of flesh at her open collar, and forced his gaze not to drift toward her breasts.

Did he mind if she talked to him? *Careful, Richie-boy. Careful.*

"I can't really go into what happened," he told her. "The matter's still under investigation."

"I understand," she said. "I wouldn't ask you anything uncomfortable. Just a couple of questions about your part in all this." She waved her hand toward the front of the plane, where Dawson and his immediate party were sequestered in the first-class cabin.

"You just said you wouldn't ask anything uncomfortable," Corrigan told her.

She turned back to him, puzzled.

He smiled. "Just a dumb joke," he said. "The truth is, I'm more or less along for the ride, that's all."

She was staring at him uncertainly.

Duh, Richie. Don't let her get away. Tell her anything. Your shoe size. Your freaking middle name.

"You're welcome to sit down," he said. "Please."

She glanced over her shoulder, then settled into the seat on the aisle. She leaned out and seemed to signal to someone farther up in the plane. She turned back to him, gave him an apologetic smile. "I'm supposed to have a few minutes with the governor," she said. "You know how it is. I may have to get up and run."

"Sure," he said. "Whatever."

"Well," she said. "This must be pretty exciting for you." She glanced at him again. "Or maybe not. What you just said, I mean."

He saw that she hadn't opened her notebook. "It's something, all right."

"But uncomfortable."

"You could say that."

"Because you feel like the governor's show pony."

"Excuse me?" He turned to stare at her.

She dropped her eyes. "I'm sorry," she said. "I shouldn't have said that." She came back with an ingenuous smile. "You're supposed to let the interviewee do the talking."

He shrugged. "You been at this long?"

Her smile was more practiced this time. "Long enough," she said.

"Anyway, it's okay," he told her. "You more or less hit the nail on the head."

Her gaze softened. "Why don't we start over?" she said. "I'm not here to embarrass you, if that's what you think."

She glanced around, making sure there was no one else listening in. But they were well toward the rear of the sparsely populated charter. One flight attendant lounged near the service galley, flipping through a copy of *Elle;* a guy with a photographer's gear jacket zipped under his chin was stretched across the row catty-corner, apparently fast asleep.

"We do *people* pieces, okay? It's not like they send *me* to cover the war in Bosnia, you know."

"You're telling me you're doing a puff piece on the governor?"

It was her turn to shrug. She flashed her more professional smile. A good one, he thought. Give this woman a couple more years in the business, she could probably slide in beside Connie Chung, nudge her right off her chair.

"The governor is positioning himself," she said. "He's going out West to brave the wilderness and prove to the American public that he's not just an East Coast guy with a God complex. He's going to climb mountains and bang Boy Scouts together to start fires. He's going to scare off grizzlies, catch trout, and shoot rapids, and when he comes out the other end, he's going to rhapsodize about the glories of the American experience, detail a plan to rededicate our energies to the preservation of the environment and our bedrock verities, and *then* announce his run for the presidency."

He stared at her, noting the flush that had arisen in her cheeks. Freckles there, too, he saw now, though they hadn't been visible before. He was also thinking maybe he'd been wrong a moment ago. Forget Connie Chung. This woman could boot Dan Rather out of his chair. "Sounds like a plan to me," Corrigan said.

"And I'll be there to record it, every step of the way," she said. "Seven days and seven nights in the wilderness, big press conference at the end." She nodded at the sleeping photographer across the way. "There's a film crew going along, shooting a documentary, but ours will be the first story out."

He glanced at her. "You're going on the trip?"

She studied him. "It'll make it a lot easier to write the piece," she said, her honest smile returning.

"I guess so." Corrigan nodded. Was he doomed forever to be so obvious to women? he wondered. Why not just let his tongue dangle, drool a few drops down the front of his chest? "So, you want to do a sidebar on the honorary chief of security?"

She shrugged. "You looked so miserable back there at the airport. I found myself wondering why."

"Yeah, well, maybe I'm not so good in crowds."

"Then you picked the wrong line of work, didn't you?"

He smiled. "I don't have to do a lot of talking to the people on the subway platforms," he said. "'Keep it moving.' 'Step back.' 'No jumping the turnstiles, now. '"

She nodded, glancing up the aisle. *Not so fascinating, Richie-boy. She still cares more about the governor than you.*

"You wanted to be a cop because of your father," she said casually.

He felt his guard raise suddenly. "You know about my dad?"

She shrugged. "Someone must have told me."

Something in her expression seemed troubled. It certainly was troubling him. He realized he'd been riding this seesaw since the moment she'd sat down next to him—salivating one instant, on his guard the next.

Things had been a lot less complicated with Angela Caravetti, sister of his boyhood pal Angelo. The last year or so— right up until his parents' deaths, anyway—they'd gone out once or twice a month: the movies, sometimes the Italian place the other side of her father's dry-cleaning shop there by Pratt Institute. Quite often they had sex, of a sort, on the couch of her parents' living room, Angela as apparently content with the arrangement as any normal, red-blooded guy not in love might hope.

But Corrigan sensed he was reaching the end of his play-it-as-it-lays rope. He was tired of feeling uncomfortable, up to his ears with holding it in. All of a sudden, he didn't care if he drove Dara Wylie away, no matter what she looked like, no matter if he ended up in her send-Fielding-Dawson-to-the-White-House magazine story as the biggest oaf in the history of fluff journalism.

"I think it's about time we cut the bullshit," he told her, his voice even.

She blinked, the color rising in her cheeks again. "I'm sorry?" she said.

"Stop with the pretense," he said. "I'm a cop, remember? Even down there in the caves, we get plenty of people running their scams. After a while, you develop a kind of radar, okay?"

There was silence for a moment. "Maybe you're a pretty good cop," she said, finally. She glanced down at her hands for a moment, seemed to make a decision. "The truth is," she said, glancing back up at him, "there is something I wanted to discuss with you—"

"Miss Wylie," a familiar voice cut in.

Corrigan glanced up and found Fielding Dawson himself standing in the aisle, his sport coat shed, the full force of his smile trained on Dara. "I'm sorry to have kept you waiting."

Dara gave Corrigan an apologetic glance. "That's all right," she said to Dawson. "You're a busy man . . . . and likely to get busier."

Dawson held up his palm to stop her. "Not on this trip," he said. "That's the very point of it, to get as far from the spotlight as is possible. We'll take up the business of the campaign, assuming I decide to go ahead with it, once we've returned."

And once the public appetite has been whipped up by seven *more* days of speculation, Corrigan thought, wondering what on earth she'd been about to say. Now he'd have to wait while she took down the plan: how Candidate Dawson was to come back from wandering the wilderness after all those lonely days and nights, bearing the balm for all our aches and fears. Maybe he intended to serve fishes and loaves at the press conference, as well.

Corrigan noticed that Dawson's gaze had drifted toward his own. "Ever do much camping, Officer?"

"You don't want to know how much," Corrigan said easily.

Dawson gave a hearty laugh. "Well, the outfitters tell me

we're going places the average person has never seen." He glanced briefly at Dara. "I understand you grew up in this part of the country, Ms. Wylie. Idaho, wasn't it?"

Dara glanced back at Corrigan. "Utah," she said, nodding.

"Mormons." Dawson nodded. "Salt of the earth. Nixon trusted them with his life. So did Howard Hughes."

"I'm not a Mormon, though," she said.

Dawson seemed not to hear. He stepped back slightly, made a sweeping gesture toward the first-class cabin. Dara stood and gave Corrigan a last, earnest look.

"I'm sorry, Richard," she said.

"If I'm interrupting . . . ?" Dawson said. He looked at Corrigan, making it clear he couldn't have cared less what he might have been interrupting.

"No," Corrigan said. "We were just chatting."

"We'll talk later," Dara said, moving away.

"Sure," Corrigan said.

Then Dawson had placed a proprietary hand on her shoulder and was guiding her away down the aisle.

Corrigan watched them disappear through the curtain, thinking that while he had *heard* of Utah, he'd never actually met a person who claimed to be from there. He was also considering that whatever she'd been trying to draw out of him, as a native of the West, she had yet another advantage on him.

The plane gave a sudden lurch, then, popping through an updraft that rattled the overhead bins and lightened him in his seat momentarily. There was a beeping sound from the intercom, followed by the voice of a flight attendant. "The captain has turned on the seat-belt sign in preparation for our descent into the Denver airport. Please make sure your trays and seat backs are locked and in the upright position. . . ."

The plane was jouncing steadily, now, the engines groaning as the updrafts swirled. As the plane began to bank, Corrigan caught sight of a much different landscape out the opposite windows, an unbroken sweep of brownish plain that ended abruptly in the distance, where it seemed that a great bank of thunderheads had massed.

He noted that the photographer was awake, now, and was struggling to get himself buckled into his seat belt. The guy glanced at Corrigan, who gestured out the window.

"Looks like we're in for a storm," Corrigan said, pointing.

The guy turned to look out, then gave Corrigan a quizzical look. "What do you mean?" he asked.

"Out there," Corrigan said. "All those thunderclouds at the horizon."

The photographer glanced out at the jagged blue-black mass, then back at him. "I don't know what the hell you're talking about," he said, "but those aren't thunderheads. Those are the Rocky Mountains."

11

At the Denver airport, they'd been transferred to a twin-engine propeller-driven plane for what was announced as a "short" flight to Jackson, Wyoming, three hundred miles or so away. While there was no first-class cabin in the smaller plane and their party took up many more of the available seats, there would have been little opportunity for conversation above the racket of these engines, even if Dara had had it on her mind to explain herself.

He hadn't seen her or Dawson get off the jet, and though Corrigan had found a seat near the back of the smaller plane, leaving a space beside him, it did no good. When she did come on board, just ahead of Dawson and Soldinger, she settled into a spot several rows ahead and had launched into a fervent note-taking session once they were off the ground—working over some of Dawson's more pungent quotes, Corrigan supposed.

Corrigan, seated alone again, contented himself with the fact that this plane had climbed to nowhere near the altitude of the jet carrying them to Denver, and spent his time studying the landforms below. To his surprise, he found that this rugged topography *did* bear a resemblance to some of the maps he had studied as a youth. Mountain ranges stood out in clear relief, green at the lower elevations, increasingly brown and gnarled at the higher reaches. Rivers etched the land clearly, opening deep chasms through layers of red and orange and yellow rock. Roads, where there were any, were just as clearly defined.

Even to a kid whose idea of the wilderness was an unbuilt lot, this was country you could make sense of, he thought, at least from the vantage point of a growling plane.

By the time the plane neared Jackson, dusk had fallen, and though the pilot informed them that the not-to-be-missed spectacle of the Teton Range was coming up just off their port side, the combination of the failing light and gathering clouds obscured Corrigan's view. Still, even in those vague, looming shadows he saw enough to know that something amazing lay out there, some gathering of earth matter even mightier than the tons of rock that lay over his head each day of his working life back in Manhattan, and that was no puny concept in itself.

They landed at the Jackson airport without incident and were whisked by limousine (Dawson and his party) and small bus (the rest of them) to their hotel, a massive turreted and clapboard structure that looked like Teddy Roosevelt might have supervised its design and construction. A broad porch surrounded the main floor, where a series of rocking chairs had been set up, all of them filled by what seemed to be tourists in stiff jeans and colorful plaid shirts, some of them sporting cowboy hats.

He found himself assigned to a far more spacious room than he'd anticipated, with a four-poster bed sitting so high that he'd have to roll into it, and a claw-foot tub in the bath. He drew as hot a bath as he could stand, and soaked himself for an hour while leafing through a paperbound coffee-table volume he'd found on his bedside table: *High Country Visions,* a series of photographs of country so rugged and striking that Corrigan wondered if they'd been faked. It was about as dramatic an array of natural formations—snowy peaks, white-water gorges, alpine meadows—as could be imagined. Corrigan had never seen an antelope or an elk or a bear outside a zoo, and in fact suspected that such creatures truly existed only in such places. But here, if the photographic record was to be believed, the creatures abounded in the nearby territory he was about to visit.

He was no fan of Fielding Dawson, but on the other hand, the man had certain instincts for what made an arresting backdrop, no doubt about it. Corrigan dragged himself out of the tub, thinking how much more interesting commuters might find the subway if there was the chance of happening on a clutch of deer scampering up a stairwell now and then. Or imagine catching sight of the odd wolf or two, howling at the end of a lonely midtown platform late at night. Rather have that than the specter of a Brooklyn posse drag-assing toward you at 2:00 A.M., wouldn't you?

Maybe he'd make the suggestion to his superiors when he got back, he thought as he stepped happily into a pair of jeans. He was beginning to mellow, he realized. There was Dara, for one thing. And, if nothing else, he'd be out of uniform for a week, the first time in several months since he and Montcrief had been assigned a plainclothes stakeout trying to catch the heinous criminal who'd been jamming a series of turnstile coin slots with gum, then sucking the tokens out by mouth. Montcrief had been incredulous, and Corrigan might not have believed it himself, but they'd finally captured the entire process on videotape, had snagged the poor bastard in the station beneath Bloomingdale's, his lips still puckered up to one of the turnstiles. Business couldn't have been so good, anyway, with more and more people using the MetroCard instead of the tokens. The guy was a loser all the way around.

But it all seemed so far away, now, he thought as he snapped his new jeans, then reached to study the handout they'd been given by one of Dawson's aides. Dinner in something called the "Sacajawea Room" at 7:30. "Briefing" to follow.

He combed his hair, decided against a shave, then made his way down to the lobby in an elevator so ponderous, so loaded with brass, he felt as if he were riding in a safe. When he asked directions of the desk clerk to the meeting room, he didn't bother trying to pronounce "Sacajawea," and neither did the desk clerk, an affable older man wearing a shirt with pearl snaps on the pockets.

"I'm trying to find this place," Corrigan said, sliding the memo across the gleaming mahogany counter.

"Right across that way," the clerk said, pointing across the high-ceilinged lobby, "and down the hall, there."

Corrigan thanked him and walked away, thinking of how the last time he'd asked directions in the city, he'd had to flash his shield to a fellow cop to get cooperation. He skirted an outcropping of overstuffed leather sofas arranged beneath a chandelier that would have looked good in the ballroom of the *Titanic,* dodged what he saw was an actual, operating spittoon beside one armchair, noted a series of stuffed animal heads mounted on the wall beneath a railed gallery on the mezzanine.

He had stopped to stare up at the array of glassy-eyed creatures when he heard the voice over his shoulder. "Not very politically correct of them, is it?"

He glanced over his shoulder and saw Dara approaching him with a smile. Her hair was still wet from the shower, and she'd combed it straight back behind her ears. She was wearing jeans, low-cut hiking boots, and a flannel shirt with the sleeves rolled to the elbows. It was a look many of the tourists had affected. On Dara it was natural.

"You look . . . . healthy," he said, searching for the right words. She looked far more than that to Corrigan, but every other phrase seemed impossible.

She looked at him. "My father might have said something like that."

Corrigan nodded. "It's a compliment," he said.

She nodded, her smile broadening at his discomfort. "I'm taking it as a compliment."

"My old man would have told you, 'If you don't have your health, you don't have anything.'"

"I'm sorry I never met your father," she said.

He stared at her. "That more or less brings us back to where we were before, doesn't it?"

She stared at him for a moment. "It does, doesn't it?"

She glanced at the open doors to the meeting room, where waiters were bustling about the seated guests. "How about I buy you a drink after dinner?"

He shook his head. "I'm a cop. We can't accept gratuities."

She smiled. "Then you can buy me one."

"You got it," he said, and followed her into the room.

12

"**H**ow come it has the head on?" he said, leaning close to Dara. They were seated near the end of one of the two long tables that had been set up in the room, one peopled by the media types, the other by Dawson and his immediate entourage.

She glanced at him. "So you can tell it's a fish," she said mildly.

"What kind of fish?" Corrigan asked.

"Trout," she said. "That's the way we do trout out West."

Corrigan was trying to think of some response, when there was an amplified thumping from the front of the room. Corrigan turned to find that one of the rugged-looking types who had been sitting at Dawson's table was standing at a podium set up near the front of the meeting room.

The murmur of conversation in the room gradually died away, and the tall man, who, with his chiseled good looks and Western attire, could have easily posed for a Marlboro ad, continued. "I'm Ben Donnelly," he said. "I run Outback Expeditions, the outfit in charge of our little foray into the wilderness."

Donnelly nodded toward the back of the room, where an assistant, an even taller, somewhat bulkier replica of Donnelly, stood by a cart bearing a slide projector. "This is my son, Chipper," Donnelly said. "He'll be with us on the trip as well." Donnelly extended his hand toward his son. "Chipper!"

There was a polite smattering of applause as Chipper, clearly not an attention seeker, nodded a greeting. He turned to a panel on the wall and flipped a switch. The lights went down, and the slide-projector beam jumped to life.

A topographically enhanced map of the Intermountain West now filled a screen, which had been lowered just to Donnelly's side. The rendering featured every aspect of the maps Corrigan had pored over as a child, and he felt an odd thrill wash over him as he surveyed the vast sweep of mountain ranges, river courses, attendant canyons and valleys. Even the dotted lines outlining the familiar shapes of the states were there: Idaho, Montana, a chunk of northeastern Nevada, northern sections of Utah and Colorado, and, of course, Wyoming. There was a sizable red dot in the northwestern corner of the latter, and a "You Are Here"–styled arrow pointing to the spot he presumed was Jackson.

Donnelly, who had donned a pair of reading glasses, was bent to the podium, his face reflecting the glow of a reading lamp. "This is the big picture," Donnelly said, speaking with the air of a man who had been through the script before. "And it *is* a mighty big picture, folks. More beautiful, undeveloped territory here than anywhere else on earth."

He glanced out at his audience over his glasses. "That's part of the point of our journey, after all. To give you all a sense of what this country is all about."

"Hear, hear," Corrigan heard someone say. After a moment, he realized it was Dawson chiming in.

Donnelly managed a smile and gestured at his son. "Whyn't you bring 'em in a little closer to the subject, Chipper?"

There was a clunking sound as the changer cycled and another view came up on the screen, this one drawn down tighter on Wyoming. The extreme northwestern corner of the state was crosshatched off to show the boundaries of Yellowstone National Park, an assemblage of rugged peaks surrounding the vivid blue sprawl of Yellowstone Lake. The peaks weren't confined to the boundaries of the park, to be sure, and in fact, some of the country farther east, on the northern border of the state, seemed, if anything, even more rugged.

Just south of Yellowstone was another area of peaks and lakes and rivers, and there Corrigan saw the familiar dot representing Jackson. "We're *here,*" Donnelly said, "and first thing in the morning we'll be flying up *here.*"

As he spoke, the slide changed once more, where a yellow dotted line indicated a semicircular course into the heart of the rugged tangle well east of Yellowstone. Corrigan found himself barraged with exhilarating images of old films, with their treasure maps, newsreels tracing Lindbergh's flight to Europe, Amelia Earhart's doomed course over the Pacific. No wonder people wanted to be cartographers, he thought. Maybe that was a career he could look into. But what was the job market like for cartographers? he wondered.

The slide changed again, depicting a vast expanse of forest, glacier-strewn peaks, deep canyons, one sizable lake at the farthest reaches. "No roads where we're headed. No houses, no people, no newspapers, no cell-phone service." There were a few chuckles. "The deer and the bears don't need any of that." More chuckles, though Corrigan saw a look of concern on the face of one of the women across the table from him.

"Now, I don't want anyone to be concerned about safety. That's why we're there. Besides, those creatures don't want anything more to do with you than vice versa. We'll see some squirrels and a deer or two. But probably no bears . . . unless you ignore the basic rules concerning food storage and the like that we'll be going over with you later, of course."

Donnelly gestured again, and this time the new scene elicited a murmur from the audience. It was a ground-level shot taken from the shores of a peak-encircled lake, perhaps the same one from the previous slide. The sky was crystal, the water cobalt. In the distance, at the head of the lake, a waterfall cascaded down a sheer rock face, a lacelike trail of white against the near-black backdrop of cliff.

"This is where we begin," Donnelly said, glancing up at them, his glasses gleaming in the reflected light. Corrigan couldn't see the man's eyes, just those glowing half-moons high up on his cheeks. Just as well, he thought. It made him seem like some kind of prophet of the wilderness. He was also beginning to understand why people would shell out whatever astronomical sum was required to take this trip.

"The first day we circle the lake, camp beside Bridal Lace Falls, there, then start through the mountains. Six days through some of the prettiest country you'll ever see, then to Garrett's Canyon, the best part of a day climbing down, and then two days on the river coming out, back to civilization." He'd said all this to a rapidly shifting panorama of rock formations, dizzying overlooks, and winding trails, capped off with a shot of a series of yellow rubber rafts hurtling through white-water rapids in a deep gorge.

Donnelly gestured again, and the lights came up. He smiled out at the blinking audience. "Of course, I didn't show you any of the best stuff," he said. "We're saving that for the trip, right, Chipper?"

Chipper colored, managing a nod for the group.

Corrigan turned to Dara. "I foresee a challenge, getting Chipper involved in your story," he said.

"If we meet any grizzlies, he's the one I want in front of me," she said.

Corrigan nodded, and turned back as a carefully groomed man at Dawson's table raised a hand. "I've heard rumors these trips are well provisioned," the man said, meaning it as a question.

"I should introduce all of you to Giles Ashmead," Dawson called, smiling out over the crowd. "As some of you know, Giles is my attorney and chief advisor. This lovely woman he's sitting with is his wife, Sonia."

The pair smiled perfunctorily, and Corrigan thought they seemed more likely to be found sitting at a society fund-raiser than at the kickoff dinner to a wilderness trip. He wondered just how eager the two of them were to be making this trek.

"You won't go hungry," Donnelly assured Ashmead. "Or thirsty," he added, to general laughter from the Dawson table.

"I was just wondering how many bearers there'll have to be," Ashmead continued.

Donnelly gave a laugh of his own. "Well, we don't use *bearers* here in Wyoming, Mr. Ashmead. We have some *wranglers* that manage our pack animals—horses and mules, that is. But they won't be with us. That would slow everything down too much. Fact of the matter, they're already up there caching what we'll need at various spots along the way. We'll just carry in a few of the basics so we can move along unencumbered."

Corrigan leaned back to Dara. "Yeah, those cases of Chateau Lafitte Rothschild get a little heavy toward the end of the day."

"I'd be happy with a Coors Lite every once in a while," she said.

Corrigan sat forward again, noticing that Dawson's wife

had her hand aloft. "I know you have a lot of experience at what you do, Mr. Donnelly, but what if something *should* happen, an accident of some kind . . . ?"

Donnelly held up a reassuring hand. "I understand exactly where you're coming from, Mrs. Dawson. And while it is important to us to maintain the sense of a true wilderness experience, we have to be prepared."

He turned back to his son. "Chipper, you got your new phone with you?"

Chipper nodded, lumbering toward the front of the room like a well-trained bear himself. He handed his father something that looked much like an ordinary cell phone. Donnelly took it, examined the keypad, punched a button. He held the instrument close to the microphone as an electronic chime sounded.

"On this trip, we'll be carrying a couple of these satellite phones," Donnelly said, holding the thing aloft. "They're not cheap—about four thousand dollars apiece—but they'll keep us in touch, wherever we go. Anything should happen—and it hasn't, yet—we can, at a moment's notice, call in a 'copter or whatever else might be necessary."

"Like a side of beef," Corrigan murmured. "Or more Pouilly-Fuissé."

Dara frowned to silence him, and Corrigan gave her a good-natured shrug.

Donnelly handed back the phone to his son and turned once again to the group. "Now, there'll be plenty of opportunity for the more adventurous among you to do some wild-game stalking—we shoot with cameras only, of course—and some rock climbing . . ." He paused to glance at Dawson, then continued: "And if you're really brave, maybe we'll let you put in the river a bit upstream from our normal spot, in case you want to get a taste of some wilder water." He paused again, waiting for some nervous laughter to die away.

"But I want to stress that you'll get your ration of thrilling experiences without having to be concerned for safety, beyond the reasonable precautions, of course. We've been at this for some years, now. I know the way in and the way out, and just in case I forget, we'll have our GPS along for good measure." He pointed back at Chipper again, who held up another electronic device a little smaller than a laptop computer. "If global positioning devices are good enough for Hertz and Avis," Donnelly said, "then they're good enough for us as well. Any other questions?" Donnelly called as the chuckles faded.

Corrigan longed to ask the man how he really felt about leading a bunch of tenderfeet through a fortnight of "wilderness experience," especially when the party had been assembled for the purpose of furthering a political campaign, but he knew he wouldn't. If he got the chance, maybe he'd ask Donnelly some version of the question over after-dinner drinks around the campfire.

For one thing, and despite all the Disneyesque overtones of the enterprise, Corrigan was beginning to look forward to seeing what was out there. For another, he suspected he knew the reasoning that lay at the heart of Donnelly's motivation. Avuncular Marlboro Man or no, Ben Donnelly surely loved the look of a healthy bank statement. For what he'd make from the trip, Corrigan thought, he'd probably be willing to escort Leona Helmsley through the territories.

"Well, if you all are through with me," Donnelly said, "then I'm through with you. I'll see you all out on the seaplane pier at eight A.M. sharp."

He left to a round of applause, and paused to accept a hearty handshake from Dawson. Waiters were hurrying toward the tables with dessert and coffee, but Dawson's entourage was up and filtering toward the door.

Corrigan turned to Dara, who was shaking her head at the offer of cheesecake.

"How about that drink?" he said.

She hesitated, then gave him a look. "I'm feeling a little worn out all of a sudden. Would you mind if I ducked out on you?"

He stared back at her. "Of course I would," he said. "But could I have a rain check?"

She nodded. "I'll buy you a drink in the mountains," she said. And then she gathered her things and was gone.

13

Lost Lake, Idaho

The vast hangar was silent, the shapes of the planes dim silhouettes in the shadows. There was a vague nimbus of light that radiated from the cockpit of one of the craft, however, enough to draw the attention of the security man, who had been about to end his cursory inspection of the company offices, a small area in one corner of the building with its own entrance, a low, noninsulated roof of particleboard partitioned from the hangar itself by a wall that was framed primarily in glass.

The dog that was with him must have sensed something as well, possibly a nervous quality about the tug on its short chain lead, some tightening in the posture of its master, for it gave a low growl as the watchman doused his light and moved toward the door in the partitioned wall. "Quiet, Oscar," the man said, and the dog obeyed, even though it was trembling with anticipation as the two of them moved quietly out into the nearly dark hangar.

The smell of oil, grease, gasoline, and the indefinable musk of a cavernous structure that had housed machinery for many years rose to the man's nostrils. There was also something else in the air, something far less tangible though no less noticeable to the watchman, whose name was McCullough. Pressed to describe it, he would have called it trouble.

McCullough had been a night watchman, as he referred to himself, for only four months. Before that he had worked for almost a year at the Wal-Mart in Rock Springs, as a stocker and sales associate, until the company had dropped all but three—one per eight-hour shift—of its full-time employees in a cost-cutting move. Prior to that, he had worked for twenty-

four years as a roustabout in the oil and gas fields in various
forlorn spots around the West, a career that had ended when a
load of drill casing burst its restraints and tumbled off a
flatbed, shattering his left leg. The accident had left him with
a limp, lingering arthritis in his knee and ankle, and an edge
that hadn't helped him much in selling power tools and lawn
mowers to penny-pinching idiots, but it was nothing his
monthly disability check and a half-pint of Green Jack over
the course of a lonely evening's tour of his present duties
couldn't assuage.

The only fly in the ointment, so to speak, was the dog.
McCullough had never liked dogs, considered them freeload-
ers on the great human enterprise at best, and the fact that this
one actually had a job annoyed him all the more. He had
learned, in fact, that the company that trained and provided
the animals was paid a monthly sum for each that was greater
even than his own salary. To be out-earned by a dog was a fact
that he had labored mightily to accept.

"Hold on, you stupid shit," McCullough said in a fierce
whisper, one hand tight on the animal's lead. He eased the
door shut behind him and fished in his windbreaker pocket for
the bottle. He spun the cap away with his thumb, palmed it,
tipped the bottle for a taste, and had it down and capped again
all in the space of time it might have taken John Elway to fire
a short dump over the middle.

"All right," he hissed, nudging the dog with his knee. "Let's
go see."

He could hear the animal's nails digging on the concrete
floor, and, he supposed, so could anyone else who might happen to be in the building. Most likely, all this was for nothing.
Most likely, the glow that lent a soft illumination to the cockpit up ahead was that of a panel light or a hand torch left on
mistakenly by a crew member, but there was always the possibility of something else, some unfathomable skullduggery
involved, and for McCullough, whose boredom had grown to
gargantuan proportions over the past four months, the possibility of actually capturing someone up to no good filled him
with an anticipatory rush that was very nearly sexual.

As it had, by all appearances, filled the straining animal as
well. The thing was breathing in harsh pants, now, its nails
tearing frantically at the floor. Though it pained him to think

so, McCullough could not deny the notion that had flashed across the readout of his consciousness: *Good minds think alike.*

McCullough patted his chest, where he kept his pistol strapped, just to be sure. Intermountain Security supplied him with a nightstick, a leather sap, and a holstered can of Mace, but he had a registered permit to carry his own .38, and none of his supervisors had ever discouraged the practice. The West was still the West, after all.

As he came around the tail of the craft and noted the shadow of the gangway that extended down toward the hangar floor in the gesture of a languid hand, McCullough paused. He considered the possibility of another taste, briefly, then dismissed it. He reached to his shoulder holster, lifted out his pistol. He bent to the insanely straining dog and gave its skull a sharp rap with the butt of the weapon, careful to keep the barrel pointed away from his own skull just in case. The dog, to its credit, did not yelp; its struggles at the lead fell off considerably.

There was the problem of climbing the gangway to consider, but McCullough did not overthink the matter. He moved stealthily to the dangling steps, stepped around the dog, thumping it in the chest with his heel to make his intentions clear. The dog waited patiently for him to pass, and when it was time, moved nimbly up the metal steps behind McCullough about as quietly as was possible for a dog to do.

McCullough needed to climb less than halfway up to get a clear view inside the cockpit, and what he saw convinced him that all his suspicions had been dead-on from the beginning. A panel dangled loose from the copilot's console, wires splayed out like a network of arteries and veins. Some sort of trouble light had been rigged up there, hooked to a line that descended from the pilot's stick. Laid out on the floorboards was a set of what looked like dental tools in a soft leather case.

McCullough wasn't sure what was going on, but he knew he was not staring at the signs of scheduled maintenance. Sometimes work went on in the hangar after hours, but doors were open, overhead lights switched on, radios were played. McCullough realized that his hands had grown slick with sweat and that he was feeling a little light-headed. He drew his head back out of the cabin and stood unsteadily on the lower step of the gangway. He reholstered his pistol, then wiped his palms on his pants, transferring the dog's lead back and forth as he did so.

Whether the dog had heard something or had just taken advantage of the slackening in its lead as he passed it back and forth, McCullough couldn't say. In an instant, however, the lead had jerked from his hand and the animal was gone—no barks, no growls, just the frantic clatter of nails on concrete, receding into the darkness.

McCullough cursed, steadying himself on the wobbling gangway. The overpaid bastard was eager, he'd have to give it that much. And if the person who'd been mucking around, trying to steal valuable airplane instruments, was still in the building, McCullough felt sorry for him. The dog's powerful jaws had already been snapping viciously as it tore away.

He was down off the gangway, now, had his hand back on his pistol, when he heard the sounds: a muffled growl followed almost immediately by a great crashing of oil drums, part of the stack near the south hangar door, he calculated. McCullough was moving quickly in that direction, but had to duck as the shadow of a wing swooped up toward him out of the darkness.

Drums were still banging and rolling as he came up on the other side of the wing he'd nearly brained himself on. In a sliver of moonlight drifting in from the little see-through window in the delivery gate, he could make out the shapes of several of the big drums tumbled over, some of them still rocking back and forth. There was something else on the floor there, too, a broad dark puddle—oil, his mind insisted, had to be oil.

But there was something moving there in the middle of the puddle, something skittering and splashing and flopping like a beached fish. *What in God's name is a fish doing in an airplane hangar?* was the question that a part of McCullough's brain was demanding, but he chose to ignore it.

He squinted, cursing the dim light, then knelt down, cautious. Maybe it was a possum or a raccoon that had been nesting among those barrels, gotten squashed in all the ruckus. McCullough had his flashlight clipped to his belt, but something, some atavistic sense of self-preservation, was keeping him from snapping it on and making a sitting duck of himself in the darkness. Not until he knew a few more things.

Meantime, whatever it was flopping around there was about done for, he realized, its movements subdued, less frequent, now. He reached out gingerly with his pistol, nudged it. One last shuddering spasm, then nothing.

McCullough glanced over his shoulder. All quiet. Was the thing that had just died before him what had gotten the dog all worked up—some poor feral creature just looking for a quiet place to sleep?

And where *was* the fucking dog, anyway? McCullough turned back and used the barrel of his pistol to rake the inert form toward him, out of the dark puddle and into the slice of moonlight that painted the concrete floor.

What he saw made his heart lurch and caused his finger to tighten reflexively on the trigger of his pistol. The explosion blew hot fragments of concrete up against his cheeks, was magnified a dozen times over inside the cavernous hangar. McCullough was on his feet in an instant, staggering backward, slapping at his stinging cheeks. He was gasping for breath and trying to squeeze out little cries of terror at the same time.

Dog's head, he heard his mind saying as he danced backward from the awful thing he'd dragged into the light. *Dog's head. Dog's head. Dog's head.*

That flopping creature down there, that beached fish. *Sure, some poor possum, dumbass.* His legs were leaden, his throat the size of a pinhole. He had a pistol in his hand, but it might as well have been a rock or a snowball. He realized that his ears were still ringing, clogged, in fact, with a noise that went beyond a roar into some other realm. At first he assumed it was the echoing of the shot he'd fired, but in the next moment he realized it was something else altogether—some sound that was new, though still familiar.

He turned, staring dumbly into the dark reaches of the hangar. *Airplane,* he thought. *The roar of an airplane engine.*

He shook his head, trying to get himself under control. The sound was deafening, disorienting.

"Here!"

A voice. Very definitely a human voice, shouting over the roaring of the engines. McCullough felt his bowels going watery and at the same time remembered the pistol. He was holding it up, pointing it toward the ceiling like a starter about to kick off a race.

"Over here!" The voice, this time from a different angle. He spun about, dizzy, now, waving his pistol aimlessly before him. He felt a trickle of wetness at his cheek. His head was throbbing. A drum was rolling toward him. He sidestepped, his feet slipping in wetness.

"Here!" The voice again. He saw a shadow coming toward him and threw his arms up too late to stop it.

Something heavy struck him in the chest. His arms curled about it in reflex. Heavy and warm and wet, this burden he now clutched to his chest. The odor of wet fur. Of blood. Of sweetness and foulness and death.

McCullough realized he had lost his pistol. He was whimpering, choking on his own breath, beyond reason, beyond any hope of combat. He knew only that something, someone, was coming for him and that he longed to be anywhere else but there.

He turned and began to run, one step, a second, a third . . .

He realized he was still clutching the carcass of the dog to his chest, and flung it away with a cry of disgust. He was still moving, still praying the darkness might save him, when he remembered that the great roaring was in fact the sound of airplane engines and that the sudden and terrible wind whirling at his face might signal a great downturn in his prospects.

Had he thought these things a moment earlier, he might have stopped himself. For that matter, had he stayed himself from panic, he might not have run in the first place. He might have held his ground and used his pistol properly, and he might have come out of all this a hero.

But as it was, he was in full panic mode, in full flight, in midstep, and there was time to do nothing but fling up his arm as he toppled into the roaring, invisible cyclone just ahead.

"There must have been easier ways," she said.

"Never underestimate what a rent-a-cop might do," he told her.

"If you think I'm cleaning up that mess, you're crazy," she said.

"No one asked you to," he said.

"I just wanted to make sure," she said. "I've got plenty of work left of my own, you know."

"You do your thing, I'll do mine."

She shook her head, moved toward the still-swaying steps that climbed to the cockpit. "Just don't get any ideas," she said. "I'm going to be a while."

"Take as long as you need," he said, surveying the scene about him. At least they didn't have to worry about using the lights any longer. "I might just be a while myself."

14

It's a Grumman Mallard," Chipper was saying, pointing at the sizable seaplane that floated beside the pier nearby. "You ever been in one?"

Quite a speech for Chipper, Corrigan thought as he shook his head. He hadn't been looking at the plane, in fact. He'd been staring at the saw-toothed backdrop of the Tetons that loomed beyond the lake in the distance, as dramatic a sight as he'd ever seen.

He'd almost forgotten how chilly it was, he thought, unwrapping his parka-clad arms from in front of his chest. The sun was rising at his back, lighting the tips of the mountains in brilliant gold, leaving their lower reaches in blue-black shadow, and it already seemed ten degrees warmer. He gave an experimental puff of breath from his cheeks, noticed that no vapor took shape, and tried to force himself to pay attention to the outfitter's son standing beside him.

The mountains' reflections seemed to stretch across the intervening water toward him, though a breeze had kicked up and a light chop had sent the inverted images dancing into an impressionist's dream. The waves sloshed against the hull of the plane with a hollow sound, and Corrigan made himself turn to face Chipper, this earnest young man who'd taken a break from his supervision of the loading of the gear and only wanted to talk.

"Looks like a boat with wings," Corrigan said. Unlike smaller seaplanes Corrigan had seen in pictures, this craft's hull rested squarely on the water. The pontoon structures, which dangled from the tips of the wings, seemed barely to touch the water.

Chipper nodded. "That's about what it is," he said. "Those

floats at the end of the wings are really auxiliary fuel tanks. We can put another fifty gallons in each one."

"I guess that's important," Corrigan said.

"This little puppy burns a hundred gallons an hour, loaded the way she is," Chipper said. "The regular tanks'll hold four hundred. She goes about a hundred and fifty knots, assuming there's no headwind. So that's plenty of fuel to get us where we're going and get the pilot back home." Chipper gave him an affable glance. "Still, you like to have yourself a margin for error, flying around this country."

Corrigan wasn't sure he wanted to ask about what might constitute "error," and he had the uncomfortable feeling that Chipper was about to tell him. "You had it long?"

"Naw, we just lease it on a need-be basis," he said. "There's an outfit up in Idaho we get 'em from."

"That where they're made, Idaho?" Corrigan was starting to get the hang of this patter. Just drift along from one inconsequential thing to another, maybe you learn something useful, maybe you don't. A lot like passing the time of day with another cop, he thought.

He glanced back toward shore where the big Chevy Blazer sat, Dara in there, talking to Dawson.

"They don't make a Mallard anywhere, not anymore," Chipper was saying. "This one was 1948, I think."

Corrigan looked at him, his attention finally caught. "It's fifty years old?" he said, hearing the surprise in his own voice.

Chipper shrugged. "I wouldn't be too concerned. There's a whole airline still uses them down in Florida," he said. "Chalk's. Takes people from Miami all around the Caribbean. They tell me Jimmy Buffett has one, too."

"It doesn't look fifty years old," Corrigan said. The part about Jimmy Buffett failed to reassure him. Unless he was mistaken, every rock-and-roll star of the fifties and sixties seemed to have died in a small-plane crash. Buffett could simply be thumbing his nose at Fate.

"They're well taken care of," Chipper said, a smile forming at the corners of his mouth. "Totally refurbished, the engines replaced altogether in the seventies, when a guy named Frakes came up with the idea of adding turbo props. The Coast Guard uses 'em for air-sea rescue in weather they'd never take a helicopter out in."

"We don't have to talk about rescue, do we?"

"Not if you don't want to," Chipper said.

After a moment, he turned his gaze toward the Blazer. "She's a pretty girl, isn't she?"

Corrigan looked to see if Chipper might be goading him, but there was nothing like guile on his round face. Give it a few years, let the wind and the rain and the sun go to work on that visage, maybe something like his old man's "Been there, done that, seen it all" expression would take shape. Right now, he was just a guy expressing what every other guy in his right mind would express, or so Corrigan thought.

"She *is* a piece of work," Corrigan said. And they both nodded at that, just as one of the doors of the Blazer opened and a peal of Fielding Dawson's laughter rolled out their way.

Seventeen seats, seventeen passengers, Corrigan noted as the plane taxied out toward takeoff. He was sitting in one of the single places near the rear, where the cabin narrowed, and he'd had plenty of time to count. Up front were Dawson and his wife, Elizabeth, the Ashmeads, and Dawson's assistant, Ariel Sorenson—an energetic young woman with plum-colored lipstick and matching dark nails who looked like she survived on a diet of wheat germ and positive thoughts. There was also the muscle-bound type who'd been with Soldinger at the airport, the last remnant of real "security," Corrigan supposed. Soldinger, it was explained, had gone off to make arrangements for the governor's press conference at the other end of the line.

Behind Dawson's entourage, Donnelly and Chipper sat together, intently trading comments over a topographical map. Close by were two other wiry, leather-skinned types who looked like they'd been flown in from wrangler central.

From Chipper, he'd learned that there were five members of the film team: a young female director who'd done a number of documentaries for the Adventure Channel, two cameramen, a sound man, and a grip. That group had clustered together as well, leaving Corrigan and Dara the last seats: Dara sat across the narrow aisle in another single place, intent on her notes.

Corrigan turned his own attention out the window. The wind seemed to have picked up, and the plane wallowed in the chop, its engines groaning louder. Though he couldn't make out the shoreline from his angle, he sensed that they had been taxiing or trolling or whatever a seaplane did for way long enough to reach their takeoff point.

Earlier, Chipper had broken off his discourse on the Mallard's features long enough for Dara to make her way past them and on toward the plane, but the moment she was out of sight, he'd relapsed. Corrigan had learned that the plane needed a good 5,000 feet of unobstructed waterway in order to take off or land. ("Don't worry, we got seven thousand feet here, and a good six thousand up in the mountains.") That much had sounded vaguely reassuring, until Chipper began to explain how payload and altitude could affect these limits.

"We'll put down at just about nine thousand feet," he'd said, shaking his head. "Air's awful thin up that high, so you *need* some extra room."

Corrigan tried to put such thoughts aside, feeling the pulsation of the engines growing. He felt a momentary surge of anxiety, then came the moment of release as the plane started forward, lumbering through the water at first as if it were trying to plow through glue. In moments, the pace had quickened, doubling and redoubling until they were skimming the wave tops. Finally they were lifting free of the water altogether and were airborne. In the next moment, the plane had banked steeply, laying out the breathtaking sight of the Tetons before him.

"Awesome," Corrigan heard himself saying. It was not a word he was inclined to use, but what else could he say?

"Leave it to a Frenchman to name them breasts." Dara's voice came to him.

He turned to see her leaning across the aisle, sharing his view. He might have said something, but he wasn't quite sure what she was talking about.

"Grand Tetons," she said, by way of explanation. "As in *big breasts.*"

"Oh," Corrigan said.

"Don't tell me," she said, "you hadn't thought about what the name meant."

"I guess I never thought about it," he told her. He wasn't sure if his face was coloring or if it was just the sudden shift in altitude. All he could think about suddenly were *her* breasts. It took a monumental force of his will not to stare.

"This the kind of place you grew up in?" he asked after a moment.

She looked up at him, seemed to decide something. She put her notebook aside, glanced out the window. "Not exactly. Salt Lake's an actual city, you know."

"But you're not a Mormon."

"Is this an interrogation?"

"Just making conversation," he said.

She nodded, leaned back in her seat. "My father taught journalism at the university in Salt Lake City," she said. "He grew up Methodist in Odessa, Texas, but believed in the Gospel according to Damon Runyon."

She tucked a lock of her hair behind her ear, and he thought she looked tired, suddenly. He didn't like thinking of her that way. He preferred bright and cheery. "How'd you get to New York?" he asked.

"You really want to know?"

He nodded. *That and a few thousand other things,* he thought.

She glanced across the narrow aisle at him. "After I graduated, I moved to Southern California with a couple of girls from school, to get away from home. I was knocking around, trying to get on with the *Times,* had picked up some work as a stringer for *USA,* when the O.J. story broke. As it turned out, I was going to the same health club where one of his girlfriends was a member. I knew this girl on a first-name basis, we were doing the StairMasters together one day, and out of nowhere she burst into tears, started telling me all this stuff about what she really believed about what he'd done."

A rueful smile crossed her face. "Some reporter I am. After a couple of minutes, I'm going, like, 'Oh, she's *that* Paula!'"

Corrigan considered it for a moment and glanced ahead toward Dawson and the others. "You're telling me you're the one who spilled this girl's mess in *USA Magazine,* therefore I can trust you not to get me in trouble?"

She shook her head. "Other people got into that part of her story. The piece I did was all about the real person behind all the headlines. I didn't write one thing she was upset with." She fixed him with her stare. "Anyway, you asked me a question, I'm answering you truthfully. I wrote that story, the L.A. bureau chief offered me a full-time job with the magazine.

When he got the New York bureau last year, I asked to come along. So here I am." She flashed him her ingenuous smile, gesturing at the rugged terrain below. "Back in the wilderness."

Corrigan nodded. "So, what was it you wanted to discuss with me, anyway? I have to warn you, though, it's not like Fielding Dawson told me where he hid his bloody gloves."

"It doesn't have anything to do with Dawson," she said.

"I already told you I can't talk about what happened down there that day."

"I know," she said, turning to him. There was a mournful expression on her face, he thought.

"Then what?"

"I'm sure no one else knows this . . . ," she began.

"I'll say this much," he told her impatiently. "You know how to string a story out."

She didn't smile. "Remember I told you I did that piece on the subways?"

"Maybe I remember something." He shrugged.

"Well," she said, "one of the things that never got in the story was this sidebar I wanted to add about some of the homeless people still living down there."

"There's a lot of them," he said. "There used to be a lot more?"

She nodded. "And some of them are pretty interesting," she said. "They've had some fairly amazing experiences."

"So I have observed," he said.

"I mean, *before* they ended up down there," she said.

"I know there is a point to all this," Corrigan said.

She'd been biting her lip. Finally she glanced up to be sure no one seemed to be listening, then leaned closer to him. "The point is, I think I know who the man was that you . . . ." She broke off, then continued, "The man who died."

He was shaking his head. "How could you know? He wasn't carrying any I.D. The M.E. couldn't even find a set of teeth. They'll never find out who that guy was."

"I can't be sure," she persisted. "But judging from his height, the way he moved and all . . ."

"How in the hell would you know what he looked like—" He broke off suddenly, staring at her as it sunk in. "You talked to Montcrief, didn't you. You pumped Rollie about all this . . ."

"Richard," she said, shaking her head, "I was just doing my job. I'd been assigned to the governor's campaign—"

"Sonofabitch," he said. "What're you trying to do, break the big story of the killer cave cop?"

She stared at him, her eyes wide. "I don't know what you're talking about. You're not in any trouble that I'm aware of."

"Then what the hell *are* we talking about?"

She sighed. "I wasn't even going to bring it up, okay? But the more I thought about it, the more it bothered me."

He forced himself to calm down, tried to focus on the steady grinding noise of the plane's engines. "Just tell me. Who is this guy you think you know?" He was ready for anything at this point. The guy had once played for the Knicks. Had invented the computer chip. He was the second fucking gunman behind the grassy knoll.

"He was nobody special," she said quietly. "Or he was, depending on how you view it. He'd been a teacher. A philosophy professor, for a time. He had some pretty unusual ideas. I suppose that's why he ended up losing his job. He'd been married, had a son and a daughter—he had no idea what had happened to them, of course. He'd been hospitalized. There was drinking, a drug problem . . . ." She broke off, biting her lip again.

"Look, Richard, I don't even know why I'm telling you all this. I—"

He raised his hand to stop her. "I think you know exactly why you're telling me. You think you've got a pretty good story here, but telling it would run against the grain of your big assignment with the governor up there, and you don't know whether it's worth the trouble until you see what's doing with the big hero cop."

She was shaking her head, ready to interrupt, but he wasn't about to give her the chance. "Well, let me make it easy for you," he said. "Let me be the first to deliver the scoop."

"Richard—"

"All this about me saving the governor's life is bullshit," he said.

She stared at him, shaking her head uncertainly.

"Shots fired, hand-to-hand combat," he said, gesturing toward the front of the plane. "It never happened. The poor bastard never even had a gun."

"But your partner said he did—"

"It might have looked like it when he came out of the bushes," Corrigan said. "What he was holding was a piece of plastic. This homeless philosopher you interviewed, he have a problem with asthma?"

"I saw a copy of the police report," she insisted, holding her voice low. "A thirty-two-caliber pistol—"

"Somebody threw it down," Corrigan said.

She stared back at him in shock.

"It wasn't me," he added. "I was chasing the guy down onto the platform; he tripped and fell before I could catch him. End of story." He paused. "The rest of it just sort of grew."

"Like Topsy," she said, still shaking her head.

"Like a lot of things," he said, gesturing toward the front of the plane. "So, here I am, Fielding Dawson's chief show pony, just the way you called it. How's that for a story?"

There was a long pause.

"Pretty sad," she said finally.

"I couldn't agree more," he said.

"You remember I said I was sorry your father had died?" she said after a moment.

"Yeah. What's that have to do with it?"

"Because I think you'd like to have him here to talk to right now."

"We didn't talk about much when he was alive."

"Still," she said. "Still."

He felt a deep ache growing somewhere under his lungs. "You talk to your old man about what stories to write?"

She shook her head. "He's dead, too. Heart attack. Right in front of his class one day."

He paused. "Your mom?"

She shook her head. "She didn't last too long after he died."

He forced himself to take a breath. A doozy of a deep breath, this time. "So, what would your old man think about what I just gave you?"

She thought about it. "He'd probably tell me to trust my own instincts."

"What do *they* tell you?"

She held his gaze. "That you're a good guy," she said, glancing out the window. "And that we're about to land."

He turned as a jolt of rough air caused him to clutch reflexively at the armrests of his seat. He glanced out, saw that they were pushing into a bank of clouds.

". . . little rough weather as we make our approach." The voice of the pilot crackled over the intercom. "Just be sure to stay buckled tight. . . ."

If he'd intended to say something else, Corrigan couldn't be sure, for his attention had been drawn away by a sudden, sickening drop in their altitude, followed by an equally sharp surge upward. He kept his grip on the armrests but felt his seatbelt pull tightly against his midsection, felt his head fly back, then dip, as if he were on some carnival ride. He glanced up at the ceiling of the plane, listening as the engines picked up a notch in volume. If he hadn't been buckled in, he thought, he would have surely bounced off those unyielding-looking panels.

Then, just as quickly, they had broken out of the clouds. As if by magic, the ride steadied and sunshine poured through the windows. Dazed by the sudden contrast, Corrigan glanced out and saw another range of snowcapped peaks in the distance.

". . . about the joyride." The still-crackling voice of the pilot came again. "But we'll be down in a minute. . . ." More crashing and hissing, then, and the roar of the engines kicked up yet another notch.

The plane was dropping through a pass between peaks, now, a green canopy spread about below, with a view of sheer granite cliffs out either window. There was snow still packed in the recesses of the mountains and, here and there, waterfalls tumbling toward the forest below.

He strained to see the bottom of the canyon beneath them, and did manage to make out one brief flash of white water far below. He wondered if that was the route they'd take on the last leg of their journey, or if it might be just one of a multitude of white-water rivers in this exotic land. He saw a dark shape rushing across the sun-washed shoulder of mountain nearby, and realized that it was the shadow of their plane hurtling along.

Abruptly they were soaring over a rock-strewn ridge, and their hurrying shadow had vanished. Ahead, Corrigan caught a glimpse of forest, then a crescent of blue mirroring an array of snow peaks. It was so perfect—as pristine as one of those perfect-looking shots from a drugstore calendar—that he found it impossible to accept at first.

But then the plane banked for its final descent, allowing him another look at the lake and the mountains and the encircling canopy of pines, and he knew that it was true, that they had arrived. Say what you might about Fielding Dawson and the reasons for this trip, Richard Corrigan believed he was staring out now at paradise.

The plane turned again, its flaps dropping, its engines groaning a deeper note as the drag increased. In moments, it seemed, they had dropped below the rocky line of the ridge and were whisking over the tops of the pines, the glassy surface of the lake looming up ahead.

He knew it was only an illusion created by his faulty sense of perspective as he glanced at the encroaching pines and looming peaks, but the plane actually seemed to be picking up speed as they arrowed toward the water. Numbers born of Chipper's monologue on altitude and landing clearances flashed through his mind with no regard for logic: Did they need 26,000 feet to land, or was that the height of some Himalayan peak? Was the lake below 9,000 feet deep, or 150 knots wide? Did anyone care?

He felt a moment of dizzying lunacy—*If this is how it ends, then what a way to go*—and then the plane kissed the water. They bounced up briefly like a huge stone skimming the surface, then came down again, this time hugging the water for good. A spontaneous cheer arose in the cabin, and Corrigan realized that he had lent his voice to the cry.

"Is this real?" Corrigan said to Dara. They were still on the pier that reached out into the lake, watching as the seaplane taxied away for its takeoff. The breeze off the lake was cool, the thin air exhilarating, the early sun hot on his forehead.

She glanced around, smiling. "About as real as it gets," she said, her voice softening.

"What are those?" he asked, pointing at a pair of sizable rodentlike creatures scuttling along the rocky shore.

She followed his gesture. "Marmots," she said.

"A better-looking grade of rat?"

She gave him a look. "More like a squirrel," she said.

"We could introduce them into the subways," he said. "Upgrade the neighborhood."

She shook her head, smiling.

"I guess you've seen a lot of places like this, growing up out West," he continued.

She gave him an appraising stare. "Nothing any prettier than this," she said.

He nodded. "You forget, where I come from, Central Park is a vast, unspoiled wilderness."

"Central Park is pretty, too."

He glanced toward shore, where Donnelly and his crew were busying themselves arranging gear. One of the wranglers—Vaughn was his name—had already started a fire and had put up a pot of coffee. Corrigan, who sometimes had coffee and sometimes not, could smell the aroma all the way to the end of the dock.

The other wrangler—Pete, was it?—was fitting together some fly rods for the morning amusement of Dawson and his friends, Corrigan assumed. The plan, as Donnelly had outlined it, was to have lunch where they were, then spend the afternoon in a leisurely trek around to the far side of the lake, where the waterfall tumbled down. They'd camp there for the evening, then strike out over the ridge and on into the wilderness first thing in the morning.

He turned, found Dara holding a camera toward him. "I'm supposed to leave the photography to the other team—Dawson will clear everything through them—but I don't suppose anyone would care about a couple of snapshots," she said. "If you don't mind, that is."

He gave her a look. "I'm not much good at it," he said. And he never had been, he thought, suspecting it had something to do with his eye.

"I trust you," she said, her gaze holding his.

He took the camera, waved at the crystal water. "What kind of fish are in here, anyway?"

"Trout," she said, with the hint of a smile. "Remember trout?"

"Roger on the trout," he said. He could still see her wielding her dinner knife, deftly lifting that latticework of bones away.

Corrigan noticed that Dawson had taken up one of the fly

rods and was waving it in erratic loops. Maybe he should try to place Dara in the foreground, try his best to catch the governor in some preposterous great-hunter pose in the background, he was thinking, when he heard the revving of the seaplane at the far end of the lake, and hesitated.

"Maybe I ought to take a picture of the plane taking off," he said to Dara. "Departure of our last link to civilization and all that?"

She shrugged. "Suit yourself."

"Move right over here," he said, motioning her toward the edge of the pier.

He steadied himself against one of the pilings, tried to focus on her and get the revving plane there in the background. He heard the pitch of the engines climb as he maneuvered the focus, saw a tiny storm of whitecaps kick up in the wash of the propellers.

He remembered back a few hours before, when he'd sat white-knuckled inside the same craft, waiting for that precise moment of release, when the urge to be aloft overcame the instinct to clutch hold, no matter what . . . and it occurred to him, staring at Dara through the lens, that he wished there was a way to capture such a feeling on film.

It was a luxuriant experience, having this excuse just to stare at her, the first chance he'd really dared to since he'd spotted her unaware, back at that press conference. He held up his hand to signal her, snapped one shot as the plane's engines grew in volume, another as they finally released. He caught a glimpse of the plane as it hurtled away, a rogue wave slapping the tail as if to finish a game of got-you-last.

He got another good shot of her with the snowy peaks in the background, shifted slightly, and took another.

"I think that's probably enough, Richard," she said.

"Just a couple more," he said, eye still pressed to the viewfinder.

Her face, the feeling of flight, the icy water, and the plane gleaming in the sun, a graceful white arrow against the dark backdrop of the cliff, where water drifted like shaken lace.

"Richard." He heard Dara's voice as he snapped, and snapped again, turning to catch the rest of the view.

"Richard, I think something's wrong."

He heard the concern, finally noted it in her face, wondered what she might be talking about, what could be wrong.

Be right with you, he was thinking. *Just one second more.*

Yes, yes, yes, he thought with each snap of the shutter. He had it, he was certain, now. He dropped the camera at last and turned to see what, in Dara's world, the trouble was, at the instant it became abundantly clear.

The explosion, magnified several times over by the surrounding rock walls, ripped across the surface of the lake like the clap of doom itself. An enormous fireball shot up the face of the cliff, obliterating the waterfall for a brief moment. In the aftermath, bits of wreckage rained down upon the lake in an awful hailstorm.

And then, suddenly, all was calm again. For a few moments, time was stilled. No sound of laboring engines, no screams of onlookers. The echoes of the explosion had died away. No scar upon the wall of rock where the water tumbled, nothing left on the calm surface of the lake.

No evidence whatsoever of what had just taken place, not to Corrigan's eyes. He stood frozen, the camera dangling, gaping out over the empty water, feeling Dara's hands clutching at his arm, trying to comprehend.

It can't be, something in him insisted. *Impossible. Absolutely, categorically impossible.*

From somewhere in the tall pines behind him came one note, the raucous call of a crow. And then, from all about him, the disbelieving cries began.

The tall man listened as the echoes of the explosion rolled away, then glanced down at the tiny transmitter he still held in his hand. With its various arrowed buttons and switches, it might have been mistaken for a sophisticated video-game controller. Except that this was one capable of guiding much more than computerized images, he thought. Receiver there, transmitter here—you could take over the electronic guidance of just about any craft. So clever, these Japanese.

He put the device back into a pocket, and turned to make his way back down the trail beneath the trees toward the campsite, careful of his footing in the sandy soil. Every pebble, every shard of wood was a tiny, old-fashioned disaster-in-waiting, and electronics was no shield. Twist an ankle, break a bone out here, it could mean your life. Particularly if you were alone.

He was not alone, of course, but he would behave as if he were. It was the best way. For him, the only way.

The woman glanced up when she heard his approach, her face spangled with sunlight and shadow cast by the pines. She had her long hair tied back in a knot, a kerchief around her neck. No makeup, a loose-fitting T-shirt, blousy camper's pants. See her in the city, you might take her for a wheat-germ lady, a tree-hugger, a nature nerd. And God help you if you did.

She'd been on her knees, shoveling the last of the soil back atop the hole he'd helped her dig. She stood, now, tossing the camp shovel aside, wiping a sheen of sweat from her brow.

"That sound I heard a bit ago," she asked. She gestured toward the top of the ridge where he'd been. "Was it what I think it was?"

He nodded, still staring at the partner Fate had brought him.

"I expect they're about to try their fancy satellite phone devices," she added.

"I expect they are," he said.

"So, let the games begin," she said with a last glance at the silent mound beside her.

And with that, they started off.

15

"Where's that goddamned phone?" Ben Donnelly shouted toward his son over the turmoil at lakeside.

Chipper had plowed into the stack of gear piled near the pier head. He finished rummaging through one rucksack, tossed it aside, turned his attention to the next. "It was in there. I *know* it was."

He glanced up at Corrigan, who'd just hurried in from the pier.

"Take it easy," Corrigan said. "You'll find it."

Chipper gave him a doubtful look, but in the next instant his face brightened. He withdrew his hand from the canvas bag, held the phone up in triumph.

Donnelly strode forward and snatched the device from Chipper's hand. He pressed a button, started to punch in numbers, then abruptly stopped.

He tried again, then turned the phone over and flipped open a compartment on the back. "Where's the battery?" he said to Chipper.

Chipper shook his head. "I don't know. It was there yesterday when I packed it. It had to be."

Donnelly scowled. "Where's the other phone?" he barked at Chipper.

"Maybe you took it," Chipper said.

"I didn't take the goddamned thing . . ." Donnelly began, then cut himself off.

"Get my pack," he said to one of the wranglers.

The wrangler found Donnelly's pack amid the stack of gear, jerked it loose, hurried forward with it. Donnelly set the bag on the rocks at his feet, then bent down to paw through the contents.

After a moment he stopped, glancing up briefly at his son.

He reached into the bag with his other hand, brushed aside some clothing, and pulled out a second phone, the twin to the first. He turned the phone over and checked the battery pack. He pressed a button, and the electronic chime Corrigan had heard at the briefing the night before sounded faintly in the thin mountain air.

A look approaching relief spread across Donnelly's face, and he turned to punch in a series of numbers on the keypad. He brought the phone to his ear, then, waiting for the connection to be made.

Corrigan stared about them at the array of silent faces. Sixteen people standing by the side of a lake in the middle of nowhere, watching a man make a telephone call, he thought. Somehow it seemed ludicrous.

Dara must have felt something similar. "Shouldn't we try to get over there?" she said, holding her voice down. She gestured at the spot where the plane had exploded. "See if someone might have made it?"

Corrigan turned to her, mindful of Donnelly's unfortunate example. "It'd take hours," he said, gesturing at the rugged shoreline that lay between them and the crash site. "I'm not sure there's much point in it."

"But we can't just stand here like ghouls," she said.

"Hold it down," Donnelly called. "I can't hear." He listened a moment, then banged the phone against his palm in frustration. He pressed another button, seemingly clearing the call, then punched in numbers once again.

"For God's sake," he said after a moment. He pulled the phone away from his ear again, glaring at Corrigan, who stood closest to him.

"What?" Corrigan asked, shaking his head.

"You listen," Donnelly said, thrusting the phone at him.

Corrigan reached out and brought the phone carefully to his ear. Unintelligible clamor, at first, but then it began to resolve itself into recognizable sound. Finally he pulled the instrument from his ear and stared back at Donnelly.

"Sounds like Japanese radio to me," Donnelly said, his voice disgusted.

Corrigan nodded. He'd heard the same excited chatter, then

music swelling up, the sounds tinny but unmistakable: a group from somewhere far away, pumping out the strains of an old Beatles tune in Oriental harmony. And, unless he missed his guess, what they were calling for was "Help!"

16

The batteries to one phone disappear, the other one picks up only Japanese radio? Is that some kind of joke?" Dara said to him.

Corrigan shrugged. "If it is, it's a pretty grim one," he said. They stood in the shade of some pines a few yards up from the lakeshore while Donnelly, who'd tried the remaining phone several more times without success, conferred with Dawson.

Odd, Corrigan thought, rubbing his arms against the chill breeze. Out in the sun, it had seemed hot. A few minutes in the shade and he was practically shivering, but then again, he could see pockets of snow still lurking here and there, sheltered by rock outcroppings and pines. "Just like those new phones they okayed for the Transit Authority cops," he said, checking the sky. The sun was well up over the mountains to the east, but clouds had begun scudding in, and large patches of shadow were gliding over the surface of the lake. "They were going to revolutionize communications underground, according to the hype."

Dara nodded glumly. "How about that GPS device Donnelly showed us at dinner last night?" she asked.

Corrigan glanced at her. "We know where we *are,* Dara. That's all a thing like that is good for."

She shook her head, glancing across the lake toward the waterfall, as beautiful, as indifferent, as ever. "Those poor men."

He nodded, remembering all of Chipper's technical jargon about altitudes and takeoff and landing clearances, remembered his own death's grip on the armrests of his seat. "A few minutes the other way, it could have been all of us," he told her with a bleak look.

They stood quietly for a moment, staring out over the water, while the conference between Donnelly and Dawson continued down by the water. Donnelly was making an effort at keeping his voice down, but Corrigan could hear the strain in the man's voice. By the agitated way Donnelly moved, Corrigan guessed there was some disagreement between the pair, though what it might be was anyone's guess. Was Dawson blaming Donnelly for the accident, for the malfunctioning phones? Could a plane crash affect a candidate's poll numbers adversely?

"So, what happens now?" Dara asked over his shoulder.

"I'm not sure," Corrigan said. "When the plane doesn't show up back in Jackson, it'll raise some flags. They'll send a search plane out."

"So, that's it? We'll just wait here to get picked up?"

He gave her a blank look. "I suppose. I'm not exactly the one in charge."

She stared back at him, her expression despairing. "Hardly what anyone had in mind, is it?"

He shook his head, glancing out at the end of the pier where the film crew had huddled, each caught up in formulating his own battle plan, he supposed. Giles Ashmead stood together with his wife, Sonia, a few feet from Dawson and Donnelly, while Dawson's own private linebacker and his female assistant hovered nearby. Corrigan noted that the young woman's plum-colored nails and lips, which might have seemed stylish once, now only accentuated her pallor.

Chipper and the two wranglers were busy rearranging the gear, moving it away from the water's edge, closer to the encircling forest. Elizabeth Dawson had walked out to the end of the pier and stood with her arms wrapped about herself, as if she were fighting some deep chill, her back to them all.

Finally Corrigan turned back to Dara, trying to find some reassuring words, when Donnelly's voice cut through his intentions. "Heads up, folks," the outfitter called. "I need everyone's attention, please. On down here, if you would."

Everyone began to filter Donnelly's way. Even Elizabeth Dawson seemed eager enough to end her exile, had turned, and was making her way quickly back along the pier.

When they all had gathered sufficiently close, Donnelly

raised his hands and began. "I know we've suffered a terrible tragedy, here, and I want to commend everyone on how well you've taken it, that's the first thing."

He glanced off toward the cliff where the plane had crashed, then turned back to them. "I've known Don Barton for most of my adult life, and I've put my life in his hands more times than I can count. He was as good as they come." He paused, shaking his head in sorrow. "I don't have the slightest idea what happened up there, but I know that Don would be the first one to say he'd rather it was him and not us."

"What are we going to do?" It was the director of the film crew. Her mascara seemed smudged, as if she might have been crying.

Donnelly nodded, anticipating the question. "Well, I presume you all realize we've got a foul-up with our communications." He sent a dark look toward Chipper, as if his son were responsible for the failure of all things modern.

"Now, maybe that'll clear itself up yet," Donnelly continued, his voice rising to carry above the growing sigh of the wind through the pines. "If it does, we'll call in immediately and report the crash."

"When the plane doesn't return to the airport on schedule," Corrigan offered, "won't they send out a search party?"

Donnelly cleared his throat, looking distinctly uncomfortable. "Ordinarily, that's exactly what would happen. We could just wait right here, send up a flare the minute we see a plane—"

"But that's not going to happen anytime soon." It was Fielding Dawson cutting in, clearly impatient with Donnelly's elliptical manner. The governor strode forward, gazing about the group. "The plane wasn't flying directly back to Jackson. It was on its way to a remote lake in southern Montana to rendezvous with a group of fishermen the day after tomorrow."

"The day after tomorrow?" Giles Ashmead said in disbelief. "Then it could be two days, maybe three, before anyone raises an alarm. . . ."

So, that explained Dawson's obvious irritation, Corrigan thought. He turned to Donnelly. "This lake in Montana, is it as isolated as the place we are now?"

Donnelly glanced around, made a helpless gesture. "Well,

not *quite* as isolated as here, but Heggen Lake's still a couple days' hike in or out."

"And how about *that* group?" Corrigan persisted. "How many functioning satellite phones do they have?"

Donnelly shook his head. "Tell you the truth, it isn't one of my groups, Mr. . . .?" He paused, looking uncertainly at Corrigan.

"Corrigan," he said. "Richard Corrigan."

"Right," Donnelly said. "You're the police officer."

Corrigan gave him a grudging nod.

"Well," Donnelly said, "the plane was leased from a company that hires out to a number of outfitters in these parts."

Corrigan nodded. It was as Chipper had suggested earlier, then. "So, even if this group of fishermen on Lake Whatever-It-Is realizes that something has happened to the plane that was supposed to pick them up, they might be in the same position we are. Nothing to do but wait and wonder."

"Up shit's creek without a paddle," one of the cameramen offered.

"Who knows *how* long we'll have to wait for help," Sonia Ashmead said, her attractive features pained.

Here, Donnelly broke in, perhaps sensing a stampede. "Well, the fact is, we don't exactly need *help*, Mrs. Ashmead." He glanced back at Dawson. "What's happened is unfortunate . . ."

Probably not the words the two pilots might have used, Corrigan thought, but he kept that to himself.

". . . but we're in pretty good shape, truth be told. We've got our gear, we've got our original game plan intact." Donnelly cleared his throat again, giving Dawson a sidelong glance. "What Mr. Dawson and I have determined is that we might just as well start making our own way back down toward civilization—"

"Wait a minute," Elizabeth Dawson said. "I thought it was going to take the better part of a week to get out of this"—she turned, waving her arm about their surroundings—"this hell-hole!"

"Well, we can shave some time off that figure, Mrs. Dawson," Donnelly said, clearly uncomfortable. Corrigan suspected the outfitter had been privy to some of Elizabeth

Dawson's thoughts on the beauties of the wilderness before this moment. "With any luck, we can be out of here in as little as three days. . . ."

"Three days?" she said, her voice rising even higher.

"Meantime," Donnelly said, holding up a hand to forestall whatever she intended to say, "we'll send Chipper and Pete over there on ahead. They can move twice as fast as all of us together can. It's even money they'll be able to get down, get the word out about what's happened, before that group up in Montana even realizes there's been a problem."

Fielding Dawson spoke up at this point. "I think we should all remind ourselves that, in fact, there is no problem where we personally are concerned. . . ."

"If the point is to get us all back to civilization as quickly and painlessly as possible, then maybe we ought to stay put until help arrives, whether that's two days, or three, or four." Corrigan turned to regard the film crew. "I know that pretty much does away with the point of the trip—"

"That's hardly the issue, Officer Corrigan," Dawson interrupted. "The truth is, we *can't* stay here."

"And why is that?" Corrigan asked.

Dawson glanced at Donnelly, inviting the outfitter to do the explaining.

"For one thing, we don't have enough supplies, and we're not really outfitted for serious hunting or fishing," Donnelly said, loud enough for everyone to hear. "We need to get down the mountainside to the first cache point, or there are going to be a bunch of hungry people among you."

Corrigan thought he heard Elizabeth Dawson mutter a curse. If he noticed, Donnelly ignored it. He ran his gaze over the group, then turned back to Corrigan and nodded upward. "For another thing, we've got the weather to think about."

Corrigan glanced up at the sky, where the clouds had thickened considerably. In the distance, over the peaks, it appeared that dark thunderheads were brewing. "That's just rain right now. But if a bad enough storm comes through at this altitude," Donnelly explained, "we could find ourselves up to our butts in snow, even in September. It behooves us to move a little lower down the mountainside."

Behooves? As Corrigan stared at the man, Dara broke in:

"Don't you check the weather before you start off on these things?"

"Of course we do," Donnelly shot back. "But storms kick up. Things happen in the wilderness. That's why we want to get moving." He broke off to survey the group.

"Well, you've heard the plan. So, unless there are any other questions . . ."

He waited for a moment, but no one else spoke up. "The boys'll rustle up a quick lunch," Donnelly said, motioning toward the fire, where Pete and Vaughn were already busy. "And then we'll be on our way." He stole one last glance toward the gathering skies. "I'd keep my poncho out where I could get to it, you all," he added, and then turned away, one hand on Fielding Dawson's shoulder.

Dawson gave Corrigan something of a speculative glance, then followed Donnelly away toward the fire, where Pete and Vaughn were adding seasonings and feathery-looking dried vegetables to a pot Corrigan supposed held soup. Corrigan, who realized his gut had tightened into a knot over the last few minutes, let out his breath in a rush. So maybe he'd annoyed Fielding Dawson, he thought, but at least he'd forced Donnelly into an admission that there were legitimate concerns about their situation.

"I'm not sure he liked your implication," Dara said.

Corrigan turned. "What implication?"

"Suggesting Dawson doesn't want to miss his photo opportunity," she said.

"That's not what I said."

"But I think you hit the nail on the head," she said, with the hint of a smile. "You let him off easy, in fact."

"I'm just a public servant," he said. "You're the reporter. Why don't you hold his feet to the fire?"

She glanced at the governor, then shrugged. "There's no rush," she said. "Let's see how things turn out."

Corrigan glanced at Dawson, who was now standing near the campfire, engaged in earnest conversation with Giles Ashmead and his wife. He noted that Elizabeth Dawson had not joined the group but had wandered off once again toward the lakeside, her arms wrapped about herself as if she were warding off some bone-deep chill that only she could feel.

It was irrational to think of Dawson as responsible for what had happened, Corrigan would have to admit, but given his rather transparent motivation to make this trip in the first place, how could he not be?

"One thing's for sure," Corrigan told her. "Neither one of us would be here if it weren't for Dawson's political agenda. That's what it comes down to, any way you slice it."

"Even if you're right," Dara said, "you just can't say things like that to Fielding Dawson."

"As a reporter for *USA Magazine,* you mean."

"Exactly," she said. "I could lose my job, Richard. It's as simple as that." She gave him a look, then turned toward the spot where the wranglers had stowed their packs. Corrigan gave a last look Dara's way, then moved for the campfire, where Vaughn was ladling out bowls of soup, which steamed in the chilly air.

17

By the time they had finished lunch and shouldered their packs—each containing a sleeping bag, water, and other essentials, and the clothes and toiletries they'd all been asked to give over to Donnelly's men back in Jackson for packing—it had begun to drizzle, forcing them all to pause while the packs came off, ponchos retrieved and donned, the packs replaced.

Finally they all were moving again, and so long as the trail cut beneath the pines, the rain reached them as more of a cooling mist than an annoyance. Inside of half an hour, they had broken out of the cover of the pines and were moving up a series of switchbacks toward the ridge overlooking the lake, where, as Donnelly had explained, they would hook on to the trail that led downward. Meantime, Corrigan noted, the rain seemed to have lessened. The clouds, though, had descended from the peaks and settled over the lake like dense fog, masking the view of the distant cliff where the Mallard had crashed.

Just as well, he thought with a last glance over his shoulder. Perhaps with the crash site out of view, something of the gloom that had enveloped them all would disappear as well.

He turned his attention up ahead, where Ben Donnelly stood at one juncture of the zigzagging trail, calling out his version of encouragement as various members of the party passed by. "Okay, this is a tough stretch ahead. Don't overdo it. Rest when you need to. It's not a sprint, it's a marathon. . . ."

Corrigan, who had purposely lagged near the end of the line, glanced up the steep hillside to see that even Elizabeth Dawson and Sonia Ashmead, burdened as they were with packs easily the size of his own, seemed to be holding pace just fine. Dara, too, was up ahead, somewhere out of sight.

Corrigan, already feeling some strain in his thighs, moved

past Donnelly, then stopped a few feet up the trail, realizing his breath had quickened considerably.

"It's the altitude," Donnelly said, moving his way. "But don't worry, this part'll be behind us in another half hour or so. You'll get your wind back then."

Corrigan, who'd been careful not to huff and puff when he passed the outfitter, considered kicking the man off the narrow path. Donnelly, however, had paused a few feet below him, well out of booting range.

"Go ahead," Corrigan said, gesturing at Donnelly.

"No can do," Donnelly said, shaking his head. "I'm the last man up the trail. My job."

Corrigan glanced back down the trail toward the tree line. "How about Chipper and Pete?"

Donnelly followed his gaze. "They peeled off a ways back. They'll head over the ridge, catch the alternate trail I was talking about. Straight down the face of Black Mountain."

Corrigan nodded. He stared out along the ridgeline but could see no one.

"There's a fold in the mountain between us and them," Donnelly said, as if he could read Corrigan's thoughts. "You'll be able to see them once we cross the other side of the ridge. They'll be on one side of Gorgeous Gorge, we'll be on the other."

"Gorgeous Gorge?"

Donnelly smiled. "It's got a surveyor's name that nobody can hardly pronounce. We call it Gorgeous, because that's what it is."

Corrigan shook his head. Donnelly did have his engaging side, he decided. "This is some country," Corrigan offered.

"First time, huh?" Donnelly said.

Corrigan shrugged. "Just a city boy. Been there all my life."

"Well, that's a shame," Donnelly said. "At least you got this opportunity, though."

"At least," Corrigan agreed.

There was a moment of silence, then Donnelly took off the billed cap he'd donned, and wiped moisture from his face. "You got under Dawson's skin pretty good back there."

Corrigan checked Donnelly's expression. "Is that what he told you?"

Donnelly pursed his lips. "He didn't have to tell me."

Corrigan shrugged. "So, it wasn't fair," he said. "It was probably just the shock of the crash and all."

Donnelly considered his response, and finally nodded. "It was a hell of a thing, Mr. Corrigan, I'll agree with you there. And I'm no more a fan of political stunts than you are. Still, it doesn't do any good to be squabbling among ourselves out here, you know what I mean?"

Corrigan nodded. "I was out of line," he said.

Donnelly ran his hand through his thick, graying hair, then replaced his hat. "Well, welcome back *into* line," he said, gesturing up the trail. "After you, my friend."

Corrigan did his best to close the gap that had opened during the conversation with Donnelly, but by the time he approached the ridgeline, the trail ahead was empty. His breath was beginning to come in gasps, and his thighs were on fire with effort. He was fighting the urge to push off his knees with every step. He'd always done well in the Department trials, considered himself in decent shape, but then again, there weren't too many steep slopes in the subway.

He turned near the top of the trail and saw Donnelly perhaps twenty yards below, the man plodding steadily upward, as if he could hold the same pace all the way up Mount Everest. Donnelly noticed him and gave a wave that Corrigan presumed was to seem encouraging. He drew a deep breath, trying to force his breathing back under control, then turned and willed his legs ahead.

It wasn't more than twenty steps—counting paces couldn't be a good sign, it occurred to him—until he had cleared the ridge, and the simple accomplishment of that alone might have been enough to restore his energy. But the view that greeted him now supplied an even greater boost to his spirits.

Donnelly had been right, he thought as he surveyed the deep cleft in the rock that soared away beneath him. The drop seemed so sheer that a person with a running start might leap off into a mile-long plunge. The canyon was at least a mile wide where he stood. As it ran into the distance beyond, the gap, with gray tendrils of fog teasing its chiseled sides, opened to twice that distance, easily. Corrigan could see occasional flashes of white at the bottom of the great chasm, and again he wondered if that was the river that would take them home.

"Something, isn't it?" Donnelly's voice came beside him.

Corrigan nodded, his gaze still locked on the spectacle. "Gorgeous Gorge?"

Donnelly nodded.

"Seems the right name for it." Corrigan nodded, still panting.

He had taken some solace in the fact that the rest of the party had sprawled on a shelf of rock fifty yards or so down the opposing slope, meantime. Most had their canteens unslung. Others were in sitting positions, as obviously done in as Corrigan felt.

He noted that one of the film crew had shouldered his camera and had it trained upon him and Donnelly as they eased down toward the rest of the group. It occurred to Corrigan for the first time then that he might turn up on some televised version of this journey someday, but the concerns associated with that realization seemed trivial at the moment.

He spotted a boulder with a flat spot wide enough for his behind, and sagged gratefully down upon it. Dara, who had shed her pack and propped herself against an outcropping a few feet away, glanced up at him, her cheeks shining pink in the cool air.

"I was beginning to think we'd lost you," she said, affably enough.

"No such luck," he said. He noticed that his heart seemed to be beating several times its normal rate. He gazed out over the canyon once more, shaking his head, fighting the urge to call out to Donnelly, to beg for assurance that it was all downhill from this spot on in. He turned to say something else to Dara, when he heard the man's voice cut the air.

"Look here."

Corrigan turned to see the outfitter approaching, holding out a pair of binoculars Corrigan's way.

Donnelly pointed to a spot off in the distance that looked like any other sheer slab of granite, and handed over the glasses. Corrigan took them, trying to focus on the spot Donnelly indicated.

"Just above that light-colored vein that looks like a lightning bolt," he said, kneeling down beside Corrigan. "Chipper's wearing a red windbreaker. Pete's in blue. He's a little harder to see."

Corrigan dropped the glasses and scanned the distant rock face until he could make out the vein of rock he presumed Donnelly was talking about. He still couldn't see any movement, and he lifted the glasses to his eyes again.

He managed to locate the place in the binoculars this time, and slowly eased them up. He saw something flash through his field of vision—a soaring bird, he thought. Then another object tumbled past, and he realized what he'd seen were falling rocks.

He raised the binoculars farther and saw the two men, no more than a dozen feet apart. Both were spread-eagled, hands and feet extended, faces pressed against what seemed a sheer, featureless cliff as if they'd been pasted there.

"What the hell are they doing?" Corrigan asked. He dropped the binoculars momentarily and glanced across the vast chasm to be sure that what he thought he'd seen was true.

He could make out the two tiny dots, now: one red, one blue, seemingly suspended on the side of a cliff several thousand feet above the canyon floor below. Corrigan knew that the injury to his eye didn't register the same depth that another might see below, but still he felt his hands going damp with sweat.

"There's that one little stretch across the face of the mountain," Donnelly said, his tone casual. "They have to do a little free-climbing along in there, but it's nothing they're not used to. Those two are like Spider-Man."

Corrigan tried to conceive of big, lumbering Chipper as Spider-Man, but it just wouldn't compute. He turned to Donnelly. "Free-climbing? As in, no ropes, no equipment?"

"They've got what they need if they get into a tight spot," Donnelly said. "They're just not tied together. It would just slow them down."

Donnelly saw the uncertainty on Corrigan's face. "There's plenty over there for an experienced climber to hold on to," he said. "You just can't make it out from here."

Donnelly turned and waved at the outcropping of rock jutting twenty feet or so above Dara's head. "You see all those cracks and knobs? Those are big-time hand- and footholds. Those boys'd go up and down this piece of rock like it was the staircase in your house."

Corrigan stared at the nearly vertical surface, wondering what Donnelly was talking about. What he saw was a sheer surface that a fly would have a hard time navigating.

He also noticed that the film crew had turned its attentions to Chipper and Pete. One of the cameramen had his lens trained in their direction, while the other seemed to be hastily reading a second, longer-lensed camera. Dara had pushed herself to a standing position and approached Corrigan and Donnelly.

"Mind if I have a look?" she asked.

Corrigan handed over the binoculars. He was ready to help her locate the pair, but she seemed to have little trouble picking them up.

"Jesus," she said after a moment of staring intently across the chasm.

"I see why we couldn't all go that way," Corrigan said.

Donnelly nodded. "It's great sport, though. Gets your heart started like nothing else. You come back out here, we'll show you how it's done."

Corrigan shook his head. "The day I sprout wings," he said.

Dara turned back his way and handed over the binoculars. Corrigan took them gladly, drawn for another look despite himself. He lifted the glasses, steadied his arms, and located the two men once more. Chipper was in the lead, Pete a few yards behind. At that distance, their careful movements were almost imperceptible. It was almost as if they were oozing their way across the rock, Corrigan thought.

He was about to turn away, to hand the glasses back to Donnelly, when it happened. Corrigan saw Pete throw his arm up, abruptly, as if toward off a blow. There was a scattering of dust that obscured his view, then a huge blur that must have been a boulder hurtling down the sheer face of the cliff. With a jolt that sickened him, Corrigan saw a fragment of blue peeling away from the rock face, tumbling out of his range of vision.

"What the hell?" Corrigan heard Donnelly call out behind him.

Corrigan had already lowered the binoculars. He stared in disbelief across the chasm, where a skein of what looked like smoke was snaking down the face of the cliff. He heard cries from above and behind him, and turned back toward the camera crew. The female director was screaming, pointing out over the vast emptiness between them, while the cameramen frantically manipulated their equipment.

Corrigan felt Donnelly rip the binoculars from his numbed hands. "It's a slide!" Donnelly cried. "A goddamned rock slide!"

The cloud of dust grew wider, a murky, yellow-brown smear that wiped out the whole of the cliffside above the jagged vein etched there. A low rumble reached them, now, the sound growing steadily like unabated thunder, like the roar of a train blasting from a tunnel, Corrigan thought.

The cloud billowed up, enormous, the sound growing with it, as if some terrible fume-spewing industry had sprouted on the side of the distant cliff. And then finally the plume lifted away, and the sound rolled over them with one final burst, and all of them were left to stare dumbly across the intervening space.

Corrigan saw no signs of the climbers there. No dot of blue. No dot of red. But there were folds and clefts that could easily hide a man, even a big man like Chipper. Hadn't Donnelly told him that just a half hour before?

With a sense of apprehension he'd never experienced before, Corrigan turned toward Donnelly, who held the binoculars clamped to his eyes, frantically scanning the distant rock face. Donnelly's lips were moving, but no sound seemed to issue from them.

After a moment, Corrigan heard it, barely a whisper at first, growing slowly to a terrible, gut-wrenching mantra. "Chipper? Where are you, boy? Come on, Chipper. Chipper? Son?"

Dara stared up at Corrigan, her mouth frozen open with a question she would never ask. Behind him, Corrigan heard shouts, Elizabeth Dawson's quavering voice. Heard Fielding Dawson's mumbled reply.

Ben Donnelly still scanned the distance with the binoculars, still called out ever more urgently toward his son. Corrigan heard weeping from behind him. Saw Dara Wylie's stricken face before him. Calamity on one side, chaos on the other. He took her in his arms and uttered something like a prayer.

18

"I **think** I've found him," the cameraman said to Corrigan, his voice quiet, his tone somber. It was the same guy who'd slept from New York to Denver in the plane seat across from him.

Corrigan glanced at the guy, then off at Dara, who had calmed by now. She'd pulled her notebook out of her pack and stood a few yards away, under the shelter of the overhang, shielding herself from the persistent drizzle while she wrote.

He was glad she hadn't heard. There was nothing positive in the cameraman's tone. And Corrigan should have known better than to have hoped for anything good, anyway. He was going to set hope aside for a while, see if that improved things any.

The cameraman's expression was beyond glum. "You want to come have a look before I say anything to Mr. Donnelly?" The guy had a vaguely Asian cast to his features, Corrigan noted, and still carried his long-lensed camera propped on his shoulder.

Corrigan glanced across their staging area toward Donnelly, who had collapsed into a sitting position not far from where Dara had been resting earlier. Fielding Dawson stood beside the outfitter, a comforting hand on the man's shoulder, but his attention had been caught by the cameraman's approach. He was staring intently at Corrigan.

Corrigan turned back to the cameraman. "Yeah, sure," he said finally. The cameraman nodded and started away. Corrigan gave a last glance back at Dawson, then turned and moved off.

"What's your name, anyway?" he called after the cameraman.

"Mal," the guy said over his shoulder. "Think of the Latin, for bad shit."

"Great," Corrigan said, hurrying through the loose rock after him. They had left the trail, now, circling around a large outcropping of rock that shielded them from the main group.

"Down there," Mal said. "You can only see it from this angle."

He pointed down into the chasm, but Corrigan could make out nothing.

"Here, use the camera," Mal told him, handing the bulky thing over.

Corrigan hefted the thing, bringing the eyepiece up to his good eye, then aimed the lens downward. It was a momentarily dizzying view, making him feel almost as though he'd dived headlong into space. He fought the sensation, steadying himself, sweeping the lens over the rugged terrain a thousand feet or more below.

"Come up a bit," Mal was saying. "To your left."

Corrigan followed the directions but still made out nothing but rock and scrub, the occasional gnarled pine. Then he saw it, a moment's flash of red. He swept the camera back slowly, fighting to stabilize the shimmering image.

Finally he had it: a vague blur at first, but then, unmistakably, the form of a man. "Focus is right by your first finger," Mal told him quietly.

Corrigan found the button and brought the image into clarity. A man, all right. A man in a red windbreaker draped facedown across a rocky slope, his arms outflung.

No doubt who it was. No doubt at all.

After a few moments, Corrigan lowered the camera. He took a deep breath, working the strained muscles at his neck. "No sign of Pete? The guy in the blue jacket?"

Mal gave him a disconsolate stare, shook his head.

Corrigan glanced back up the slope. "Okay," he said. "Let's go tell Donnelly."

When Corrigan returned with Mal, they found that the outfitter had regained his feet and had drawn Vaughn away from the rest of the group. The two stood well down the slope and were involved in a heated discussion.

Dara started toward Corrigan as they edged down the slope toward Donnelly, but Corrigan held her off with a look and a raised hand.

"You can't go by yourself, Mr. Donnelly," Vaughn was saying as Corrigan and Mal approached.

"And I can't leave all these people here by themselves," Donnelly responded. He glanced briefly at Corrigan, then turned back to Vaughn, gesturing at the sky where the dark clouds were beginning to boil over the ridge from the direction they'd come. "A thunderstorm hits while we're still out on this exposed slope, and every damned one of them could end up toast."

"There's nothing you can do over there. Even if . . ." The man broke off, unwilling to voice his suspicions. "Look, you don't have any equipment, you don't have enough hands—"

"It's my *son,* goddamnit. You think I'm just going to sit here and do nothing—"

"Mr. Donnelly," Corrigan interrupted.

Donnelly whirled upon him, his eyes flashing. "What do you want?"

Corrigan stared back at him evenly. "I think there's something you should see," he said simply.

Donnelly seemed ready to explode once more. Then he registered something in Corrigan's tone of voice, noted his lowered gaze.

Raindrops had begun to spatter the rocks about them. Corrigan felt an icy tap on the back of his neck, another at his cheek.

"Where is he?" Donnelly said at last, his eyes hooded, his once-commanding voice ready to break.

Corrigan, who had seen his mother buried only months before, who could still remember the pain of his father's passing, realized that what Donnelly felt at that moment was worse beyond measure. Difficult as it was, sons and daughters would have to bear the loss of parents. It was the very way of the world.

But it was not supposed to happen the other way around. No parent should have to endure what Corrigan saw going on behind the man's watery eyes.

Been there, done that, seen it all. Corrigan rebuked himself for his earlier thoughts about the man. He put his hand on Donnelly's shoulder and led him off to see and, after that, to mourn.

19

So why did we put the tents *here*?" Corrigan asked, glancing around the forested area where they'd finally put up. They'd hiked down only another hour or so from the place where they'd witnessed Chipper's fall, but given everything that had happened, it seemed like they'd been on the move for days.

Dara left off an inspection of her notes and glanced up at him speculatively. She was sitting Indian-style on a ground cloth beneath the fly canopy of her own tent. "As opposed to where?" There was a hint of managed patience in her voice.

Corrigan shrugged. "Down there, maybe," he said. "On top of all those pine needles."

She followed his gesture down a slope to a cleft in the rock where a thick carpet of needles had collected. She nodded. "They look soft, huh?"

"That's my point."

"You *could* move your tent," she said. She was nodding, contemplating the possibility. "But I wouldn't, if I were you."

"And why's that?" He was already calculating the effort involved in pulling the pegs he'd banged in under Vaughn's supervision, the disentangling of the tension poles, the removal and carrying of his soggy equipment. But on the other hand, he'd already tested the hard and rocky ground beneath his sleeping bag where the tent presently rested.

"Flood," she said mildly.

He stared at her. "We're on the side of a mountain."

"And that's a little canyon you want to move to," she said. "Rain runs down the sides of mountains. If it gets any worse, it could turn into a little river right down there."

"Ah," he said, nodding, though the needles still looked inviting. "Woodscraft."

He glanced at her own seating arrangement, then spread out

his poncho beneath the tiny canopy of his own rain fly and sat down with a sigh. "Your legs sore?" he asked.

"A little," she said. "Going downhill's almost as bad as going up."

He nodded, kneading at a cramp in one of his calves. He spent his entire days walking the caves. He'd never expected a downhill trek was going to tax him.

He pulled off one of the lightweight hiking shoes—he'd bought them only the day before, he reminded himself, wriggling his toes experimentally. He wasn't going to take off his sock. He already knew where the blisters had burst—there was a brown smudge of trail dust gathered at each spot. And this after little more than a half-day's trek. At least he'd resisted the impulse to buy a pair of the bulky, stiff-soled monsters, he thought. He'd be looking at amputation by this point.

"So, how do you figure our candidate's holding up?" he asked her.

"Physically?" She let the question hang a moment before she continued. "Actually, he's in pretty good shape. He told me he and the Ashmeads have been training for the last couple of months for this."

"Are you serious?"

"Donnelly sends out a little booklet. You have to agree to the training regimen, send in progress reports, or you don't get to go on the trip."

"You, too?"

She stared at him. "Media excepted, of course. I don't think Donnelly was too crazy about it, but what was he supposed to do?"

"Then there's me," he offered.

"You're doing pretty well for a city boy," she said.

"And Dawson's bodyguard," he said, nodding in the direction of the linebacker, who stood off to the side, inspecting his tent dubiously.

"Uh-huh," she said. "That guy is fat like Mark McGwire is fat."

Corrigan nodded agreement absently, letting his glance travel around their campsite, where the small red and yellow and orange tents glowed almost cheerily in the dim light that filtered down beneath the pines. Most were small affairs, barely big enough for one person and a bit of gear. The Dawsons' and the Ashmeads', however, were considerably larger, big enough to stand in. Corrigan could make out the shape of Fielding Dawson even now, silhouetted by an electric lantern, struggling into dry clothing, or so it seemed.

Earlier, after supervising the pitching of the tents, Vaughn and Donnelly had organized Corrigan and the others into a wood-gathering foray, then had busied themselves building a fire. Now the two men were engaged in preparing dinner. "It won't be anything fancy," Vaughn had warned. "We couldn't make our first cache point tonight, not with all the time we lost."

Corrigan watched the two men bustle about, Donnelly stoking the fire, Vaughn lugging water he'd gathered in a collapsible bucket from a stream on the opposite side of the camp, Donnelly dumping packets of premixed foods into steaming pots. Corrigan felt vaguely guilty about sitting on his duff, but he didn't know what he might contribute at the moment. Dragging a couple of reasonably dry logs back through the forest had just about exhausted his repertoire of wilderness skills.

"I'm impressed, watching Donnelly carry on like he is," Corrigan offered. The picture of Chipper's motionless body lying on that distant mountainside was still vividly etched in his own mind. He could only imagine what the memories were doing to Donnelly.

She nodded, following Corrigan's gaze. When she spoke, her voice seemed weary. "What choice does he have, Richard? He's got fourteen other people he's responsible for, and one of them happens to be the governor of the state of New York."

"Big frigging deal," Corrigan said. "If it was me, I'd be tempted to tell us all to take a flying leap. Find our own way down the mountainside."

"I'm sure it crossed his mind," she said. There was silence between them for a moment.

"Could we?" he asked after a bit.

"Could we what?"

"Get out of here on our own?" he said.

He leaned toward her, close enough to the edge of his canopy for the never-ending mist to bathe his face again. "I mean, you ask a cop, any cop in New York, is there any jam you couldn't get out of, and he's going to tell you, 'No way,' because that's how most cops think. Hundred crackheads coming at you, it's kickass time. Nerve gas loose in the subways, suck it down like exhaust fumes and keep on hauling. But out here," he said, waving his arms about, "we're walking through clouds, we're building campfires. . . . I don't exactly know where I am, you know what I mean?"

"That's very reassuring, Richard." She glanced toward Dawson's tent, where the light had abruptly switched off. "I'm sure your charge would be happy to hear your feelings on the matter."

Corrigan followed her gaze and saw Elizabeth Dawson pushing her way out through the tent flaps, her husband, clad in fresh clothing, coming after her. Vaughn had turned from his duties at the fire and was banging a rod on a dinner gong, just like some character out of a Western movie.

Corrigan hesitated. *Find some rejoinder, Richie-boy, some bit of hero's trash talk.* But it simply wouldn't come.

He sat back, watching her stow her notebook and rise wearily to answer the call for dinner. Forget it. He'd think about such matters tomorrow, as the lady said. Tomorrow was bound to be a better day.

"I thought I might have a word with you, Officer Corrigan."

Corrigan, who'd found a seat a bit away from the others, glanced up from his dessert—a handful of trail mix with raisins, owing to their reduced circumstances, Vaughn had explained apologetically—to find Fielding Dawson standing over him, his expression back to its normal emanation of earnest good will.

"Sure," Corrigan said, pushing himself up from the fallen log where he'd been sitting. Corrigan grimaced, straightening his legs in turn, and Dawson gave a knowing nod.

"Just wait until tomorrow," the governor said. "I'll need a block and tackle to get me out of my sleeping bag."

Corrigan gave him a look. "Glad to hear I'm not the only one."

"You don't see anyone up dancing, do you?" the governor said.

Corrigan scanned the faces reflected in the glow of the fire. Donnelly and Vaughn idled together, each holding a tin cup of instant coffee. Dara was chatting with an exhausted-looking Giles Ashmead and his wife, while the film crew was huddled in a knot of its own, probably discussing their own battle plan for the next day, he presumed. Elizabeth Dawson was already back in the couple's tent. There was no sign of the governor's taciturn bodyguard, nor of Ariel Sorenson, his assistant. Those who were there did seem a subdued group, but given the events of the day, why expect anything else?

"It gets better," Dawson added. "Once we're up and moving, the joints loosen."

Corrigan glanced at the governor. "You can skip the 'officer' part, you know."

The governor shrugged, staring at him expectantly, as if it had been Corrigan who'd wanted to talk.

"Look, maybe it came off wrong, what I said earlier," Corrigan offered.

Dawson raised a hand to forestall him. "It's forgotten," he said. "Truth is, I don't blame you. I've been kicking myself all the way down this mountainside."

Corrigan glanced toward the fire, then back at the man. Why was it so difficult to accept the sincerity of the words? he wondered. Why couldn't he just buddy up with Dawson, take advantage of an opportunity most poor saps would die for? Suck up, his old man surely would have told him. Suck up, Richie-boy. Never mind the governor's word on behalf of that transfer application. Think big. If he played his cards right, he could be one of the governor's permanent bodyguards. He might even take over Soldinger's job, join the Secret Service, become White House chief of security one day.

"It's hardly your fault, those accidents," Corrigan said. "Such shit happens."

The governor nodded thoughtfully, as if he might be hearing the expression for the first time. "Still and all, we wouldn't be here if it weren't for me," he said. "And the implication that my political aspirations were in a way responsible . . ." He broke off, shaking his head in the perfect gesture of contrition.

"I don't know, Governor. When it comes right down to it, we're all here because we want to be, one way or another."

Dawson glanced up as Corrigan continued.

"Take me, for instance. It wasn't exactly my idea to come along, but I let it happen, you know?"

Dawson nodded. "You haven't seemed very comfortable. . . ."

"I'm not," Corrigan said. "What I did back in the park that day, that's what anybody would have done—"

"I suppose that's where we differ," Dawson cut in. "I don't think those were ordinary actions. I think what you did, whether you believe you acted on instinct or out of duty . . . I don't think that most people would have found it within themselves to take such a risk. . . ."

"Governor . . ." Corrigan protested. He could feel it building up inside again, this urge to protest the whole miserable mess. Was he actually about to tell the governor everything he'd spilled to Dara? The very thought made him giddy.

"It goes beyond *you*," Dawson hastened on. "Your reticence, your humility, that's all quite understandable, even charming. But holding your deeds up to the public eye says something to all of us, reminds us that we are all capable of valiant, selfless actions. In a day and age like ours . . ." He swept his arm about the darkness. "Well, let's just say we've had about all the politics of selfishness a nation can stand."

Corrigan stared back, trying to fathom the vast distance between the grandiosity of Dawson's vision of what had taken place and his own picture of smudge man toppling into the path of the train.

"That's why I love it out here," Dawson went on. "Nature is a great teacher. She reminds us that we're pretty frail and unimportant creatures, ultimately. That our time here is well spent only in regard to how responsibly we spend it on behalf of the greater good. That's why I do what I do, Richard. God only knows I'd have an easier time of it if I let up on the gun lobby or called off the watchdogs from the practices of industry, but then I'd be just like the rest of them. What's the point of it?"

For a moment, Corrigan felt what he supposed most of the governor's ardent supporters felt on a regular basis: an actual rush of energy that seemed to emanate from the man, like the heat and light pumping out of Vaughn's campfire on the other side of the clearing. As Rollie Montcrief had said, this man, he was good, there was no getting around it. And perhaps he was so good because he sincerely believed the things he said. As politicians went, wasn't it better to have someone arguing on behalf of fewer guns, less acid rain? *Come on, Richie-boy, lighten up.*

If the governor had been motivated to make a positive example out of him, then why not just go along, ride it out? Never mind that in fact he'd chased an addled philosopher into the path of a speeding train; never mind that he hadn't been able to do a damned thing to stop his father from blowing himself to kingdom come. *Just be a hero, Richie-boy. Play the part. Play it as it lays. Besides, what's the point of fighting?*

"The guy didn't have a gun, Governor," he heard himself saying.

Dawson blinked. "What's that?"

Corrigan shook his head. "The guy I chased down into the subway," he insisted. "He wasn't armed."

The governor stared back at him in confusion. "But I saw the pistol myself. One of the investigators showed me—"

"It was a throw-down," Corrigan said. "A plant. One of the other cops was afraid I'd get in trouble."

Dawson stared about the campsite, as if he was worried the others might have heard. Corrigan thought he could see the gears whirling inside the governor's head—trying to calculate the political downside. What would people think if he had brought along a hero who wasn't really a hero?

After a moment, however, his features eased and he leaned toward Corrigan, confidentially. "Well, tell me this, Richard. Did *you* think the man was armed when you were chasing him?"

Corrigan shrugged. "I wasn't sure. I had to assume he was."

The governor nodded. "There you are, then," he said, a satisfied smile returning to his face. "It's all a matter of perspective. What you've just told me doesn't diminish what you've done."

Corrigan stared back at him. "Perspective," he repeated. You had to give the governor credit for his unflappability, that much was certain.

For Dawson, the matter appeared to be closed. He reached out, clapped a hand on Corrigan's shoulder. "You're a good man, Richard. And you're a credit to your fellow officers."

Yeah, Corrigan thought, watching the man walk away. *But I wish you could tell it to that poor bastard who went over the side in the subway. I wish you could tell it to my old man.*

20

The cry cut the cold night air with startling clarity, causing the horses tied near the edge of the clearing to set up their own chorus of snorts and whinnies.

"What the hell was that?" one of the men near the campfire said. He had started at the sound, his boot heel striking the end of a log that jutted from the nearly spent fire. A stream of brilliant sparks soared up into the darkness. Maybe he'd just started a forest fire, his partner thought.

"Beats the jack out of me," this second man said. He favored a bit of whiskey before turning in, especially once their work was over, and in this case it was. They were employed by Ben Donnelly, their job to carry in provisions and cache them for the tenderfeet Donnelly guided through the wilderness. The provisions had been cached, he and his partner would begin their trek back out of the wilderness in the morning, and now there was time for R and R. All in all, he was not concerned by the sound. "Maybe it's that asswipe C.T. out there, fooling around."

"C.T.'s in Cody by now," the first man said, glancing at his watch. "Besides, it sounded like a woman."

"C.T. can make hisself sound like a woman when he wants to," the one with the half-pint in his hand said.

"Think it could have been a mountain lion?"

The older man had another sip of whiskey. "Was a lion, those horses over there would have run straight up a tree by now." He had a healthier sip. "Wasn't no lion."

The first man moistened his lips, staring out into the darkness from which it seemed the sound had come. There was another cry, then, lower in pitch, more guttural, and the man rubbed the back of his neck, as if he had felt the hair prickle there.

"Someone's hurt," he said as he got to his feet. The horses were dancing at the tether, now.

"Shit on a stick," the older man said. He stood as well, capping his bottle.

The first man was already off into the darkness, flashlight in hand. The older man followed, stopping briefly at his saddle pack, where he kept his pistol. It was a long-barreled Colt Peacemaker with a carved ivory handle and a stiff cocking mechanism, the kind of gun Wild Bill Hickok had been on the wrong end of. He didn't have to check to see if it was loaded. It was always loaded. He stuck the pistol in his belt and went after his partner, thinking to himself that only an idiot would go off unarmed in the night toward sounds of trouble.

"Leo," the older man heard. "Goddamnit, Leo, over here!"

Leo saw the wavering beam of his partner's torch and moved toward it, past a tangle of manzanita and scrub oak, down a slight incline to a ledge where the trail they'd traveled earlier cut the forest. His footing was unsteady on the talus slope, and he wondered briefly if he might have had one too many nips from the bottle that was sloshing in his hip pocket.

"Good Lord of living," he said when he saw what was caught in the beam of his partner's light.

"Look at her face," his partner said.

Leo didn't particularly want to look at her face, but it was hard to avoid. She lay on the rocky ground at the base of a stunted piñon pine, one arm twisted behind her back, the other outstretched toward them in entreaty. Her face was a mass of blood, her long black hair tangled and matted with it. *Horror show,* that's the phrase that leapt into Leo's mind. Something right out of a horror show.

"What the hell's been at her?" his partner was saying.

He bent down toward her, his hands outstretched as if to calm her. "It's all right," he said. "Just lay still. We'll help you. . . ."

Leo saw it happen, but he wasn't sure he understood what he was seeing, exactly. Maybe it was the chancy lighting—just the reflection of that torch beam, not much moon at all. Or maybe it was the effects of the whiskey that were blurring his senses.

What he thought he saw was the woman's hand circling around the back of his partner's neck, pulling him down sharply. Caught off guard like that, his partner toppled forward, his boots shooting backward through the loose talus like a mule trying to kick.

"Careful, now," Leo wanted to say. "Settle down." Any words to calm her. Because that's what he was thinking, at first: The woman had panicked, like a swimmer going down in a deep lake and some poor soul comes trying to help.

But then he realized that wasn't right, that wasn't what was happening at all. That bloody hand had a death grip on his partner—all locked up in the hair on the back of his head, all right—but panic had nothing to do with it.

She'd used her grip to lever herself off the ground and had brought her other arm—the one he'd assumed was broken—from behind her back, driving her hand toward his partner's gut. Leo saw a flash of steel, heard his partner's surprised gasp.

The speed of it all was what stunned Leo. She'd drawn back and struck again, and his partner had uttered an awful groan before Leo was able even to will his own hand toward the revolver at his belt. So many things crowding his unprepared and fuzzy mind, so many questions that seemed impossible to phrase, let alone solve.

His fingers seemed numb, clawing at the pistol as if they'd grown to twice their natural size, as if the bones had turned to flab, as if this all were some awful dream. He stumbled as he went backpedaling up the slope, felt his feet go out from under him. He came down in a sitting position, felt the half-pint shatter beneath his hip.

A stab of pain, warm wetness at his backside, spreading down his legs, but whether it was blood, whiskey, or himself pissing his own pants, what did it matter? For his partner was on the ground, now, hacking wet, terrible coughs. And the woman they thought they had come to save had rolled out from under his partner and was coming Leo's way, moving as quick and sure across the uneven ground as a great human spider.

Leo dug his heels into the gravel. He swung one hand back blindly, found a limb he could haul himself up with.

His other hand had finally come back from the dead. He felt the pistol grip against his palm. His thumb on the hammer. His trigger finger in place.

He was on his feet. Moving backward up the slope. She was coming at him like some dervish from a nightmare, and even though he heard strange whimpers of panic from his own throat, he was going to be fine. Anybody might whine, given what he was facing.

He was raising his pistol. He had plenty of time. *Blow this bitch back to hell,* that's what he was thinking . . .

. . . when the heavy arms encircled him from behind.

"All right." He heard a man's calm voice, almost a whisper, at his ear. "All right, now."

Leo's thumb slipped off the hammer, and his trigger finger tightened in reflex. The roar seemed deafening, the explosion of rock at his feet seemed that of a mining detonation.

At first he hardly felt the pain. It began as an icy stab, then grew almost instantly to a blaze. His foot, he thought, unwilling tears in his eyes. His own damned foot.

He blinked, stared down dumbly, the pain so terrible now that he was almost glad for the darkness. He didn't want to see it, didn't want to know what he had done to himself.

Would he still walk? That was the thought that coursed through his mind just as he saw the flash of steel swoop under his nose. He felt something warm flood his chest.

He was fumbling for the hammer of his pistol, wanting to fire again, or so he believed. But it surely could not have been, for now he saw the pistol sliding down the rocky slope between his feet. Why had he dropped his pistol? Why had he come this way? He felt the heavy arms loosen at his sides, felt himself go weightless.

"Say you're sorry," the man's voice intoned behind him, and Leo thought that an odd thing, indeed.

"Say you're sorry," the man repeated. "It's the way it's done." But Leo had ceased to care.

Sharp rock kissed his cheek, and he felt his legs and his feet vault up and over—the pain strangely vanished as quickly as it had come—his legs toppling over his head.

"Sorry for what?" He heard a woman's voice drift across the starry night. Puzzled. Disdainful.

Leo didn't blame her. He understood none of this. He understood nothing. He was tumbling freely, cartwheeling down the mountain, leaving all things terrible behind.

21

Though Corrigan had not slept in a tent since an outing up the Hudson he'd taken with his cousin half a life before, and though he felt instantly claustrophobic in the mummy-styled bag provided for him, and though he was wet and cold and one rock in particular jabbed its way easily through the Ensolite pad that was supposed to serve as a mattress, painfully gouging his hip, his back, and his ribs, he nonetheless fell asleep almost instantly after he had finished his chat with the governor and hobbled back to his little warren to burrow in.

The next morning, he awakened with an ache in his kidneys and, without bothering with shoes, walked a few yards into the misted woods to relieve himself. He was zipping himself up, his bare feet already chilled, and was about to turn back for his tent when he realized someone was standing nearby, a ghostly presence materialized out of the fog. For an instant, it was one of those bears from out of the hotel's picture book, but then the figure resolved into something more familiar.

"You gotta love this wilderness shit, huh?" It was Dawson's bodyguard standing there, taking a thunderous leak of his own.

"Dumbest fucking idea *I* ever heard of, I'll tell you that much," the big guy continued. He finished up, shook himself off, worked hard at sucking in his gut while buttoning up his jeans. He rolled each of his sweatshirt-clad shoulders in turn, and regarded their surroundings darkly. "Gotta be a lot of fun taking a dump out here," he added.

Corrigan looked back at the guy evenly. "You get used to it," he heard himself saying.

"You done a lot of this, huh?" There was a satisfying hint of surprise in the big guy's gravelly voice.

"My share," Corrigan said, enjoying the look in the guy's eyes.

The big guy nodded. "But you're from the city, right?"

Corrigan nodded. "Brooklyn."

"Uh-huh," the guy said. "You look familiar."

Corrigan felt his head snap up. "You don't," he told the guy, after what seemed a suitable pause.

The guy was still looking at him, then finally shrugged. "Happens to me a lot," he said mildly. "I used to be a cop. I'm always seeing people I recognize off the street. Curse of the job."

"I guess so," Corrigan said.

"Fucking faces, man. You're always looking for the assholes, the ones with something in mind." He broke off, regarding Corrigan anew. "Am I right, or am I right?"

Go three thousand miles away from the city, lose yourself in the frigging wilderness, look who you meet. "I hear you," Corrigan said.

"Fucking-A," the guy said. He reached out, cuffed Corrigan on the shoulder. Corrigan knew it was a gesture of friendship but still felt himself rocking on the unsteady ground. His feet were freezing, but he willed himself to ignore it.

"So, what's your name, again, ace?"

"Corrigan," he said, meeting the guy's gaze squarely. "Richard Corrigan."

"That's right." The big guy nodded. "You're the hero. Mine's Lou. Lou Vida." He glanced down at his thick hand. "I'd shake, but I just took a piss and all."

Corrigan glanced down at his own hand. "Right," he said. Lou Vida, hygienic woodsman.

Vida had turned in the meantime and gestured off toward the camp, where a figure was backing out of Dawson's tent. "Not such a bad ass for an older lady," Vida observed. It was Elizabeth Dawson who had emerged from the tent, Corrigan saw. And she was a handsome woman, even dragging herself sleepily out of a tent on the first morning of the camping trip from hell. She straightened, ran a hand through her hair. She glanced in their direction, then moved off toward a clump of underbrush.

"Maybe you want to take over for me, help her find a spot," Vida said, pointing after her.

"I think I'll pass," Corrigan said.

Vida, who was still staring in the direction that Mrs. Dawson had taken, made a sound that might have been intended as a laugh. He raised his arms, brought his hands together, cracked his knuckles noisily.

"Yeah, well, time to go back to work, I guess," he said, giving Corrigan another comradely cuff as he moved away. "What a circus, huh?"

And with its own trained bears, Corrigan thought, watching Vida move off in his waddling, muscle-bound walk.

They had breakfast—an oatmeal-like cereal with milk that had come from powder—then took their last turns warming themselves at the fire before Vaughn undertook its drowning, scattering what was left of the embers, dousing the hissing coals. Corrigan picked up an extra camp shovel and lent a hand with tossing dirt over the steaming remains. Vaughn didn't say anything but gave him a look that Corrigan interpreted as appreciative.

Donnelly, though he still looked ashen and drawn, made a show of calling them together after the tents had been stowed and the packs readied for the day's trek. As he prepped himself for whatever speech was to come, the big man rubbed his hands together vigorously, a gesture that reminded Corrigan how much cooler this new day seemed. Donnelly broke off the gesture abruptly, glancing around the group as if he'd been caught at some secret act. He glanced up through the canopy of pines toward the gray sky, and Corrigan followed his gaze.

The drizzle had stopped for the time being, but the prospects of its return seemed ripe to Corrigan's eye. The day was about as promising as a gloomy workday morning at the butt end of autumn. For some reason, Corrigan found himself thinking of smudge man and all his homeless allies, huddled together on a lonely, unheated platform somewhere in the bowels of Manhattan. Meantime, Donnelly had cleared his throat, breaking the expectant silence. "Yesterday was about as miserable a day as a man can have in this life," the outfitter said. He paused for a moment, as if the events were replaying themselves behind his eyes.

"I've spent a life at this work, and in all that time together there haven't been four lives lost doing what we do. To see all that happen, to lose your own son . . ." He broke off, there, turning his gaze from them momentarily, his head dipping as if in disbelief, as if he might be absorbing Fate's blow all over again.

When he turned back, his face was composed. "Still, we've got a job to do . . . . we've *all* got a job to do." He looked at them all. "There isn't a hell of a lot of choice. We've got to get ourselves safely down this mountain before the weather gets worse."

Fielding Dawson seemed about to step forward at this moment, but Corrigan saw his wife catch his arm, saw her fingers tighten into whiteness. The two stared at each other with such intensity that it seemed to Corrigan as if a force field had sprung up between them, a beam of fury great enough to kill anything unfortunate enough to stumble through it. He glanced about to see if anyone else had noticed, but all eyes seemed to be on Donnelly. When he glanced back, Elizabeth Dawson's arms were once again clutched in front of her chest, and Fielding Dawson was staring off into the trees, his jaw set, his lips clamped tight.

"We'll reach our first cache point by noon, as long as the weather holds," Donnelly was saying. "We'll have a decent meal, at least, and a chance to rest up a bit."

"Rest for what?" Corrigan found himself saying. There'd been an undeniable implication in Donnelly's words.

Donnelly turned to him. "There's something of an uphill stretch from that point on," the outfitter said. "Normally, we'd be climbing it first thing, after a good night's sleep." He shrugged. "But we're off schedule, now. We'll have to change our response accordingly."

Corrigan heard muffled groans from around the group. He felt the stiffness in his own legs and knew he couldn't be the only one. "You can look at the bright side, though," Donnelly continued. "Going uphill will stretch some of those sore muscles. In the end, you'll be better off for it."

To Corrigan, the remark sounded like something his father might have said. He might have even said so, but by then, Donnelly had turned and was leading them away.

22

"Oh my God." Corrigan heard Dara's voice from somewhere on the trail ahead, her tone filling him with dread.

He'd fallen behind a bit, had been trying to get the straps of his pack adjusted out of the inch-deep troughs they seemed to have chiseled into the flesh of his shoulders. He'd read stories of explorers lost in the desert, men who'd piece by piece tossed their weapons, their equipment, their food aside, leaving a grim trail toward the inevitable in their stumbling wake. He'd always wondered what degree of exhaustion would trigger such jettisoning, and now he was beginning to understand.

The note of alarm in Dara's voice wiped those thoughts away, however, and he found himself nearly bounding up a rise that blocked his view. He came over the top of a hummock, puffing, found her standing just at the down slope, frozen by the heart-stopping sight before them.

A deep gorge sliced the mountainside abruptly, as if a gigantic ax had cleaved the earth there, leaving behind a two-hundred-foot wound defined by sheer granite cliffs on either side, gushing white water for blood down a narrow canyon floor far below. Corrigan had heard all those stories as a schoolboy: Paul Bunyan and Babe the Blue Ox stomping across the American landscape, the lumberjack's footprints creating the depressions for lake sites, the ox's tears stocking them brim full. Given the landscape of his Brooklyn neighborhood, the tales had seemed too fanciful for his imagination to contain. But staring down past the cliffs to the frothing ribbon of water, he found himself light-headed, a new appreciation of the myths boiling up inside.

"I can't do it," Dara was saying. "I really can't." Her voice was uncharacteristically tight. Though Corrigan stood perhaps half a dozen feet away, she might have been talking to herself.

It took Corrigan a moment to realize what she was referring to. Then he saw it. The trail curved off a bit to the right, edging at an oblique angle behind a screen of low-growing scrub down to the edge of the precipice. And out there, past the juncture of pathway and cliffside, human beings were actually hovering, as if they were suspended in the ether. Of course she couldn't do that, he thought for one crazed micromoment. Neither could he. Walking on air was out of the question.

In the next instant, the shock had dissipated and the mirage reassembled itself into something that made perfect sense. Corrigan's eye had caught the lines anchored in the far side of the cliff, the rugged planked flooring that dangled down from those lines, edging out toward those people he'd taken to be floating in space.

In actuality, they were walking slowly, making their way carefully across a swaying suspension footbridge that spanned the gorge. Corrigan nodded. He had been on a rope bridge once. It was about a dozen feet long, spanning a drainage ditch that lay all of a foot or two beneath ground level. It connected the parking lot with the boat ramp where he and his father had launched their Boston Whaler the day he nearly lost his eye. Corrigan could still hear the pounding of his father's feet on those rough planks as he rushed him, bleeding in his arms, back to the family car.

He noted that the film crew had set up at a vantage point on the near cliffside, both cameras rolling as the rest of the group picked its way off across the wobbling bridge. "So, the show goes on," he said to Dara.

She glanced up, as if she'd just noticed he was there. "I can't do it," she repeated.

"What are you talking about?"

She pointed. "The bridge. I *can't.*"

He turned back, glancing out over the gorge. Donnelly, leading the way, had nearly reached the far side. The outfitter turned, urging the Ashmeads and the Dawsons along. Dawson's assistant was next in line, followed by Lou Vida, who moved in teetering, uncertain steps, like a rhino trying to tip-toe across a floor full of marbles.

Corrigan saw movement near the place where the path led to the bridge, and saw Vaughn coming up the trail a bit to check on them. "Everything okay?" the wrangler called in his twanging voice.

Corrigan raised a reassuring hand. "Just catching my breath," he called back. "We're coming."

Vaughn nodded, and turned back toward the bridge, saying something to Mal, the cameraman.

"I don't get it," Corrigan said to Dara. "You've been skipping along these cliffs for two days, now."

She shook her head. "It's different," she said. "I know it doesn't make sense. I tried to go across one of those things when I was in high school. It was even longer and higher, across Devil's Canyon in Colorado . . ." She broke off, shuddering at the memory.

"I got about halfway out and just froze up. Something about the perspective, I guess." She glanced up at him, her face pinched. "Or maybe it's the motion of it, the fact that there's nothing solid under my feet. I don't know. The others had to turn around, carry me back."

Corrigan looked out at the bridge, shrugged. "So, I'll carry you," he said.

She shook her head, then bit her lip and closed her eyes momentarily. "I'll do it," she said. When she opened her eyes to look at him, her face seemed a notch paler. "I'll try, anyway. If I get stuck, you just grab hold of me, drag me on across, all right?"

"Don't worry," he said. "I'll be there."

She managed a brief smile, then, and moved past him, walking quickly down the path, her chin thrust forward as if she were forcing herself toward her own execution.

"Here's the last, then," Vaughn called to the camera crew when he saw them coming. The wrangler stood aside, motioning Dara out onto the planks of the bridge.

The roar of the stream below was far more pronounced here, Corrigan noted. And the sound was familiar, somehow, rising up the steep cliffs, doubling and redoubling as it came.

And there was something else suddenly different, though it took him a moment before he could pin it down. If the temperature had not warmed significantly as they had hiked that morning, neither had it dropped. But the draft that rushed up at them here seemed ten degrees cooler, a damp slap from the frothing river.

Dara hesitated, then reached out to clamp one of the moist support cables in either hand. She moved carefully out onto the planks, some of which were dark with moss and mold.

"Watch your step," Vaughn called above the roar.

If Dara heard these words of encouragement, she made no sign. She'd made two steps, then three, seemed to be managing it after all.

Corrigan waited until she'd passed the dark-coated planks onto what seemed surer footing, then moved out after her. He glanced ahead, and gauged the distance across the chasm at a hundred feet or so, about half the distance to the furious water below. He saw that Lou Vida had made it across, now. The bodyguard was standing on the opposite side and was watching their progress, rolling his muscled arms as if he were throwing punches in slow motion.

Corrigan felt the planks wobble beneath his feet, felt their sideways sliding on the accumulated slime. He tightened his grip on the chill, damp lines, glanced over his shoulder to see that Vaughn had stepped out onto the bridge behind him.

Mal was back there too, squatting on the bank by their jumping-off spot, the lens of his big camera aimed their way. The director was higher up on the slope, offering directions to the other cameraman. The soundman was moving cautiously toward the edge of the cliff, dangling his boom out over the precipice as if it were some odd fishing pole, while the grip played out cable behind.

"You want to keep moving," Vaughn called. "Don't look down; don't freeze up."

A man with the knack for saying exactly the wrong thing, Corrigan thought, hoping that the words hadn't carried to Dara. He turned to check, but she was well out in front of him, now, moving slowly but steadily ahead. He noticed that she was dragging each foot across the wobbly planking, planting it firmly before taking the next step. Still, she seemed resolute, and he found himself hoping silently that she'd do just as Vaughn had said.

He glanced down at the tumult, saw a dark log shoot up from the froth, flip over, then fall back and disappear in an instant. If the huge thing had made a splash, there was no way to tell.

Corrigan tried to reconcile what he saw down there with the rivers he had known, but there seemed little correspondence. Unlike those languid, cow-spirited ditches of the East, the thing beneath him was a creature alive, one that seemed to writhe with angry intention. You might survive a plunge into the East River, for instance, so long as you didn't swallow anything. But fall into that havoc water below and you could surely kiss your ass good-bye.

So many things in this landscape you had to be careful of, he thought as the planks beneath him heaved and shuddered. People might conceive of the city as dangerous, but it struck him what a misperception that was. The city itself—its landscape, that is—was largely benign. It was the people you had to watch out for. Here, it seemed, things were precisely the other way around.

Still, there was nothing in the physical perspective that daunted him, he noted. Not like what Dara must be experiencing right now. Maybe it was just the way his mind worked, or maybe there was something good about that depth-altering injury to his eye after all. Whatever it was that worked against any physical disorientation, however, it did not keep him from having a profound respect for the power thundering beneath him. He would keep a firm grip on those slick steel cables every step of the way.

Dara, meanwhile, was nearing the end of her ordeal. Corrigan saw Donnelly move toward the end of the bridge to offer a hand her way, but she ignored him, propelling herself onto land with a thrust that sent a ripple out along the guidelines. Corrigan picked up his own pace, then, his last dozen strides over the unsteady planks more like nervous jogging.

And then he was off and with the others.

"You did it," he said to Dara as he joined her on the rocky platform where the others had gathered. He felt his own breathing even out as he saw how far from the edge he'd come. Maybe twenty feet in from the side of the cliff, and the sound of the river was a background mumble once again.

She nodded. Her face had regained most of its color. "I had my eyes closed the whole time," she said.

"That's no problem," he said, gesturing back across the chasm. "Your back was to the cameras."

She managed a smile, and he turned, watching as Vaughn

made his way off the bridge and stationed himself to wait for the film crew to join them. Mal was already moving across the bridge, steadying himself with one hand, keeping his camera rolling with the other. The second cameraman had left off filming and was helping the grip and the soundman with their equipment, while the female director moved out onto the bridge, bringing up the rear.

"All right, folks," Donnelly called. "Get your things together. We've still got a ways to go."

Corrigan drew a breath, reaching to adjust his backpack on his shoulders. "Do I remember something about an uphill part?" he said to Dara. He felt a drop of rain on the back of his hand, and glanced up at the steely sky.

"It doesn't matter," she said. "But as long as there aren't any more rope bridges, I really don't care."

Corrigan nodded, checking again on the progress of the film crew. A thick gray squall cloud was swooping down the canyon toward the group on the bridge, rain already beginning to pelt them. Great, Corrigan thought. Just where you wanted to be in a storm.

Mal, meanwhile, had stopped filming and had slung his camera across his back. He turned to help the second cameraman with one of the bulky bags of gear, and the entire procession had to stop momentarily while the transfer between the two was completed.

Mal had just turned, the bag tucked under one arm, when Corrigan saw a bucking motion ripple through the guylines, as if some giant unseen hand had picked up one end of the bridge and popped it like a whip. Mal staggered, the heavy bag tumbling from his grasp. The bag went over the side, hurtling down toward the water, where it disappeared without a trace.

Another shock wave bucked through the bridge, and Corrigan felt his stomach turn. He was already running down the slope, Dara's cries ringing in his ears, when he saw the far end of the bridge anchors tear loose altogether.

The grip, who had both hands clutching a long coil of wire to his chest, was the first to go off as the long string of planking snapped down. The soundman managed to keep his hold on one of the guylines for a moment. But the cable in the grip's hands was still connected to the folded-up boom. And the boom was slung over the soundman's shoulders.

The slack played out in an instant. The soundman was ripped away with his boom after his partner, and the two spun downward in a tethered whirl before disappearing into the water.

Corrigan caught himself at the edge of the cliff, clutching one of the heavy bridge supports just as the tongue of the bridge slammed against the side of the cliff. He could feel the force of the blow vibrate the post like a tuning fork, a note that ran on through his body. The impact sent the second cameraman backward off the broken bridge, his hands clutching at nothing, his mouth frozen in a scream that never rose over the roar of the river.

The director had slid to the end of the bridge, where she was flung about upside down, her foot caught in a tangle of cable and planking. The splintered bridge rebounded off the face of the cliff, its tail snapping like the end of a whip.

As Corrigan watched, stunned, the bridge slammed back into the rock wall a second time, bringing her along with it. This time, the tangle of rope and wood blew apart, and the director tumbled free, her form pinwheeling down after the others.

Corrigan felt his legs going weak, his mind spinning. He clutched at the support post as if gravity itself were trying to yank him off his perch. He shook his head, trying to bring himself back, trying to find the place where there had once been a normal world.

And then he saw Mal. Somehow, the cameraman had managed to keep his grip on one of the bridge lines. He dangled there against the face of the cliff, staring up at Corrigan with a look that went beyond terror.

Corrigan was frozen for a moment, staring down at Mal's battered face. He was only a few feet away, his hands locked to the bridge cable, his feet beating a frantic tattoo against the rock, searching for some crevice, some knob, the slightest place to dig in.

Corrigan hardly noticed the rain. He fell to his knees, then threw himself flat on the ground, one arm wrapped around the stanchion, the other flung out over the edge toward the cameraman. He stretched down as far as he dared, his fingers tantalizingly close to Mal.

Corrigan twisted his head up and shouted over his shoulder

into the torrent from the skies. "Lou!" he called. "Lou Vida, for God's sake."

The few moments it took the burly man's face to appear above him seemed an endless expanse of time. "What the hell . . . ?" Vida began, his eyes widening in disbelief.

"Grab my legs," Corrigan cried. "Lower me down a couple of feet so I can grab him. See if Donnelly's got a rope. Come on, goddamnit!"

"We need a rope," Vida called over his shoulder. Then he was down on his knees, bracing himself against the stanchion.

Corrigan felt Vida's big hands lock about his ankles as if iron had been welded there. He would never again demean the man's physique, he thought. Never again question the wisdom of steroid usage.

"Let me down," he called, fighting the light-headedness that came as his torso edged off the rain-slicked rock ledge and out into space. "A little more! Come on."

He was upside down, now, grasping toward Mal, willing his arms to telescope, his fingers to stretch just a few more inches. Mal stared up at him in agony, his face clotted with effort.

Another foot, Corrigan thought. *Just one more foot.*

He twisted his head back over his shoulder to call to Vida. "Where's the rope!"

Vida glanced back into the forest, then down at Corrigan. "Donnelly's coming. Tell him to hold on!"

Corrigan heard a commotion above him, had to turn away as a sheet of loose sand and gravel fell down over him, pelting his shoulders, the back of his head. Mal took the same debris full in his already rain-spattered face.

"We got a rope!" Donnelly called down breathlessly. "Let me get a loop in it—"

"Fuck the loop," Corrigan cried. "We're going to lose him!"

"He'll never take the strain if he's not locked in," Donnelly shouted back, working frantically at the rope. "Tell him to hold on."

Corrigan let his head fall back toward the cameraman. His own vision was pinging, now, his ears roaring with pressure. Rainwater ran down his arms, coursed from his chin.

"Come on, Mal," he said. "The rope's coming. You gotta hold on. Come on. Just one foot. Come on, buddy. Just reach up and grab my hand."

Mal's eyes were bulging, his face purple. His head fell back a bit, his mouth opening, fishlike, as if he were straining to reply. For a moment, Corrigan thought that it might be the roar of the water below that hid whatever he was trying to say. But in the next moment, he saw it: There was a heavy strap wrapped full across Mal's straining throat, and at last Corrigan understood.

"His camera," Vida called down at the same moment. "His camera's choking him. Tell him to get it off!"

Mal must have heard, for he shook his head, helpless. And Corrigan mirrored the gesture in his own mind. How could he get the strap off? Let go of the cable with one hand, Mal would never be able to maintain his grip. Yet his eyes were already rolling back, his tongue protruding.

"Here," Donnelly cried, flinging one noosed end of the rope out into space. "Get it down to him."

"Too late," Corrigan called to Vida. He felt the knotted rope smack against his back. "Lower me one more foot."

Vida glanced about, helpless. "How?"

"He's going to die!" Corrigan screamed.

Vida gave him a look, then slid down onto his chest, bracing one of his blocky shoulders against the stanchion.

Corrigan felt a jolt as he slid farther down the cliff. He swung about, ignoring the swirling disorientation in his head, grabbing the wet rope Donnelly had tossed with one hand.

He flung his other hand out for Mal, but the effort sent him swaying a bit and his hand slapped hard against Mal's now-darkened face. Mal seemed hardly to notice.

"Mal!" Corrigan cried. "Take my hand!"

"We're tied off up here!" Donnelly called.

Corrigan saw one of Mal's hands peel away from the heavy cable. "Grab my hand, Mal!"

Mal's arm fell away limply to his side, the movement of a mime simply overwhelmed by whatever he'd worked out in his silent play.

"Mal!" Corrigan screamed.

He lunged for the hand that remained, just as it loosened from the cable. For a moment, he felt Mal's wet fingers clutched in his fingers, palm pressed to his palm. He let go of the rope, then, flinging his other hand to him, but it was all weight and gravity, all beyond his strength.

Mal's fingers slid away: one inch, then two, and then he was gone. His body bounced off the face of the rock, his heels brushing the rope intended to save him. As his body spun away in the crude semblance of a dive, the camera strap came loose from his throat, and the heavy camera was finally tumbling free.

The heavy thing struck the rocks near the foot of the cliff and burst into pieces. Mal's body plummeted directly into the water and vanished.

Corrigan felt himself being pulled up the side of the cliff. In moments, he was back on solid ground with Donnelly and Vida. Dara stood a few feet away, in the shadows of the forest, her face a pale mask. He turned and glanced back down over the edge of the precipice. The rain had stopped, he realized, gone as quickly as it had come.

He saw a dangling rope. The wreckage of the bridge. The endless torrent of white water. But not a trace of anything human, not a hint of all those who had died.

It was then that he finally realized why the sound that rose up toward him had seemed so familiar.

The sound of a train, he thought. Of a machine roaring out of a tunnel somewhere, of a thing shot straight up from Hell.

23

"You want me to try and get folks moving, Ben?" The voice was soft, almost apologetic. Corrigan glanced up to see that Vaughn had made his way back up the trail to the edge of the cliff. The wrangler had addressed the question to his boss, who had yet to lift his gaze from the raging waters below.

It was as if the three of them—himself, Donnelly, and Vida—were waiting there for some indication that what they had just witnessed hadn't really happened. As if they were hoping that it was some kind of collective nightmare, some hallucination of doom spawned by the weather, by the memories of disasters that had already befallen them.

But it wasn't that way, of course. The shattered bridge still trailed down the cliff, the forlorn length of rope they'd hoped to use to save the cameraman still tossed aimlessly in the stiff updrafts, the pieces of Mal's camera still lay strewn about on the rocks far below.

Finally, Donnelly lifted his gaze, focusing in on his wrangler like a man who'd been summoned back to the world from a great distance away. "You tell them . . ." Donnelly began, then stopped. He hung his head, swinging it back and forth like an old fighter trying to muster a last store of energy.

After a moment, he looked up at Vaughn. "Just hold on," he managed. "I'll talk to them in a minute."

Vaughn nodded and moved off, back down the trail to where the others had huddled beneath a clump of pines, out of the blast of the worsening storm. Donnelly was still shaking his head. "Just when you think it can't get any worse," he said to Corrigan, "it'll be something come along and show you how wrong you are."

Corrigan murmured agreement, his eyes on Dara, who stood with the rest of the group, a comforting arm around

Dawson's assistant, Ariel. The young woman had her face in her hands, her shoulders heaving with what Corrigan presumed were sobs. He could hardly blame her—it seemed the perfect response to what had taken place. Either that or some fist-shaking rage at the heavens, take your choice.

"Ten little Indians," Lou Vida said.

"What are you talking about?" Corrigan said, turning to him.

"With those pilots, it's nine down, ten to go," Vida said, nodding at the rest of the group. "Count for yourself."

The look on Donnelly's face defied description. The outfitter leaned forward as if he might send Vida over the side, reverse the count in an instant. Corrigan found himself placing a hand on Donnelly's shoulder.

"What did Vaughn mean about getting people moving?" Corrigan said to Donnelly. "Maybe we ought to pitch camp right here for the night."

Donnelly gave Vida a last withering glance, then turned, wiping rain from his craggy face with a sweep of his hand. "We can't do it. We don't have any food left. We've got to get down to that cache point, for a lot of reasons . . ." He broke off, staring up at the leaden skies above them with uncharacteristic concern. The rain had picked up again, and Corrigan felt a new chill in the wind gusting at the edge of the gorge.

"What's the rest of it?" Corrigan prompted.

Donnelly held two fingers up in a pinching gesture. "We're about this close to snow."

"You have to be shitting me," Lou Vida cut in.

Donnelly glanced at Vida, too tired, it seemed, to waste any more energy on contentiousness. "I wish I was, my friend. I surely wish I was." The outfitter ran both of his hands over his face, then, as if trying to massage new life into his features.

Corrigan felt a fresh wave of dread. What had Donnelly said a few minutes ago? *Just when you think it can't get any worse . . .*

Corrigan glanced down the sheer canyon wall beside him. The updrafts were strong enough to drive him backward, now, and he clutched at one of the bridge supports.

"Any way we could haul that bridge up here?"

Donnelly gave him a look, then glanced down at the long trail of planks and cable. "If you had a heavy-duty winch or a twenty-mule team, maybe." His faded blue eyes had narrowed when he looked up at Corrigan again. "Why would you want to do such a thing?"

Corrigan shrugged. "I'd like to have a look at the ends of those lines, that's all."

"For what reason?"

Something in Donnelly's tone made Corrigan feel he already knew what the reason was. "I don't know," Corrigan said. "I'd just like to see."

"See if maybe somebody had been sawing on them, is that what you mean?"

Corrigan turned up his hands in a gesture of uncertainty. Lou Vida was staring at the two of them, his brow furrowed with suspicion.

Donnelly nodded. "A hell of a lot of accidents, isn't it?"

"At least three too many," Corrigan said.

"You guys trying to say somebody set all this up?" Vida said.

Corrigan gave him what he hoped was a neutral glance. "You used to be a cop. What do you think?"

Vida rolled his shoulders, clearly uncomfortable with the question. "Who the hell would do it?"

"*Why* would be my question," Donnelly said.

"Maybe someone who doesn't want Fielding Dawson to be president," Corrigan offered. He hadn't consciously formulated the thought, but the moment the words were out of his mouth, he realized he'd suspected it for some time now. "This is militiaman country, isn't it?"

Donnelly shrugged.

"Then maybe there's someone who doesn't like the governor's proposals on gun control, for instance, and doesn't want to take any chances."

The three of them turned to stare down the trail toward the others. Dawson was squatting in front of his wife, who was seated on a boulder, her head in her hands, her long black hair draped shroudlike over her face. He seemed to be talking earnestly to her.

"I guess anything is possible," Donnelly said.

Corrigan glanced at Vida. "Did Soldinger say anything about this to you?"

Vida stared back, his face a blank. "He said it was going to be a long walk in the park, that's all." He gave a ponderous shrug. "See a bear, shoot it. See two bears, run."

"Maybe we ought to talk to Dawson, see if he's received any threats lately. Some group he's offended, something like that," Donnelly suggested.

"You guys can't be serious," Vida said. "Yo, Governor, anybody pissed off at you, bad enough to follow you out to Bumfuck, Wyoming, blow up an airplane, start a rockslide, cut the ropes on the bridge you were going to walk across?"

Corrigan hesitated, pondered the situation, then glanced back at the lowering sky. "We will talk to him, but I'm not sure what the good of it would be at this moment. Like you say, Donnelly, if we don't get down out of this weather, we won't have to worry about who might have it in for Dawson. Mother Nature'll make the question moot."

Already, Corrigan was feeling the sting of rain cold enough to turn to sleet. One thing about working the tunnels, he thought. Rain or shine, it didn't make a hell of a lot of difference.

"We're agreed, then," Donnelly said.

"I still think you guys are nuts," Vida said.

But his words were swept up in a great gust of wind and rain, and besides, they were already on their way.

24

The first four or five hundred yards took the group away from the site of the bridge disaster along a gradual downhill slope. Thank God for small favors, Corrigan was thinking as he made his way along. But he was also wary of whatever climb lay ahead. If he was bone-tired, the others had to be hanging on by a thread as well. The weather, the lack of food, the exertion . . . all were bad enough. Add on the psychological battering they'd taken, it was a wonder everyone was still walking.

But walking they were, and though the brave chatter that had characterized the procession earlier in the day had vanished, there was no grumbling, either. Even Lou Vida had buttoned it up, once Donnelly reiterated the situation with the weather to the rest of the party.

While Dara had shot him an inquiring glance, there'd been no chance for the two of them to talk. There had been no dissension, no questions, just resigned glances and a quiet shouldering of packs. No more fun and games, Corrigan thought. Certainly no more fun. Just a group of survivors bent on climbing down from Hell.

The trail switched back around a deep fold in the forested mountainside, giving him a clear view of the party. Vaughn was leading the way, followed by Dawson, his wife, and Dawson's assistant. Next in line were Giles Ashmead and his wife, followed by Lou Vida and Dara, who glanced up, giving him a look as she circled around on the opposite side of the cleft. Corrigan sent her what he hoped was an encouraging nod, but she turned away without any response. They hadn't spoken, in fact, since he'd urged her out across the bridge. It gave him the uncomfortable feeling that she somehow blamed him for what had happened. An irrational feeling, Corrigan knew, but it nagged at him just the same.

He heard the sounds of footsteps behind him, and paused as Ben Donnelly came half jogging down the sloping trail toward him.

"We call this the shepherd's position," the outfitter told Corrigan as he approached.

"As in sheep?" Corrigan asked, grateful for a moment's rest.

"Exactly," Donnelly said. "Trouble is, I've lost a hell of a lot of the flock."

"I'd hardly say it was your fault," Corrigan said, wiping the dripping rain from his chin.

"It's my party," Donnelly said, his voice firm. "I'm responsible for what happens every minute we're out here." He gave Corrigan a steely look that suggested they'd lingered long enough.

Corrigan nodded as he moved off, even if he thought Donnelly was being too hard on himself. Like Fielding Dawson said, it was the kind of attitude that seemed in short supply these days. Still, he doubted he'd ever hear Dawson taking public responsibility for this string of calamities—not exactly the sort of thing to make for stirring speechifying on the campaign trail: "I know what hard times are, my fellow Americans, for I have led nine decent people to their deaths."

Corrigan knew it wasn't fair of him to blame Dawson and his ambitions for what had happened, and, if pressed, he might have to wonder whether his suspicions of foul play were the natural product of a wounded psyche. He'd seen it often enough in the course of his duties, after all.

Once, an enormously fat man—easily four hundred pounds—had keeled over on his way up the steps of Penn Station. His heart had stopped beating before Corrigan had arrived. He'd administered CPR to no avail, and nothing the arriving EMS team had done had been able to start the man's heart again, either.

The man's widow, however, had hardly seen their efforts as heroic. She'd arrived on the scene in shrieking hysterics and had immediately accused the EMS team—all white—of giving indifferent treatment to her husband—a black man—because of his race. There had been much talk of legal repercussions and one appearance on Channel Four by Al Sharpton, but as far as Corrigan knew, nothing had ever come of it.

And, as Corrigan well knew, things might just as easily have turned out differently in his own case. A witness comes down a dimly lit stairwell, glances across a subway platform, sees a white man struggling with a black man, and . . . "Yessir, Officer, I saw it all with my own eyes. He pushed him. That's right. He pushed him into the path of that express train."

Corrigan shook his head, noticing that the trail had swung upward once again. He wanted to ask Donnelly if this was the signal of what was to come—that last dreaded, uphill push—but he decided against it.

Why think about it? Just gut it out, take what comes. The trail turns uphill, then lean into it and climb. Some terrible accident takes place, why try to attribute the matter to some malevolent force, torture yourself with whys and wherefores? Like Donnelly had said, there was only one thing that mattered right now, and that was getting out. There would be time to resolve the matter later on.

"The sad thing is that it's so beautiful."

Corrigan came out of his reverie to find Dara waiting for him at a juncture where the trail switched back. "Look," she said, pointing over his shoulder.

Corrigan turned. There was an opening through the pines, there, affording a view back down toward the canyon they'd crossed earlier. Gray tendrils of mist cruised the dark pine canopy like benevolent smoke. In the distance was the dramatic gash of the canyon, sheer walls, the rock blackened by rain, and a glimpse, far below, of that electric white ribbon he knew to be a river. No sound at this distance, though—just a writhing, ever-shifting, indifferent trail of brightness.

"That it is," he said. He'd seen pictures of this in museums.

After a moment, she spoke. "You think that was just another accident, what happened at the bridge?"

"Pretty hard to say, Dara."

"What do your cop's instincts tell you?"

"Probably the same thing your reporter's instincts tell you," he said.

"Militia crazies?"

"Could be," he said. "Of course, Dawson was also a tough nut when he was a prosecutor. And some of the environmental programs he's pushed would put a dent in some pretty big wallets if he got the chance to go nationwide. . ." He broke off, still trying to puzzle it through. "The question is, who would be capable of something like *this?*"

She stared about the forest. "Say there *was* someone out there, someone or some group who'd planned all this; say they were watching us right now . . ."

"What could we do about it, that's what you're wondering."

"Exactly."

He shook his head. "Step carefully," he said. "Keep our eyes open; hurry on home."

"Maybe I'm just being paranoid," she said, tossing her hair. A brave gesture, he thought. It made her seem all the more desirable.

"Just because you're paranoid," he told her, "it doesn't mean they're not after you."

She managed a smile, which soon faded as she glanced up the trail after the rest of the party. "After Dawson, you mean. It's all about him."

"If there is someone behind this," he said, stretching his sore shoulders against the straps of his pack. "We could just be having a lousy run of luck, that's all."

"One of the worst," she agreed.

"We get to wherever we're supposed to be going, I'll talk to him," he said. "Right now I think that's our prime concern."

She nodded, shifting her pack up on her back. "I guess so," she said. She gave one last forlorn wave toward the vista stretched out before them. "But you should come back one day," she said. "You should see this when . . ." She broke off, searching for the right words. "It's not the fault of the place," she said. "I know it sounds ridiculous. . . ."

He reached out, then, encircled her with his arms, pulled her close. They must have looked like a couple of awkward, orange-humped bears locked in a dance step, he thought, but he didn't care. All that seemed to matter was that for a few brief seconds, the sense of calamity was gone.

"Better pick it up." Donnelly's voice came from behind them. Dara stepped back as Corrigan glanced down the trail to see the outfitter making the turn around the switchback toward them. He'd donned a fisherman's cap, but that too was soaked, the rain running down his cheeks and dripping from his chin. "We've got about an hour's climbing, now," he said, gesturing up the slope as he strode their way, "and at least that much down the other side of the ridge before we reach the cache point."

Corrigan checked his watch, surprised to see that it was nearly five o'clock. "When does it get dark?" he asked, trying to remember what time they'd pitched their camp the night before.

"We've got time," Donnelly said, waving them along. "As long as nothing else happens."

"Now, there's a cheery thought," Dara said. Then she turned and began to climb.

25

It was sleet at first, an almost imperceptible shifting from icy rain to ice and finally back to rain as it caught in Corrigan's matted hair and slithered down his neck and cheeks. They were back above the tree line, now, and had been for ten or fifteen minutes.

He glanced up and counted the entire party strung out along the barren, tundralike landscape, everyone but him with a cap or hood drawn up against the weather. He saw a vague shadow that loomed through the thick mist farther up, but whether that was the ridgeline to which Donnelly had referred or just one more ledge to be surmounted, Corrigan had no idea. He was a foot soldier, now, he thought, scrabbling at the collar of his brand-new, rain-soaked, water-resistant coat. The same clerk who'd sold him his *trés* hip hiking shoes—now themselves soaked, his feet freezing—had sold him the coat as well, had shown him where the hood was tucked beneath Velcro tabs, and Corrigan struggled to untuck the thing with his numbed fingers, wishing he'd paid more attention at the time.

Finally he had the hood unfurled and pulled it over his ears, tied it securely under his chin. Ridiculous, he thought, but what did it matter how he looked? He was a grunt. Like Fielding Dawson said, a flyspeck on the canvas of the universe. His job was to keep his feet moving to climb and climb and climb some more.

He glanced ahead, eyes fixed on the steady trudge of Dara's boots along the trail. If he *were* to come back, it would be on a sunny day, and he—*they*—would be in a divan held aloft by bearers, he thought, his mind going bleary with fatigue.

He heard a shrill whistle from below, then, and turned, startled, to see Donnelly waving his arms in some kind of signal. He raised his fingers to his lips and gave another piercing

blast. This time Vaughn, who was at the head of the party, perhaps fifty yards up the slope, heard. He stopped and held up
his hand to halt the others.

Donnelly, meantime, was gesturing frantically at the leaden
skies. Vaughn turned to look, and Corrigan swiveled his head
as well. He noted that the shadow he'd taken to be a ledge, or,
better yet, the ridgeline, seemed to be moving, advancing
ominously down the slope toward them.

Not the ridgeline, not a ledge, no earth formation at all, he
was thinking. This was weather. Some dark, heavy cloud that
looked as formidable as an avalanche, rolling rapidly down
the barren mountainside toward them, with nothing in its way
that might stop it.

Donnelly was practically sprinting up the trail, now, elbow-
ing past Corrigan on his way toward Vaughn. "Turn around,
get back down the slope," he shouted as he passed. "Try to get
back to the trees. If you get caught in it, don't wander around.
Get your tent up. Stay inside and hope it passes."

Then he was gone, struggling on up the slope toward the
others. Corrigan turned to Dara. "Caught in it? Caught in
what? What's he talking about?"

She pointed at the dark mass of advancing clouds. "That,"
she said, her voice grim. "That snowstorm."

Corrigan stared at her for a moment, frozen streaks of rain
slashing the air between them. The stinging bite of sleet at his
forehead, his cheeks. The unmistakable flutter of snowflakes.
He glanced down at the distant tree line below. Only a
moment before, he'd been so proud of how far he'd
climbed . . .

. . . and then everyone was on the run back down.

26

It was something out of a nightmare, like trying to outrun a bus or an iceboat on a frozen pond, but instead of skates you were wearing snowshoes, or, actually, shoes that had turned to blocks of ice, Corrigan thought. Dara was in front of him, half running, half sliding down the rubble-strewn switchbacks.

The terrain was too rugged and too steep to make a direct run down the slope for the trees, and even on the trail, the footing was too uncertain to move on the dead run, no matter how much they might be tempted. The snow had caught them, now, was steadily increasing in volume. The back of Dara's pack was plastered white, and so were her pants, the sleeves of her coat. It was getting hard to see, to keep the white stuff out of his eyes, and the footing was almost impossible.

Corrigan made a turn and stole a glance upward to see how the others were faring, but he could have saved himself the trouble. There was nothing to see but a blur of white and a blast of wind and snow that struck him like a slap.

He turned back and made out the ghost that was Dara just before the full force of the storm swept over them. He lunged forward, caught her hand. He paused momentarily to make sure of his bearings, then pulled her over the side of the trail as the wave of whiteness enveloped them.

"What are you doing?" she cried as they stumbled down the rocky slope.

"Just hold on," he called back, shouting over the rush of the wind. "Whatever you do, don't let go. We've got to make it to the trees."

No sooner had he said it than he felt his feet go out from under him. He went down hard on his back, his elbows cracking painfully into the rock. His coat rode up, bunching under his arms as he slid, and rock and slush piled up beneath the fabric, soaking his back, scraping his flesh raw.

He had taken Dara down with him as well, he realized, hearing her cry out as he rolled over her. They tumbled together for a moment, then he felt something—a rock, a stump—jam into his side with the force of a driving linebacker or a cabby's fender, and she was gone from him.

He was falling freely now, cartwheeling out of control down the slope. First his shoulder digging into the rocks, then his feet whipping by, sending him into an ever faster whirl. He felt his feet touch the ground again, and for a moment he was actually running, hurtling down the mountainside at incredible speed. No sprinter, no prey, had ever run so fast, he thought, and yet he knew he could not maintain this pace, never catch up with his fleeing self. . . .

In the next instant he was blindsided and down again, swatted by something, a great and heavy arm . . . feathery, and also limber. A tree limb, he realized, and realized, too, that he was still falling.

He sensed the crackling of underbrush around and beneath him, a shattering of limbs, one more moment of weightlessness, and finally . . .

. . . free fall—the end of his life, the end of it all, he was thinking—then a final jolt, and all was still.

He lay quietly for a moment, scarcely daring to breathe. He was on his back, in a tangle of deadfall at the base of a tiny cliff, an outcropping of rock perhaps a dozen feet high, no more. Pines towered above him, shielding him from the full fury of the storm, though snow still whistled over the lip of the rock above him and drove in sheets about the treetops.

He raised one arm gingerly and pulled himself upright. His other arm was numb from the blow he'd taken from the first limb, but he found that he could move that as well. He flexed one leg, then the other. He ran his hands over his face, then checked his hands. No blood.

He was whole, then, he thought, and yet he sensed some injury, some terrible absence. He had barely registered what it was when a great flurry of snow shot from the top of the ledge above him, and in the next instant she was falling toward him, plummeting down from the sky like something delivered from a dream.

She landed with her arms tucked over her head, driving so far into the tangle of brush that only her orange pack was still visible as he made his way to her.

"Dara," he called out. "Dara?"

There was no answer, no movement, and he felt his pulse thudding as he struggled through the interlocking maze of limbs. There was a snapping sound, bright as a rifle shot beneath him, and he pitched forward as a rotted limb gave way. He found himself lying helpless, suspended in a springy net of branches like an insect in a spider's web.

He managed to turn his head, then caught a glimpse of orange above him, a glimpse of cloth, of flesh. He reached out carefully and took her hand. "Dara," he called again.

He squeezed. "Dara?"

He felt an answering pressure, then, and relief washed over him. He struggled until his feet found a limb that seemed solid, then fought through the tangle toward her, like a man swimming through an ocean made of trees.

Finally, he had her in his arms, and she was staring up at him, her eyes blinking slowly into focus. There was a knot on her forehead, a scrape on her cheek. She was staring at him, now.

"Richard," she said, as if they'd just bumped into each other back on the city streets.

"You okay?" he asked. He scanned her arms, her legs. One knee of her jeans was torn out, but there was no blood, no awkward angles.

"I think so," she said, her eyes regaining focus as she slowly tested herself.

She stopped, checked him over in turn. "Where's your pack?"

He reached over his shoulder, realized it was gone. He glanced about the deadfall, then back at her, shaking his head. "Who knows."

The wind was driving the snow in sheets over the lip of the cliff, and he realized that they had tumbled out of the grasp of the storm only momentarily. Dara worked her way into a sitting position, then pulled herself upright. She pointed to a spot farther down the slope, sheltered by the cliff and the deadfall. "There," she said to him.

"There what?" Corrigan said.

"We've got to get the tent up," she said. "Come on." She was struggling out of the tangle of limbs, holding on to one branch to keep from falling as she emerged.

"What about the others?" Corrigan said, scrambling over the fallen brush toward her.

She glanced up in the direction they had come, had to hold up her arm as a blanket of white drove itself down upon them. He was beside her, then, the two of them limping toward the spot she'd indicated. The floor of the forest had still been dark with fallen leaves seconds before. Now it was already covered with a mixture of snow and frozen rain.

"Get the tent out of my pack," she shouted as she kicked the frozen snow away.

Corrigan dug into the pack, found the nylon sack, jerked it free. She was already facing him, digging at the ties with her fingers. "You remember how to do this?"

He nodded.

She handed him the spikes that would serve as tent pegs. "Use a rock to pound them in," she said. "I'll handle the frame."

Corrigan snatched the pegs, kicked about the frozen needles until his foot struck something hard. He reached down, found the rock, went to work on driving the pegs through the grommeted holes around the perimeter of the tent.

It was September, he found himself thinking. Not January, but September. He shook his head and forced his aching hands about their business.

One peg struck something solid an inch below the surface. The rock he was using for a hammer glanced off the steel head and cracked his other hand so hard he thought he'd broken something. Even if, he thought, even if. He cursed, jerked the stymied peg out, reset it, and drove it down with a single furious blow.

Dara was already inside the nylon shell, her movements sending the thing into a writhing dance. He'd barely managed to pound in the last of the pegs when the top of the tent sprang into shape, showering splinters of ice everywhere.

Then Dara emerged, head and shoulders. She spotted her

pack, brushed off the worst of the snow that had already piled atop it, then jerked it inside.

He was still in a crouched position, she on her knees, when their eyes met.

"I've got to go see about the others," he called above the howling of the storm.

She grabbed the front of his coat and twisted. "You can't," she called back. "Look at it."

He glanced over his shoulder. Utter whiteout, now. Nothing to see but wind and snow; even the trunks of trees he knew to be a few feet away vanished in the blast.

"You can't help anyone, Richard," she cried. "Not in this. Get inside. Get inside, now!"

Already his face was frozen with ice and snow, and yet still he hesitated. In his mind he saw smudge man, his face tumbling away into an abyss of pure white. He saw his mother adrift on the snowy backdrop of her hospital bed. He saw his father's face surrounded by a radiant halo of light. "Heroes are for the movies, son."

He felt Dara's hands desperate at the collar of his coat. He gave one last glance toward the icy nothingness about him. And finally he let himself be drawn inside.

27

But we're going *uphill*," Sonia Ashmead cried as Fielding Dawson bent to pull her from the drift where she had fallen.

She was standing, now, panting for breath. She leaned against him, her face shielded momentarily from the driving storm. "The others were headed *that* way," she shouted above the noise of the wind, pointing back down the slope. "I'm sure of it."

"It doesn't matter," he called back. "We're almost at the top. We'll find shelter on the other side of the ridge."

She shook her head, clinging to him. Her legs were rubbery, her throat on fire. "I can't do it, Fielding. I'm exhausted. I can't climb anymore."

The look he gave her in response was chilling. She'd expected exasperation, and that would have been all right. Exasperation she could have handled. But this was different. Something in the way he was looking at her made her think he was actually contemplating the possibility of leaving her. But then the moment passed, and he was leaning toward her, his hands on her shoulders, shaking her in exhortation.

"You've got to, Sonia. We're almost there..A hundred yards, no more than that."

A hundred yards, she thought. Why not a hundred *miles?* "What about Giles? And Elizabeth?"

"We'll find them later," he said. "We've got to take care of ourselves right now."

A violent gust of wind swept over them, blanketing them with snow. Her face was covered, her throat filled. She was choking, trying to catch her breath, trying to stem the panic that rose up inside her. *Don't panic,* she told herself. *Just stay steady, Sonia.*

"I'll try," she gasped, finally. "I hope you know what you're doing."

"Just trust me," he called. "Stay close!" And then he was climbing again.

She had resorted to counting each stride, now, planting her hands on her burning thighs, pushing off with every step. *Forty-five*, she thought, and just as quickly doubt gripped her. Was it fifty-five? The wind slamming into her, the snow so thick she could hardly see her boots below her. She glanced ahead, caught a glimpse of Fielding, who had paused to motion her forward. Impatience in that gesture of his, she thought. Maybe even contempt. She wanted to rest and catch her breath, ease the aching in her throat, but he was already turned and lunging forward again, threatening to disappear in the storm.

She felt a flash of rage. She wanted to kill him, she thought, shoot him right between the shoulder blades. Fielding had one of those big Bowie knives on his belt. Shoot him, then use his own knife to gut him, hollow him out like an Eskimo hunter did to polar bears, climb inside the carcass, ride out the storm that way.

She'd heard a famous poet read a long poem at the Ninety-second Street Y years before about just such an occurrence. Her friend Deirdre, wife of a bond trader, who'd talked her into going to the reading—"Broaden your cultural horizons, Sonia"—had screwed the poet on top of a pile of coats in the bedroom of a townhouse where the postreading reception was being held, while Sonia sipped cheap white wine in the overlit kitchen and talked to an economics professor from Sarah Lawrence about cigars, of all things. . . .

She shook her head, forcing herself back. She sensed she had wobbled off course during her reverie, and glanced around her surroundings in a panic. No sign of Fielding, goddamn him. So, she was alone, now. Her heart rate seemed to triple over the space of an instant.

She thought back to that look he had given her earlier and decided that he *had* wanted to leave her then and there. He'd only been feigning any concern for her. He *wanted* her to die.

She felt tears at her eyes, tiny traces that constituted the only specks of heat in her entire body, and those only for an instant or so, until the tears froze solid on her cheeks. Oh, yes, she thought, it *was* true. He had left her to die on the side of this godawful mountain, and why, oh, why hadn't she taken the kind of vacation a sane person would have? Why hadn't she left Fielding to his macho-man pursuits; why hadn't she just let her suck-up husband go along, as he always did whenever Fielding snapped his fingers?

God, she wanted to kill him, she thought. The only thing was, he had beat her to the punch. He'd just walked off and left her to die in the middle of a blizzard, and if she had just had the good sense to anticipate it, she would have taken that knife off his belt, stabbed him silly when she'd had the chance.

Sixty-seven, sixty-eight, sixty-nine . . . she counted to herself, straining with every step, no longer certain if she was moving up, down, or sideways, for it was nothing but white all around, and her mind was a corresponding blur. *One hundred take away seventy leaves forty,* she was thinking, and the fact that she had lost the capacity to subtract seemed the final indignity.

She wailed something out into the whirling storm and was about to collapse in the snow, just give it up once and for all, when she saw him, sidestepping back down the slope until he'd caught his arm under hers and began to pull her along.

"Right ahead," he shouted, wrapping his arm about her shoulders. "I've found it. Just a few more steps."

"I thought . . ." she began, but her feet were slipping beneath her, and it seemed too much energy to continue.

"You thought *what?*" he called back, still holding her tightly, propelling her up the slope.

"Nothing," she said. How could she have hated him, this savior, this angel of mercy come to gather her in? "It was nothing."

"Well," he called out, heaving them around a jutting outcropping of rock that loomed up suddenly from the gloom like the prow of a frozen boat. "Here we are."

She blinked her eyes, astounded at the sudden shift. One moment caught in the grip of an arctic blizzard, the next plopped under a bell jar of calm. They were standing in the lee of the rock formation, now, a kind of shallow cave that faced the direction opposite the onslaught of the storm. Snow swirled off the tops of the rocks above their heads, then disappeared into the turmoil farther down the slope below the ridge—but where they stood gave her the sense of having ducked into the lobby of a warm office building while a blizzard raged down Fifth Avenue. *Saved,* she thought. *Great God Almighty, saved at last.*

"I told you," Dawson said, giving her his typical self-satisfied look. She might have told him, then, might have confessed her earlier intention to have shot him in the back and cut him into pieces for scaring her so, but something had diverted her.

"You saved us," she admitted, finally able to breathe again. "But who is that?"

"Who is who?" he asked blankly.

She gestured over his shoulder at the man who had appeared at the mouth of their little shelter. "Him," she said, indicating the tall, parka-clad man with the rifle pointed their way. Something in his pose, in the way he held the weapon, suggested that he was not there to guide them to safety.

"Can you help us?" she heard herself saying, and she knew instantly it was the dumbest question she had ever asked.

28

"**H**ere," Giles Ashmead called, turning to Elizabeth Dawson, who had been trailing him down the mountainside through the storm. He caught a glimpse of her face, tucked under the hood of the thin blue windbreaker, then she ducked away again. It was just the two of them, now. God knows what had happened to the others.

"I'm here!" he called again.

He was shouting as loudly as he could, but the words seemed smothered by the driving snow, whipped away by the wind the moment he'd uttered them. He leaned back into the shelter of the rock overhang he'd stumbled across, felt a moment's relief from the blistering storm. He could see here, at least, could breathe air that wasn't half ice.

He wiped frozen crystals from his burning face and glanced back up the path toward the vague shape of Elizabeth, who was stumbling down the slope with her arm raised against the blast of the wind. It was no surprise she'd chosen him to stick close to. When the chips were down, you went with the one you trusted, wasn't that the way it was supposed to work?

"Elizabeth," he called, his hands cupped to his mouth this time. "Down here!"

Ten feet away, fifteen at most. But she seemed not to hear. She veered away from the overhang as a fresh gust swirled, bringing with it a vortex of snow that nearly obliterated her.

"Goddamnit," Ashmead cried, pushing himself away from the rock face where he had been resting. *"Over here!"*

In the next instant he was blind, the snow pelting his face like pea rock shot from a great cannon somewhere. No wonder she hadn't seen him, he thought, flinging his own arm up for protection. Superman couldn't see through this mess.

And how was it possible, anyway, a frigging blizzard in the month of September? Goddamn Fielding Dawson and his ideas. Just one more idiot notion in a long line of schemes that Ashmead had been stupid enough to go along with. But this was the end of it, once and for all. The minute they got back to civilization, it was all coming to an end; Giles Ashmead was going to see to it, just as he and Elizabeth had discussed.

"Liz!" he cried again, but his throat was filled with ice.

He staggered sideways, disoriented in the white that was everywhere, now. He took a step that he would have sworn led uphill, but felt nothing but air beneath him. His weight shifted, and he tumbled awkwardly, felt jarring pain at his elbow, something tearing in his knee.

He slid down the steep slope a few feet, then stopped. He lay paralyzed for a moment, his breath knocked away, one arm throbbing, his leg twisted under him. He felt something warm inside his mouth and realized he'd bitten his tongue as he'd fallen.

The snow—the never-ending goddamned snow—was already piling against his cheek, his twisted leg, his side. He was going to die, he thought, right there, right then. He was going to be frozen inside a glacier like some goddamned wooly mammoth or saber-toothed tiger that some archaeologist would chisel out of the ice in about 10 million years, and it was all Fielding Dawson's fault.

If only he'd had the courage to do what should have been done long before. Though he might never have, he realized, if it hadn't been for Liz.

The thought reminded him of why he'd ventured out into the icy blast, and he felt a pang, a profound hopelessness that brought stinging tears to his eyes. She would die, too, lost out there now in the white nothingness, and there was nothing he could do to save her, the woman he had come to love.

He realized he could breathe, then, that his lungs had unlocked themselves, that little wheezes were erupting at his throat. *Hell, yes, Giles,* he told himself. *Just the wind knocked out of you. You've had worse. You'll live. Up on your feet, man. Suck it up. Go find Elizabeth, now.*

He managed to roll onto his side, then his stomach. But when he tried to push himself up, he discovered that his right arm would not cooperate. He stared in its direction, blinking, feeling the leaden sensation of a limb gone deep into sleep.

And there was the pain in his knee, searing. He tried to get the knee under him, push up from the frozen mountainside, but the response was electric. He went down, rigid with pain, gasping as his cheek thudded off the frozen snow.

He lay there for a moment, weeping silently in frustration, waiting for the pain in his leg to subside. When he could think once again, it occurred to him that he could not have come far from the haven of that overhang. If he could just manage to drag himself uphill a few yards . . . *If you can do that, Ashmead, you just might live.*

The process was tedious, filled with more pain than he had ever endured, but the prospect of survival pushed him on. One foot levered against a rock or a crevice below, one hand scrabbling in the frozen ice and snow above. He push-pulled himself one foot, gritting his teeth against the stabbing pain in his other leg, then managed another foot, and another.

A yard, then two. His knee had begun to go numb, and though he took that as a blessing, he also knew that it meant that he was freezing. He found himself laughing at the absurdity of it. *Happy to be freezing to death. Oh, Giles. You are a card. . . .*

And then he felt his hand strike something hard and massive, and he glanced up to realize that he could see again. *The overhang,* he thought. He was out of the weather. Had made it. Might survive, after all.

He pulled himself on into shelter, managing to roll onto his back. He dug his heel into the rock and shoved—*Ignore the pain in your knee, fuck, fuck, fuck*—until he was in a sitting position, his back jammed against a vertical slab of rock.

He was staring out into a blast of white nothingness, still, but comparatively speaking, he felt as if he had crawled onto a tropical beach. No wind, no driving, freezing, unbreathable air. He might yet make it, he thought. He just might make it yet.

One arm dangled uselessly at his side, and the opposite leg was rigid with pain, but he was alive and out of that icy wind. Maybe Elizabeth had stumbled into her own place of shelter. Surely she wouldn't have been so clumsy as he. She'd always been so graceful, so tolerant of his own awkwardness. As if she'd needed someone like himself to take care of, to indulge such feelings, he thought, all those years with a husband whose idea of pleasure derived from a Marine Corp drill instructor's manual.

Yes, let her have somehow found shelter, he thought. Please. And God forgive him for being unable to help her. That most of all.

He was blinking away tears again when he saw it. At first he thought it was a mirage, some vision born purely out of his desperation. A shadow moving out there, someone coming through the storm toward him. The shadow wavered in the great blast of whiteness, disappeared for a moment, then came back, clearer this time.

He sat up straighter, feeling his throat constrict with unreasoning hope. *Elizabeth,* he found himself thinking, at the same time warning himself away from such a notion.

Still the shadow moved and grew, until he was finally able to see that it was indeed a person—a very oddly shaped and bulky person, moving slowly, awkwardly, up the slope.

A few steps closer and he could see that it was someone in a hooded parka, one of those Peary-at-the-Pole coats, bulky, almost knee-length, with a halo of fur that virtually obscured the face. And carrying something—no, *someone*—fireman-style across the shoulders.

Ashmead caught a glimpse of Elizabeth's blue nylon jacket and was ready to weep again. The figure bearing her stumbled into the lee of the rocks, turned, eased his burden down in one swift motion.

"Elizabeth," Ashmead called, trying to make his way toward her inert form. But the pain in his leg was so great, and the figure stood in Ashmead's way and seemed disinclined to move. There was something odd about the way Elizabeth was lying there, Ashmead thought, but the pain and the circumstances and the surprise had mixed him up so.

He glanced up at the man in the heavy parka, perhaps meaning to offer some expression of thanks—or maybe he'd simply intended to ask the man where he'd come from. The man was wearing dark snow goggles and was staring down at Ashmead in a way that made him feel strange, somehow, like a specimen, like an earth creature under observation by an alien.

"You saved her," Ashmead managed.

"Yes," the creature in the parka answered, and Ashmead realized it was not a *he* hidden behind those goggles and that great coat at all. *A woman,* he marveled. *A woman has saved Elizabeth.*

But where? And how? Question after question, suddenly, all of them piling up, along with a worm of uncertainty.

"I'm hurt," he told her. Why had he said that?

She nodded. He felt her eyes roaming over him from behind the goggles.

"But you can get us out of here?" Ashmead heard himself saying.

"Of course," the woman behind the goggles said.

Ashmead wanted to take heart from that, but somehow he could not.

She bent to take Ashmead's head in her hands, then. One hand beneath his chin, the other opposite, just above his ear. Cradling him gently but firmly, as if she understood just how forlorn he was.

"Like this," she said, her voice almost soft.

Ashmead saw the movement, felt a moment's pressure, observed one instant of a world that had turned upon its edge. And in the next moment, he felt himself go free.

29

Take your boots off," Dara was saying over the whistling of the wind, the rasp of its force against the tent fabric.

Corrigan stared at her, his face still burning from the wind and the freezing snow. Only now, out of the gale, did he realize how cold he'd really been out there. His hands were numb, and, he realized, so were his feet. He wouldn't have lasted five minutes out there in the blizzard.

"We've only got one sleeping bag," Dara said. She was already struggling to unfurl the thing, was working intently at the zipper in what little light filtered in. "Damnit," she cried suddenly, bringing a shattered nail to her lips.

"Let me do it," Corrigan said. He found the zipper mechanism, located a jammed wad of nylon by feel, willed his numbed fingers to work the fabric out of the catch. A lovely way to work, he thought. No light to speak of, hands as brittle as ice, two people squeezed into a tent that was snug enough for one. He felt a suffocating wave of claustrophobia but fought it away with an answering surge of anger. What else? Just what the hell else could happen?

And as for claustrophobia, it could go screw itself. What was he going to do, go running out into an ice storm to die?

He jerked savagely at the zipper, which gave way so suddenly that he backhanded himself across the face.

"Goddamnit!" he cried. Blood was already trickling from his nose.

"What?" Dara called. He could hear the note of panic in her voice.

"Nothing," he grumbled through the mask of his hand. "I just punched myself, that's all."

He heard silence in return. "I fixed the zipper," he said after a moment.

"Good," she said. He felt her take the bag, heard the whine of nylon as she pulled the zipper open. "Get your feet in here," she said. "Hurry up. I'm freezing."

He reached down, pulled blindly at the laces of his boots, kicked his numbed feet free.

"Lift up so I can get the bottom under you," she said.

He lifted up on the twin points of his feet and one hand, a kind of sideways push-up. She slid the fabric under him, knocking his braced hand out from under him. When he came down, the crown of her head smashed into his already throbbing nose.

"Fucking-A," he groaned, clutching at his nose again. He sank onto his back, his fingers clamped against the renewed gush of blood from his nostrils.

"I'm sorry," she said. She was writhing about, both her hands clutched to her forehead.

After a moment, her movements had calmed and the steady flow of blood that leaked down his throat had slowed. "You okay?" he asked.

"I think so," she said. "How about you?"

"I'll live," he said, then thought of the storm that still raged outside, separated from them by the sheerest millimeter of nylon. "For a while, anyway."

"I'm starting to feel my feet again," she said. "How are yours?"

"I can feel *your* feet," he said. And it was true. He had the sensation of movement at the bottom of the sleeping bag, not much more than that. He tried flexing his toes, felt something resembling a response.

"Keep that up," she said. "You don't want frostbite."

Visions of blackened digits, gangrenous limbs flashed through his mind. He wriggled his toes vigorously, felt icy stirrings, wriggled more.

"I have to tell you, Dara. I'm taking back what I told you earlier. I am never going camping again."

"I was wondering when you'd get around to telling me that," she told him. "Now, how about your toes?"

"Still numb," he said.

"Okay," she said. "Hold on. Put your hands over your nose or something. Just so I don't bash you again."

"But—"

"Just do it," she said. "Just lie there and shut up."

He did as he was told, cupping his hand over his throbbing nose while she maneuvered herself into a 180-degree turn beside him. In moments, he felt her hands kneading at the flesh of his feet.

"Feel anything?" Her voice came muffled from the other end of the tent.

"Why couldn't Dawson have had a thing for the tropics?" he responded.

"Just tell me when they start to hurt," she said, squeezing roughly at one little toe.

"All right!" he cried, jerking his foot in reflex.

"Good," she said, her voice calm. "Now for the next little piggy."

It might have been ten minutes, it might have been half an hour, but finally she had restored feeling to all of his toes and was back upright in the bag. The light outside was gone—either that or they were now entombed beneath vast drifts of snow, Corrigan thought. He reached out gingerly, felt the inwardly bowed curve of the wall of the tent that had faced the direction of the wind. Frozen, he thought. A frozen wall of ice.

The other side of the tent gave under his touch, however. A good sign.

"What are you doing?" Dara asked.

"Checking the tent," he told her.

"You'll make it leak," she said. "Any place you touch it, that'll wick the water right through the fabric."

"You're full of good news, aren't you?"

"Then again, if it gets any colder, everything will just freeze solid; we won't have to worry about it."

"Why don't we talk about something else?" he said.

There was silence, then. The wind outside seemed to have died down.

"You think it's letting up?"

"It could," she said. "Sometimes these things go as quickly as they come. I don't think we'd be up here if there had been any kind of a serious weather front on the way."

"Don't be so sure," Corrigan told her. "I don't think Fielding Dawson would let a little bad weather stand in the way of his campaign."

"You're not going to start that again, are you?"

"No," he said. "I'm not."

"Good," she said.

He shifted on his elbow, then, felt her backside pressed warmly against him. His hands and feet were back to something resembling normal feeling, and the fiery sensation had faded from his cheeks. There was a time—and it seemed so long ago—when he would have given anything to find himself tucked into a sleeping bag with Dara Wylie. Right now, however, what he mostly felt was glad to be alive.

He shifted again, felt something digging into his shoulder. He was on her pack, he realized, then thought of something. "Do you have a flashlight in your pack?"

"Somewhere," she told him.

He snaked an arm awkwardly behind him, groped about until he had his hand inside the pack, the chill handle of a flashlight in his palm. He brought the thing out and around slowly, careful not to smash his still throbbing nose again. A drunk had swung his elbow wildly once while Corrigan had been assisting in an arrest on a platform. It occurred to him that maybe he'd finally straightened it out.

He found the switch, pushed it up with his thumb. A brilliant sheen of light erupted, nearly blinding him. Then, just as abruptly, the light was gone.

"What was that?" she asked. He suspected she was blinking into the darkness the same as he was.

"The bulb burned out," he said dispiritedly. He worked the switch off and on a few times, just to be sure.

"Burned out? It was just on, bright as anything. How can that be?"

"In line with everything else, Dara," he told her. He sighed, tossing the light aside. "The filament probably cracked when you fell."

He heard her sigh, and there was silence for a bit.

"I thought you'd killed us," she said finally. "Running us straight down the hill like that."

"Give it time," he said. "I don't exactly hear the sound of cavalry out there."

More silence.

"I wonder what's happened to the others," she said finally.

"They got their tents up," he said. "That's what we'll have to hope." And if they hadn't, he thought . . . then he didn't want to know.

The silence returned. The wind *had* died down, he was sure of it. Or perhaps it was just a momentary lull in the storm.

"We were really lucky, Richard," she said finally.

"You'll have to try that one on me again, Dara."

"It was incredible luck that we stayed together," she insisted. "Think about it. If you were on your own, without your pack, without a tent—"

"I'd have kept going down the mountain until the snow stopped," he told her.

"Well, it would be nice to think so," she said.

"I'm not complaining," he assured her. "I'm glad I didn't end up with Lou Vida. Or Dawson."

He felt her tense, and he wondered if what he had said had upset her. Sure enough, when she spoke again, her voice had changed. "You know, it's not like this storm rolled in on purpose," she said. "I mean, there's nothing personal involved."

"I'm glad to know it," he said, listening to the rattle of the tent in the wind.

"I'm serious," she said. "It's hard not to feel that way, like all this is directed at us, somehow. But the mountain doesn't care one way or the other, Richard. It's just there."

"I know there's a reason you're telling me these things," he said.

She let out her breath in frustration. "Like earlier, when I was trying to lay everything off on some conspiracy against Fielding Dawson, for instance. It's an energy waste. It really is paranoia."

"Cops like to call it suspicion, Dara."

"Suspicion of what? Someone creating this storm?" Her voice was rising, and he could feel her beginning to fidget inside the sleeping bag.

"Forget it," he told her. "You're right. It just makes me feel better to blame somebody, okay?"

There was another pause, and he felt some of the tension slip away. "When it comes right down to it, we're just not that important," she said, and he thought he heard a note of resignation in her voice.

"You're important to me," he said.

He felt her shift slightly. "I'm talking in the cosmic sense."

"So am I."

"We *could* die, Richard."

"I'm not planning on it." He managed to get his arm away from his side, wrap it tightly around her.

"But if we did—"

"I'm glad I'm here, Dara," he told her. "I could do without the blizzard, but I'm glad I'm here."

He felt her long intake of breath. "I'm glad you are, too," she said.

There was something in what she'd been trying to get across to him, of course. The world turned and turned, and soon enough he and she and Fielding Dawson and everyone else on the planet would be distant memories, if that . . . and there was not one thing personal about the process.

But all that granted, he found himself now in a place he wouldn't trade for anything, storm or no storm, his arm tucked around a woman whose presence seemed more precious than anything he'd ever known. Maybe it had something to do with the circumstances, with the threat, with the possibility that this storm would cover them, lock them into a glacier that would not melt for months . . . . but he had never felt so much alive.

There was nothing sexual about it, but it was as if in intertwining inside a single nylon sack inside a flimsy tent that wasn't even a dot from the perspective of a high-flying plane or to the eye of a "cosmic" observer, if there was such a thing . . . it seemed to him as if he and she had recombined somehow. Like the alchemists had insisted: They'd become gold, even radium.

"Dara?" There was no response, and he felt an irrational surge of panic. He reached to her shoulder, shook her gently.

"What?" Her voice came out muffled, bewildered. "What is it?"

"Did you go to sleep?"

"Maybe. I'm just a little tired, Richard."

"Sure," he said. He patted her shoulder. "You rest, then. I'll keep an eye on things."

"I don't want to sleep," she protested.

"What else did you have in mind, yard work?" he said.

For a moment, he thought she might have drifted off again. Then: "You never told me how you hurt your eye," she said.

He paused. "Is that important?"

"Maybe," she said. "I don't know. Is it?"

"It was a long time ago," he said.

"But it's why you ended up a subway cop, isn't it? Instead of on the regular force."

He felt a brief surge of resentment but fought it down. *At a time like this, Richie-boy. At a time like this . . .*

"So, Rollie told you about it? My eye, the transfer, all that?"

"He didn't tell me how it happened," she said.

The silence held, and he felt her shrug. "A guy whose father was NYPD, there had to be a reason."

Sure, he thought. She was just being a good reporter, after all. And why would Rollie Montcrief turn down the advances of a good-looking woman, no matter what her motivation? He sighed, and raised his voice a bit as the wind picked up outside.

"It was a fishing trip, my dad and me," he began. "We'd do it a couple times a summer, maybe, our father-and-son thing, you know. I didn't give a rat's ass about fishing, but I liked going out with him. My mom'd pack a lunch, he'd borrow this Boston Whaler from a friend, we'd go out to the bay and putt around for the afternoon."

He closed his eyes, squinted hard until the little coil of fire that he could still feel deep inside every time he thought about the accident burned away. He took a breath, felt her stir.

"You okay?" she asked.

He thought about it. What he felt at that moment wasn't necessarily bad, but okay didn't seem quite to cover it. He realized that he wanted to kiss her. Instead, he continued his story.

"So, on this particular day, we came in a little late, we were in a hurry, maybe the old man had an extra beer or two, I dunno. It was a lot of things, or it was nothing, just Fate. Anyway, the boat kept sliding sideways while he was trying to winch it up onto the trailer—they're heavy bastards, you know—and he finally told me to mind the winch while he got into the water to guide the boat up."

"And . . . ?"

He realized he'd paused again. He shook his head as if to clear some blockage, then continued. "So, he's out there, slipping around on the boat ramp, which is all crapped up with mud and algae and stuff—I think he must have fallen a couple of times—and he's yelling at me to take in the slack, which I try to do—give it a great big yank, like a kid might, you know." He shrugged. "When at that moment, there's a gust of wind that pushes the boat sideways, knocks him ass over teakettle, and the line just snaps."

She put her hand to her mouth, as if she could anticipate what was coming. "Oh God."

"The loose end came back across my face like a bullwhip," he said. "I heard this pop, but I never knew what hit me. Before I know it, I'm in the hospital, most of my face already bandaged up. The doctors were sure I'd lose the eye, but my old man told them to shut up about it, he'd kill them if they said anything to me."

She shook her head. "How long before you found out you could still see?"

"I can see fine," he told her, stiffly. " I don't have much peripheral vision on that side, and my depth perception—"

"I'm not an examiner for the force, Richard," she admonished.

"I'm sorry," he said after a moment. "It took a long time before I could use the eye." He managed to get a hand up, put a finger to his left cheek. "In and out of doctors' offices, sometimes two and three times a week. And I was a kid—a geek, all of a sudden—with a patch on his eye."

"I can't imagine you were ever a geek," she said.

"Well, I was," he said. "You know how kids are." He broke off for a moment. "I was pretty upset; my old man was upset with himself, you can imagine. All in all it was pretty grim . . . until one day the patch came off, and by the time school rolled around that fall, things more or less went back to normal."

He touched his cheek again. "The doctors used some terms for what I'd be faced with, but I put all that aside. I don't know if I can really explain it. It's okay. I'm used to it. It's the way I see the world."

"Did your father ever tell you how he felt about what had happened?"

"This some kind of shrink session?"

He felt her stiffen again. "You said he was upset with himself. . . ."

"It was obvious. He started in on the sauce right about then, so that's what I've always assumed. My father wasn't the type for your regular heart-to-heart," he said.

"So, when he . . . died," she said, "you hadn't really talked. You've just been assuming that he felt this guilt about what he'd done to you."

He took a deep breath. "Did I say that?"

"You implied it."

"Jesus Christ, Dara, what are you getting at?"

"That you shouldn't assume anything. When he killed himself, it didn't necessarily have anything to do with you."

"Whoever said it did?"

There was another pause. "You don't have to shout," she said finally.

"I'm sorry," he said, feeling the tent rock with the gale. "I guess I'm not used to talking about these things."

"So it would seem."

"It was a hell of a feeling, I can tell you. Seeing him there, ready to . . . ready to pull the trigger, and not a damn thing I could do to stop it."

"Same thing with the guy in the subway?"

He was ready to shout at her, then felt something give inside. "Same thing," he said.

"And Mal?"

"Goddamnit, Dara . . ."

"It's okay, Richard," she said. She was moving, now, twisting her hips about, her shoulders, until she was facing him. "No one blames you."

Her arms were around his neck, and she was drawing herself tightly against him.

"*I* do," he told her, his voice muffled in her hair.

"We're going to work on that," she said.

"It'll take a lot of work," he said.

"Just shhhh," she said, her voice sounding drowsy again. Wind rattled the tent, doom railing out there, he thought—the end of them both just on the other side of a sheet of nylon.

She lifted her chin, then, lifted her lips to his. He felt his mouth on hers, sliding to her throat, felt her mouth upon his ear . . . and what sounds came after that had almost nothing to do with speech.

30

"Who *are* you?" Sonia Ashmead asked the man with the rifle propped between his legs.

The man glanced up at her, then at Fielding Dawson, who sat on a rock on the opposite side of the fire the man had built, holding his palms up to the blaze. The snow had turned gradually to rain as they had descended the mountainside. Over the past hour, even that had diminished to a drizzle that was more like mist than actual rain. If only she weren't so wet, she thought, suppressing a shudder.

She longed to change out of her soggy clothes. She longed for a hot shower. She longed for comfort was what it came down to, but comfort seemed to be in short supply.

A log popped, shooting a glowing coal toward the darkness, but the man's gaze held level on hers. Dawson turned to her.

"Leave him alone, Sonia," Dawson said. "He's not going to tell us anything." They had been in this camp of sorts for what seemed like hours, and the man had said nothing. A glare here, a gesture with the rifle there. That was the extent of his communication. Simple but effective.

"So, we just sit around, eat pork and beans, pretend nothing has happened?"

"What would you suggest?"

She stared back at him, astonished. "That we *do* something. There are eight people on the other side of that ridge somewhere, your wife among them. My *husband* is up there."

Dawson regarded her for a moment. "Leaving aside the presence of our armed guard, here, you're worried about my wife and Giles all of a sudden?"

Her face darkened, and she cut a glance at the man with the rifle, as if he might understand Dawson's remark. "Go to hell, Fielding. We're all human beings, here. At least I think we are."

"Your husband has been having an affair with my wife for more than a year, now," Dawson said. "You and I haven't ever discussed it, but we both know it's true." He stared at her evenly.

"You're unbelievable."

"I'm a pragmatist," he told her, gesturing at the man with the rifle.

"They could be in serious trouble, Fielding." She broke off, glancing up at the looming ridgeline. There was a pale glow in the sky up there, but not much that a person might navigate by, not any longer.

"I hate Giles from the tip of his toes to the last strand of his thinning hair," she said after a moment, her voice calm once again, "but that doesn't mean I want him to die out here."

Dawson shrugged, then gestured at the man with the rifle. "I don't think it matters very much what you and I want," he said. "I think it is only this man's opinion which counts."

The man with the rifle sat impassively, watching the two of them. When the man's eyes lifted to hers, she felt an involuntary chill. Men had stared at her in an impersonal fashion before—just meat before their eyes—but she'd never sensed such utter indifference as that in this one's eyes.

"What is it with you?" she demanded. "What do you want with us?"

She turned back to Dawson. "What the hell is it, what plank in your platform has the mountain men up in arms, Fielding?"

"Who can say?" Dawson shrugged. He turned to the man with the rifle. "Is that why you're holding us?" he asked the man. "You don't like my politics?"

The man glanced at Dawson, then bent forward and spat into the fire. Dawson turned to Sonia. "I don't think he's going to tell us."

She turned away, exasperated, her hands jammed into the pockets of her jacket. Only one thing left, then. When she turned back toward the fire, she was holding a small, nickel-plated pistol in her hand, had it pointed at the man holding the rifle. Both men stared at her in surprise.

"Sonia," Dawson said, his voice almost admonishing in tone. "Where did *that* come from?"

"I wouldn't walk across the street in Manhattan without it," she told him, her eyes on the man with the rifle. "What makes you think I'd come all the way out to this godforsaken place unarmed?"

She waved the pistol authoritatively at the man with the rifle. "Put your hands behind your neck," she told him. The man, whose expression had regained its former impassiveness, did as he was told.

"Get his gun, Fielding." She gestured with the pistol for emphasis. "I go to a range in Westchester once a month," she told the man with the rifle. "The targets they put up look a lot like you, in fact. You so much as twitch, and I'll shoot you dead."

Dawson was smiling, now. "Don't let those good looks fool you," he told the man. "She's a tiger."

"Stop fooling around, Fielding," Sonia said. "Get his gun."

Dawson nodded, stepping around the fire. He reached for the barrel of the rifle that was still propped against the leg of the man, eased it carefully away.

"Be careful, Fielding," she said. "Step away from him before he tries something."

"You don't have to worry, Sonia," Dawson said. He backed away from the man, the rifle braced before his chest, now.

He was moving back toward Sonia, when he stopped abruptly. "Jesus Christ," he said, staring at something in the darkness over her shoulder. "Just when you think things are finally going your way."

Sonia cut her glance to him briefly, keeping her aim on the man sitting by the campfire. "What are you talking about?"

He used his chin to point at something at the edge of the campfire's glow. "I'm afraid there's another one," he told her.

Sonia turned just in time to catch the blow high on her cheek. As she was falling, the woman who hit her spun deftly on one foot, aiming a kick at Sonia's hand. There was another sharp crack, and the pistol sailed harmlessly off into the darkness. The woman completed her turn, driving another kick that caught Sonia near the ear with a dull thud.

Dawson stepped back quickly as Sonia tumbled to the ground at his feet, her head turned at an odd angle. He sensed the man at his side, felt the rifle being lifted from his grip.

The woman was bent over Sonia's inert form, checking her pulse. She glanced up at the two men, then stood, dragging Sonia's body toward the nearby stream.

Dawson heard a splash and turned toward the man, who held the rifle again. "Is that really necessary?" Dawson asked, gesturing off toward the woman, who stood near the stream above Sonia's inert form. Sonia appeared to lie facedown in the shallow water, the woman's foot pressing between her shoulder blades.

The man shrugged. "Just as well she drowns," the man said. "Makes more sense that way."

"But—" Dawson began.

"Have to do you the right way, too," the man was saying. And he swung the stock of his rifle heavily into Dawson's face.

"I don't think he's going to like that," she said to Bright as she stared at Fielding Dawson's crumpled form.

Bright turned and regarded her for a moment.

"The man is hardly in any position to complain," he said mildly.

"I hope you know what you're doing, that's all."

He shrugged. "I've been paid to do a job. I intend to see that it gets done properly."

"I think you've gone a bit beyond the call of duty," she said.

He allowed himself a smile. "That's what keeps me in demand," he told her. "So many people these days are content to do only what's been asked of them, not one whit more."

She was shaking her head. "Still and all," she said.

"Don't worry," he told her. "Just don't worry. All is well that ends."

31

Corrigan awoke to darkness, to aching everywhere and a profound numbness in both his arms. At first he thought it was the cold, that his limbs might have frozen . . . but after a moment he realized that it was a result of the confined space in which he'd slept.

He managed to disentangle himself from Dara, roll over on his deadened arms, and maneuver his watch in front of his face. He blinked until his eyes could focus on the dimly glowing phosphorus, saw that it was nearly six, and in the next moment found himself replaying the events of the night before.

It was still as dark as one of the subway tunnels inside the tent, he thought; the only thing missing was the ever-present smell of ozone. But no ozone here. Instead, the faint hint of the muskiness they'd managed to create in the tiny space.

Amazing, he thought, what humans could manage even under the most unlikely circumstances. Or perhaps the circumstances had brought them to the act, he thought. Some stubborn impulse to celebrate life at the moment it seemed most tenuous. He felt Dara shift about, heard her breath catch, then resume its steady pace.

Was that it? he wondered. Just a couple of desperate people grasping for some psychological lifeline? Put them back in normal circumstances, all the fire would go out? Somehow he doubted that. And in any case, whatever had allowed it to happen, he was damned grateful, that much was certain.

And now the next issue at hand: how to make sure they survived. Got back to Normalsville, found out what would happen between them next.

He nodded to himself, trying to come up with a reasoned assessment of the situation. How long until dawn, for instance? He glanced at the glowing dial of his watch again.

Either the sun was not yet up, or they were buried beneath several feet of snow. He listened intently but heard nothing aside from Dara's rhythmic breathing.

He also realized that the incessant wind was gone, leaving an immense silence in its wake. No chirping of birds. No banging of pots and pans around a cheery campfire. Nothing.

He maneuvered his numbed right arm about until there was a welcome tingling in his fingertips. He reached above his head, found the zipper of the tent in the darkness, pulled.

The zipper refused to budge. He felt a nudge of anxiety, and struggled to get his other arm free from under him. He ended up having to lift one hand with another and shake it himself until he got the circulation going again.

This time he worked at the zipper with two hands, jerking at the mechanism until it broke free, sending a little shower of ice crystals down across his face.

"What?" It was Dara's voice, heavy with sleep. "What are you doing?"

"It's morning," he said, then remembered how dark it was. "According to my watch, anyway. We slept all the way through."

She was quiet for a moment. "Did we do what I think we did?"

"Unless we had the same dream," he said.

"I guess that's possible," she said.

"Pretty good dream," he said.

"Yes," she said. "Even more than that." He felt her hand rest briefly against his chest.

"So, you are here," she said after a moment. "And we're still alive."

"You sound surprised," he said.

"A lot of people aren't," she said, her tone shifting. He felt her struggling beside him. "What do you suppose we're going to find out there?"

"Assuming we can get out there," he told her.

There was a pause. "What are you talking about?"

"This," he said, smacking his hand against the inner wall of the tent flap. It felt as if he were slapping the side of a bank vault.

He took her hand, guided it to the frozen entryway of the

tent. He could feel it dawning on her. After a moment, she pulled her hand away.

"Shit," she said.

"About what I was thinking," he said. He sank back on his elbow, staring into the darkness, willing himself to keep his breathing under control, his mind from spinning into places it would do no good to visit. He'd read Poe's "Premature Burial" with one eye when he was laid up after his childhood accident, and had trouble sleeping for weeks afterward. Now a hodgepodge of images was crowding back upon him: a man clawing at the sheeting of his own coffin, a thick wood lid just inches from his face, every lifeline from the grave cut, every safeguard failed. . . .

Corrigan felt his nerve ends going fiery, his muscles coiling. A few more minutes and he'd be hot enough to melt them through a glacier. What a grand idea he'd had, taking this trip. He wasn't sure what day of the week it was, but he knew one thing for certain: If he'd stayed in New York, he'd be rolling over in his bed, readying himself for a nice long sleep-in on another of his days off.

He twisted onto his stomach, levered his chin and chest up off the ground. He took a breath, drew his right arm back, his forearm angled at his side.

"What are you doing?" Dara asked.

"Lie down," he told her.

"But—"

"Lie still!" he said. "Keep your head down."

He heard her sigh, felt her flatten beside him. He grunted, and drove his forearm toward the door of the tent. It was a shot he thought John Madden might approve of.

His arm cracked hard into the frozen snow, sending a jolt all the way into the muscles of his neck. But he'd sensed something, the slightest give, beneath his forearm. He sucked down another breath, drew back, then lunged again, making some noise this time—one of those Monica Seles tennis grunts, about as loud, he imagined, as that poor bastard in his tomb must have yelped when he realized every one of his careful little plans had gone haywire.

He was still in the middle of his noisemaking when his arm burst through the frozen crust, sending him halfway out the front of the tent. He landed face first in a crusty pile of snow, his legs still tangled inside.

He pushed himself up, gulping for breath. He swiped ice crystals from his face, then pulled his legs out of the tent and struggled to his feet. The sun was still hidden, but the sky was clear, a few stars still hanging on against a backdrop tending from indigo toward blue. At least it had brightened enough for him to make out the vague shadows of trees, the nearly buried mound of their tent.

He glanced down and saw that he was standing knee-deep in drifted snow. The air at his face, though, seemed unaccountably warm. Snow up to his ass, everything balmy beyond. What kind of a world had he fallen into, anyway?

He was aware of an odd series of sounds all about him. Unusual pops and creaks, interspersed with soft chuffing noises, as if small animals might be dropping from the tree branches into the drifts. Along with that, the rustling of Dara, struggling out of the tent. He bent, caught her under the elbow, and helped her stand, just as a clump of snow fell from an overhanging branch and burst across his shoulders.

"I'm guessing the storm is over," he told her, brushing wet snow from his head and arms.

She nodded. "It's already melting," she said. "Listen."

He stopped swiping at the snow on his neck and concentrated on the sounds around them. Everything that he had noticed before, along with the sounds of trickling water.

"What kind of weather . . . ?" He broke off, shaking his head.

"That's the way it is up here, this time of the year," she said. "One minute it's summer, then bam, it lets you have it. Next day it's back to normal. We might have another month before it snows again."

He stared about the slowly lightening landscape in disbelief. "It could snow again?"

He thought he saw her shoulders rise in a shrug. "It might," she said. "It's not likely."

He nodded, thinking about the possibilities. "Doesn't a guy like Donnelly take these things into account?"

"Sure," she said. "But you heard him. We should have been

two thousand feet down the mountain by now. We'd have had a rainstorm to put up with. That's all."

"Right," he said. "A simple miscalculation."

"So, now it's Donnelly's fault?"

"No," he said. "It's still Dawson's."

"You do maintain your focus," she said. "I'll give you that."

"He'll have that story he wanted to tell, if he ever gets out of this," he told her.

"*When* he gets out," she corrected. "We all will."

"So maybe we should try and find him," he said. "We wouldn't want them to take off and leave us."

The gloom was steadily lifting. A few more minutes and they'd have enough light to maneuver by. If the others had found shelter, they'd be ready to move now as well, make their way down to that rumored cache point where who knows what delicacies awaited the intrepid, well-heeled camper. And if they hadn't, well, Corrigan didn't want to think a whole lot about that.

He glanced doubtfully at the snow-covered forest floor surrounding them. His feet were already cold. How much slogging lay ahead of them? Which way to go? Dear smudge man, he thought. Maybe the guy was up there on a cloud somewhere, strumming a harp, smiling at their predicament.

"We'll find them," Dara was saying. "They'll have done just what we did. They can't be far."

He turned to find her staring at him, her expression demanding some encouragement, some response that might resemble encouragement, at least. And it wasn't just about Dawson and Ben Donnelly and the others, of course.

She was the one who knew this country, the one who'd hiked and climbed and fished and camped all her life, and he was a pissant cave cop who'd never been higher than the top of the Empire State Building, never been west of the Hudson River except for that one plane hop to Chicago, which hardly counted as a foray into the wilderness.

Still, the expression on her face was one he'd seen countless times before. You're in trouble, you find yourself a cop. And if you manage that much, how can you not expect help to be forthcoming, never mind if the cop had suddenly awakened to find himself in the middle of absolutely nowhere and couldn't tell the difference between a pinecone and a pine tree?

He wanted to tell her to get real, not to expect anything special from him. But it just didn't work that way. To do it would be the same thing as turning to some poor guy on a subway platform, some desperate bastard who's just had his wallet lifted or his laptop snatched and saying straight out: "What are you bothering *me* for, pal? I'm just on my way to a costume party."

And Corrigan couldn't do that. He simply could not. Not to Dara; not to anyone. Maybe it was what made him a cop. It was certainly part of *him*. Worms crawled off hot sidewalks if they could; it was Corrigan's instinct to give aid and comfort.

"Sure, we'll find them" is what he said to her. He glanced about the forest again, trying to calculate the most likely route by which to begin.

She managed something of a smile. He nodded. And all the while, he prayed that he was right.

32

By the time they fought their way up the slope to the place where they had tumbled over the ledge, it was fully light. Corrigan pulled himself to a level spot by the branch of a pine, then paused to catch his breath. The legs of his jeans were soaked, his feet numb with cold from slogging through the slushy snow. But the sky above had turned clear, with wisps of feathery clouds drifting brightly above the peaks, and he felt sweat trickling between his shoulder blades. Bizarre country, he thought. A bizarre set of circumstances altogether.

"Give me a hand."

It was Dara, coming up the slope below. He pushed away from the pine where he'd been leaning, and reached to haul her up. He realized his palm was covered with pinesap, but he supposed she'd be willing to put up with it.

Their hands clung together briefly, and she gave him a look as she joined him on the little shelf of rock he'd found. "Stuck on me, huh?" she said.

She was smiling, but it made him hesitate for a moment. Suppose he had lost her, tumbling down the mountainside. Where would he be now?

"Yeah," he said, "I am," and got a brief smile in return.

She turned after a moment, wiping her face on her sleeve. "I guess this is where we went over," she said, glancing down.

Corrigan looked. He *knew* it was a formidable drop, but there was none of that empty-stomach feeling he supposed others might have experienced. "I'm glad I couldn't see it coming," he told her mildly.

"I can't imagine you being scared," she said.

"I get scared," he said. "Anybody doesn't, then they're in real trouble."

"What you're talking about is different, though," she said. "More like a way of thinking."

He shrugged. "I get scared," he repeated.

They were quiet a moment, their breathing the only sounds under the hushed canopy of pines. He wiped his sticky palm on his wet pants, then cupped his hands to his mouth.

"Anybody there?" he called. His voice seemed to go nowhere, the sound soaked up at once by the feathery boughs, the spongy ground, the soft light.

"Anybody hear me?" he called again.

He might have called a third time, until he saw the expression on Dara's face. "I'm wasting my breath?" he asked.

She shrugged. "I don't know. Sound works funny on the mountain. You might hear people having a normal conversation fifty yards away, if they're in the right spot. Or you could be just the other side of a ridge, an outcropping of rock, somebody could drive a mule team right past and you'd never know."

"That's comforting," he said.

"That's just the way it is," she said.

"So, what do you suggest?"

She glanced speculatively up through the pines. "Keep climbing," she said.

"You figure they might have found a place to camp up that way?"

She shrugged. "That's the way we've got to go, regardless."

He followed her gaze, nodding slowly. "I had two granola bars in my pack."

"I've got an apple."

He turned to face her. "So, the point is, we can't spend a lot of time looking for the others."

She stared at him, her expression solemn.

"I mean, I'm no woodsman . . ."

She nodded, stamping her feet to get the circulation going. "We've got to get down the mountain, get ourselves dried off, find some food," she said.

"We'll have to assume that's what the others are doing," he said.

"Right," she said.

There was a certain fatality in all of this talk, he thought.

Maybe it was the same way the Donner party had gone about their plans.

"You have any idea where this cache point is?" he asked.

She looked away. "There's a trail up there, where we were headed," she said. "It's got to lead down. We'll find the place."

"Sounds like a plan to me," he said. "You want to lead the way for a while?"

"Sure," she said. And then she started out.

By the time they approached the tree line, the sun had cleared the distant ridge. Jays darted through the thinning branches above, their raucous cries an apparent protest against the pair of humans struggling through the soaking drifts, circling around steaming deadfalls. It didn't seem possible that they had covered so much ground in that mad dash the previous evening, Corrigan thought. But maybe that's what panic could do for you.

By now, Dara had stretched the distance between them to fifty yards or more. She glanced back to make sure he hadn't fallen too far behind, and he gave her a reassuring gesture. The moment she turned around, picking her way out over the barren landscape that lay between them and the ridge, he wheezed to a halt, leaning heavily into a big pine, gulping for air.

He could do with a few days of light rations, he supposed. Compared to her, he was carrying an extra fifty, sixty pounds of flesh up the mountain. No wonder she was so far out front. It was like a water bug blazing the trail for a water buffalo.

So, *moo,* he thought, or whatever it was that water buffalo said. No point in complaining. Just lumber along. He had just pushed himself away from the tree and had headed out into that stark landscape ahead when he saw it happen.

Her foot slid off a patch of exposed rock and into a crusted skiff of snow that collapsed under her weight. In the next moment, she was on her back and sliding sideways down a narrow chute, picking up speed as she went.

Under other circumstances it might have seemed funny, Corrigan thought, hurrying sideways over the slope. Worst thing, she'd end up in a pile right about tree line and she'd just have to start over again. That's what he was thinking, anyway, until she began to scream.

33

He was gasping for breath by the time he reached her, his legs numb from the struggle across the slope. It was no more than a forty-yard dash, first to last, but it was worse than running through mud.

All the while, his mind had been racing, calculating the possibilities: She'd sprained an ankle—or, worse yet, broken something, an arm or a leg. Still, he was thinking, they could make it, somehow. He'd fashion crutches, carry her if he had to. . . .

And then he was over the side himself, half running, half stumbling down the narrow chute where she had tumbled just moments before. She was sitting at the bottom, now, her legs tucked awkwardly beneath her, and she was no longer screaming.

She stared up at him, her face grim, her hands cradling something in her lap. Or some*one,* he saw as he neared, his mind already fighting the thought. *Someone else? Someone else is in trouble?*

"It's Lou," she cried as he slid-stumbled toward her. "Lou Vida."

And he knew from the look on her face that *trouble* did not begin to cover it.

"His head," she said softly as Corrigan knelt beside her. "His head." Her voice was a near whisper.

Corrigan glanced at her, then at the battered creature—the face swollen and blue-black where blood had pooled—this person who once had been Lou Vida. He felt instinctively at Vida's throat but knew at once that there hadn't been anything like a pulse there for a long time.

Abruptly, Dara turned away and began to vomit into the

snow. He held her shoulders until she stopped, then eased her out from under Vida's form.

"Dear God," she said as Vida slumped sideways, revealing the back of his skull.

Corrigan caught a glimpse of splintered bone, matted hair, other things he didn't want to identify. Dara struggled up and leaned heavily into him. He held her as much for his own comfort as hers.

"Maybe he fell," she said, her words muffled against his chest.

Corrigan glanced up the slope, squinting against the brilliance of the reflected sun. Broad swathes of snow, punctuated here and there by rocky outcroppings and upthrust boulders. He supposed it could have happened that way.

"He could have," he said.

"But you don't think so," she said, stepping back.

Corrigan glanced down at the body, then back at her. "His head hit a rock, there's no question about that. The exact physics of it, I'm not so sure about."

She stepped away and stared at him for a moment. She was fighting to control herself, that much he could see. And he could see also that she was about a feather's swipe from losing it altogether. "But why wait?" she cried. "Why fool around, going after us one by one? Why not just blow everyone up in that plane before we ever landed?"

He gripped her shoulders. "Maybe that's the way it was supposed to happen," he said. "Maybe it's been a game of catch-up ever since."

She turned, and glanced back down toward the snow-dusted tree line. That canopy had looked inviting the day before, something out of a calendar or a coffee-table book. Now, he doubted that even Dara found the prospect inviting.

"If you were right, then they could be down there right now," she said. "Watching." She whirled back upon him. "What if they have guns, what if they want to kill us, too—"

"Stop it!" he called, his voice sharp. She broke off, staring uncertainly at him.

"If there *is* someone out there, we don't have to worry about getting shot. Not right now, anyway."

She hardly seemed reassured. "And why is that?"

He gestured at Vida's body. "Think about it," he said.

"Everything that's happened *could* have been an accident. They find a couple of bodies with deer slugs in them, that might raise a few questions."

She considered it a moment, and glanced over her shoulder again, toward the looming pines. "So, what happens to us, then? An avalanche? Grizzly attack?"

He shrugged. "There are quite a few ways to die out here, that much I've learned."

Her eyes traveled to Vida's body briefly. She clutched her arms about herself, shuddering.

"So, what do we do now?"

"We press on," he said. "Hope we find the others."

She nodded, almost imperceptibly. "What about . . ." She squeezed her eyes tightly for a moment, then looked back at him. "What are we going to do with Lou?"

Corrigan stared down at the body. Lou Vida was just a dead man, now, hardly in a position to complain about whatever they might decide, but that was hardly the point. It seemed they had to do something. He bent and tugged a loose boulder up from the rubble-strewn slope. His hand slipped on a patch of melting ice, and he felt a fingernail snap.

Probably take an hour, probably break every nail, probably end up with frostbite. Still, he told himself, they had to do something, didn't they? And if you weren't sentimental, Corrigan thought, you could chalk it up to preservation of evidence. Whatever you chalked it up to, it was going to be done. He rolled the stone over, propping it as gently as he could against Lou Vida's massive shoulder.

"I'll help," Dara said, bending to the rocky patch at her feet.

"Sure," he told her. "That'd be fine."

He managed to flip another rock up from its resting place, and eased it beside the first. Dara was on the other side of Vida's body, gasping as she pulled a slab the size of a drum lid into place. Tears streaked her face, now.

He looked away and worked on. He worked steadily, without pausing, without looking up, until he knew that they had very nearly circled the body, until he could see Dara moving at the fringes of his vision as he worked.

He turned to an area behind him, at last, searching for a large rock, something that might finish their gruesome job. He swept his numbed hand across a mound of melting snow, spotting the edge of what seemed to be a suitable slab. He swiped at the stubborn mound of snow again, and paused.

He glanced back at Dara, who was hunkered back on her heels, breathing heavily, watching him work. "What?" she said when she saw the expression on his face.

He stared at her for a moment, unable to find the words. He turned back to the mound of snow he'd been working on.

There were fingers there. Four delicate fingers, each with a plum-painted nail, each as still as his own heart seemed to be.

"No," Dara was saying behind him. "No!"

Corrigan was digging at the snow more quickly, now. He grasped that cold hand in his and pulled gently, but firmly. The mound of snow rose up in a piece, almost as if it were alive, he thought.

But it was nothing living, of course. He heard Dara's sobs behind him. Sobs that grew as he pulled up the body of Ariel, Dawson's once-pert assistant, the body of yet one more.

34

It had taken them another half hour to fashion a second makeshift grave, this for Ariel, another forty-five minutes to climb up out of the worst of the snow that had drifted down off the ridgeline during the storm. Every bit of it exhausting, both physically and mentally, he thought as he rested, waiting for Dara to catch up.

But one good thing about being ground down, he mused as he stared over the cliff edge, where he'd been leaning against a boulder, was that if he hadn't been so tired, he might have missed what he had just seen. He heard the sharp call of a crow, glanced up as the shadow of the soaring bird cut between him and the fully risen sun. Wasn't that appropriate, he thought. The perfect cosmic touch.

"Dara," he said, turning, as she struggled up the steep slope toward him. He'd been tired before, but suddenly he was approaching his limit.

She joined him at the place where the trail switched back toward the top of the ridge, no more than a hundred yards away. "What is it?" she said.

"Down there," he said, pointing.

She followed his gesture down the side of the narrow fold to the bottom, a hundred feet or more. There were clumps of brush dotting the floor of the canyon, there, and a few spindly trees, but not enough cover to fully hide the man in a bright-red parka who was moving about, engaged in some task. Lifting something. Turning to place it. Then turning back to bend and lift again. A clatter of rocks rose toward them, echoing off the sides of the narrow cleft.

"Ben Donnelly," she said. She stared at Corrigan eagerly, finally registered his concern. She glanced back at Donnelly. "What's he doing?"

Corrigan shrugged, following Donnelly's movements. He spoke without turning to her, hearing the weariness in his own voice. "I'm going to guess it's the same thing you and I were doing a little while ago."

It took a moment for it to dawn on her, but he heard it in her voice soon enough. "No," she said flatly. "It can't be. . . ."

He met her stricken gaze. "Maybe I'm wrong," he said. Sure, maybe Donnelly was prospecting for gold, or trying to dig a hole to China.

She cupped her hands about her mouth, was about to call down into the canyon, when Corrigan pulled her back.

"Don't," he told her.

She turned to him in surprise. "Why? What's wrong?"

He gave her a look. "Maybe nothing," he told her. "But hasn't it occurred to you . . ." He hesitated, glanced back down to where Donnelly continued his work.

"Oh, no," she said, giving him an ashen look. "You don't think Ben Donnelly . . ."

"Could have murdered his own son?" He shook his head, let his breath out in a rush of frustration. "No. I don't think that." He raised his hands in a gesture of helplessness. "But ever since we found Lou and Ariel, I've been wondering how all these things could happen without *someone's* help. . . ."

"But *who*?" she demanded. "Who is left?"

He shrugged. "That's a pretty good question."

"Come on, Richard. You said yourself there could be people—militiamen, money men, some screwed-up group that has it in for Dawson—simply out there, watching." She glanced around, her face twisted with concern. "Watching and waiting for just the right time for the next one of us . . ." She broke off, glanced down into the canyon once again. "One thing I'm sure of. We don't have to worry about Ben Donnelly."

They stared at each other for a moment, and finally Corrigan turned. She was right, of course. She had to be. But still . . .

He shook his head, cupped his hands to his mouth. "Donnelly," he called. "Ben Donnelly!"

The man stopped what he was doing and straightened, shading his eyes to gaze at the top of the opposite slope. "Up here," Corrigan called. "Behind you!"

"Over here," Dara joined in, her voice echoing in counterpoint down the cliffside.

Finally Donnelly turned, still shading his eyes. Dara was flapping her arms, repeating her cries. After a moment, Donnelly raised his own arm in signal. He turned to glance at the mound of stones by his side, did something with his hand. Corrigan wasn't sure, but he thought the man might have been crossing himself.

He felt Dara's hand on his arm, felt her cheek brush his shoulder. "He did bury someone, Richard." She turned to him, her expression one of anguish. "This can't be happening, Richard," she said. "It can't."

He had his gaze on Donnelly, who was moving, now, down the canyon, where snow still lay in patches. He was headed toward that spot, where the tiny canyon played out onto the main slope, Corrigan saw. That's how he'd gotten in; that's where he would turn.

Donnelly would climb up to join them, then, and give them all the news. But it would take a while, he thought, and that was just fine with Corrigan. He felt in no hurry to hear about it, no hurry at all.

He stared out over the picture-postcard scenery below him, saw that a second crow had joined the other soaring in the sun-spawned updrafts. If you were a bird, he thought, you wouldn't give a damn about any of this. Wake up, cruise the thermals, croak your best thoughts to the world below all the livelong day.

He reached out beside him, put his arm around Dara's shoulders. "It's happening, all right," he told her, trying for something like a smile. "But there's some good news."

"What's that?" she asked, her tone doubtful.

He turned to her, struggling for an encouraging tone. "It still hasn't happened to *us*."

35

Poor Vaughn," Donnelly said, shaking his head, staring out over the canyon. He turned back to face them. "I was right about here when I saw him lying down there . . ." He trailed off.

Corrigan found himself watching the man closely, but Donnelly seemed not to notice.

"He might've gotten confused in the storm," the outfitter went on, glancing down the sheer slope beside them. "Neck was broke. At least he didn't suffer."

"Small consolation, wouldn't you say?"

Donnelly heard something in Corrigan's tone and glanced up. "I suppose it is," he said after a moment.

"You figure Lou Vida and Ariel Sorenson's deaths were accidents, too?" Corrigan asked. He'd been grappling with the impossible thought that Donnelly was responsible. That the man had bludgeoned Lou Vida, smothered Ariel Sorenson in the snow, thrown his own outfitter Vaughn over the side of the cliff . . .

It simply could not be, and yet, as he had so glibly said to Dara, paranoia had its insidious appeal.

"Could've been," Donnelly said. "You saw what happened to the two of you. If you'd hit a rock on your way down, you could have ended up the same as them."

"Ariel didn't have a mark on her," Dara broke in. "At least not that we could see."

"It happens," Donnelly said. "People get disoriented, exhausted. Sometimes they just sit right down in the middle of a blizzard and die."

"But you don't believe that's what happened to her, do you?" Corrigan said.

The outfitter glanced up at him. "Not any more than you do," he said. His gaze held Corrigan's for a moment, then broke off. He turned to look out over the canyon, let out a pent-up breath. "What happened to Chipper back there, it seemed like an accident at first, and that was bad enough. But now," he said, turning back to the two of them, "I find myself praying I'll find the one responsible. And God help him if I do."

Corrigan nodded, shamed anew by his own unspoken suspicions. Sure, there might have been fathers who'd killed their own in the heat of some raging passion, some terrifying feud, some moment's unfathomable suspension of reason. But no way a man like Donnelly could have sent his own son off coldly to his death, no way a man like Donnelly could be feigning the emotion that fairly pulsed from him now.

"In a way, it helps," Donnelly was saying, his voice intense. "You know what I mean. I think about getting hold of the person who might have planned all this, and I . . ." He stared down at his meaty hands. "Two wrongs don't make a right, I know it, but I'd get great satisfaction out of killing someone right now."

Dara turned away, brushing at her eyes suddenly. Corrigan stared back at Donnelly, transported momentarily. He knew exactly how the man felt, that boiling mixture of outrage and helplessness that demanded some target. Corrigan had felt it very clearly that night when he stood staring openmouthed at the back of his father's shattered skull. He too had wanted to find someone responsible, to wrap his fingers around some throat, to squeeze so hard he might bring his father back to life . . . but there had been no one to take hold of but himself, now, had there?

His father, smudge man, Mal. All the others. Dropping like lambs at his feet. Corrigan the cop. The one folks looked to for help. To serve and protect. He thought he might have given a bitter laugh. The only such feat he'd managed lately had been an utter sham, and look where that had brought him: to a place where he could witness more slaughter. Standing by helplessly while whatever malevolent force worked its way steadily down the list.

He broke away from his reverie and put a hand on Donnelly's shoulder. "We'll find out who's responsible," he said. "The first thing's to make it out of here. But once we've managed that, we'll find out who's responsible."

Donnelly stared back at him for a moment, nodding solemnly. The outfitter's face was leaden, the flesh seeming to sag on his cheeks and jowls. Just a day or two before, he'd looked like the Marlboro Man, Corrigan thought, the picture of a man chiseled out of a block of granite. At this moment he looked ready to disintegrate, to shatter at every seam.

"I've been thinking," Dara said, her tone hesitant. Corrigan turned. "Dawson and the others," she said, her face pained. "I mean, if something happened to them . . . God, help me, I know it sounds terrible, but—"

"It's all right," Corrigan broke in, shaking his head. "The same thought occurred to me."

"They wouldn't stop now," Donnelly chimed in. "Even if it's all about Dawson. Whoever it is wouldn't want anybody left to talk."

Dara stared back at the two of them, her face ashen. "Dear God . . ." she said, her voice trailing off.

"You didn't see any sign of them?" Corrigan said to Donnelly.

"Neither the Ashmeads nor the Dawsons." Donnelly shook his head bleakly. "We could be the last ones."

And then there were three, Corrigan found himself thinking. Lou Vida's gruesome nursery rhyme.

"Maybe they just kept going down the slope, back the way we came," Dara said, gesturing toward the great sweep of pines below.

"I hope not," Donnelly said. "That's nothing but a dead end. The only way back over that canyon is on that bridge we crossed. The rest of it gives out onto a mesa, just breaks off at a cliff, a thousand feet or more above the plains, in some places." He shook his head in dismissal.

"If you had climbing equipment, you might be able to get down, but . . ." He paused again. "Out there is where the Indians used to chase game—deer, elk, whatever—drive them right off the edge of the cliffs. Whoever was down below could just walk along and pick up the fresh meat."

"That's cheery," Dara said. She stared down over the pines. "Still, if they didn't realize it, they could have gone that way. Maybe we should try looking for them. . . ."

"You could send a dozen people into that country," Donnelly said, waving out over the vast expanse of forest. "A dozen *well-provisioned* people, with all the time in the world, and you still could walk right past them."

"They wouldn't have gone that way," Corrigan said. "Dawson knows that much."

"I just hope they're *some*where," Donnelly said. He gazed down the slope speculatively. "Somewhere alive, that is."

He was quiet for a moment, and when he did speak, it sounded almost as if he were talking to himself. "Vaughn was carrying a flare pistol in his pack," he said. He looked at Corrigan out of the corner of his eye. "Never found the damned pack."

Corrigan glanced over at the somber outfitter. "That's a little strange, wouldn't you say?"

Donnelly turned to meet his gaze. "Almost as strange as Vaughn running uphill from that storm," he said. After a moment, he went on: "You armed?"

"In *my* pack." Corrigan raised his hands helplessly. "Wherever it is."

Donnelly gave a mirthless laugh, staring back down the mountainside. Several more crows had joined the pair soaring in the updrafts, their calls piling on top of one another, echoing raucously in the distance.

"I've got a pistol," Donnelly said, his voice sounding as weary as Corrigan felt. "Just as soon have a rifle, but it might come in handy."

"You figure they'll want to work in close," Corrigan said.

Donnelly glanced at him, nodding. "Like you said, everything so far *could* be taken for an accident."

Corrigan nodded. Donnelly would have made a good cop, he was thinking. Or maybe it meant that Corrigan would have done all right as a wilderness guide.

"Time the predators get finished, what's left to find gets found," Donnelly continued. "There's going to be damned little to suggest otherwise—"

"Of course, we don't know for sure that there is any *they* out there. Isn't that right?" Dara broke in. She was staring at Corrigan, her expression seeming to demand he give her that shred of hope.

Corrigan gave Donnelly a look. "That could be," he said. "It *could* be the worst string of luck known to man. But I don't know that we want to take that chance."

"If they *are* out there, why aren't they coming after us right now?" She gestured toward the top of the ridge. "Why don't they just get it over with?"

Donnelly shrugged. "They don't have to."

"And why is that?"

"Like he just said," Corrigan cut in gently. "There's only one way off this mountain. They know that. Whoever's waiting, they know that sooner or later we'll have to come to them."

"So, what are we going to do?" she demanded.

"Go to them," Corrigan said.

And so they did.

36

It was only a few minutes' climb to the top of the ridge, a vantage point that offered a stunning view in both directions. At least, a view that would have been stunning in another life, Corrigan thought.

Behind them was the backdrop Corrigan had already wondered at the day before, before the storm had swept down upon them: a broad sweep of pines, the chasm they'd crossed in the distance, the snow-dusted peak of Black Mountain looming over it all.

Ahead was an area of bare, boulder-strewn landscape similar to that which they had just climbed through, leading down to another unbroken stretch of pines. On the horizon beyond the pines, a series of snow-covered peaks rose up, leading off to the north like a chain of imaginary pack animals arrayed for a march to the Pole. A dozen or more peaks, the last simply fading away into the blue mists of distance. Despite it all, despite every awful thing that had happened, Corrigan found himself caught momentarily by the sight.

The breeze that cruised the top of the ridge was cool, but hardly the killer wind of the previous day, the sky as bright as it had been threatening. As if the wilderness were schizophrenic, he thought. Hell one day, paradise the next.

"It's something, isn't it?" Dara said.

"It's more than that," he said. "I don't think the guys back home would believe me if I told them about it."

She gave him a thoughtful look. "But you're *going* to tell them about it, aren't you?"

He turned to her. "That is my undeniable intention," he told her.

"Good," she said. "I like that plan."

Donnelly, who'd found a resting place on a boulder beneath a massive overhang, glanced at the two of them. "Over there's where we're headed," he said, gesturing down toward the forest. "A couple more hours, once we get down below tree line."

"Over *where*?" Dara asked.

"Take a look," he said, pointing. "See if you can spot something looks like a dark line in the trees."

Corrigan stared out, saw what might have been the slightest seam twisting through the otherwise unbroken canopy. "Maybe I've got it," he said. "Almost at the horizon?" he asked.

"That's Bell's Canyon," Donnelly said, nodding. "Trail leads to our cache point, there. Little bit of a scramble down the side of a cliff to the river just beyond, and that's where the rafts are."

"Rafts?" Corrigan asked.

Donnelly had a shoe off and was kneading one of his feet. "We get that far, the last part's just a boat ride. There's three rafts stashed down by the water."

Corrigan noticed Dara looking at him. "We'll get there," he said.

"What I *meant* to say." Donnelly nodded.

Corrigan looked down at the placid-looking sweep of pines, thoughtful for a moment. He glanced at Donnelly. "Once we're back in the forest, that's where we have to be ready."

"Yeah," Donnelly agreed. "Maybe they're set up between there and the canyon. Or someplace around the cache. Doesn't really matter, does it, so long as they make sure nobody gets home to talk."

"You don't really think we're supposed to get out of this, do you?"

"Do the math, Dara," Corrigan said. "For all we know, there are only three of us left. Why would people who've done what they've done already take that kind of chance?"

"But like the two of you point out, what have we witnessed? A bunch of accidents, when it comes right down to it. I'm no cop, but I don't see much evidence lying around. No bullets or anything. What are people going to do, dust the pine trees for fingerprints?"

She paused, then, and the shadow that crossed her features sent a pang through Corrigan. *Maybe not the best way to boost the morale of the regiment, General Corrigan.* Maybe next he could give her his rendition of "The Charge of the Light Brigade."

He stared down across the rocky moraine that separated them from the forest, pondering who and what might be waiting for them, just inside the shade of that inviting canopy, trying to imagine what kind of accident might have been reserved especially for the hardiest of the three.

Of course, he could be altogether wrong. The Dawsons and the Ashmeads could be down there, rollicking along the trail, or already at the cache point, roasting weenies and singing camp songs. But he wasn't going to put any money on it.

After a moment, he turned to Donnelly, who had his sock back on and was working his foot back into his boot. "Is there just one trail to where we want to go?"

Donnelly finished tying his boot, finally looked up at Corrigan. "Well, there's deer tracks and so forth winding all over down there. Nothing you'd call a real trail."

"Could we get through that way?" Corrigan persisted.

Donnelly paused, then finally blew out a stream of breath. "I suppose so." He glanced at Dara's pack, then patted his own. "There's just the three of us, and we're traveling pretty light. It wouldn't be the express route, mind you. Your basic elk doesn't really care about the straightest line between two points."

"You said it would take us a couple of hours on the trail once we hit the tree line." Corrigan checked his own watch. "How much longer would it take if we went this other way?"

Donnelly shrugged. "Hard to say, seeing as how I never tried." He looked off, thinking. "There'd probably be some dead ends, some backtracking and all." He turned back to Corrigan. "I don't know. Say, twice as long, give or take."

"Let's count on six hours," Corrigan pressed. "Would that be safe?"

"Ought to be," Donnelly said. "Unless somebody throws a wheel or something."

Another cheery prospect, Corrigan thought. He checked his watch again and glanced up at the angle of the sun. "We would have to do this at night, I'm thinking."

"At *night*?" It was Dara, disbelief in her voice.

Donnelly was nodding agreement. "Makes sense," he said.

He waved in the direction of the distant line of peaks, where a pale disk hovered, almost invisible in the shimmering sky. "That's a three-quarters moon up there. Plenty of light so long as it doesn't cloud up or storm again."

"Please," Dara said.

"So, we wait until dark, cross this open stretch," Corrigan continued. He stared at Donnelly. "It'd be up to you to lead us through these trails you're talking about from there."

Donnelly's gaze turned inward briefly. He checked the canopy below, glanced at Dara, then back to Corrigan. "I don't see what choice we have. Do you?"

Corrigan shook his head.

"Then that's the way we'll do it," Donnelly said. He eased down off the boulder where he'd been sitting, found a spot deeper beneath the overhanging rock. He turned his pack on its side, punched a spot for his head to rest, then leaned back, his feet stretched out on the smooth rock floor of the natural shelter.

"Might as well find a place to rest," he said to them. "We're not going to be doing much sleeping tonight."

Corrigan turned to Dara, who shrugged. "I guess my vote doesn't count," she said.

"What is it?" he asked.

She looked off toward the forest below, then sighed in resignation. "That we wait till dark," she said, mustering a smile.

"Then of course it counts," he said, and gestured toward the shallow cave where Donnelly already appeared to be sleeping. "Now, let me show you to your room."

37

I don't know about the two of you, but I'm so hungry my big guts are starting to gnaw on my little guts," Donnelly was saying.

Corrigan glanced out from their shelter. The sky was nearly dark, the moon gathering strength over those distant ghostly peaks. "Something like that," he said, though he felt a bit too wired to be hungry. They'd shared Dara's apple, had plenty of water from the melting snow. As for hunger, it was as if he'd moved to some other plane of need.

"A girl never minds a chance to drop a few pounds," Dara said, a slight quaver in her voice.

When Corrigan turned to see how she was holding up, she shook her head before he could say anything. "I'm just cold," she said, clutching her arms about her. "I'm ready to roll, to tell the truth."

Corrigan nodded. It was a good ten degrees cooler since the sun had dipped below the horizon. And though he'd felt an odd sense of comfort here in the shallow cave—the subway cop in him, he supposed—he knew it was time to move. "Okay with you, Ben?"

The outfitter was a vague shape in the gloom, now. "Ready as I'll ever be," he said.

"Then, let's do it," Corrigan said, and rose to lead them out.

The first hundred yards were nearly straight down, the path grooved as smooth as the rock where they'd been resting above, their descent aided by the last of the glow reflected from a cobalt sky. The plan was to move without speaking, insofar as it was possible, keeping within sight of one another at all times, and so far there had not been a sound, not even the clatter of a rock or the scuff of a boot sole.

Corrigan paused at the first switchback, waiting for Donnelly to pass him and take the lead. He felt oddly exposed there, his back turned to the forest another hundred yards or so below them, imagining that the crosshairs of some nightscoped sniper's sights were, at that moment, merging into focus somewhere between his shoulder blades. There were people down there who meant them harm, of that much he was certain. And the only thing protecting them right now was their unproven belief that whoever it was could not use a bullet—just that supposition for a shield, along with the thin veil of darkness that covered them.

The darkness was in fact the greatest comfort to Corrigan, who was beginning to realize just how much of a cave fish he had become. He was used to dim light and close quarters, it dawned on him. In the darkness, whatever shortcomings of perspective the injury to his eye might have caused were erased, the shadings of light and darkness as vivid as an old movie shot in black and white. He hadn't planned it that way, but he felt it wash over him, now, an exhilarating sense of unexpected advantage.

"You take it," he said as Donnelly approached, and the burly outfitter put his hand to Corrigan's shoulder as he passed.

"Stay close," Donnelly murmured. "Whatever happens."

Corrigan nodded, but Donnelly was already past, angling down the path that appeared to Corrigan like a luminescent slash across the mountainside. He hesitated a moment longer, waiting for Dara to join him.

He noted the brightness of her eyes, the shining planes of her cheeks, the shadow at the hollow of her throat. He had fallen big-time, he knew, had given himself over in a way he never could have anticipated . . . and yet, look where they were now.

"You go," he said quietly. He grasped her hand tightly for one brief moment. She returned the pressure, hesitated, then moved along.

Good, he found himself thinking. *This is as good as we can make it just now.* And then he took his place in line.

The trail leveled out as they approached the dark line of trees, but loose stones littered the path, forcing them to slow their progress as they picked their way along. Donnelly was a dozen yards or so in the lead, Corrigan an equal distance at the rear.

He watched Donnelly slow, apparently waiting for Dara to join him. The moment she caught up, Donnelly pointed at something, then moved carefully off the trail, leading her straight down toward the shadows.

Corrigan hurried to the spot and found another, dimmer trail peeling away through the loose talus there. The two of them were into the shadows, now, and Corrigan moved as quickly as he dared after them, realizing that he was holding his breath. *Is it now?* he asked himself as he hurried toward the ragged line of darkness. *Or now?*

But there was nothing but blessed silence, and soon he felt himself swallowed by the same darkness, the path leveling out beneath his feet. The smells were different, suddenly, the vanillalike scent of pine bark, the musky smell of the earth, still damp from snowmelt, the tang of needles brushed by someone who had recently passed this way.

He felt a hand on his arm, then, and though he had not expected it, he felt no urge to jerk away. "So far so good." He heard Donnelly's gruff voice, surprisingly soft in his ear.

Corrigan's eyes had already adjusted, giving him Donnelly's silhouette clearly, and that of Dara, standing a few feet away. The pines rose up like dark pickets all around them, and the moonlight fell between the trunks like paint splashed randomly on a blackened canvas.

"We're a couple hundred yards up the slope from the main trail," Donnelly continued. "And this track's pretty well worn."

He produced a compass with a glow-in-the-dark needle jiggling on its spindle like a luminescent worm. Corrigan thought briefly about having a compass in the tunnels back home. Would the thing still work down there, still home in faithfully on north? Or more likely send a person directly toward the live third rail?

"Just keep yourselves in sight," Donnelly told them quietly. "I'm not going to try and set any speed records. Stay quiet, but if something happens, let me know. I don't want to be walking off, leaving anybody in the dark, okay?"

"I'll let you know," Dara said.

Corrigan simply nodded.

He heard a rush of sound above them, and glanced up to see something darting through the intertwined limbs above. Whatever it was stopped abruptly, the sound stopping with it. Corrigan searched the dark crosshatching of limbs, passing over a vague hunched form, before he realized he'd found what he was looking for.

"Owl," Donnelly said, glancing up at the looming creature, a broad-shouldered shadow at least a foot tall. It had something of the shape of a manta ray, Corrigan thought, and something of the same forbidding aspect. "Probably wonders what the hell we're doing out here."

"I don't blame him," Dara said.

"How do they fly through all that tangle?" Corrigan wondered.

"Just the way they were made," Donnelly said. "Now, let's go before he gets any big ideas and comes down here to carry one of us off."

Corrigan had marked their entry into the forest at seven-thirty. It was nearly eleven by the time he checked the dial of his watch again. They'd had to abandon the trail they'd used originally when it began to curve dangerously close to the main track, according to Donnelly's calculations. They spent considerable time struggling along an overgrown passage that curved back up the mountainside, a part of the trek marked by tedious clambering over deadfall and ducking through vine-tangled brush—even that owl he'd seen couldn't have maneuvered through that mass, Corrigan had thought, yanking barbed tendrils from his face and neck. Not and keep its feathers on, anyway.

The upside of the struggle was that it kept them warm. The temperature had not dipped anywhere close to what it had been the night before, but it was still somewhere in the thirties, cold enough to turn his breath to steam when there was enough moonlight filtering through the trees to see. And yet he could feel the sweat forming beneath his jacket, stinging the spots where brambles had scraped him raw.

The night remained clear, however, the moon affording them enough light to keep moving by, at times painting the forest floor with intricate patterns that lent an otherworldly sense to their passage. Corrigan was tired, now, and his muscles were tight with the constant threat of some unknown watcher out there, just waiting, but all the same there were moments when his mind would drift and he'd find himself moving almost without volition along the slope, weaving through the sentinel trees and the splashes of light and shadow like a spirit from a storyteller's fable. *And so, lost and alone, the three wandered through the forest* . . .

His mind had always worked that way, Corrigan mused, creating these little internal dramas, fanciful scenarios in which his most mundane tasks—a stakeout at the turnstiles, shepherding the boisterous traffic pouring down into the tunnels following a Knicks game, or on the way to Times Square at New Year's—became the background counterpoint to some daydream with Corrigan at its center, the hero of his own oddball tale. It was the sort of thing that kids did all the time—or at least he had, on those long afternoons he'd spent in the family apartment during the recuperation from his injury—something that had apparently never left him.

And a nice sort of dream it would have been to inhabit right now, he thought, rousing himself back to the real world. In fact, there was nothing mundane about the reality he was caught in, was there? No time for fantasy. No time for kid stuff anymore. There were very real forces that would end his daydreaming forever, send him and Dara and Donnelly into oblivion without regard for the vast importance they all placed upon themselves. Oh, yes, Corrigan thought, very definitely time to grow up.

Donnelly, who had found them a better path to travel this last half hour or so, had stopped up ahead there, in a deep pool of shadow, and, with Dara at his side, appeared to be consulting his compass once again. "We screw up again?" Corrigan asked softly as he joined them, already dreading another side trip through thick brush and fallen limbs.

"Quiet," Donnelly told him. He replaced his compass and seemed to be listening intently for something close by.

Corrigan glanced at Dara, who was staring off into the darkness as well. What would it be? Corrigan wondered. The sound of footsteps, snapping twigs, feet scuffing through the carpet of needles that surrounded them? Or a series of animal calls—little whistles and clicks that mimicked birds or frogs but were really the signals of killers moving in?

But there was none of that, no cricket noise, no sounds of breezes moving branches about, nothing but stillness and the palpitating quiet of the forest. Then, just as he thought his ears would clog altogether with the hiss of nothingness, he became aware of it: a kind of rumbling noise, so faint and low as to be almost indistinguishable. Corrigan turned to Donnelly, who nodded.

"That's the river," the outfitter said quietly. "We're not far, now."

"Sounds like a serious river," Corrigan said.

"Yeah, well, some of us like to call it *Balls* Canyon," Donnelly said, glancing off in the direction he'd indicated. "On account of that's what it takes to ride the river that made it."

"That's not exactly how you described it earlier," Dara said.

"That was earlier," Donnelly said. "I like to focus on one problem at a time."

"Speaking of which," Corrigan said.

"Yeah," Donnelly said. "We have to decide just how to play this next part."

"How far over to the canyon?" Corrigan asked. Maybe it was his imagination, but the rumble of the water seemed to have grown in the past moments.

"It's a little rougher from here," Donnelly said. "Maybe half an hour."

"And then we could make our way down toward the cache point?"

"We could."

Corrigan nodded, thinking. "So, we could move in close enough, set up a stakeout, see if anybody's lurking around, waiting for us. If we don't see anything by dawn, we could load up some supplies and take that boat ride you were talking about."

Donnelly considered it. "Sounds as good as anything," he said. "If there was somebody there waiting on us, I'd like the idea of taking the bastards by surprise."

"Then that's what we'll do," Corrigan said. "That sound all right to you, Dara?"

She turned back to the two of them. "I'm thinking that derring-do is not my department. But if there's a chance we'd catch someone who's responsible for all this, I'm for it." He thought he saw her shoulders move in a shrug. "What's the worst thing that could happen, anyway?"

Corrigan found himself wanting to smile. So what if he'd won a free cruise on the *Titanic,* he thought. They could still keep this ship afloat. And that was enough for now.

38

Donnelly had been proven correct about the change in the nature of the terrain, Corrigan thought. As they moved ahead, homing in on the sound of the water, they found themselves struggling through an ever-thickening screen of underbrush so dense they had to give up and backtrack several times. On occasion, the slope seemed practically vertical, and the overhead canopy had thickened as well, forcing them to navigate almost entirely by feel and instinct. They'd long ago lost any trace of the fast-dimming path, as if even the deer and the elk had found the going too rough.

At the same time, the rumble of the water grew steadily louder, almost enough to vibrate the ground itself. In its ominous way, the sound was a summons, a suggestion of hope that kept them stumbling on through the darkness, although Corrigan couldn't shed himself of Donnelly's characterization of the river. *Yes, come ahead,* you could interpret that steady rumbling to say. *Make your way to me. There are much more terrible things in store.*

He pushed the thoughts away, and paused to lean wearily against a slender pine, his body held from pitching over backward solely by its answering thrust. He checked his watch and saw that it was well past midnight. Donnelly's estimate of the time it would take them to reach the canyon had more than doubled already. It wasn't really a problem. They had all night, if it came to it. Just so long as they could make it to the cache point before dawn, with enough time to be sure there were no more surprises waiting.

He glanced up the slope to see Dara pulling herself through a particularly thick tangle, jerking her feet high like someone trying to wade through glue. She wasn't cursing audibly, but he thought he could hear every one of the violent oaths that had to be traveling through her mind.

But it had taken them at least fifteen minutes to climb to this point of the slope they were on. No way were they going to backtrack now. Besides, Donnelly had apparently made his way, somehow. They surely could, too. Corrigan drew a deep breath, shoved away from his resting place, and moved upward to see if he could help.

By the time he reached the thicket, Dara had disappeared, leaving something of a passageway for Corrigan. He stumbled once, his foot caught in the clutch of a root, and found himself looped beneath the chin by a thick curl of vine. *Just great,* he thought, flailing about, trying to ease the pressure on his throat. *Make it this far, get yourself strangled by a goddamned vine.*

He managed to grab a limb with one hand and pulled, raising himself off the ground, and finally found he could breathe again. He pulled his foot free of the root, then leaned forward and sideways at the same time, charging through the last screen of brush like a lineman bent on a downfield block. *Forget the subtleties of the owl method,* he thought, his legs churning, limbs raking at his face.

He felt the hold of the underbrush give at last, felt himself tumbling freely, his knees cracking against rock, then his shoulders . . .

"Holy shit." He heard Donnelly's voice above him, then felt the big man's bulk toppling onto his.

The two of them slid forward, then stopped abruptly. Corrigan felt his legs oddly heavy, then, and realized they were dangling in space. The roaring of the water, which had been loud enough before, was almost deafening, now. He blinked, opened his eyes, and found himself staring over the edge of a precipice that dropped away toward a roiling band of white far below.

The river, he realized. They'd finally made it. And he'd nearly driven both of them off the edge of the cliff.

"Don't move," he heard Donnelly saying. "Just lie still, right where you are."

Corrigan felt himself teetering, then, felt all the grains of sand and earth between his body and the rocky lip of the cliff turning into tiny ball bearings that wanted to roll him right off into the void.

"I've got you," Dara was saying somewhere behind him. He felt a hand clamp on to his ankle, and he dared a glance over his shoulder.

She was holding on to a branch with one hand, his pant leg with the other. Corrigan looked back toward Donnelly, who was on his back, his heels dug into a crevice coursing the tilted shelf where they lay. The outfitter had his palms flat at his sides, his body held as rigid as a plank.

Corrigan, who was pointed in the opposite direction, head down toward the water, worked his own hands forward, pressed his palms to the rock, and began to lever himself backward, aided by Dara's steady tug at his leg. *Inch by inch,* he thought. *Never hurry anything again in your life, Richie-boy. Who needs bad guys when there's someone like yourself around . . . ?*

He felt some odd resistance beneath him, realized his belt buckle had caught on something, and sucked his gut up toward his spine until it released with a snap. In the next moment, he felt his balance point shift and the knot in his stomach relax. *On solid ground at last,* he thought, and heard Donnelly's cry just a few feet away.

"I'm going," Donnelly was saying, his voice oddly calm. "I can feel it. . . ."

Corrigan flung himself sideways, breaking Dara's grasp on his leg. He ignored her cry, then rolled over completely, hooking one leg around a spindly-looking tree that had found a way to sprout at the very lip of the cliff.

In the same motion, he lunged toward Donnelly and caught the big man by the collar, steadying him for the moment.

"Let go, damnit. We'll both go over," Donnelly said.

"No, we won't," Corrigan told him. "Just hang on."

"A fly couldn't hold on to this," Donnelly said. "Birds couldn't land here."

"Use your heels," Corrigan demanded. "Your palms. Grab the rock with your ass if you have to."

"You make me laugh, we're going to die," Donnelly said.

"Nobody's going to die," Corrigan said. "Not this time. Are you steady, now?"

"I think so," Donnelly said. He seemed to be staring down

at the water between his splayed-out legs. "Maybe we're dead already, we're just dreaming this."

"There's spray on my face all the way up here," Corrigan said, glancing down at the boiling water. "You really think people can take a raft down that?"

"It's not so bad downstream," Donnelly said. "That's where we put in."

"I'm glad to hear it," Corrigan said. "Let's not put in up here, then. Not like this."

"Roger that," Donnelly said. "How do you intend to prevent it?"

"I'm holding on," Corrigan told him. "Now, try to push yourself up, hands and feet together. *Will* yourself."

"I'd levitate if I could," Donnelly said between clenched teeth. "I'm going to stop talking, now. I think it's shaking me toward the edge."

"I've got you," Corrigan told him. "Now, push."

He could feel the tiny tree shuddering at the strain behind him. *Grow, damn you,* he thought. *Get some real fucking roots.*

He thought of smudge man, of Mal, of Lou Vida and Vaughn, of all those dead or missing, felt his grip tighten to steel on Donnelly's collar. If Donnelly went, he would have to go, too, Corrigan thought. No way around that, no way at all.

He was vaguely aware of Dara's hands at his other ankle, then, realized she was tying something there. He struggled to turn his head toward her. "What are you doing?"

"One of those vines," she said. "I wrapped the other end around a big tree."

"I couldn't break the sonofabitch before," he said. "I guess we'll have to trust it this time."

He turned to Donnelly. "I'm going to pull hard, now. Are you ready?"

"That's a waste of breath, Corrigan."

"Here goes," Corrigan said. And gave it all he had.

39

I never thought you'd be the one to try and kill me," Donnelly was saying.

"I already said I was sorry," Corrigan replied. He knew Donnelly wasn't complaining about the accident. It was the big man's way of saying thanks, about as direct a statement as was likely to come, too.

It happened the same way back on the job, Corrigan thought: One cop pulls another's fat from the fire, saves a partner from certain death, no big valentines get exchanged. You nod your thanks, go on, and do your job. Maybe tomorrow your partner returns the favor. Arrangement understood.

And it was okay by Corrigan. He hadn't done anything intentional to smudge man, he hadn't been able to save Mal, but he'd somehow managed to jerk Donnelly's 200-plus pounds up the cliff. They'd dusted themselves off, found their way down to this spot overlooking a clearing, thirty yards or so from the place where Donnelly indicated their supplies were cached, and had gone on to the next order of business—staking out the cache point—virtually without comment on the near disaster. Attending to matters of life and death in a place so dark you couldn't read a rulebook even if one existed. So, what else was new?

The moon had long ago sunk behind the mountain at his back, and they were reduced almost entirely to guesswork, now. He raised on one elbow, turning to Donnelly, who had gone to reconnoiter the opposite side of the clearing and was back, now, easing down on his haunches beside him.

One he'd managed not to lose, Corrigan thought. One he'd pulled back from the brink. Perhaps it meant their fortunes had taken a turn. He could always hope.

"See anything?" the outfitter asked, his voice barely more than a whisper, as much a thought as an utterance.

"Not even a gopher, or a marmot, whatever you call them out here," Corrigan told him, his response equally quiet. "Not enough light to see much, though."

He knew that Donnelly would be nodding agreement.

"Wasn't anything over on that side, either," the outfitter said. "It *feels* deserted, doesn't it?"

Corrigan nodded in turn. He suspected Donnelly could feel his gesture as well. Spend enough time out here in the wilderness, wander long enough through the dark, he could probably communicate with bark beetles, he thought.

"Maybe someone'll show up at dawn," Corrigan said.

"Anything's possible," Donnelly said.

"We'll wait until we can see, give it a few minutes, then make our move, right?"

"Sounds good," Donnelly said. "Still, I'd like someone to show up. I'd like to get my hands on one of these people."

"Maybe we will," Corrigan said, though he'd heard that sentiment from countless victims before. Count your blessings, the cop in him wanted to say. Be happy it didn't happen to you; get on with your life. But somehow those bromides weren't holding up so well any longer, not even in his own mind. He could only guess what fantasies of revenge raged in Donnelly's mind.

He glanced toward the place where Dara lay. The barest glow of light formed in the sky above, now. Enough to trace her quiet form, her head tucked in the crook of her arm. Sleeping, it would seem. At least he hoped she was. One of their party deserved a few minutes away from the unrelenting threat of doom, that much he was sure of.

A few more minutes and the light had grown appreciably, enough for him to make out a low-slung structure on the far side of the clearing below. "Right there," Donnelly said, nudging him. "That's where we're headed."

Corrigan nodded. A sod hut, he was thinking. He'd seen such structures in one of his schoolbooks. This one was dug into the side of a bank, its roof part of the rising slope above. You could keep things cool in such a place, all right. Keep them hidden as well. A person who didn't know what he was

looking for could walk right by the cache. A skiff of pine needles had piled up in front of what must have been the door to
the thing. A limb from a pine had tumbled down over the lip
of the sod roof. It was the picture of abandonment, he was
thinking, and then he caught something at the edge of his
vision.

Something there, in the trees on the far side of the clearing,
a form moving stealthily, silently toward the hut. Corrigan felt
his breath catch, his scalp prickling.

"Something . . ." he whispered to Donnelly. "Over there . . ."

"Yeah," Donnelly said in a voice that Corrigan thought
sounded eager.

His gaze was focused on the source of the movement, now,
straining. He'd give anything to have that rifle with its
nightscope back, he thought, home in on the bastard, take him
out before . . .

"Sonofabitch." Corrigan heard Donnelly's voice beside
him, heard the big man's breath release and the note of disappointment there.

Corrigan was puzzled for an instant, but in the next moment
could see it himself and understood: Not a killer come to do
them harm, not a man there at all.

Deer, he thought next, but the creature was far too big for
that. An elk, he realized. With its ponderous, antler-capped
head and massive chest, it was as perfect-looking an animal
as those he'd seen in that pictorial layout. It seemed a hundred years ago, that evening at the hotel in Jackson. Back
then the wilderness had been all about peace and beauty,
hadn't it? Sure. In that other universe where he once had
lived.

The creature picked its head up as if it had heard something,
seemed to glance across the clearing directly at them. In the
next moment, it turned and bounded back into the shadows,
vanished as suddenly as if it had never been. Corrigan realized
he had not heard the huge creature make a single sound.

He turned to Donnelly, then. "Did I really see that?"

Donnelly nodded. "Granddaddy elk," he said. "Not exactly
who we were expecting, was it?"

Corrigan rolled onto his stomach, glanced back toward the
sod hut. An amazing sight for a city boy, all right. He was
going to take it as an omen, he decided. As a good omen.

After a moment, he turned back to Donnelly. "You sure your guys have been here?"

"I'm sure," Donnelly said. "If they forgot, I'm going to fire them."

Corrigan saw a smile cross the man's weathered features.

"To the right is where the trail comes down," Donnelly continued, pointing. "About opposite, that's where the trail goes down the side of the canyon. You'll find a sandbar down there, on this side of the river. Walk upstream, you'll find a spot tucked under the cliff where the rafts are."

Corrigan saw that Dara was awake, now, her eyes narrowing as Donnelly spoke.

"What are you talking about?" Corrigan said. "Aren't you going with us?"

Donnelly glanced back at the clearing, then back at the two of them. "We don't want to waste any time," he said. "I'll take your pack, too." He pointed to Dara. "While I'm loading up, you two can get one of the rafts dug out. Make sure there's enough paddles. By the time you've carried the rafts back down to the put-in, I'll have joined up with you."

"I'd feel better if we all stuck together," Dara said.

Donnelly shook his head, then gestured at the surrounding forest. "We're clear right now, but we don't know when the wrong people might show up. It'll take both of you to wrangle those rafts down. That's the way it has to be."

"No point in arguing about it, Dara," Corrigan said, checking his watch. "Let's give it another minute or two. If we don't see anyone, we'll make our move."

"Agreed, then," Donnelly said. He waited for Dara to hand over her pack, raised up to hook one of its straps over his burly shoulder. He reached for his own pack, unzipped a pocket, and dug about for something.

"Here," he said after a moment, handing something to Corrigan. "You know how to use this, don't you?"

Corrigan stared down at the pistol Donnelly held out, butt-first. A Smith & Wesson .38 with a lanyard ring dangling beneath the wooden grip. He glanced up at Donnelly. "Hadn't you better keep that?" he said, nodding at the clearing below.

Donnelly shook his head. "We know they're not up here . . ." he said, leaving the thought unfinished.

Corrigan glanced at Dara, then back at the outfitter. "All

right," he said, taking the weapon. He checked the cylinders, made sure the hammer was resting on empty. He eased up to jam the pistol in his waistband. "I'd be happier with an Uzi," he said. "But we'll make do."

"Just a precaution." Donnelly nodded, with a glance of his own at Dara. "Now, if you two are ready."

They all rose carefully, then, checking their surroundings one last time.

"I'll wait till you're circled around to the trailhead," Donnelly said. He paused. "Somebody *is* hiding someplace I can't figure," he said, nodding over his shoulder toward the clearing, "then maybe we're saying good-bye, here." He put out his hand, and Corrigan shook it. Dara stared at him for a moment, then took the man's big hand in both of hers.

"Whoever's responsible is going to pay for this," she said.

Donnelly nodded, giving her a grateful look. "Let's just get ourselves home, first, what do you say?"

They parted, then, Corrigan leading the way through the trees toward the spot that Donnelly had indicated. In minutes they reached the edge of the cliff, where the trees thinned, and a narrow track dived through a screen of brush toward the river far below. Though he couldn't see the water from where he stood, Corrigan could hear it. Maybe that turmoil was not quite what he had experienced the night before, but still it was formidable enough, he thought. He glanced at the steeply descending path before them. Why couldn't anything seem easy?

"There he is," Dara said, pointing back across the clearing. Donnelly had emerged from their hiding spot, was standing fully exposed at the edge of the open space. He gave them a high sign, then moved on across the clearing toward the cache at a trot.

Corrigan watched the man go, felt his own hand moving for the pistol he'd jammed into his belt. Not a lot of good that would do if something went wrong, but still it gave him the illusion of doing something useful.

Donnelly was at the entrance to the cache, now, examining something. He turned to see them still standing there, watching, then waved them emphatically on.

"Shit," Dara said, glancing at Corrigan. "I don't feel right about leaving him."

"He's got his job, we've got ours," Corrigan said. "Come on."

And they began to pick their way down toward the growling water.

40

Donnelly spun the dial through the numbers on the combination lock for a second time, cursing the dim light, cursing his failing close vision. He clicked on the last digit, then tugged on the lock again . . . but nothing doing.

He actually had a pair of reading glasses stowed somewhere, but he was damned if he wanted to take the time to fish them out. Maybe he'd just blow the goddamned lock off, he thought, before remembering he'd given his pistol to Corrigan.

He took a deep breath, closed his eyes momentarily, then began again. A couple of free spins to clear the tumblers, then a very careful application to the task. Four, forty-four, fourteen. How in the hell could you screw up a series like that? And then a paralyzing thought struck him. Maybe it was forty-four, four, fourteen?

Stop it, he commanded himself. He had it right. The same damned numbers it had been for a dozen years. Every goddamned combination lock he owned, though nobody else knew it. Month, year, day of his birth. Could have made it year, month, day, but he hadn't. He liked the rhythm of the way he'd done it. Just missing the mark, here, in the piss-poor light, that was all. This time didn't work out, he'd dig out his glasses.

He stopped on fourteen, made sure of it, counting the little notches off with his thumbnail before he pulled on the lock. *This time, baby,* he willed. *This time.*

And nothing. The dial of the lock stared up at him through the dim light like an angry eye. *All right, I'll get the goddamned glasses out,* he thought, giving the lock a last, angry yank . . .

. . . and felt the first shock wave of the blast, felt himself go weightless with surprise.

41

Corrigan and Dara had just reached the trail's first switch-back when the explosion thundered behind them, sending rock and debris straight out over the cliff edge above. The shock wave rolled through the ground, earthquake-style, flinging Corrigan forward onto his face as if he were a skittle. He felt his chin grind against rock, felt the taste of blood in his mouth. He dug his heels in, splayed out his arms, managing to stop his slide, then rolled onto his back, searching frantically for Dara.

In the next moment he found her, blown off the side of the trail into a thicket of undergrowth. She was in a sitting position, her mouth open in surprise, her eyes wide as wave after wave of aftershock rumbled through them. Echoes of the blast still reverberated down the canyon walls.

"Ben . . .?" she cried to Corrigan.

But Corrigan was already on his feet and sprinting back up the trail. He barely paused as he crested the top.

The forest seemed preternaturally quiet in the aftermath of the explosion. If it had been dim in the clearing before, it might have turned to night again. A thick pall of dust hung between the trees, the air so thick with the taste of cordite and ash that he could scarcely breathe.

He sensed footsteps behind him, realized that Dara had caught up. "Oh my God," she said, choking on what passed for air around them. Like breathing evil itself, Corrigan thought, his eyes tearing in the stuff.

After a few moments, an updraft cut along the top of the canyon, and the pall began to lift. Across the clearing where the cache had been tucked into the hillside, there was nothing left but a rocky gash a dozen feet across, maybe five or six feet deep. One great pine had collapsed across the wound in the earth, another had toppled backward, propped up in the clutch of others up the slope.

Beyond that evidence of what had happened, there was nothing. No scrap of paper, no cloth, no hint that anything human had ever come this way. Corrigan gaped in disbelief.

"Why would they do this?" Dara cried at his shoulder. "You said they wouldn't. You said they wouldn't shoot us. You said . . ."

He turned and caught her shoulders. "Stop it!" he shouted. His voice sounded magnified in the unearthly quiet.

She stared back at him, her eyes gradually coming back into focus, beginning to water, shifting over from shock to pain. "Oh, Ben," she said, collapsing against him. "Poor Ben."

Corrigan scanned the forest floor about them once again, hoping against hope. . . . *Come on, Donnelly, out from behind that tree over there, turn yourself in.* But there was nothing, not the barest testimony there had ever been a man named Donnelly.

"We're the last ones," Dara murmured, her face against his chest. "We're going to die."

"We're not going to die," Corrigan said. The words came automatically to his lips, even as he witnessed the faces of the lost receding behind his eyes.

All those people. And now Donnelly, too. The man he'd once been ready to blame for all this, the man he thought he'd saved. And that action, which he had been foolish enough to take as an omen of good fortune. *Richie, Richie, Richie. It's never too late to die.*

"If they can do this," Dara said, "they can do anything."

He held her close, part of him understanding how she felt. Experience enough calamity, the spirit simply wanes. Go ahead, get it over with. Why prolong the agony? Probably what his old man had been thinking. Or something along those lines. *Wife gone, job gone, everything gone. So long, Richie-boy, give my regards to Broadway station.*

Sure. Maybe Corrigan could understand it. But that didn't mean he bought into it. Just kneel down before the man with the ax and hang your head?

"No way," Corrigan heard himself saying to Dara. "No one can do everything."

She stared up at him, shaking her head in confusion.

"They're not going to do it to us," he told her. "We're going to take that boat ride, just like Donnelly said, and we are going to make it home."

She stared at him, still shaking her head. "Don't you see?" She swept her arm at the gaping crater across the clearing. "Don't you see what we're up against . . . ?"

He glanced in the direction she'd indicated, then turned back, shaking his head. "I see *you*," he told her. "I see *me.* Maybe it's a problem of perception, but right now that's all that counts."

He took her hand, then, and began to lead her down.

42

It was fully light by the time Corrigan and Dara neared the bottom of the narrow trail. He turned at the last switchback, where a clump of willowy trees had sprouted in the seep of a cliffside spring. Ahead, the trail broadened out into a gentle descent, twenty yards or so, to the sandbar Donnelly had mentioned.

Through the screen of overhanging branches he could see the river: no frothing rapids, here, just as Donnelly had predicted. Just a swift ribbon of gray-green current—maybe fifty feet across—that whisked between the canyon walls with a deceptive fluidity. A pair of canyon birds skimmed along the surface, and somewhere in the nearby brush some other bird cousin was pumping out a complicated song. The temperature seemed to have risen another ten degrees, at least, giving the humid air an almost springlike balminess. If you didn't know better, Corrigan thought, you might get the feeling that not a hair was out of place in the greater scheme of things.

Corrigan, however, had witnessed more than enough evidence to the contrary. And he was well aware of the dim rumble of the maelstrom far upstream. Plenty of unseen power beneath that apparently calm surface. It was like watching a subway train from a bad dream, hurtling silently down a greased chute. And God only knows what was waiting around the next bend.

"Wait here," he said as Dara caught up. "I'll go on out there, see what it looks like."

She'd been bent over, hands on her knees, her breath coming in gasps. She glanced up, shaking her head.

"No way," she said. "You heard Donnelly. It'll take both of us to manage the raft."

"We don't even know if there's a raft there," he said. "Or who might be waiting with it."

"I don't care if it's the whole Aryan Nation," she said. "I'm not staying here by myself. If something happens, it's going to happen to both of us together." She paused.

He took a breath, threw his hands up. "All right," he said, "but stay behind me, at least. I'm the one with the gun."

She nodded grudgingly. "Let's go."

He moved cautiously down the broadening slope, the pistol in his hand seeming something less than a comfort. If these people had been willing to do what they'd done to Donnelly, then why would they worry about taking him and Dara out at long range? Bodies were made to be buried, after all. What would a missing subway cop and a reporter matter, given all the other carcasses that would be found?

He was walking on soft sand, now, leaving dim footprints as he went. No other tracks that he could see, but then there was a broad band of gravel closer to the side of the cliff. A person could easily have used that path to move upstream ahead of them.

He veered toward the gravel, motioning for Dara to follow him. Better cover closer to the cliff, anyway, just in case. He scanned the low-lying brush ahead and saw nothing. But that's the way the African veldt probably looked, too, he thought. Then you take a step into the long grass and find your leg going down a lion's throat.

"Up there," Dara said behind him.

Corrigan stopped, his feet scattering gravel, his hand going toward his gun.

"The rafts," she said, pointing. "Right where Donnelly said."

He willed himself to relax, following her gesture to a place on the rocky cliffside just above where the sandbar narrowed almost to nothing. He found it, then, a hollowed spot in the rocks several feet above the waterline, and a broad shelf where the rafts had likely been stored. If there had been any camouflaging brush stacked up there, however, it was long gone. He saw one bright yellow craft leaning out over the lip of the shelf, another dragged partway down toward the water. *Three* rafts, Donnelly had told them, Corrigan was sure of it.

"*Someone's* been here," Dara said.

"I think that's what Goldilocks said," Corrigan told her, scanning the surrounding cliffside, his grip still firm on the pistol. "Right before they all came back."

He checked the top of the cliff, then the opposite rim, and turned to glance behind them.

"You see anyone?" he asked Dara.

She shook her head, but he was already moving forward. They struggled through the low-lying screen of brush toward the tumbled inflatables, Dara having an easier time of it, leading the way, now. She pulled herself free from a last wiry clump that resembled an anchored tumbleweed, then broke into a run toward the one that lay near a pulsing eddy.

She stopped abruptly and turned to call to him. "Richard," she said, pointing down at the raft with a stricken face.

He hurried up to join her, expecting anything at this point: more bodies, a killer lying on his back inside, a submachine gun pointing their way . . .

What he saw had its own grim portent. From a distance, the raft had looked fine, and in fact, the inflated side closest to them was intact: a big puffy cushion of yellow rubberized fabric swelling with air. But the rest of it, floor and sides alike, had been hacked to shreds, one long chunk of fabric draped over the rocks like an exhausted tongue.

Corrigan glanced up quickly toward the rocky shelf, where the other raft lay. This one seemed fine, however, a pair of oars propped up by a forward seat.

"What's going on, Richard?"

Corrigan shook his head, trying to puzzle it out.

"Maybe there's a bomb in that one," Dara said.

He turned, scanned the still empty sandbar behind them. "I don't think so," he said.

"But why cut one raft to pieces and leave the other one alone?"

"Maybe someone has plans for it," he said, his eyes roaming up the trail that zigzagged down the cliff toward them.

"What do you mean?"

He heard the uncertainty in her voice. "There's someone who still needs a ride out of this place," he said. "I don't think they left it for us."

"But what if it's a trap?"

He gestured at the river. "You have any other suggestions?"

She stared back at him, shaking her head glumly. "I just hope you're right."

He gave her the best smile he could manage. "I'm going to bet my life on it," he said, and hurried up the slope toward the raft.

43

As he grasped the nylon line that ran through a series of guides along the top of the raft's flotation chambers, Corrigan felt a moment's hesitation. He glanced back at Dara, who stood a few feet away, her jaw set. No wavering there, he thought. As she'd said earlier, what was the worst that could happen? If he was wrong, if this was another trap, then they'd go to kingdom come together.

He bent down, tucked his fingers beneath the line, and lifted the nose of the craft. He hadn't taken his gaze from hers, nor did he look away as he started toward her, dragging the heavy thing over the lip of the ledge where it had been resting. He heard a dull thunk behind him—the oars tumbling together onto the rubbery floor of the craft—but he didn't even flinch.

He thought he saw Dara press her eyes together in a momentary gesture of relief, but he couldn't be sure. She was already hurrying his way, had caught one of the rear lines, helping lift the raft clear of the gravelly verge. She helped him maneuver the raft past the place where its ruined counterpart lay. He nodded, and together they tossed the raft toward the shallow eddy at the top of the sandbar. It slapped down with a splash, and Corrigan steadied the nose while she clambered in.

She leaned forward, grabbed one of the paddles, then sat back against the rear bumper. "What are you waiting for?" she said mildly.

"Nothing," he said. He was ankle deep in the frigid water, felt his shoes filling quickly. He glanced back across the expanse of sandbar toward the place where the trail angled down. No sign of anyone.

He stepped into the raft with one foot, felt it slide away from the shore with the pressure. He pulled his other foot from the muck, heard a sucking sound and a pop, then tumbled awkwardly into the raft. He felt a moment's scrape of gravel under his shoulder, then the smooth slip of the water's cushion sliding beneath him. He struggled into a sitting position and discovered they were twisting slowly out into the pool.

He found the other paddle, then turned back to Dara, who was using her blade as a rudder, angling them toward the current that raced past, just a few yards away. "You ever done this?" she asked.

"I had a rubber duck once," he said. "I think it was lost at sea."

"Just try and keep your end pointed downstream," she said. "I'll do what I can back here."

Corrigan nodded. He felt a tug beneath him, and suddenly they were in the grip of the current, moving broadside, threatening to spin about already. He dug his paddle, felt it nearly ripped from his hands by the water's force. He managed to hang on, and pulled back violently, sending them into a spin in the opposite direction.

He saw a flash of the rock wall on the far side of the canyon, then a glimpse of the sandbar whisking past. "Not so deep," Dara called. "Use the tip of your paddle, not the whole thing."

He nodded, lunging to the opposite side of the raft, stroking to bring them back around. The nose of the craft steadied, aiming them squarely downstream, now. He glanced over his shoulder and was startled to see the sandbar receding rapidly in the distance. Anybody'd intended to come that way, he thought, they'd just missed the last bus.

"Keep your eyes forward," Dara cried.

He turned back in time to see a huge boulder jutting out from the near canyon wall. He brought his paddle quickly to that side of the raft, and stroked, resisting the urge to gouge deeply into the greenish water. He saw a white swirl as his paddle dipped and rose . . . then the raft swung to the right obediently and the boulder slid harmlessly by.

"You're getting it," Dara called.

He raised a hand in acknowledgment, then quickly brought it back as a fulcrum for his paddle. The floor of the raft shuddered rhythmically beneath him, a strangely comforting feeling, he thought, given the fact that it was just a thin rubbery cloth separating him from the icy current.

He began to find his own rhythm, a couple of strokes on the left, a couple more on the right. With the force of the current what it was, the process wasn't exactly like work. And the walls of the canyon seemed to be narrowing, the speed of the current picking up steam.

He tried to remember what Donnelly had said. *Just a boat ride home,* right? A few hours of this and they'd be out of it, back into something resembling civilization. That's what Corrigan had dared to think, anyway, when he heard the low rumble building up ahead.

44

Is that what I think it is?" he called to Dara over his shoulder. The muffled echoes of his own voice bounced off the narrow canyon walls, interspersed with the piercing cries of the birds that cruised the surface of the water all around them, now. The rumbling sound that came from up ahead was still something he felt as much as heard, a sensation that made it seem even more threatening.

"Rapids," she called. "Don't worry. It always sounds worse than what it is."

"Sure," Corrigan called back. The rumble had already risen a notch or two, the sound of a half dozen trains thundering abreast. The birds soared and darted, apparently oblivious to the sound. They were too small to be vultures, Corrigan reassured himself. Dara had the right take.

"Just paddle like hell," she was saying. "Try to keep away from the rocks. If we go over, try to stay with the raft."

Corrigan nodded. How about a few more tasks as well? Walk on water, make the blind man see. His arms already felt leaden. He still wasn't hungry, but he knew the lack of food had taken its toll. Soon enough, though, he told himself. A few more hours at most.

He tried to clear his mind, brace himself for what was coming. He thought he could see an actual dip in the course of the river up ahead. As if the water were pouring off the edge of the earth. He saw a tendril of white froth shoot high into the air somewhere beyond that lip, then snap into nothingness, as if something had eaten it.

The raft bucked beneath him, suddenly, jouncing like a worn-out truck on a potholed stretch of road. They were sliding sideways, he realized, and he dug his paddle frantically into the opposing current, fighting to right them.

Then he saw it, a stretch of white water just seconds away, a roaring chute that seemed to tumble away forever. Go sideways into that, he thought, they might as well hang it up. He pulled hard at the water, realized he had overcorrected, then had to switch sides quickly to bring them back into line.

They clipped past a jagged rock on his left, then bounced off an even bigger boulder opposite. He tried to fend themselves off a third boulder with his paddle, but they were spinning with the full force of the rapids, now. His paddle glanced off the rock face, driving the handle back against his cheek with a stunning blow.

He bounced off the side of the raft, feeling the paddle sliding from his grasp. He lunged after it, but it was like trying to hold a boated fish. In an instant the thing was gone, vanished into the froth of whiteness that was everywhere. He was gasping, fighting to find something like air along with the freezing mist.

He realized he had been driven onto his back, his feet jammed against one side of the raft, his shoulders braced against the other. He could see Dara still battling the current, swinging her paddle from left to right, then back again. The current steadied momentarily, and she cut her gaze to him.

"Richard . . ." she began . . . and then it happened.

She had her paddle in front of her and was about to switch sides once again. He saw the grimace of pain flash across her face, saw her fling her arms high into the air and fall backward into the water. He was struggling up from the floor of the raft toward her when he felt the bottom of the river drop away beneath him.

He felt himself going over backward, caught a glimpse of Dara's heels as she hurtled past. In the next moment, he was under the water, the roar of the rapids gone silent. His shoulders slammed into a rock, and his body twisted away, spiraling into a deeper channel.

He clawed, fighting to bring himself up toward the surface, but it was useless. It was like being a balloon tethered to the back of a speeding bus. He managed to get himself turned around, his head pointed downstream, then began swimming again.

This time, he felt himself beginning to rise with the current. He sensed a vague, greenish glow before his eyes, a glow that lightened with every stroke. He came up out of the water, then, gasping, managed to catch one good breath before he found a boulder rushing squarely toward his face. His urge was to throw out his hand for protection, but some impulse reminded him of what had happened when he'd tried to use the paddle that way. At this speed, he would snap his arm like a dry stick.

Instead, he did the only thing he could: He tucked his head into his shoulder and rolled, taking most of the force of the blow on his back. He spun dizzily away, his shoulder on fire, but nothing broken, that much at least.

He was trying to get himself turned around, get himself braced for the next blow, when he realized it was over. He was lolling in a pool that had formed off to the side of the last stretch of rapids, his feet bumping against the sandy bottom. The raft was there, too, he saw, upended, its still-intact floor turned toward the sky, a paddle twirling slowly in the eddies beside it. He glanced up, made out a narrow line of blue that twisted between the cliff tops high above.

But Dara, he thought, panic surging through him. He flailed in the sluggish water, spinning himself about, ignoring the flash of pain where his shoulder had smashed into the rocks.

"Dara!" he called, his voice bounding off the sheer walls. There was a narrow sandbar rising up from the backwaters, there, a tiny version of the place where they had put into the river upstream. "Dara!" he called again.

He turned back to the river, his mind racing, trying to calculate the possibilities. Had the current swept her on downriver? Was she somewhere upstream, still struggling in that froth or, worse, pinned somehow beneath the current? And what had happened, anyway, what had caused that odd dive she'd suddenly taken into the water?

All the while, some outraged clamor was going on inside him—*not fair, not fair, it can't be happening*—but he pushed it away. No time to bitch, no time for feeling sorry.

Into the water, Corrigan. Find her. Sure, it's impossible. But find her, just the same.

And then, in the next moment, he saw that he had.

45

She lay motionless in a matching set of shallows directly across the quietly rushing river from him, one arm outflung on the sandy bank, her hand still clutching her paddle.

Corrigan was about to dive straight toward her when he realized the current would never let him make it across. Cursing, he turned and dived into the pool where he'd come out of the rapids, stroking back upstream until he was even with the last of the frothing steps. He launched himself into the current, then, feeling himself swept away like a twig. He stroked quickly, trying to keep himself pointed sideways across the canyon, but it was like fighting the worst riptide imaginable. He saw Dara's form rushing up toward him, and for a moment, it seemed that his idea would not work after all, that he might be swept by altogether, carried on down into that deep canyon and away.

He ducked his face back into the icy water, stroking on willpower alone. *Never mind if you wear yourself out, Corrigan. If you don't make it, just go ahead and drown . . .*

. . . until, with his lungs burning, his body going numb, he felt his hands clawing down through shallow water and into sand.

He struggled onto his hands and knees, blinking water from his eyes until he had his bearings. *Up there, up there, you jerk.*

He managed to get to his feet and began to run toward her, every footstep plunging deep into the soft sand. He stumbled back to his knees beside her, reached to turn her face up toward his.

Her eyes were closed, her mouth slack, and he put his ear to her chest, fighting back panic. He thought he felt her heart beating, and brought his paired fingers to her throat to be sure.

It *was* her pulse he felt there, he assured himself, though his own was pounding in his ears. He rose, got his hand under the back of her head, was easing her out of the water altogether, when he saw the blood.

He stared at the bright blossom that seeped high on her right shoulder, stunned. Then it began to fall into place: that sudden grimace on her face, her awkward, inexplicable dive . . .

"Bastard," he said, his head swiveling toward the top of the opposite cliff. "Sonofabitch fucking bastard . . ."

He felt her coughing, then, and turned back as her eyes flickered open. She coughed again, turning as water trickled down her chin. "Richard . . ." she said, her good hand going for his shirtfront.

She locked a wad of fabric in her hand, pulled herself up with a gasp of pain. She steadied herself momentarily, her eyes gradually coming into focus.

She glanced down at the wound on her shoulder, then back at him. "I thought I'd dreamed it," she said, her voice barely audible against the echo of the rapids behind them.

He shook his head, struggling to find words.

"Someone's up there," she said, glancing listlessly toward the distant rim. "We stole his boat, and now he's really pissed." She started to laugh, but the sound turned into a cough as more water passed from her lungs.

"At least it's not blood," she said, wiping at her chin.

Corrigan pressed his forehead to hers, fighting the urge to weep. "Ah, Dara," he said. "Whatever it takes, I promise you. Whatever it takes."

She leaned back hard against him, and he felt her breath come out in a sigh. "Whatever happens," she said weakly. "I appreciate the thought."

46

He can't stay down there forever," Nelia Esteban said.

Bright glanced up, noticing that the sun was balanced, now, at the jagged line of mountains to the west. Half an hour of light left, not much more. He found himself thinking of the Indian he'd met, the proprietor of that bizarre trading post. Just a few days before, really, but it seemed so much longer.

"He will if he's dead," Bright told her.

"There's a point," she said.

"If he isn't, he'll have to make his move soon," he told her, his eyes fixed on the water far below. The rapids where the raft had flipped were on their right, upstream. On their left, downstream, stretched a long straight course where the water ran swiftly. There was just one place where the man could be hiding, *if* he had somehow managed to survive that formidable stretch of rapids, that is: One spot directly beneath them, where their view of the water was blocked by the jutting cliffs.

"Maybe he'll wait until morning," Nelia offered.

"Would you?" Bright asked. "Cold and wet, without food, without shelter?" No, if the man *had* survived, he would be making his dash any moment, now. Hoping to cross that long straight course ahead with just enough light to guide him to a safe landing above the next set of rapids beyond. Hoping that someone like Bright was not up there to stitch the length of his spine with blue dotting.

"I don't know what I would do," Nelia was saying. "But it might have been better if you'd shot the man first."

Bright glanced at her. He had been thinking about how that Indian would have handled this matter. Hold his position atop these cliffs forever, Bright supposed. Or at least for the amount of time it would take for the white man's carcass to rot, for his bones to bleach white in the sun. That's how the Indian had struck him, after all: a man who had always been here, a man who would outlast them all.

He turned to Nelia, offered her the rifle he was holding. "Maybe you'd like to take over."

She raised an eyebrow, shook her head. "I do my best work close in."

He gave her a smile. "I can attest to that."

The sun had slipped below the horizon, and Bright saw a dark shape whizzing past them, soaring out over the dizzying space of the canyon. A bat, he realized, as another and another followed. There was a narrow fissure opening out onto the platform where they stood. Bright had examined the cave far enough to satisfy himself that no predator was using the place as a den, but now that the sun had begun to sink, he realized that he'd been wrong: Certain creatures *had* found a home there after all, were hurtling out to hunt with the steadily increasing breeze pouring out of the cave's mouth. It was as though the mountain itself had life, he thought, as though the old rock were exhaling a sigh at the end of another wearying day.

"Better go inside and check on our charge," Bright said, motioning toward the entrance to the cave. "We may have to be moving soon."

She gave him a look, then glanced over the side. "Couldn't we just toss him down there with the others?"

"Wish we could, love." He smiled at her. "Wish we could."

He checked his watch as she moved grudgingly off toward the cave. Perhaps fifteen more minutes of light.

He glanced down toward the bottom of the canyon, fifty feet, he guessed. Perhaps a little more.

Reason told him they were both dead—one shot, the other drowned in that mass of rapids—and his plans did not call for a lengthy vigil. Things had already become messy enough. He'd hoped the explosion at the cache point would have eliminated the last of them—another unfortunate mishap, this one to be explained by the inadvertent detonation of trail-clearing dynamite left in storage too long—but then that was the thing about the best-laid plans, wasn't it? Whatever might go wrong would. That's why they had taken up this post, why Bright had not truly been surprised to see the two of them coming down the river.

He regretted having to shoot the woman, for her death could hardly be explained away as an accident, but their choices had become limited, and the fallback plan would have to be employed: Bright would be sure to see that the rifle he had used to kill her ended up in the hands of the authorities. Her death would be clearly attributable to that fearsome party of militiamen who'd bought their last weapons at Mighty Malcolm's Arsenal and Ordnance. Two deaths by gunshot, if the man who might be hiding down below turned up, that is.

Bright tried to put himself in the place of this hypothetical man. It was highly unlikely but still possible that he was not drowned, that he had washed up on some spit of sand like Crusoe, hunkered now beneath the overhanging rocks, perhaps with his life raft bobbing nearby, perhaps not, mourning the loss of his companion, and surely burdened by the awareness that he was the last.

Five minutes of light left, Bright reckoned, and noted that the steady breeze from the cave had dropped off. The sun was down behind the distant peaks, the river beginning to glow in what was reflected high above. No way the man would venture out at night. Trying to run that mad river in the dark would be suicide in itself.

Bright turned back to the canyon and eased his rifle up. He activated the nightscope mechanism and used its unearthly glowing eye to scan the river. He made out the light rifflings where the last of the turbulence from the rapids gave out and the river began its long, smooth descent. The hulk of a flood-deposited tree was lodged at the base of the opposite cliff, there, part in, part out of the water. One of its bare limbs shuddered in the current, disappeared beneath the surface, then rose up quivering again.

Bright followed the main trunk back toward the overhang, but the jutting rocks cut off the view before he could reach its base. The great tree was just one more casualty of nature, he mused, a different sort of body washed up on shore.

He was about to turn away when he saw it, a vague blur of yellow nudging out along the length of the fallen tree. *Ah, yes,* he thought as his finger eased inside the trigger guard and he firmed the rifle's stock against his shoulder. *At the eleventh hour, he comes.*

The nose of the raft inched out a foot, then two, then three, bouncing against the trunk in the current. Another foot, and another, and then the whole of the raft was in view, oddly hesitant in its motions when it should be whisking away with the current.

He scanned the raft back to front with the scope, then back again, squinting to be sure. But there was no one inside, and the raft had stopped its forward progress altogether, was bobbing obstinately in the current beside the fallen tree.

He thought he could make out a line trailing off the back of the craft and into the water, and shook his head. The thing had probably been hung up in the tangle of half-submerged brush all this time, had only now worked itself along to the point where Bright could see it.

The raft's appearance had answered his questions, at any rate. Had the man survived the rapids, he already would have made his way to where the raft was tangled. Instead, the craft itself was simply making its own way along, trying like a riderless horse to find the way home.

Bright stared down at the shuddering craft, wondering if he should send a few shots into the flotation chambers or if he should simply let nature take its course. He was still considering the choices, still held the wavering craft in the sights of his scope, when he heard the sounds behind him.

He turned toward the mouth of the cave, thinking that it might be Nelia. Or bats, possibly. More of the creatures squeaking and clicking their way out of the cave. But as he turned, he realized that he was wrong. The sounds were coming from the other side of the rocky platform, something over the other side of the cliff, it seemed.

"Nelia," he called toward the mouth of the cave. "Better come out here, now," and he hurried off to see.

47

Corrigan felt his foot give way momentarily, heard the clatter of rocks falling away beneath him before his boot slid into a crevice and steadied him. He was nearly horizontal, braced across the narrow fissure that climbed the last several feet toward the ledge above, his shoulders pressed against the rock behind him, his feet jammed against the rock face opposite.

He fought the urge to look down, knowing that the sight might freeze him. No point in looking down, anyway, not again. The light was nearly gone, now, and he'd already had the signal from Dara, just as they'd planned. She'd used her good arm to swing what was left of her shirt as a banner, what they hadn't had to use for bandage and a sling, that is.

It meant she'd sent the raft floating on down the river, as far as the tether line would let it, anyway. In the dim light it might attract the attention of whoever might still be up there, waiting, bring a shot or at least serve as a distraction for Corrigan to make some final move those last few feet toward the top. Not much of a plan, but they were just about out of options.

There was no way to have foreseen the matter of this last obstacle, however, not from the bottom of the canyon where they'd hatched their plan. A dozen feet of nearly vertical rock face, no other passage, simply no way . . . This eroded chimney where he'd managed to wedge himself upward bit by bit was the only hope of making it to the top.

Corrigan, still willing himself not to look down, took rapid inventory. The raft sent out as decoy, no shots fired. Which meant that maybe no one was up there, after all, that he and Dara had been given up for dead.

On to the bad news. His ass was stuck in a very literal

crack, and he'd just made enough noise to alert even the most distracted of snipers.

He wriggled his shoulders a few inches higher, moved his feet a corresponding distance. He had had his eyes on a loop of gnarled root dangling beneath the overhang of the platform, had been inching himself toward it for the last several minutes. The root *looked* strong, a wilderness version of a passenger's strap, just waiting for him to grab hold, pull himself on over.

He prayed that his feet would hold in place this time—*kiss it good-bye if they don't*—and lunged for the root. He felt his hand catch the rough surface, felt the root give way a bit. A fine and sandy dirt showered down into his eyes, his mouth, the sweaty folds of his neck, but the root shuddered and held.

Corrigan was holding his pistol in his right hand, now. He took a deep breath, clutched the root tightly, and allowed himself to swing backward, trusting all his weight to that single handhold. He would bounce himself off the rock, use his momentum to swing himself over the edge, and he would either make it or go sailing out into oblivion, all or nothing at all, he was thinking . . .

. . . when he heard the explosion just above him, felt rock fragments burst hot against his cheek.

His backward motion was all that had saved him, it occurred to him, even as he bounded off the rock face, his feet sliding out into space. He swung out into nothingness, caught a glimpse of a figure standing above him, a rifle braced his way.

In the instant he had, Corrigan squeezed off two shots, all instinct, no aim. Then he was back under the lip of the cliff again, still dangling by one hand. He flailed about with his gun hand until he caught hold of the root and could finally pull himself back into the fissure, get himself wedged again.

He heard a clattering sound—something falling to the rocks up above—then silence. He got his feet tucked, steadied himself, waiting for more shots, for shouts, a general alarm . . . but there was nothing more.

He'd been lucky, he told himself. His shots had been true. Or the man had simply gone off for reinforcements. In either case, he could not wait. His legs were already trembling from the strain. A few more moments and he'd lose what little strength remained, it wouldn't matter whether there was anyone waiting up there or not.

He closed his eyes for an instant, forcing himself to visualize once again how the movement would work. Then he let himself swing back again, letting his momentum build, banging hard against the rock, kicking with everything he had, his feet flying out into space . . .

. . . and this time carried it out, flinging himself up and over, onto the rocky ledge. He rolled once, came up in a crouch, his pistol braced . . .

. . . and found the tall man who had just tried to kill him moving back across the platform, his rifle dangling from his arm. He had his hand clamped to his opposite shoulder, blood flowing from between his fingers.

"Stop right there," Corrigan said, fighting to get his breath under control, feeling his finger tighten on the trigger of Ben Donnelly's pistol.

The man stared evenly back at him. No fear there, Corrigan saw, not a hint of submission. Just simple acceptance of the situation. There was no way he could lift that rifle in time, not with a pistol already leveled at him.

"Let it slide off your shoulder, ease it to the ground," Corrigan said, and the man obeyed.

"Now, step back," Corrigan continued. "Very, very slowly."

The man took one careful step back, and Corrigan straightened, then began edging toward the weapon, when he saw the man's eyes flicker. Corrigan sensed movement in the shadows, something coming at him out of a dark gash in the sheer rock face at the back of the platform, and how in the hell could that be . . . ?

He spun around, trying to bring his pistol up, even as he realized it would be too late.

A woman was standing there, a step or two out of the mouth of a cave, he saw, her own pistol braced in both hands, its muzzle as big as a howitzer's, or so it seemed, and aimed just below his chin as she squared up to fire. She would be just a split second ahead of Corrigan, who was still swinging his pistol up, but a split second was all it took, wasn't it?

So, there he had it. *A fine job, as far as you've taken it,*

Richie-boy. Good work, for a transit cop. But now it was over and all the struggling could stop. . . .

He saw the muzzle of the pistol blossom into fire, heard the explosion and the shattering of fragments at his feet, then stared in amazement as the woman went onto her knees with a groan, her pistol clattering over the side of the cliff. There was a man standing there behind her, Corrigan saw, a familiar-looking man with a silvery shock of hair and a badly bruised face. He was holding a jagged rock, its point smeared with blood where he'd just brained her.

Fielding Dawson, Corrigan realized—his face was battered, his stare was dazed, but there was no mistaking who it was. This pair had been holding Fielding Dawson captive. . . .

Corrigan heard a scraping sound behind him and spun to see the tall man going for the rifle that lay on the rocky floor of the platform between them. Instinctively, Corrigan strode forward and roundhoused his gun hand into the man's wounded shoulder. He felt maximum resistance, heard a wet crunching sound as the heavy steel cracked into flesh, heard the man's grunt as he went down.

Just as quickly, his own legs went out from under him, and he fell hard on the rocks, his pistol tumbling away as the woman clawed atop him. Blood was streaming down her forehead, but it made no difference. She'd scrambled up in those brief seconds, and tackled him. In the next instant, she was astride him, her knees pinning his arms, the rifle raised high in her hands. She wasn't going to bother trying to get it into a position to fire.

She lifted the weapon high, until the heavy stock was level with her nose, then brought it down toward his face. At the last instant, Corrigan twisted aside. He felt the shock as the heavy weapon slammed into the rock a millimeter from his skull, sensed her jerking back for another blow. She was about to bring the rifle down again, when the shot rang out, and she stiffened.

The rifle slid from her hands, banging onto the rocks by Corrigan's side. There was another shot, and a patch of flesh erupted high on her cheek. Then she went over on her face.

Corrigan scrambled up to find Fielding Dawson advancing toward the woman's fallen form, his face contorted in rage.

"Bitch . . ." he snarled, and jammed Corrigan's pistol into the flesh behind her ear. "Fucking bitch!"

He was about to squeeze the trigger again when Corrigan pulled his arm away. Dawson turned in surprise. "She's responsible," he said. "I saw her kill Sonia Ashmead. She wanted to kill us all—"

"She's dead," Corrigan told him, prying the pistol from Dawson's grasp. He gestured around the empty platform, at the mouth of the cave. "We may need the round."

Dawson stared at him dumbly. It took a moment, but finally he understood. He turned to regard the dark maw of the cave, where the man had disappeared. "You're going in there?"

Corrigan stared at him. "You want me to let him go?"

Dawson stared. "No. Of course not." He pointed down at the rifle. "We've got his gun, though. . . ."

"Unless he's got another stashed in that cave," Corrigan said. "We can't take that chance."

Dawson nodded, glancing at the cave. "I'm going with you."

Corrigan shook his head. "You stay here. I'm the guy who saves your life, remember? If I'm not the one who comes back out of that cave, you'd better use this."

Corrigan picked up the rifle, then handed it over to Dawson.

He gestured toward the river. "Dara's down there, waiting," Corrigan said. "She's alive, but she's hurt. You might be her only chance. Can you get her out?"

Dawson glanced over the edge, then back at Corrigan. "You can count on it," he said.

"Good," Corrigan said. Then he turned and hurried inside the cave.

It had been dark enough outside, but a few steps inside the cave and he was moving almost totally by feel. He'd been in the subway during power outages, of course, but there had been emergency lights, and he'd always had his flashlight, too.

He heard a rasping, whirring sound as something came at him, and he ducked away instinctively. At first he thought it was something thrown, but then he realized. A bat. Noiseless as a shadow. Then another, and another after that.

Corrigan stood quietly as the creatures whisked out the entrance of the cave. He was listening, trying to calculate the odds, trying to put himself inside the skin of the one he was following. No smudge man, this time, scared witless and just trying to find a place to roost. Corrigan had seen the look on the tall man's face: *One of us will die, my friend.* Still, the man was unarmed, presumably, and wounded, no telling just how badly. It was always possible, wasn't it? *He's just crawled in here to die.*

Corrigan wanted it to be true, of course. He wanted more than anything to walk away and leave it just like that. He'd seen the blood spilling from the man's body, proof that at least one of his shots had been good.

But he'd seen worse messes before . . . so much blood on the platform, so much trailing up the subway steps you'd think there'd be a pile of bodies on the landing above . . . but you go on up with your gun hand ready and find nothing, no bodies, no one dead, maybe some guy propped against the tiles, playing a jolly tune on a violin—*Wassup, Officer?*—just some folks passing through and bleeding, had their little fun and gone home. . . .

Sorry, Richie-boy, you're going to have to keep on going, finish this business firsthand. . . .

Corrigan shook off the thoughts and moved forward.

It was utterly dark and quiet, now. The last of the light and even the sound of the river below were snuffed out the moment he eased around a bend in the narrow passage. He sensed the press of dank air against his face, a breeze that coursed through the cave like the musty tunnel drafts back home. Two thousand miles into the wilderness, and he'd managed to get himself right back where he'd started.

He felt something wet on the rock where he'd let his hand rest, and brought his fingers near his face. Warm and coppery, the greasiness of blood. He wiped his fingers quickly on his pant leg.

He could wait this out a bit, he reasoned, give the man a chance to weaken. But on the other hand, what if it worked the other way around? What if the man was not as seriously wounded as it seemed? What if at this very moment he was gathering steam, about to make a charge?

Or what if there was another entrance somewhere? That draft moving through the passage, it had to come from somewhere, after all.

What if that's how the man had gotten here in the first place? Another entrance. He could be on his way out right now. Or headed toward some cache of weapons, a band of reinforcements . . .

Corrigan turned and glanced behind himself, still wavering. He could see the dregs of light reflected past the bend in the passageway, there, his trusty, screwed-up vision doing the best it could, feeding him the last scraps of brightness as if it were silver plate itself. Everything in him yearned to go that way, just go back outside and forget his quarry. . . .

He was still debating it when he felt something change in the nature of the cave draft at his back, the most subtle of shifts in its course, in direction. Nothing like those great drafts that burst out of a tunnel's mouth, ahead of the charge of a train, of course. But what was coming at him now was every bit as powerful, and deadly.

Corrigan crouched instinctively as the shadow hurtled toward him with a roar all its own. The man's weight slammed into him, and he fell forward, felt his hand crack against a rocky wall, felt the pistol fall free.

There was an arm locked around his throat, another hand that levered his head forward. His breath was already gone, stars pinging behind his eyes. He felt his feet stumbling awkwardly beneath him, tangling in other feet. He was a double creature, now, four arms, four legs, one half bent upon destroying the other. His own arms flailed in the darkness, useless, unable to reach the creature at his back.

Darkness piled on darkness. A few moments more, and it would be endless night.

He heard rasping breath at his ear, sounds of effort, as they stumbled over a rift on the rubble-strewn floor. *He's hurt, Richie-boy. Remember? You hit him with one of those shots.*

Corrigan's knees cracked painfully into a wall of rock, then his face. He managed to get his hands in front of himself, and shoved back at the rock with everything he could muster.

They were stumbling backward, then, two sets of feet in a blind dance . . . *Still dying, here, Richie-boy . . .*

He caught a glimpse of light as the mouth of the tunnel

whirled past and was gone again . . . then came a moment's
weightlessness, and they both were going down.

He landed on his back on top of the man, who uttered
another groan with the impact. Corrigan felt the pressure
loosen at his throat—a passage the size of a thread there, now,
perhaps. He choked for air and pistoned his elbow backward
against the man's blood-soaked shoulder.

He felt the man's grip give, and he bucked forward, twisting free at last.

He was on his hands and knees, gasping, forcing himself to
focus. *Only a second before he's back on board. Go after him.
Now. Go for him before he goes for you.*

Corrigan turned and lunged through the darkness, felt his
hand brush over wet cloth . . . then there was nothing but the
sounds of receding footsteps.

He groped about for his pistol, but it was impossible in the
darkness. No more time for that, he thought. He scrambled to
his feet, started moving in the direction the man had gone, the
breeze that coursed through the tunnel full in his face, now.

There had to be another entrance that way, Corrigan
thought. That's where the man was headed. *Just let him go,* a
part of his brain willed. *Let well enough alone.* But the same
body that had propelled him after smudge man, that had propelled him all this way, disregarded those orders. He didn't
want to hurry off into that darkness ahead. But his feet carried
him there nonetheless.

He couldn't see a thing, of course. No more than a dozen
steps forward, and his forehead cracked off a low-hanging
shelf. Another dozen steps, and he ran squarely into a wall
where the passage made a turn. He paused, straining for any
sound. Possibly the sound of a dislodged stone up ahead, but
so hard to tell.

He put out a hand to guide himself forward, and felt something live whisk against his arm. He staggered back, his hands
held high to ward off another blow, then released his breath
when he sensed the flutter of wings past his face and realized
he'd simply dislodged a sleeping bat.

He pushed himself off the rock wall, rounded the turn, took
a few more steps, and found himself stymied. He groped in
the darkness like a blind man, searching for the continuation
of the passage at chest height, then dropped to his knees, but it

was useless. He realized that the breeze that had pressed against his face was gone.

A dead end. He'd missed a turn somewhere. Or he'd been mistaken and the man had escaped past him in the first place. He was out there on the platform, had killed Dawson, was waiting for him to blunder out so the job could be finished. . . .

He forced himself to calm, to turn back the way he had come, one step, two, three, then back to the cleft where he'd been moments before . . . and felt the rush of the tunnel's breath back on his face.

He sensed the slightest change in the character of the darkness around him. Still inky, to be sure, but one click lessened, or so it seemed. He held his breath, listening, heard another stone dislodged, this time he was sure of it. He groped about, puzzled. The breeze told him there was another passage, but there was simply no opening, just the one narrow passage back the way he had come, the way that led to the front of the cave. . . .

There was flittering movement from somewhere nearby, and he hesitated even though he sensed it was too far away to be a threat. A shadow passing across a shadow, he thought . . . and then, as a fine skein of dust drifted down over his face and shoulders, he realized.

He swung his gaze straight upward, then, squinting as more fine particles drifted down, and saw it: a square of twilight sky a dozen feet or so above his head, and the vague shape of a man levering himself out of the hole.

A natural chimney that climbed up through the rock, Corrigan realized. He groped above him for a handhold and pulled himself up, twisting his shoulders to make the fit. Once he had pulled his feet up after him, it was like climbing a steep staircase, his back pressed against the upper wall, his feet digging into what felt like primitive steps carved into the rock.

He hesitated near the top, raising his head cautiously . . . in time to see the man poised with what looked like a shard of tree limb high over his head. Corrigan ducked back as the heavy limb shattered against the rocks just inches away.

The man raised his club for another blow, but Corrigan caught the end of the limb and shoved upward with all he had. He felt resistance up there, but the man was standing and Corrigan had a tunnel rat's advantage, wedged against the rock as he shoved.

He felt the man go over backward, and in the next instant, Corrigan tumbled out into the twilight.

They'd come out atop a platform jutting from the surrounding forest, a ledge that seemed much higher than the place where the man had set up his sniper's post. The tethered raft was a vague glowing dot from this vantage point, the river squeezed to a dim narrow line of silver.

The man who'd just tried to kill him had fallen halfway down a steep slope covered with loose rock, but was clawing himself back up toward Corrigan like a machine, thrashing upward a foot at a time, then sliding back two. Near the edge of the precipice, where dislodged rocks cascaded off in a knee-weakening shower, the man slid finally to a stop, balancing himself on a narrow ledge that snaked away toward the forest.

The man glanced off in the direction of the trees, then up at Corrigan, then over his shoulder at the drop below.

Still favoring that arm, Corrigan saw, and there was a dark stain on the side of the light jacket he wore. But it was only a few dozen steps along that narrow parapet into the forest. Once he made that cover and was gone, he could wait patiently for night, circle around, come back for them in the dark. . . .

At Corrigan's feet lay the limb the man had tried to kill him with. He bent and picked it up, tested the heft. It would do in a pinch, he thought. And this was very definitely a pinch.

It was the last thing on earth that he wanted to do, but what choice did he have? Using the limb as a prop to keep from skidding down the treacherous slope to his death, he began his own uncertain descent toward the ledge.

By the time he'd slid to his own stop, the tall man was halfway across the ledge. But things were a bit trickier than they'd seemed at first.

The ledge, narrow enough to begin with, had narrowed to mere inches where the man stood now. To make it all the way across, you'd have to lean into the rock, edge your way along, pray nothing—not the slightest breeze, not the merest nudge of a worm—came along to urge you off. Corrigan thought of Chipper, suddenly, that benign giant picking his way across a similar rockface. A few feet away stood the man who had killed him, Corrigan was sure of it.

Corrigan saw the look on the man's face as he glanced back, calmly measuring distances, calculating odds. Corrigan glanced out over the yawning chasm beside them, toward the rocks and the water below.

Corrigan shrugged. He knew what it would mean to take that fall, of course, but he felt a curious detachment at the sight.

"Frightening, isn't it?" the man said to him.

Corrigan watched him carefully. "Not so bad," he said. "Of course, my perspective is a little messed up." He pointed at his eye as he moved out along the shelf. "I *know* it's a long way down, but it just doesn't look like it to me."

Corrigan flicked his foot, toeing a sizable rock out into the void. It hurtled down and down, cracked off the steep face a hundred feet or so below. He had the limb raised up like a prod, now, judging the distance left between the two of them.

"Why don't we talk," the man said, his eyes on the end of the limb. "No need for us to be taking such chances."

Corrigan paused. He gave the limb an exploratory thrust, a fencer with a prehistoric sword.

The man edged back.

"I want to know who put you up to this," Corrigan said. "What crackpot group are you involved with?" He moved in another foot, jabbed again. "Or is it something personal?"

The man steadied himself, glanced over his shoulder again at the narrowing ledge behind him.

"Last chance," Corrigan said. He jabbed the limb at the man's midsection, stopped an inch short.

"You seem to have me at a disadvantage," the man said evenly.

Corrigan thought his control was impressive. He'd hate to have their positions reversed.

"Just back off a bit. Give me room to stand," the man said.

"Who was it?" Corrigan repeated. He sent the tip of the limb at the man's head, dislodged another chunk of rock, which rolled off his shoulder, down into nothingness.

"Edward Soldinger," the man said, his gaze steady.

Corrigan stared, dumbstruck. "Dawson's security chief?"

"He hired me two months ago, along with Nelia," the man continued, without acknowledging Corrigan's surprise. "My name is Bright, by the way."

The man's tone suggested he was ready to shake hands. Corrigan shook his head. "Soldinger . . . . ? Responsible for all this? It doesn't make sense."

Corrigan saw something in the man's eyes, realized he'd nearly lost his focus. He brought the tip of the limb up, one hand braced on its top, the other ready to piston it forward, into the man's gut. He'd have one chance, he thought. Just one.

"Perhaps someone should have looked more thoroughly into Mr. Soldinger's background." The man affected a smile, but his eyes were intent, again seeming to calculate the distance between them, the odds of his own best shot. "He has many friends in this part of the country, men who hold fast to their causes, Mr. Corrigan."

"Soldinger's a closet militiaman? That's what this is all about?"

The man didn't move, though his expression reflected a shrug. "We did not dwell upon his reasons for the work at issue."

"In other words, you're just a hired hand."

This time the man did lift his shoulders slightly. "I do a job," he said. "Politics are no concern of mine. You of all people should understand. A police officer who chases a frightened, unarmed man into the path of a speeding train. To some, your actions seem heroic. To those who know the truth . . ." He shook his head, and Corrigan fought a pang despite himself.

It was a slight distraction, but it was enough. In the next instant, the man made his move. He rushed forward, his arms outstretched, giving Corrigan no time to think.

He brought the point of the limb up in reflex, and the tip of it traveled perhaps half a foot before it met the point of the man's chin. The man tottered, made a lunge, got one hand around the limb's jagged end. He jerked hard, trying to yank the weapon from Corrigan's grasp, but his foot slipped on the rocky ledge.

Corrigan had expected strength, there, but he wasn't really

prepared for this. He felt the force jolt him all the way to the muscles of his back. *No contest, Richie-boy. Better go to Plan B . . .* and as the man jerked again, Corrigan simply let go.

"Damnit . . ." the man said, his eyes widening as he realized that the limb was all his, now, that his balance had made an entirely unexpected shift. His mouth formed an "O" of surprise. And in the next instant he was off into space.

He toppled backward, his gaze burning into Corrigan's, his arms whirling backward as if he might be trying to swim in air. A second more, and his face was lost in the gloom. His body turned over once, twice, then began to tumble wildly until he was gone altogether, the darkness so deep in the narrow canyon, Corrigan never saw him hit bottom.

Corrigan stood there for a moment, staring down into the abyss, thinking that it might as easily have been himself. And then he turned and began to climb.

48

On his way back through the cave, Corrigan spent a few moments searching for the pistol he'd lost during the struggle, but he was no more successful this time than he'd been before. When he emerged quietly from the mouth of the cave, he saw that the moon had already cleared the crest of the canyon top above, had bathed the rocky platform in a dim light.

Fielding Dawson's form was outlined clearly at the edge of the cliff. The governor held the rifle pointed toward the bottom of the canyon, his eye pressed intently to the nightscope's port as Corrigan moved toward him.

"See anything down there?" Corrigan asked, barely a step away.

The governor turned with a start, dropping the rifle at port arms. "Good God. You scared me. I could have fallen."

"That would be a hell of a note," Corrigan said, glancing down.

"I thought I heard noises a while ago," Dawson said, staring at him. He gestured over the side, then, and shook his head. "I couldn't see anything." He hesitated. "No sign of Dara, either."

"I told her to sit tight." Corrigan nodded. "Mind if I have a look?" He reached out for the rifle, and the governor handed the weapon over.

Corrigan quickly scanned the bottom of the canyon through the otherworldly glow of the nightscope. As Dawson said, there was no sign of Dara, but that didn't mean anything, did it? He turned back to the man at his side, his mind still whirling with what he'd been told on the ledge. So much had happened, so many people had died, he was so exhausted. . . .

"What happened to Bright?" Dawson asked.

Corrigan hesitated. He thought about telling him what

Bright had said, about Soldinger, but this was hardly the time. The important thing was to get out of there, and he didn't need Dawson distracted. Besides, what was he going to say? *Hey, Guv, I was just talking to this hired killer. He told me your security man was the one trying to kill you.*

Even if it was true, why should Dawson believe him? And even if he did believe him, hero junkie that he was, Dawson would be bound to confront Soldinger himself once they got back to the lodge, give the man the chance to deny everything.

What witnesses, what proof did Corrigan have, after all? Two dead killers? Corrigan shook his head. He needed a plan, and right now he couldn't take the time to form one. He glanced back down into the canyon where Dara awaited. Cold and hungry, a bullet lodged inside her, no idea what was going on up here . . .

"He fell," Corrigan said finally, gesturing with his chin. "Off the side of the cliff."

Dawson stared back at him for a moment. "Jesus." He took a deep breath. "So, what do we do now?"

Corrigan hefted the rifle, thinking about what it had taken to climb up here, wondering just how long it would take to duplicate that feat in reverse, if it would even be possible in the dark, without ropes, without any kind of equipment. He thought of Dara lying down there, the time ticking away. He stared over the precipice, down at the swirling pool where he and Dara had tumbled out of the rapids. The water was directly below them; they were half again as close to the bottom, here . . .

After a moment, he glanced up. "Can you swim, Governor?" he asked.

"Of course I can swim," Dawson said. "Why . . . ?"

"Then get ready," Corrigan said, and pushed him over the side.

The governor went out into space with a cry, his arms whirling, legs kicking as if he were pedaling a runaway bicycle. Corrigan watched him go for a moment, hoping Dawson would forgive him, then tossed the rifle aside onto the rocks.

He heard the splash from far below and hoped the governor had been telling the truth about the swimming part. It was a long way down, Corrigan thought, but the way he saw it, he was fresh out of options. He wished there had been someone there to give him a push as well, but in this case he was on his own. He took a deep breath, then, and followed after Fielding Dawson.

49

It seemed to take forever, his breathless plunge through the air. He'd caught a glimpse of the bright disk of the moon on his way over the edge, but that sight was quickly gone, leaving him rushing down through the darkness, his hands at his sides, his feet arrowed firmly beneath him.

When he hit the water, it was like entering liquid ice. The water slammed up against him, jolting his head back, but wrenching at his billowing clothing as well, braking his descent. There was no way to know how deep he plunged, but by the time his feet struck the sandy bottom, his ears were throbbing and seemed ready to burst from the pressure.

He bent his knees and shoved off the bottom, clawing his way toward the glittering orb of light above. When he came back out into the air, it was like entering the grasp of the moon itself.

"Richard?" He heard the voice bounding off the sides of the canyon. "Richard! Are you all right?"

He treaded water, glanced about blindly, holding himself against the gentle current of the pool. He shook the water from his eyes until he could focus, made a half circle in the frigid water, then finally found her: Dara, propped against a boulder at the shoreline of the sandbar at the far side of the backwater. "Over this way," she called, her voice weak and quavering over the low rumble of the rapids upstream.

He lifted a hand in acknowledgment, tried to raise his head up for a better look. "What about Dawson?" he cried, still gasping for breath.

"Dawson . . . ? I don't know. I heard something . . ."

"Down here," a strained voice called from the darkness.

Corrigan managed to twist himself around and stared downstream, oriented at last. He saw Dawson's form floundering about in the water near the raft. "Just hold on," he called across the water. "We'll be with you in a minute."

He turned, then, and began to swim toward shore. He felt his knees strike the rocky verge first, then felt the clutch of her hand at his back.

"Oh, Richard," she said, her own voice weak and breathless. She was on her hands and knees as well, pressing herself against him. "When I saw someone falling . . ." She stopped, her face buried against his shoulder.

"It's all right," he told her.

He got his feet under him, eased her back against the boulder where she'd been lying.

"What happened up there?" She shook her head dazedly. "I heard shots. I was so afraid. . . ."

"There were two of them," he said, cradling her in his arms. "At least I think that's all there were. They had Dawson. Both of them are dead, now."

"But how . . . ?"

"It doesn't matter," he told her. He glanced downstream toward the spot where the raft bobbed on its makeshift tether. Dawson had clambered up onto the limb of a tree that jutted from the water like a giant, desperate arm.

Corrigan put a hand on her forehead, smoothed her damp hair back. "All that's important now is getting you out. That's what we're going to do."

He glanced down at her face, her eyes squeezed shut with pain, with fatigue. "Can you hear me?"

She managed a feeble nod, still clutching tightly to his shirt. "I'm going to get the raft, now," he told her. "You just hang in there, rest until I get back . . ." But the last was a waste of breath, he realized, for she was already out.

He hesitated for a moment, made sure her pulse was steady, her breathing regular, then slipped back into the frigid water and swam downstream. It was only a few easy strokes before he was able to leave off swimming altogether and guide himself along to the raft by the tether. He felt his legs tangling in the submerged limbs of the fallen tree, and used that leverage to hold the raft steady while Fielding Dawson picked his way along the big, half-sunken limb.

"You could have killed me," Dawson grumbled as he made his way into the shuddering raft.

"There wasn't time for legislative debate, Governor."

Dawson managed a nod. "I suppose there wasn't."

Corrigan shoved them out from the tangle of limbs and began to swim upstream, one hand still on the tether. "I could use your help, now."

Dawson picked up a paddle and went to work. In a minute or so, they were back at the sandbar, dragging the raft through the shallows toward Dara's limp form.

"Is she . . . ?"

"She'll be all right," Corrigan told him. "But we've got to get her down, get her to a hospital."

Dawson nodded. He had his arms clutched about him in the chill, was staring up at the sky. "Can we handle it in the dark?"

"We don't have any choice," Corrigan said. He gestured at Dara's inert form. "She's in no shape to wait for morning."

"Besides," he said, glancing up at the looming cliffs. "We can't risk more of these lunatics showing up."

Dawson nodded grudgingly. "You're right, I guess. But what if there are more rapids like those?" Dawson pointed upstream.

"Then we'll pull over and wait for better light," Corrigan said. "But we can't just sit here."

He pulled his end of the raft up onto the shore, then, and bent to get his hands under Dara's shoulders. He glanced up at Dawson, but the governor was already bending to help.

50

Did they say anything to you?" Corrigan asked Dawson as they paddled down a long, straight course of river.

"Very little," Dawson said. "They just went about their business, seemed almost contemptuous of me. The only time they said the slightest thing revealing was when that woman looked at me and said, 'I'll bet you wish you could get your hands on a gun, now.'" Dawson shook his head.

"It made me think that this all had something to do with my gun-control proposals." His voice faltered. "When I think that all this could have been prompted by my own convictions . . ."

He trailed off, and Corrigan nodded, softening his voice. "They say what happened to your wife?"

Corrigan thought he saw the man's shoulders stiffen. "Nothing," he said. "They simply ignored me when I asked. They were monsters." Corrigan heard the tone of loss and outrage in Dawson's voice.

"So, what were their plans for you?"

Dawson stroked again, then brought his paddle across his knees and turned over his shoulder. "They didn't say, not in so many words. 'We'll give them something that they won't forget,' that's all Bright said. I didn't see the point of pressing them on it."

"I can understand," Corrigan said. He'd had a bit of time to think as they'd made their way downstream. He thought he'd finally formed something of a plan regarding Soldinger.

"I'm just glad you happened along when you did," Dawson added.

"Well, Governor, it wasn't exactly like I intended it that way," Corrigan said.

"Just the same," Dawson said. "You saved my life. Again."

"Whatever," Corrigan said. "You can buy me a beer when we get in."

"I'll do more than that," Dawson said.

Corrigan nodded, noting that they had begun to twist sideways. He pointed over Dawson's shoulder with his paddle.

"Better pull on the right, now."

He let Dawson's strokes guide them back toward the middle of the swiftly flowing river, leaned forward to check on Dara. They'd arranged her sideways in the raft, her head elevated on one cushion, her feet dangling over the opposite side. Corrigan had peeled off his shirt, draped it over her as best he could. If you didn't know better, he thought, it might have seemed a cozy picture.

He was exhausted, himself, he realized, almost woozy. How nice it would be to simply topple over there, float along on a soft current of deep, dark water. But there was always that distant rumble of trouble up ahead, wasn't there? He lifted his head resignedly as the sound of another set of rapids grew in volume.

They'd already managed to pick through several stretches of rough water, none of them nearly as violent as the set where they'd nearly died, however. With the full moon at its apex and Dawson proving a more than adept oarsman, they'd had no trouble to speak of: a few bumps, a little water shipped, that's about all.

"That doesn't sound so good," Dawson called over his shoulder.

Corrigan nodded, casting a quick glance at the ground that rose up on either side of the river. The moon was hidden, now, but there was still enough light to see that it was rugged country. Nothing as sheer as those cliffs they'd cut through earlier, of course, but there was no point in taking any chances, not at this stage.

"Pull toward that boulder over there," he said, pointing across the channel. "We'll try to put in behind it, have a look. . . ."

Dawson nodded his agreement with the plan, turned to sink his blade into the water, when the raft gave a sudden lurch, whirling about as if a giant hand had reached up from the bottom to set them spinning.

"What the hell?" Dawson cried as he toppled backward in the raft.

"Dara," Corrigan called, thrusting himself forward, doing his best to protect her, to wedge her in, as the silent whirlpool slung them about.

The raft rose up on the far edge of the vortex, teetering there for a moment before their centrifugal force won out, sending them on into the rapids themselves.

"Get up," he shouted to Dawson, scrambling for his own paddle. "Dig in, get the nose about. . . ."

Dawson was on his knees, jabbing his paddle to this side and that, when a huge wave crashed down, obliterating sight of him for a moment. Corrigan felt his paddle twist from his hands and fly away, glancing off his cheek as it went. He forced himself forward, got his arms around Dara, and held on desperately as the raft heaved and bucked along, slamming into boulders, twisting like a live thing itself. They weren't underwater, Corrigan realized, but they might as well have been, the air around him roaring, turned to raging foam . . . all he knew was that he would never let her go, not if they went over the side, no matter what . . .

. . . and then, as suddenly as it had begun, it was over. The awful sound was a muted roar behind them, and the nearly swamped raft twirled lazily in gently flowing waters that seemed a dozen times as wide as the river they'd been riding. On either side of them, the land fell away in mildly sloping contours, a veritable flatland compared to where they'd been.

Dawson glanced back at him, clearly exhausted. "The lake," he managed. "It's got to be the lake. We're out. We've made it!"

Corrigan glanced down at Dara, made sure her face was well out of the water sloshing about the bottom of the raft. He nodded at Dawson, then gazed blearily at the surrounding countryside.

"Maybe we have," he told Dawson. "But I don't see any brass bands just yet."

Dawson glanced around himself and sighed. "How far do you figure we have to go?"

Corrigan shook his head. "It doesn't matter," he told the governor. "What we do now is bail and row."

51

"Where are we?" Dara asked, her voice vague, drifting to him faintly in the early light.

Corrigan felt his head pop up at the words, realized he'd fallen asleep sitting up.

He glanced toward the front of the raft, where Dawson had slumped over the front cushion, his face pressed against the rubberized fabric as he snored gently.

"Almost home," Corrigan said, bending toward her. He was at the back of the raft, had been working hard with the one paddle that remained for what he guessed were hours, now. Or maybe it just seemed that way because of the fire in his shoulders and back. Two strokes to port, two to starboard, hope they would find civilization soon. Hard to know where they were, given the thick fog that still cloaked the broad waters of the lake.

"You hang in there," he said. "We'll find help soon." And they would, he thought. "I'll get out of this damned boat, walk on water if I have to. . . ."

But she was already out again, he realized. He could leave off the reassurances and simply paddle.

He glanced her way, grimacing at the ever-widening blood-stain that continued to leak through the makeshift bandages, through his shirt and jacket. If something happened to Dara, if they had come this far . . .

He heard a sudden whizzing noise, then, and whirled about as something struck his shoulder, bounced to the bottom of the raft. Something bright and shiny skittered there, a glimpse of gold, a bit of bright featherwork. As he stared dumbly, the thing—whatever the hell it was—leapt back into life with a little jangle, whisking across the floor of the raft until it lodged in the fabric of the starboard pontoon and held.

He stared at the thing, listening to the faint hiss of escaping air, feeling the unmistakable tug on the side of the raft.

"Mama." He heard a child's voice cutting excitedly through the fog-draped air. "I've got one, Mama. I've got a big one."

Oh, yes, indeed you have, Corrigan thought, staring at the lure that had fastened itself in the side of their craft. He glanced up at Dara and dug his paddle into the water, his eyes already beginning to fill, happy to lend this fisherman a hand.

52

They had come ashore at a campground less than a mile from the dock of the Absaroka Lodge, as it had turned out, and their battered party must have parted the mists like some nightmare apparition before the astonished eyes of Maurice Hanson. Maurice, eleven, had taken one look at what his fishing line was attached to and had run screaming toward the early morning campfire where his mother and father, who'd brought him all the way from Fort Lauderdale to see actual mountains, were brewing up a pot of coffee.

The Hansons had carried a cellular phone into the wilderness, "in case of emergency," only to discover they were well beyond the reach of any service provider when the occasion presented itself. While Mrs. Hanson comforted her shaken son, Mr. Hanson helped load Dara into the back of his rented Explorer, then sped off with Corrigan and Fielding Dawson for help.

"There's nothing but a Park Service clinic out in these parts," Hanson told them as they rushed through the forest, dust flaring up from this twisting, unpaved road in their wake. "But the lodge is hopping, all these reporters come in for the governor. I saw two helicopters fly in yesterday. They'll be able to get her to a hospital quick."

And in fact there had been one small helicopter there, about to take off from the hotel's sweeping front lawn for Jackson, where another contingent of media waited to be ferried in.

Hints of disaster had leaked, Corrigan discovered while he fumed, waiting for the chopper's return. There had been enough room for only the pilots and the lodge's doctor to tend to Dara on the flight. But not to worry, Officer Corrigan, the doctor had assured him. Dara was in good hands, now. She was suffering from loss of blood, exposure, a slight case of shock, but she would be fine. He could count on it.

Edward Soldinger had been there to whisk Dawson away before the reporters could get to him. Corrigan had thought of warning Dawson but decided against it. Soldinger would never try anything against Dawson in so public an arena. The governor would be safe—for now. But Corrigan would have to act soon.

Another room had been arranged for Corrigan in the same wing, its entrance blockaded by a phalanx of hotel security, a group of hard-eyed types in snap-button shirts and jeans who looked like they'd be equally at ease on the meanest city streets. He had been given a cursory examination by para-medics, then left alone for a few minutes to clean up and change into fresh clothes, before he was to appear for a debriefing with the local authorities in a command post hastily arranged in a suite at the end of the secured wing.

There had been a tray of food wheeled into his room while he was in the shower, Corrigan noted as he stepped out, towel-ing himself dry. Enough cold cuts and soft drinks for a squad picnic. On the bed were three folded pairs of Levi's, the tags still tacked to the back pockets, a similar number of bright Western shirts, a stack of packaged underwear and socks. He found the right sizes, struggled into the stiff clothing, smoothed his hair in the mirror.

He glanced at the food, then at his watch. Twenty minutes until he was due to appear at the debriefing. He went quickly to the phone.

It took a few minutes, but finally he heard Jacko Kiernan's familiar voice come crackling across the lines. It took a while longer to sketch out the basic details of what had happened and what he wanted Jacko to do, but in the end, Jacko went along.

"I hope you know what you're doing, Richie-boy," Jacko told him before he hung up.

"We'll find out soon enough, won't we?" Corrigan replied. And then came the knock on his door.

53

"Before we begin, Governor Dawson," the network correspondent was saying, "I would just like to extend my own personal sympathies. I realize what a difficult time this must be for you."

Corrigan stood watching from across the room beside Soldinger, who had arranged this single interview following the lengthy debriefings, where they had repeated their accounts of the horrific events to law-enforcement officials and search-and-rescue team coordinators. The media interview was necessary for a number of reasons, Soldinger had explained to a reluctant Dawson, not the least being "an opportunity for the governor to share his grief with the nation." Nor was it a coincidence that Soldinger had chosen the highest rated network journalist for the honors, Corrigan supposed, his eyes on this veteran who was so well known for her gripping one-on-one interviews.

"Thank you," Dawson said. He had settled himself in an embroidered bergère arranged catty-corner to the correspondent's. There was a marble-topped table in between, something out of the 1890s, or so it appeared, with a small vase of flowers and a cup of coffee for Dawson, tea for the correspondent.

In accordance with the arrangements Soldinger had made, there were but two cameras facing the pair, a minimal lighting arrangement, one sound technician, and a couple of grips. "We don't want to let this turn into a media circus," Soldinger had just whispered to Corrigan.

And we must strive to keep this looking normal was Corrigan's silent rejoinder. *The obedient servant caring for his master.* He looked at Soldinger. There was nothing in his face, no hint of anything beyond concern for Dawson. It was a commendable performance, Corrigan thought.

Once word of Dawson's emergence from the wilderness had gotten around, the already formidable crush of media had swollen geometrically: Every helicopter not pressed into the service of the search efforts for survivors, every seaplane, every rental SUV between Salt Lake City and Cheyenne was said to be on its way toward the remote Absaroka Lodge, constituting a media crush beyond all possible expectations. Outside, the broad lawn of the venerable hotel had become a sea of clamoring reporters ringed by media vans sprouting satellite dishes and RVs with awnings spread to shelter the endless string of ancillary interviews and gatherings of pundits.

But Dawson had been adamant. So long as the search efforts continued, so long as there was the slightest glimmer of hope that anyone else might be discovered alive, Fielding Dawson would withhold himself from the circus. One interview, brief, intimate, dignifed. And then . . . silence, until all the facts were known.

"I appreciate your taking the time to speak with us," the correspondent said. "And your confidence in us, of course."

Corrigan noted the slight emphasis on *us*. He also had noticed that the correspondent was decidedly more attractive in the flesh, as it were. While on camera she sometimes seemed to him standoffish, even tough; here she seemed quite warm, almost alluring.

Dawson, meanwhile, leaned forward, clasped his hands together, adopted the expression that he wanted the world to see. "I want to keep this brief," he said. "I realize that some of my policies are unpopular, particularly among certain groups . . . and the thought that the things I believe in may have contributed to this terrible tragedy is extremely painful to me."

He waved his hand before his face. "But my greatest concern is with the outcome of the search efforts," he said. "And very shortly I will be going out to see what I can do to aid in those efforts."

He paused, with a look of infinite sadness. "My own wife is still out there, somewhere. I'm hoping for her safe return. And I know how the families and friends of the others who are still missing must feel," he said, extending his arm toward the distant mountain. "My prayers and very best wishes are with them."

The correspondent had made a sound in her throat that Corrigan took for a sympathetic murmur, when a soft knock came at the rear door of the suite. Soldinger glared, then hurried to the door, opened it a crack. He started to say something, then stopped and stepped out into the hallway. Corrigan heard excited murmurs from the other side of the doorway, and nodded to himself.

Meanwhile, across the room, the network correspondent had continued: ". . . from what I gather," she was saying, "you actually managed to overcome two of your captors out there, Governor Dawson, which sounds like an amazing feat to me."

Dawson shrugged. "Once again, I'll have to thank Officer Richard Corrigan for his heroic actions," he began. He gestured across the room, then, and the network correspondent turned as well. Both seemed a bit puzzled when they found that neither Corrigan nor Soldinger was there.

54

"Where is he?" Soldinger demanded of the nurse behind the desk of the Absaroka Clinic. The clinic was housed in a low-slung building on Park Service land, tucked in among the pines roughly halfway between the lodge and the nearby campground, part of a complex of similar institutional structures, about as appealing as a clutch of tract houses dropped down in the middle of the wilderness.

The woman, a tough-looking sort in pale green trousers and a matching starched shirt, glanced up at him skeptically. "And who might *you* be?"

"I'm Edward Soldinger, chief of security for Fielding Dawson," he snapped. He gestured at the man beside him. "This is Special Agent Plummer, with the National Security Agency's field unit."

The woman apprised them for a moment. "Is that like the FBI?"

"It's much more than that," Soldinger said, impatiently. "I've been informed that this man Bright was found at the bottom of a cliff, in some trees that cushioned his fall. If he is still alive, I insist that we speak with him."

"I don't know that he's up for a conversation." The woman shrugged. "And there's not much we can do for him, here. The doc's gone. We've called for a Medivac unit out of Cody—"

"This is a matter of national security," Soldinger snapped.

She shrugged again, jabbed a pencil she was holding over her shoulder. "You go down this hallway, make a right. There's a sheriff's deputy outside the room. Talk to him about it."

Soldinger nodded to Plummer, and the two of them started

off. "You never did show me any ID," the woman called, but neither one of them bothered to turn.

"Can I help you?" the deputy said, glancing up from the folding chair he was sitting on.

Soldinger repeated his introductions, and this time the man with him flashed a shield. The deputy stood.

"Agent Plummer will relieve you, now," Soldinger said. "I'm here to speak with this man Bright."

"I dunno about that . . ." the man began. "They told me not to let anyone in. . . ."

Soldinger turned to the agent. "This man is interfering with a federal investigation," he said.

"Now, hold on . . ." the deputy said. They were the last words he spoke before Plummer clipped him sharply behind the ear. The deputy went over in a heap. Plummer bent down, eased the deputy back into his chair. He pulled his cap down over his eyes, then followed Soldinger inside.

The room was dimly lit and stuffy, the blinds drawn tight over a single window set high in the opposite wall. There was a single hospital bed beneath the window, an IV bag dangling from a silver stand, its line attached to the arm of a still figure who lay there, a tall man with most of his face covered by bandages.

"Bright?" Soldinger said.

There was no response from the figure on the bed. Soldinger turned to the agent with him and nodded. The agent stepped toward the bed. He withdrew something that resembled a pen case from his pocket, unfolded it, and took out a syringe filled with a clear liquid. He checked the syringe in the dim light, then inserted its tip into a port on the IV line. He was about to shove the plunger when the man on the bed flung himself up and wrapped his arms about Plummer.

"You're under arrest," the man with the bandaged face cried. The sheets had pulled away, revealing the uniform shirt of a Park County sheriff's deputy. The hastily tied bandages fluttered like streamers as he and Plummer toppled to the floor.

Soldinger stared in astonishment. He had turned, was moving for the hallway door, when it burst inward and a pair of burly deputies rushed inside to pin his arms behind him. A third man was there as well, Soldinger realized, and felt a wave of fury as he recognized the face.

"Time's up, Edward," Soldinger heard as he gazed back into the eyes of Richard Corrigan.

55

"**W**hat's happened to Soldinger?" Dawson asked as he ushered Corrigan into his room. "What did you want to tell me."

"You'll want to sit down," Corrigan said.

He was moving across the thick carpeting toward the broad windows that overlooked the lake at the rear of the lodge. In the distance loomed Black Mountain, its peak glowing purple, now, in the fading light. "Not bad," Corrigan offered. "All you can see from my room is trees."

"You said you needed to speak with me," Dawson said. "What's it about?"

Corrigan sat down in an embroidered, turn-of-the-century loveseat arranged by a corner fireplace. There was a tufted leather armchair nearby, a nicely fashioned antique coffee table beside it, bearing a couple of outdoorsy magazines, a half-drained tumbler of Scotch bleeding moisture onto its gleaming surface. You could sit here in front of a crackling fire, watch the light die on the distant peaks, convince yourself you were in paradise, he thought.

He reached into the pocket of his jacket, and lay a pistol down beside the sweating drink.

"What is that?" Dawson asked.

"There was a scuffle a while earlier," Corrigan said. "Your man Soldinger dropped it from his pocket."

Dawson's face creased. "I don't understand."

"That's not exactly how Soldinger tells it," Corrigan said mildly. "He says the whole thing was your idea to begin with."

There was a pause, then Dawson shook his head. "That's impossible." He glanced at the door, then at the phone. "I've got to speak to someone."

He lifted the receiver to his ear, listened for a moment, then jiggled the little switch in the cradle a few times. Corrigan stared back into his uncertain gaze, shaking his head in mock sympathy.

"Hell of a thing, isn't it? Something simple like a phone going out, just when you need it most?"

Dawson replaced the instrument, saying nothing.

"I figure it was you who disabled the satellite phones, Governor. Who else could it have been?"

Dawson stared at him. "You can't *believe* whatever nonsense Edward's been spewing. . . ."

Abruptly his expression changed to one of sympathy. "It's been a terrible strain for you, hasn't it? This whole ordeal. It could affect anyone's judgment. Especially on top of your guilt over that innocent man's death in the subway. . . ."

Corrigan shook his head sadly. "That was something I started thinking about during that last long ride down the river," he said. "The only people I told about that throw-down gun were you and Dara, and I didn't say anything to you until we were into the wilderness. How did Bright know?

"I started wondering how it would have come up between the two of you," he continued, "how you and this Bright got to be so chummy. And I kept seeing you standing up on top of that cliff with your eye pressed to the scope of that rifle as I came out of the cave . . ." Corrigan trailed off for a moment, then leaned forward.

"That's when I hit upon my little plan to draw Soldinger out. Once we had smoked him out, it didn't take much to get him to talk. *He* can expect some consideration for his cooperation." Corrigan shrugged doubtfully. "But in your case . . ."

Dawson was ashen, now. "This is nonsense. I don't know what Edward Soldinger might have said to you, but—"

"Don't hold it against him, Governor," Corrigan broke in. "He was just trying to cut the best deal he could. He even brought up a few points in your favor. He said you never meant for everyone to die, just your wife, who was planning to leave you and take all her money along with her. And Giles Ashmead, whom she was leaving you for, would have to go, of course. He'd been your lawyer for too long, knew where too many of the bodies were buried, so to speak."

Corrigan turned over his palms as if to offer a compliment.

"It was a great plan—get rid of two obstacles, and at the same time gain the sympathy of the American people."

Corrigan broke off, drew a breath. "Soldinger says it was Bright who decided to kill everyone, just to keep things tidy. Personally, I suspect it was Soldinger who came up with the 'tidy' part. He's got a flair for the dramatic, after all. A couple of unfortunate deaths, who cares? Turn it into wholesale slaughter, look at the coverage you get . . ." He waved his hand toward the front of the building, where earlier Dawson had sat with the network correspondent.

"This is absurd, Corrigan. How can you possibly believe—"

"Soldinger says you *were* a bit upset when you two discussed it after you'd made it back. But he says you calmed down, finally. After all, the mission had been accomplished, or so the two of you thought: You'd wanted to turn a liability into an asset, keep that fortune of your wife's to fuel your campaign, and garner the sympathy vote in the bargain. A hell of a kickoff to the race, no question about it."

Dawson's face seemed even paler, now, but maybe it was just a trick of the fading light. His eyes flicked down to the table, where the pistol lay between them.

Corrigan followed his gaze, leaned back with his arms spread along the top of the loveseat.

"You could go for the gun, Governor. After all, you know I'm not really the hero you told everybody I was."

Dawson glanced up at him. Their stares locked for a moment, and then Dawson turned away.

Corrigan nodded. "I didn't think so."

Dawson shook his head, speaking as if he hadn't heard. "I simply can't understand all this. If Edward Soldinger has taken responsibility for these heinous actions, then he is the one who will have to pay for them—"

"That's good, Governor," Corrigan cut him off as he stood. "You can try that line of defense in court. But Soldinger wouldn't be much of a security man if he hadn't been careful to wear a wire during most of the conversations he'd had with you about all this." Corrigan smiled. "Any way that the matter goes down, I think the party's going to be looking elsewhere for its standard bearer, wouldn't you agree?"

Dawson's gaze held his defiantly for a moment longer, but then something seemed to tip inside the man, some seismic shift, some inner landslide of staved-up resolve. He dropped his gaze, then, and eased his way into the leather armchair as carefully as if his bones had turned to glass. "My wife was behind all this," he said, but his voice lacked a certain conviction. It was almost as if he were trying it out on himself, trying yet another story on for size.

"She *was* planning to leave me. She was a bitter woman, entirely unreasonable. We could have reached some sort of arrangement, carried on as others have, but that wasn't good enough for her . . ." He caught himself, then.

"She and Giles Ashmead cooked this whole thing up. Paid off Edward Soldinger, hired this man Bright . . ."

Corrigan stepped forward, bending to clap Dawson on the shoulder. "You keep working on it," Corrigan said. "But I don't think it'll do you much good. Meantime, I'll just leave the gun," he said. "You might find some use for it."

Corrigan started for the door, then turned to look back.

The governor sat stiffly in the chair, hands gripping the armrests like some parody of Lincoln frozen in his memorial. Corrigan couldn't see his face, just his form outlined against the window, a dark shadow against the backdrop of the glowing, distant mountain.

He'd witnessed this tableau once before, Corrigan thought: a man at a table with a pistol and a glass of whiskey, reading the runes in the melting ice. Though on that occasion he would have done anything to change the course of events.

Corrigan shook his head. "Good-bye, Governor," he said quietly.

He turned and walked to the door, and didn't look back. He was outside, was halfway down the corridor, before he heard the muffled shot.

56

It was nearly midnight before the Park County sheriff's helicopter delivered Corrigan to the clinic in Jackson, where Dara had been taken for treatment. He arrived to find her asleep in her room, but the nurses had assured him she was resting comfortably. The surgery had gone well. No complications. Not to worry, Officer Corrigan. A full recovery for Dara ahead.

They'd dragged a more comfortable chair into her room, arranged it in a corner across from her bed, found a pillow for him, told him to get some rest and wait. She'd awake soon enough, they told him. Be patient. Let nature take its course.

He glanced across the room at her still-peaceful form, reassured himself with the steady rise and fall of the sheets that covered her, then checked his watch. Light outside, he saw. Just past dawn. It hadn't seemed he'd been there that long. Perhaps he'd drifted off; he'd been so exhausted he hadn't even realized it had happened.

Her eyes flickered open, then, and her gaze gradually gathered into focus.

"Hey," he said.

Her features fell into a weak smile. "Hey," she said.

"How are you feeling?" he asked.

She nodded, straightening a bit on her pillows.

Someone appeared at the doorway, and he tensed reflexively.

"Everything all right in here?" It was the charge nurse standing there, her voice mild.

"Everything's fine," Corrigan said finally.

He reached to take Dara's hand. She was a little pale, but still, looking at her made his heart race.

She nodded, and returned the pressure in her grip.

He watched her for a moment, glanced at her heavily bandaged arm. "They told me you'd be okay," he said.

She nodded. "Couple of weeks, I'll be back to typing."

"That's good."

"I've got some story to write, don't I?"

"Almost as good as the one about O.J.'s girlfriend," he told her.

She stared at him for a moment. "I was watching the news, earlier," she said. She gestured at the television screen dangling from a bracket across the room. "You heard about what happened to Fielding Dawson?"

He glanced at the darkened set, nodding.

"You surprised?" she asked him after a moment.

He thought about what to say. "Are you?" he asked finally.

She shook her head. "Not really, given the prospects. I think it was the decent thing to do, save the public all that money for a trial." She lay back against her pillow, sighing. "Maybe it'll start a trend."

He shrugged. "Maybe it will," he said. One day he'd tell her about the conversation he'd had with Dawson. But this was not the day.

Another nurse glanced into the room from the doorway, smiled to see her awake. She gave Corrigan a thumbs-up, then disappeared.

"They make them perky out here, don't they?" he said, watching the young woman walk away.

"Don't get any ideas," she said.

He smiled. "What are you going to put in this story about us?" he asked after a bit.

She raised her eyebrows. "Some things," she said. "Not every last detail."

"Good," he said.

She gave him a smile, patted the bed beside her. "Come up here," she said, beckoning.

It didn't take him long to obey. "A pretty girl invites me into her bed," he said, edging down gingerly beside her. "This must be my day."

"It's your day, all right," she said.

She reached to straighten the collar of his shirt with her good hand, held his gaze momentarily.

"So, you're ready to go back to New York, be a regular old cop again?"

He shrugged. "I was never a regular cop."

"You can be whatever kind of cop you want to be, now," she said.

He shrugged again, thinking briefly of his father. "I guess," he said. "I don't mind going back. As long as you're going, too," he added.

She smiled. "Of course I am," she said. She hesitated, and a different look came upon her. "I know this may sound strange right now . . ." she began.

"Nothing will ever seem strange to me again," he said.

"I know," she said. "But this may." She pushed herself up straighter. "It's just that, like I said before, someday I want to come back out here. I want to go back up into those mountains." She paused, gave him an earnest look. "I'd like it to be the two of us. Would you be up for that?"

He glanced out the window of the clinic, saw the jagged outline of peaks hovering blue in the distance, thought of all that storybook grandeur they had seen. At the same time, he could also conjure Bright's form crashing down into the water, could see the whole awful nightmare beginning to take shape in his mind once again.

"You really want to do that?" he said.

"I do," she said. "It's so beautiful up there. We can't let them ruin it, Richard. We have to chase the ghosts away."

He hesitated, thinking of all those faces hovering in the shadows of his mind. All those lives lost, all the sadness there. He saw smudge man hurtling over the side of the platform, saw his father's mournful gaze locked on his, saw that trigger finger about to squeeze.

He turned his gaze back from the window, took Dara's hand and gripped it tight. "Anywhere you want to go," he told her.

She smiled and leaned to kiss him, and for those few moments, at least, all he could see was her.

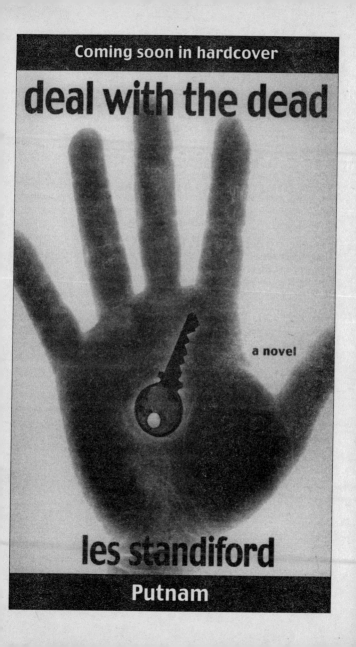